I0527066

Inquires about bulk orders or to book appearances/ book signings by the author please contact the author himself at _____ or email mike.axsom@yahoo.com

This book is dedicated to my dad, James "Jimmy" Axsom.

Introduction

James Andrew Exum III has everything at his disposal that a man his age could want. At thirty years old, he has wealth beyond belief, and good looks. After his father's death, James moved to New York City where his father had just opened up a sales and distribution center for the company before his death. James did not come home to visit much, and when he did, it was mostly because of business. James had memories of that house he cared not to think about. Although his father taught him the family business, he robbed James of a childhood that he could not get back, and he could not forgive his father for that.

During a business trip home to Exum Textiles in Greensboro, NC, if by chance or destiny, they had to pull into a small little town of Elon College to make car repairs. While waiting for the repairs to be made, James was able to walk around the small town and take in the charm and beauty of the college campus and absorb the hospitality of the town. He could not get over how friendly everybody was. James had never attended public school or college. From the age of four, his father, James Andrew Exum Jr., had the best tutors that money could buy to educate him at home. James could speak three languages and, by the time he was eleven, he had passed the exams at Harvard and Princeton. James was remised that he never had the chance to experience the life that these young people were having.

As he headed back to the limousine, he passed a corkboard that had a local posting for a roommate needed. After discussing it with J.J. the president of the company, they came up with a plan for him to enroll in college and start living the life he dreamed of as the college student, Jim Andrews not James Andrew Exum III.

Chapter 1

It was 1969, a decade steeped in revolution: love and war, politics and space exploration, human rights and fashion. All facets of culture were breaking traditional boundaries and reshaping the future landscape of American life. In the fashion industry, James Andrew Exum III was leading the charge.

For a young man, James was a giant in textiles. As the youngest CEO of the largest denim manufacturing company in the world, James was already a business tycoon at 31 years old. Newspaper and magazine editors invariably called him a genius at research and development. While most CEOs would have been flattered by the characterization, James always cringed at the word. He knew genius wasn't what built his company. Rather, his renowned business acumen was acquired at a heavy price. As his limo sped down Interstate 40 from the Raleigh-Durham airport towards Greensboro, the price he paid to become a legendary captain of industry would soon be revealed. It was a hot mid-August morning when an evocative mix of happenstance and childhood memories profoundly changed everything James thought he knew about his life.

The limo driver slid back the separating window and said, "Sir, we have a vehicle that is overheating. We need to stop and have it checked out."

After some consideration, James nodded and replied, "Yes. That will be fine."

As the limousine pulled off the interstate, they drove into an idyllic village, sitting next to the Elon College campus. James admired the charm of the Victorian homes alongside the two-lane street. They were white gingerbread creations, encased with black shutters and, wrap-around porches.

Driving into town, James noted a small fire station nestled to his right. As they crossed over the railroad tracks and through the town of Elon, the driver made a left turn into a service station. The attendant walked up as the driver got out of the car. The attendant and the driver exchanged words as the limo's hood was raised. The billowing steam cleared quickly enough, and the attendant gave it an inspection.

Finally, the driver walked back to Jame's window, knocked, and waited for James to roll the window down before giving his report. "Looks like it might be the thermostat or a leaky hose. The attendant said it will take 45 minutes to an hour to have it repaired."

James replied, "That'll be fine, Charles. I'm just going to take a walk around and I'll meet you back here in 45 minutes."

James stepped out of the car and walked to the front of the building before starting down the sidewalk. The first building he came to had a sign which read, 'Soda Shoppe.' James decided to stop in and get something to drink. As he entered, he noticed a group of young kids inside having a drink and laughing together. A few had thick textbooks with them. James stepped up to the counter and asked for a Coke. The waiter asked if he wanted plain, vanilla or cherry. James paused for a moment. Curiously, he replied, "I've never had anything but a 'regular coke'. What's a vanilla Coke?"

"Well, it's a Coke with a little vanilla flavoring in it. Cherry Coke has a little cherry flavoring in it," the waiter answered.

"Let me have a vanilla Coke. I'll try that."

The waiter nodded once and turned to the dispenser, where he poured the drink and pumped a bit of vanilla into the soda as James reached into his pocket and asked, "How much?"

"That'll be ten cents."

James laid a quarter on the counter and walked out of the soda shop. He stood, drinking his newly discovered vanilla Coke, and looked at the architectural structure of the campus buildings across the street. The age of those buildings had to go back over a hundred years. The campus was laid out in a half-circle, horseshoe design. From this point of view, there appeared to be 6 buildings. Each of the buildings were three stories tall. Steps led up to identical porches perched under A-framed roofs. There were large windows encased in dental molding. All of the woodwork and tall columns were painted white. The brick walkway followed the half circle of buildings around, circling back to the street sidewalk about a football field in distance from where it had begun. The leaves were already beginning to change to beautiful fall colors. Red and yellow leaves floated to the ground against neatly trimmed green grass. The entire campus, set against a Carolina blue sky, was a beautiful sight to see.

As he walked down this busy sidewalk, admiring the view, he passed several small businesses and even more students. He couldn't help but notice most of the young men were wearing loafers and no socks. Some wore khaki pants and some donned dress slacks. A majority of the guys had long hair growing over their ears and shirt collars. Some of the girls had skirts which fell about four inches below the knee, while others wore mini-skirts with boots and sweaters. James smiled and thought, "The times are changing in clothing, design and style."

All the students were carrying books and were laughing and joking with one another. As he casually continued down the street, he passed by older gentlemen carrying briefcases. Some wore plaid sports coats with patches on the elbows. James assumed these men were professors. Some business owners were out sweeping the sidewalks in front of their businesses. Almost all of the small businesses were one-story structures although a few reached two stories. James looked down the street and saw a statue of a Confederate soldier sculpted in granite standing at attention in the middle of the intersection, facing north. Below the monument the engraved letters read, "Standing for Liberty."

James surveyed the beauty of his surroundings. He noticed the professors and students passing him on the street. Some said, "good morning", and smiled and offered nods. Everyone seemed very friendly although they did not know James. James was more accustomed to New York, where the people did not acknowledge you as they passed, let alone wish you a 'good morning' if they did not know you. James loved the friendliness of the community here and he immediately knew this was a place he would like to stay for a while.

He stopped to look in the window of one of the businesses. As he looked, he noticed his reflection in the glass. A young man with short hair, wearing a dark blue serge suit peered back at him. White sleeves stuck out from the suit, each adorned with a gold cufflink. He wore a maroon neck tie, black wing-tip shoes. It didn't take him long to realize why everyone was staring at him as he passed He looked completely out of place. James turned around and started to walk back to the soda shop when a young lady about his age stepped out of a business and walked to the edge of the sidewalk. James stopped in his tracks. She was the best-looking woman he had ever seen.

She had auburn hair which fell down her back and wore a cloth belt cinched tightly around her waist. She stood on black high heel shoes and waited to cross the street. James found that he could not move until she started across the street. After a car passed, James crossed to the other side, too. He kept his distance as she walked up the street. She turned left and headed up the brick walkway, she continued through a set of large, wooden double doors into the building. After a moment, James followed her inside and noticed as she turned and entered a room at the lower end of the hall. He paused and saw on his left, a chart of room numbers and professors' names. He counted the row of names until he noticed the only female name. Miss Sandra Wilson, Professor of History, Room #5. James committed her name to memory and left the building headed back to the soda shop.

As he reached the shop, a three-legged dog hopped across the street toward him. The dog ambled over and began to sniff James' shoes and pants leg. James had no idea what was coming next, but one thing was certain: that dog could not lift his back leg because the other was missing! James accommodated and reached down to pat the dog's head. The dog was colored like a beagle with black, white and tan fur. "Even the dogs are friendlier here," James thought as he watched the dog hop away.

He turned to continue on his walk when a gentleman with a briefcase and wearing a sports coat and tie greeted him. The man said, "Well, I see you've met the village dog. Everyone here calls him Bandit. He doesn't belong to anyone; he just hops around and visits the business district. A lot of the professors, students and business owners take care of him. No one knows where he stays at night, either. He just shows up and makes his rounds visiting everybody. By the way, I'm Roger. I'm a professor here, just heading to class."

James took all of that in, and replied, "Nice to meet you, Roger. I'm James."

"Well, you have a good day, James. I'm late for class."

"You have a good one, too, Roger."

James watched the man hurry across campus before continuing. Even here, in the 'business district', people were friendly. James was raised a southerner but, until now, he hadn't really understood the term, 'southern gentleman.' He recalled growing up in the small town of Greensboro, North Carolina. People never locked their doors in Greensboro. On cool nights, the windows were kept wide open and you could sleep on the front porch swing. Most people had not yet acquired air conditioning; it was still a rare thing in the south. James had moved to New York City when he was 20 years old and had forgotten just how friendly people in the south could be. He missed the casual pace of their daily lives. Most New Yorkers walked fast with their heads ducked, making no eye contact and uttering no cordial words. "The south is where I belong," James decided to himself.

James crossed the street and saw that the limousine was waiting. Charles, the driver, was waiting patiently beside the car. As he passed the soda shop, a corkboard on the side of the soda shop caught his attention. There were several notices pinned on the board; cars for sale, books for sale, etc. But there was one card James read twice. He plucked the card from the board and held it between his fingers as he read it again, 'two guys looking for a roommate. Private bedroom with private bath, $50 a month. Call David at 9888." James pocketed the card.

As James reached the car, Charles nodded, "we're ready to go," he said as he opened the door for James.

As the limousine sped down Interstate 85 towards Greensboro, James picked up the rotary-dial car phone and called the president of his company. J.J. Washington was, at 33 years of age, the youngest black president of any textile company of its size.

"J.J., I'm running late. We had car trouble on the way to the plant; can we meet at the house after you get off work?" James asked.

"Sure, James. I'll be there about six."

"That's great," James replied before asking, "Do you know what Grammy is having for dinner?"

"Whatever your favorite is, I'm sure. She knows you're coming in today. I'm sure she'll be ready for you." The man on the other end chuckled, lightly.

James smiled, "Great. I'll see you at dinner!"

Chapter 2

Elizabeth Washington was a light-skinned black woman. She was a strong woman; tall, with European features and long, black hair. She worked as a nurse in one of James' father's plants in Greensboro. She was a graduate of A&T College in Greensboro and had been the company nurse for about three years when James' mother became pregnant with him. James mother's pregnancy was problematic and his father had brought Elizabeth in to care for her. After four difficult months, Mrs. Exum passed away during delivery. James' father, grateful for Elizabeth's help and perhaps also a bit lost following the death of his wife, asked Elizabeth with her two-year old son, Jonathan Jefferson Washington (everyone called him "J.J."), to stay and help raise James.

James only knew Elizabeth as 'Grammy'. She raised him as her own and took care of his dad until he died of diabetes about 20 years later. Grammy had been there ever since, managing the household. She had a housekeeper and a guard at the gate, named Mr. Sparks. Mr. Sparks had been employed there ever since the family installed a fence around the property thirty years earlier when the Union had threatened his father's life. It was the only home J.J. and James ever knew.

James knew Grammy was born around Washington, D.C. She claimed that she was one of the descendants of the slaves at George Washington's plantation and that is how her family assumed the last name of 'Washington'. She had moved to Greensboro and attended A&T College. James could remember that Grammy always made sure his dad had the right meals to ease symptoms of his diabetes. Even when his father was confined to bed, Grammy would sit by his side and talk to him and feed him. Grammy dressed his father every day. She shaved him, cleaned him up and read his mail. She was by his side day and night and was holding his hand as he passed away.

As Charles pulled up to the guard house, James rolled down the back window. Mr. Sparks walked over and shook James' hand.

James nodded, "how are you doing, Mr. Sparks?"

"I'm doing fine, James. How are you doing?"

"I'm doing well, sir."

"Well, I know Elizabeth is looking forward to seeing' you. She's been cooking all day. She'd done called me three times, making sure I'll be here when you arrive. Well, go on in 'fore she calls me again." Mr. Sparks smiled, "Welcome home, James."

Charles pulled through the double black iron gates and around the big water fountain. He stopped in front of the house and the door opened. Grammy came running out as James got out of the car. He met her halfway up the steps and the two gave one another a big hug.

"James! I have missed you so!" Grammy laughed, "This ol' house just ain't the same without you! You come on in, now, and get changed out of those clothes."

James walked beside Grammy, up the long hallway and into the kitchen, which was a little ways up from the dining room where their meals were always served. When J.J. and James were children and James' father wasn't home, Grammy, J.J. and James always ate in the kitchen. As a matter of fact, James always hated eating in the dining room, with its chandeliers and candlesticks and fuzzy wallpaper. As they walked into the kitchen area, Grammy said, "You look pale, boy. Don't the sun come out up in New York?"

"I've just been working inside, Grammy," James replied. "I haven't had much time to get outside."

"Well, tomorrow you can get outside and help me with the flowers. But for now, sit down and I will fix you a big, cold glass of iced tea before dinner."

"You might as well fix J.J. a glass of tea, as well. He'll be here in a few minutes."

Grammy grinned, "It's so nice to have both of you boys at home with me tonight."

As James sat, he looked at Grammy. He could see there were a few more gray hairs and a few more wrinkles here and there although she still had her hair fixed perfectly and still wore her white nurse's apron. James could not remember a day when she had not worn that apron, she only seemed to take it off to sit down and eat.

James and Grammy were sitting at the table, drinking their iced tea when the gate buzzer went off.

"Yes, Mr. Sparks?" Grammy asked.

"J.J. is on his way in," the guard replied.

"Thank you."

About then, J.J. opened the back door. He had driven around the back of the house. That is the way he always came in whenever he visited. Grammy met him at the door with a big hug and James stood up. The two men shook hands and leaned into a brief sort of what might pass as a masculine hug.

"Well, how's it going in the big city?" J.J. asked.

"Busy, busy, busy. As usual." James responded.

They both laughed out loud.

"You boys are somethin' else," Grammy quipped as she started setting the table for dinner. She placed a bowl of snap peas and fat back right in the middle. The next bowl to be delivered was sliced cucumbers and onions in vinegar. A plate with fried corn bread patties arrived not long after. Finally, Grammy appeared holding a big, black steel pot by the handle and placed it in the center of the table. It was piping hot and filled to the brim with chicken and dumplings. J.J. and James could see the broth floating on the top. This was James' favorite meal.

"Boy, it's been a long time since I have had a meal like this, Grammy. I can't wait to dig in," James said.

"Well, you'd better wait until I get my apron off and say the blessing. Then, you can dig in." Grammy scolded.

James, being a country boy at heart, reached up and loosened the knot on his tie and unbuttoned the top button. He grabbed a napkin, tucked it inside his collar and rolled up both sleeves. J.J. was doing the same. Grammy just sat for a few moments and watched both of her boys serve themselves and eat. Very few words were spoken as they ate.

"Grammy, this sure does bring back a lot of good memories," James said.

After making some small talk, James asked J.J. to walk with him upstairs. As James got up from the table, he reached over and gave Grammy a big hug and kissed her on the cheek.

"You're the best, Grammy, and that's why I love you," he said.

J.J. stood, as well, and also gave Grammy a hug and kiss.

"Well, you boys go on and do your business and I'll clean up," Grammy replied.

As James and J.J. left the kitchen and started across the huge living room, James stopped and looked around. There was a large fireplace that would fit six foot logs in its mouth. Above him hung a chandelier in the center of the room which was as big as a Volkswagen. There were two camelback sofas and two leather wingback chairs. A winding staircase led up three stories and James turned to J.J. and said, "I can't count how many times I have slid down those rails."

J.J. laughed and confided, "I burned my butt coming down those rails too fast."

"We have had a lot of fun here, haven't we?"

"You can say that again, James."

As they continued to walk up the stairs, making small talk about their shared childhoods, James opened the door to his father's office.

Chapter 3

James looked around as if he were seeing it for the first time. It brought back a long-forgotten world of memories. The oriental carpet he used to play on was still in the middle of the floor and a small desk remained beside his father's huge mahogany desk. The mahogany bookshelves that lined one side of the wall were filled with volumes of books revolving around textile research and development and the advancement of textiles in the United States. James recalled reading most of those books by the time he was about 17. His father would assign a book for him to read and they would discuss what he had read over dinner every night. J.J. would sit and listen as they discussed textiles and the future of the industry.

James casually walked over to the big bay window. He looked down at the driveway which circled the big water fountain in the front yard. It was the same driveway which J.J. would walk down the driveway and through the black gates, waving as he left to get on the school bus.

"Do you know how many times I would have loved to have gotten on that school bus with you, J.J.?"

"I know, James. I wish you could have gotten on it with me, too."

"While you were getting on that bus, my tutors were coming through the side door. Over there, in that small room was my classroom, J.J.. All day long. It had one desk and one chalkboard on the wall. That's where I spent most of my days learning the world of textiles in Spanish, French and German. Dad always felt that, if doing business in foreign countries, you should be able to speak the language."

As James looked around the room, he saw a big oil painting of his grandfather, behind his father's desk. James Andrew Exum came south in 1895 from Worcester, Massachusetts to start the first Exum textile plant. James' father had been brought up as James, himself, had; knowing nothing but textiles most of his life.

J.J. said, "Well, James, I guess it's just a family tradition."

Over in the corner were a confidential table and six leather wingback chairs. "Let's go over to the table and have a seat, J.J.," James said.

The two walked over to the table and pulled out a chair.

"OK, James," said J.J., "I know you have something on your mind, so get it off your chest. What's up?"

James laughed, "You can read me like a book, J.J.. By the way, how is Sally?"

"She is doing fine. After four months, she's finally over the morning sickness."

"That's great J.J.," James said, "I hope I get to see her before I leave."

"Well, you better. She'll be mad as hell at you if you don't go by and see her."

"I'll make sure I do." James said. He paused, then, "you met Sally in college, didn't you?" James asked.

"Sure did, best thing that ever happened to me. I knew the first time I saw her she was going to be my wife. I passed her in the hallway, I looked at her and she looked at me, and I knew she was the one. She said she thought the same thing the first time she saw me. Sometimes that's just how it works. But I will have to say, it was the best four years of my life. I enjoyed college life. I still have buddies that I met in college; we stay in touch."

"I knew you were having a good time, J.J.. I could tell when you would call home, but it was a long four years for me. I felt a little lost when you weren't here. Dad would always ask Grammy to see your grades. I heard him say that he was proud of those grades. I guess you could say that you not being here made me dig in a little harder to do well with my studies, just so dad would be proud of me, too. He had a way about him that would make you want to work harder."

"I can remember one time; I was walking down the sidewalk when this big, long, black limousine pulled up beside me. The back window slid down and there sat your dad. He opened the door and slid over and told me to get in. You could have knocked me over with a feather. He was the last person I expected to see. When I got in, he told Charles to take a right around the block. He just wanted to know how I was doing. Did I like college, was I having any problems… And he told me that he was checking my grades. He said that he was pleased at just how hard I was working to make good grades, and he wanted to let me know that it was going to pay off for me one day. He asked if I needed some money, and I told him I didn't. He looked at me and smiled and said, 'a young man in college, J.J., always needs a little spending money.' He reached into his pocket and pulled out a money clip with a few bills and handed it to me. He said, 'you may need this, J.J..' He tapped Charles on the shoulder and Charles pulled over to the side of the road, and I got out of the limousine. I looked back at him and he just looked at me with a smile on his face and winked and gave me one of those 'so long' waves. I will never forget that day as long as I live." J.J. continued, "When I got back to my apartment, I got out the clip and started to count the money. When I gave the clip a closer look, I noticed it had my initials engraved on the front. On the other side, it read, 'with total admiration.'" J.J. reached into his pocket and produced the same clip. He showed it to James. J.J. had carried it ever since that day.

James looked at the clip and smiled as he produced an identical clip, only with James' initials. The two men looked at one another and grinned.

James recalled how that was one of the few times his father had showed any affection towards he or J.J..

"When I got back to school the next day, I worked twice as hard to please your dad by having good grades," said J.J..

"I know, J.J.. I did the same thing. But, I have to say if it wasn't for Grammy taking up the slack while you were gone, I couldn't have made it. She pitched ball with me and we played all types of games. I think she knew that I missed having you around. If it had not been for her, I don't know what I would have done. She was not only raising and caring for me; she was my best buddy, as well. On the way up here today, Charles told me that we were having car trouble. The engine was over heating and we'd best pull off as soon as possible to have it looked at. As we turned off the interstate, we came to a small town named Elon College. As we drove through town, I couldn't help but notice all the old homes lining the street. You could tell there was money in this town just by looking at these homes. It was all quite charming. There was even a fire station with two firemen washing down the engine up front wearing the whole fireman get-up; black boots and suspenders. People waved at them as they passed by. Everyone was so friendly. Throngs of young people were crossing the street towards campus as we waited at the light just in front of the Texaco station. It was truly a beautiful campus. We pulled into the station for servicing and Charles was greeted by a guy in a Texaco uniform, with a big red star in the center of his chest. I decided to walk around while we waited. It was amazing to see young folks carrying books, some of them with long hair and loafers with no socks. I felt comfortable just being there. On my way back, I passed a corkboard with an advertisement for a roommate with a telephone number on it. This got me to thinking... Would it be possible for me to go to that college? Just for a semester? Two or three months? I feel like I need that interaction to see what it was like to go to college. I'd like to see what college life is all about. Does that seem crazy to you, J.J.?"

J.J. paused for consideration before replying, "If you feel that strongly about it, James, I think we can do it. I really think you do need that time." Another short pause "let me make some calls."

"The problem I have, J.J., is that I don't want to let anyone know who I really am. I'd like to be treated just like any other student. If anyone knew who I was, I feel that they would treat me differently and that is the last thing I want."

"Let me make those calls, James," J.J. Reassured, "I'll get back with you tomorrow night. We'll decide on what to do to keep your identity between you and me then."

James smiled with some amount of relief, "that'd be great, J.J.."

Chapter 4

The next day at about 1 o'clock in the afternoon, J.J. called James. J.J. sounded pleasant on the other end of the line, "good morning, James."

"Morning, J.J.. How're you doin'?"

J.J. chuckled, "I'm doing well, college boy."

James paused, letting that sink in. "College boy? Were you able to work something out?"

"Well, I talked to the President of Elon College this morning. We worked out a deal. You will be attending classes through a continuing education program for adults. You will only participate in one class; US History. Your teacher will be Miss Wilson, but you won't get any credit for this semester. You will go on record as attending the school and will get grades within the class as well as attendance credit. Your semester will last about three months, but it's up to you how long you want to go. I told them it would probably be three to four weeks before you would be able to attend. I figured I would take you about that long to get everything figured out and set up here before heading off to college. "

"That's fantastic, J.J.! I really do appreciate your setting this up for me."

"Oh, by the way, James. There is going to be an addition to the library, named the 'James Andrew Exum III Library'. Congratulations, James." J.J. said with a laugh.

"I don't know how this is going to work out, but I am going to give it a try. Could you drop by in the next week or so to work out the logistics of how things will run with me being gone?"

"Just call me and give me the time, and I will be there." J.J. assured.

Three weeks passed with frequent visits by J.J. and occasional times with Grammy in the flower gardens. During the day, James made phone calls to secure business while he was away. He discussed with Grammy his plans and was pleased to receive her support. She began to tell him how she had to work her way through college, washing dishes at night at a local restaurant and working as a cook on weekends just to get by. She paid her way through college and received a degree in Nursing.

Once, when he was about 12 years old, James asked Grammy about her husband. He thought now that he was 29, she might talk about him as they were weeding the grass from around her pansies. James casually mentioned, "Did your husband help you at all when you were going to college?"

She didn't say a word for a few minutes. Then she stood and placed both hands backwards on her hips and said, "James, I love you every bit as much as I do J.J. and one day I will discuss it with you both so that I don't have to repeat myself. But for now I'm going to keep it to myself."

James simply said, "yes, ma'am." And that was the end of the discussion.

Grammy told James that, when she finished college and received her degree that no one would hire her as a nurse. There were only a very few colored nurses, and none of them in the south. She said she had some money, so she went to Exum textiles to apply for a job.

"They gave me a cleaning lady job on the second shift. I would get there in the afternoon at about 4:00 and would clean all the offices by 11 o' clock at night. After working there for about 5 months, I was cleaning offices at about 5:00 when this young man came rushing up the hall, screaming. 'Someone call the doctor! Jones has cut his hand off!' I went running out into the working area and here was this white man sitting in this chair, blood all over the place, just spewing from his hand. He'd gotten it caught real good in a machine, but he hadn't cut it all the way off just yet. I reached down, and took one of his laces out of his shoe and wrapped it around his wrist, real tight. It stopped the bleeding and we rushed him to the hospital. I rode along to keep an eye on the shoe string and talked to him to keep him calm. When we got to the hospital, they rushed him right in and they were able to save his hand. That man worked there until he retired. The next day, someone told your dad what had happened and what I had done. He called me in to his office and asked me where I learned to give that type of medical care. I told him I had gone to college to be a nurse, and had a degree to show for it. He said, 'well, I guess we don't need you cleaning offices anymore.' And that was that. From that day on, I worked as the company nurse."

As Grammy and James walked back towards the house, they saw J.J. drive up.

As he got out of his car, he said, "Well James. I see that Mamma's keepin' you busy."

James laughed, "I think it's more to get me out in the sunlight than it is working. She says I'm too white. I don't know what that means."

J.J. laughed.

Grammy said, "Ya'll go into the house and sit down at the table. I'll fix us a glass of iced tea, and then you boys can talk business."

Chapter 5

As they were drinking their tea, James said, "All the arrangements are made, J.J.. Starting Monday morning, everything concerning the business has been turned over to you. All my duties and responsibilities are now in your hands. I have set it up where you will make all final decisions. You have the authority to hire, fire and make any changes you see fit in the New York office. I will be checking in with you once a week and here is the number where I can be reached. You can call me anytime, day or night." James turned to Grammy, "I am leaving you the number, as well. You and J.J. will be the only two people who will know where I am and know what I will be doing. I don't care what it is, Grammy, you call me of you need anything." After a moment, James sighed, "Well, I am going to go find that card with the ad for a roommate and give the guy a call."

When James dialed the number on the card, David answered after just a couple of rings.

James responded, "I'm calling in reference to the room you have for rent."

"Yes, we have a bedroom for rent. It has a full bath. My roommate and I are looking for a third roommate. It'll be $50 a month, plus your share of the utilities and phone and you pay for your own long-distance."

"Do you think I could come down today before lunch and have a look at the room?"

David said, "That should be fine. The address is 2424 Center Street. Head North on Main Street and turn right at the third light. It's the third white house on the left."

James nodded as he wrote the information down, "Thank you, David. I'll be there at 12 noon."

James went back downstairs and asked J.J. if he would mind giving him a ride down to Burlington and have a look at the room. As the two men headed down the interstate, James turned to J.J. and said, "Well, J.J., this could be a big beginning for me."

"Yes, it could, James. I wish you the best. You definitely need this time for yourself. Just stay out of trouble."

James laughed, "I'll try, J.J.. I'll try."

As the car pulled onto Main Street, J.J. said, "Yes, this is a typical small-town college. It's very clean and neat."

As he drove through town, J.J. looked at the businesses along the street. "This really is a neat little town. I need to make it down one day and look at where they plan to put the new addition to the Exum library."

They drove along Center Street and pulled up alongside number 2424. It was well-kept and nice. As J.J. pulled up, James asked him if he wanted to come in. J.J. replied, "James, you are on your own. This is your decision to make. I'll be right here, waiting in the car for you. You just take your time."

James got out of the car and walked up the sidewalk and stepped up onto the porch. He noticed a swing to the right, which had been freshly painted gray. The front door opened and a young man stepped out. He was about 6 feet tall, with light-colored hair which fell just past his collar.

The man stuck his hand out and smiled, "Hi. I'm David Keller."

James shook his hand, "I'm James, but everyone calls me 'Jim'." James and David walked inside the house. The house had hardwood floors in the den and hallways. The back door led onto a screened-in back porch.

There was a young man sitting in a chair drinking a beer. When he saw David and James, he smiled and stood up. "I'm Drew Harris, David's roommate."

"It's nice to meet you, Drew. You can call me 'Jim'." James said.

David offered, "Well, come on in and we'll show you the room."

The three went back through the large kitchen which had a table with four chairs, stove and what looked to be a new refrigerator.

David opened the door at the left of the hall and they walked inside the bedroom. It was large, with a small bed and dresser. The private bathroom had a large shower. It all looked good to James.

They walked back out into the hall and then entered the den. It had a sofa, recliner, TV, coffee table with a lamp and an oval rug in the center of the floor. Everything was impressively neat and tidy.

James nodded, thoughtfully and said, "Everything looks great." He smiled, "I'd like to take the room."

The men talked over the details and before leaving, James said, "I need to pick up some linens and things. I'll come back tomorrow. I'll probably see you guys when you get done with classes."

David nodded, "That's fine, Jimbo." He handed James a key and asked, "By the way, what classes are you taking?"

James said, "Well, just history for now. What about you guys?"

Drew smiled, "We're getting our engineering degrees and someday we hope to own our business together."

"That's great," James said.

David concluded, "We will be in about 2 p.m. tomorrow and we'll see you then. There's beer in the refrigerator if you decide to have one before we get here."

"OK," James nodded, "see you guys tomorrow then!"

When James got in the car, J.J. turned to him and asked, "Well? How did it go?"

"It went great. They seemed like two nice young men, and are studying to be engineers. The room was more than suitable, and was the biggest of the bedrooms."

On the way back to Greensboro, James and J.J. picked up a few things for his room. James packed one suitcase and told J.J. he'd pick up anything else when he got there.

The next morning, J.J. picked up James and they headed back to Burlington. When they arrived, J.J. helped James carry his luggage and took the opportunity to look around.

"It's not bad, James. A lot better than what I had in college." J.J. finished his tour and turned back to James. "Well, buddy," he sighed, "I guess this is it. You have to call and stay in touch."

"Thanks for all the help, J.J.. I couldn't have done it without you." James stuck out his hand to shake J.J.'s, but J.J. took his and pulled James into him for a hug.

"You be careful, James," J.J. said, "don't get in trouble. Call me if you need me, night or day."

"I will, J.J.. Thanks."

J.J. left and James made his bed and put his things away before heading into the kitchen. He got a beer and went out to the back porch to wait. At about 1 o'clock, David and Drew arrived home.

"Jimbo!" David called, "are you on the porch? Do you want a beer?"

"I have one," James answered.

About that time, music came on the on the back porch, around James and the other men joined him.

"We're glad to have you, Jimbo," David said, smiling, "do you like rhythm and blues?"

"I like all types of music."

"Well, in the house we only play rhythm and blues. Do you dance?"

"No," James confessed, "I don't."

"We'll teach you, then," David slapped James on the back. "If you can dance, you can get the girls. Do you have loafers?"

"The only shoes I have, I'm wearing," James said, looking down at his feet.

David looked down at James feet and laughed, "We've got to get rid of those wing tips, and you look like you work at a funeral home. We'll go get you some loafers."

Drew nodded and stood, "Y'all, let's go now. It's just up the road."

The men set their beers aside and left for the shoe shop. As they walked along the sidewalk, David asked Drew where the shoe store was.

"About one block up," Drew replied.

In just a few moments, the sign for Edward's Shoe Store came into view. When they went inside, Drew greeted the owner, "Mr. Edwards, this man needs a pair of loafers. Oxblood colored."

Mr. Edwards sat down in front of James, new loafers in hand.

"Take off your socks, Jim." Drew said, "You have to learn to wear them without socks. That's how we all wear them."

James took off his socks.

"My God! Look how white this boy's feet are!" Drew exclaimed, "They are as white as snow."

David agreed, "It looks as if they have no blood in them."

Drew and David laughed as James completed the purchase and put his old wing tips in the shoe box, wearing his new loafers out.

It was about 2 o' clock when they started up the sidewalk and headed into T.M.'s Men's Clothing Store. As they turned the corner to the store, a very attractive lady walked out of a store and crossed the street. James stopped walking when he saw her. Drew and David made it two steps further and then stopped and turned back to James.

David saw the lady and said, "That's Miss Wilson, the history professor."

Drew raised his eyebrows, "My God," he breathed, "she's prettier than a speckled pup lying under a red wagon." He turned to David and smiled.

James couldn't speak. He finally started to walk again, with Drew and David flanking him. The clothing store was two buildings down on the right. As they entered the store, David asked James, "What size do you wear?"

James found his voice, "32 length, 34 waist."

"OK," David nodded, "let's have a look around."

David and Drew chose about five pairs of pants and five shirts from the racks, all in different colors.

"OK, Jim," said Drew at last, "this should do you for a few days."

David nodded, "Let's take Jimbo's things back to the house and head over to the Hole in The Wall to have a beer." Turning to James he explained, "That's the local beer joint, Jimbo."

James grinned and nodded," let's do it!"

At the Hole in the Wall, they grabbed a table and ordered a round of beers. Beach music played on the radio.

After his first swig, David looked up at James. "So, you really can't dance?"

James swallowed a mouthful of beer and shook his head, "nope."

Drew laughed, "We need to teach him, David. You can't get the girls if you don't know how, man." He turned back to James and pledged, "David and I both know how to dance, and we have no trouble getting dates."

James surprised himself by tapping his foot to the rhythm of the music, which he had never before done.

When they finished, David turned to Drew, "I have to go home and do some studying for a test in the morning," he said. "Monday is always tough."

Drew nodded, "tell me about it."

The boys walked along the streets, back to the house James now called 'home'.

Chapter 6

The next morning, James woke and showered. Then, he put on his new khaki pants and black bandlon shirt; the type that bloused out over the top of his pants. Finally, he put on his new weejun loafers; without socks.

In the kitchen, there was a note:

'We had to leave early. See you this afternoon.'

There was a bowl of gravy on the table with some canned biscuits. James was pretty nervous. It wasn't that he didn't like gravy, quite the contrary. It was that he didn't have much of an appetite. Today was the beginning of something new for him. Today he was doing something he had always wanted to do – Go to college.

On his way to campus, he happened to glance over and see his reflection in one of the store windows. He paused for a moment, then just laughed and shook his head.

As James entered the classroom, Miss Wilson was standing at her desk. James slowly walked toward her and she turned, smiling. James just stared back, again unable to speak. He managed to stick his hand out.

Miss Wilson took the offered hand, "I'm Miss Wilson," she said.

Miss Wilson shook his hand like a dishrag and all James could do was grin and nod his head. Finally, James said, "Nice to meet you. I'm Jim Andrews."

Miss Wilson returned, "Nice to meet you too. Have a seat, Jim."

James walked over to the first available desk and sat down, thinking just how stupid he must have looked to her.

Miss Wilson looked over the students and began to talk. She couldn't keep her eyes from looking back at James. He seemed to be her age. The way he sat in his chair was unlike her other students. James looked dignified and professional, and very handsome. She was having a hard time focusing on what she was saying to the class.

James sat unmoving for the next hour. When the class ended, Miss Wilson stood and announced, "Class be sure to take plenty of notes. There will be a test next Friday."

James walked by her and managed a smile for Miss Wilson. She managed a smile, in return.

On his way back to Main Street, James stopped and looked around. He decided to walk around some more, to get to know the place a little better. As he walked through the village, he continued to admire the architecture of the houses. Some looked like the New England saltbox houses while others had white picketed fences with little gardens. People sat on front porches and waved as James walked by. James waived back, although they were perfect strangers. Flags hung on front porches; University of North Carolina at Chapel Hill flags, North Carolina State University flags and Duke Flags. The people here were big basketball fans, it seemed. As James walked, his feet continued to become sore. He made his way back to his room where he took off the loafers and fell asleep.

James woke to David shaking him and saying, "Wake up, Jimbo! We're going to the Hole in the Wall to get a beer."

"My feet are so sore, I don't even know if I could walk there," James said.

"By the looks of your feet, it looks as if you could use some Band-Aids," David laughed. He grabbed a box of bandages and handed them to James, "put these on and get a move on!"

James put about five Band-Aids on each foot and hobbled slowly to the Hole in the Wall. The building was brick with two double doors for entry. There was a large, black circle on the door which read, 'Hole in the Wall.' There was a deck on the back where all the kids would sit and drink beer, smoke and listen to music. Inside, the room was dark. There were tables and chairs as well as a juke box and a floor for dancing. The bar extended one entire side of the wall. Music and the sound of kids laughing and talking permeated through the entire building.

The three men sat at a table on the inside and ordered a pitcher of beer. They had only been there for about 5 minutes when a young lady walked up to Drew and asked him for a dance. Drew jumped up, grabbed her hand and left for the floor.

Drew was about 6'3" and weighed in at a slender one hundred sixty pounds, but to watch him dance was something to see. He was really good at it. James asked David if he could dance as well. David said he could dance, but that no one could dance as well as Drew.

"Drew is a natural," said David.

The next song came on the juke box and Drew stayed on the floor. David got up and walked across the floor and asked another girl to dance. The beer arrived at the table and James helped himself. The more he drank, the better it tasted. By the time the guys arrived back at the table, James had drank about half a pitcher. It was hot in there, after all. David ordered another pitcher and James drank while David and Drew danced. This continued until about 9:30 p.m. About 6 pitchers of beer later, they decided to leave. When they stood from the table, James began to walk sideways and David grabbed him and pulled him back in line with him and Drew as they walked out the door. Outside, James had to stop for a moment to take a breath of air.

James said, "Man, it's hot in there!"

Drew said, "Yeah, it's hotter than a preacher on his wedding night!"

Then David said, "I bet that's hot fella's."

James' feet were hurting so bad he could barely walk. David grabbed one arm and Drew grabbed the other and put James' arms around their necks. And off they went walking home.

As they were crossing the street a car pulled up to the stop sign and stopped. James looked over at the car and there sat Miss Wilson and some guy looking over at them. James was totally embarrassed as the car pulled off. They all finally made it home. David and Drew took James to his room and he fell back across the bed. One of them took his shoes off but he didn't know which one.

The next morning when James woke up he didn't think he had moved… all he knew was he had to go to the bathroom. He almost went back to sleep standing there urinating. It seemed like it took 30 minutes to finish. Not only did his feet hurt but his head hurt just as bad. David and Drew were gone to school already. After James took a shower and changed clothes he headed downtown to be at class by 9 o'clock.

When he walked into class he was taking small and easy steps like someone trying not to wake somebody sleeping. James went over and sat down, his head was hurting and his feet were swelling. He eased off one of his shoes, the foot that hurt the most. After class, Ms. Wilson said, "Jim, would you mind staying for a few minutes? I need to talk to you."

"Yes Ma'am," said Jim.

After everybody left Ms. Wilson turned to James and said, "What's wrong with you?"

"I'm trying to break in these new shoes, Ms. Wilson."

She looked down at his feet. "My goodness Jim, come with me. We need to put something on your feet."

James put the shoes on and down the hall he went slow and easy. "Come in here James. It's our first aid room. Sit up on the table and slip off your shoes," said Ms. Wilson as she reached up into the cabinet. James was looking at her from behind and was amazed by her figure. When she turned around she could tell James was looking at her legs. She had a bottle of alcohol in one hand and cotton in the other.

"Okay Jim, take a breath. This is going to burn."

There were many places on James' feet that were raw. She just poured the alcohol all over his feet, one at a time. "Jim, was that you I saw last night with David and Drew?" asked Miss Wilson.

"Do you know David and Drew?"

"This is their fourth year. After four years you know most everybody attending the school."

"Yes, it was me. We were coming from the Hole in the Wall."

"I knew where you were coming from. Do you get that way often, Jim?"

"No, that was my first time."

"Well, all I can say is that if you continue to do those things then you won't amount to much in life. I hope this is not a regular thing for you."

"Oh, it's not Miss Wilson. That was a onetime deal and my feet were hurting, so that's why they were carrying me."

She just smiled as James was sliding off the table easily to land on his feet softly. Miss Wilson put her hand around his arm to steady him as he looked over at her. Their eyes met and just for a second, neither of them could move. Finally, Miss Wilson turned and went over to the medicine cabinet to return the alcohol.

"Go home and keep your feet up for a while Jim. I hope they feel better tomorrow. See you in class."

"I'll be there!" said James.

As James was walking down the sidewalk toward home he could not get her face out of his mind. When he looked at her all he could see was those green-blue eyes and that expression she had on her face. It wasn't a smile, and it wasn't a sad look. It was a look that he would never forget. Whenever he thought about it, he had a hurting in his stomach. He had never had that type of feeling before. When James got home, he just went to his room and lay down on the bed and thought about the time that he had with her by himself. About the hand she put on his arm and how it made him feel.

Chapter 7

After about four or five days James was able to walk in his shoes without them hurting. The shoes had gotten softer and his feet had healed. He also had made an A+ on his history test. Miss Wilson was impressed, but to James, the test was elementary. Still, he was pleased that Miss Wilson was impressed. He also had called Grammy and J.J. and the business was running fine without him. Grammy was doing well also. He was pleased that everything was going well.

He had just gotten home when David hollered out, "Grab a beer and come out on the porch." James did just that, grabbed a beer and went out on the porch where David and Drew were sitting and listening to the radio.

"Hey James, have a seat. They're going to have a band down at the Hole in the Wall tonight. They are going to be playing rhythm and blues music tonight. And if you are going to dance we need to teach you how to dance the shag. There's only about three or four steps that you have to learn, James... you can do it. So after you drink your beer we are going to teach you."

James said, "How are you going to do that?" The radio was playing 'The Tams' and James patted his foot on the floor.

David said, "He has rhythm! He's keeping time with the music with his foot. So he will be a natural."

David got up and took his belt off and made a loop of it and put it around the doorknob on the back porch. "Now James, you just hold on to one end of this belt and you are going to pretend that it's a lady's hand. I am going to show you a few steps but you've got to keep time with the music when you dance."

James did not understand, so David said, "Then stand beside me and hold the belt and just do the steps that I do and feel the music."

After about 30 minutes James had three of the steps down. He would make two or three steps forward and step back two or three. He just had to work on the rhythm part more but it was coming to him, if slowly.

David said, "James, you have about six hours to get ready then we are going shagging." James would hold the belt and go back and forth trying to get into the rhythm. So he had one more beer, and then one more, and one more. After about four beers, the rhythm was setting in and he was feeling good. David and Drew were laughing at him. Then James began laughing.

"You're going to do alright, Jim," David said.

After three hours James knew he had done all he could do for now, and he had to get ready to go. So after taking a bath and changing clothes he stepped into the den where Drew and David were. They both had a pair of shoes in their hands.

James asked, "What is the extra pair of shoes for?"

David held one shoe up and showed him the soles of the shoes. The entire heel was gone on the shoes except about a quarter of an inch and the nail in the shoe had been driven back into that quarter of the shoe.

"It's our dancing shoes, Jim. We take the heels off so we can dance smoother and slide easier on the floor. When you are making turns and other steps it helps. You will see when we get there and start dancing. We have two ladies that are going to meet us there and are holding us a table."

So they started walking down the sidewalk. It was a cool night. The streetlights lit up the sidewalks and in the distance you could see a lot of lights and cars parked on both sides of the street. You could hear the music that was coming from the Hole in the Wall. People were standing around in the parking lot smoking and talking. Some of the ladies had on miniskirts with boots. Some had on long dresses. The miniskirt was coming into fashion and all the guys liked that. Drew said guys that didn't like them had Moms that wanted a girl and Dads that wanted a boy and both were satisfied.

As they started into the door they paid two bucks each and the man at the door stamped their hands with a big blue circle to ID the ones that had paid. The music was loud. The place was elbow –to-elbow with smoke and laughter everywhere. A girl came over and grabbed Drew by the hand and led him over to the table. As they followed Drew, James saw another girl sitting at the table holding three chairs for Drew, David and James. David introduced the two girls to Jim.

"Girls, this is Jimmy Andrews, he's our roommate. Jim, this is Linda, and this Helen. They're going to be our dance partners for tonight and they're going to work with you on your dancing. They know this is your first time dancing so they're going to work with you on it. So, just listen to these girls and you'll do fine."

Linda was tall and slender with dark hair, young and attractive. Helen was blonde and slender and also attractive. She had on a red miniskirt and boots. The guys ordered two pitchers of beer.

David looked at Drew and said, "Jim looks really nervous."

Drew turned and looked at Jim, then turned back to David and said, "My God, he looks as nervous as a virgin at a prison rodeo."

"It will take some time and about a pitcher of beer for him to get loosened up," David said.

James looked around. Sweat was running down the side of his face and his back. His hair had fallen down on his forehead.

James was thinking to himself, 'What have I gotten myself into?' As he poured himself a glass of cold beer from the pitcher Helen looked over at him and said, "Come on Jim, let's break the ice and get you started." She grabbed him by the hand and started pulling him towards the floor, making room as they went because the dance floor was full.

When they stepped out on the floor she took her right hand and grabbed Jim's left hand and stood beside him. She bumped him with her hip against his hip. She stepped backwards one step and then went forward and stood in front of him. She nodded her head for him to start dancing so he started making his three steps forwards and three steps backwards. Helen was moving back and forth with Jim, keeping in time with the music. When the dance was over Jim thanked Helen for dancing with him and told her he would try to do better next time. She said, "Jim, you did fine! You just need to dance more, that's all." James was pleased with her comment.

Another pitcher of beer was brought to the table. Linda was on the floor dancing with Drew. They would really dance well together. They had been dancing together for about three years now. David took Helen by the hand and led her to the dance floor. About that time a young lady came over to the table and asked if James would like to dance. He had never had a woman ask him to dance before that he didn't already know. So he got up from the table and went to the floor with her. He just sort of started going back and forth just like he did when he was dancing with Helen. He could see that this young lady was dancing with no problem, so he got a little looser thinking that he was doing something right. He was getting a little bit braver.

The beer was kicking in by the time the song was over. On the way back to the table David walked by James and said, "Man, you were looking good! Just keep doing what you are doing."

They ordered another beer and about the time James finished his glass Linda said, "Come on Jim, it's my turn now." The band was playing 'What Kinda Fool' by The Tams, one of the most requested songs of the night. It was a great song to dance to but James also liked the lyrics. James was singing along and really enjoying himself. Now, he was beginning to feel comfortable.

He knew what David and Drew told him about being in rhythm with the music. His timing was coming in and the beer was kicking in. James had never been a drinking man, so it didn't take much for him to get that buzz on that he had heard about.

One of the band members stepped up to the microphone and said, "This will be the last song for tonight. Thank you folks for coming! We've enjoyed being here tonight. Drive safe leaving." Linda leaned over the table and asked Drew, David and Jim if they would like to go with them to get something to eat before going home. All three said, "Yes!" at the same time.

They all left and went to the parking lot where Linda's car was. It was a 1965 Mustang, candy apple red, and two doors. Linda opened the driver's door and unlocked the other side. Drew hollered, "Shotgun" and pulled the seat back for David, Jim and Helen. It was a little tight in the back seat with Helen sitting between David and Jim. Her miniskirt went a little higher when she sat down.

David said, "I'm really hungry."

"I'm so hungry I could eat the ass end out of a skunk," Drew said.

"That is really hungry!"

They all laughed as Linda drove to Carter's restaurant up the road about 5 miles. Drew turned to David and Jim and said, "Guys, we've got to get us a car. We will need it when we go to Myrtle Beach."

"You are right, Drew," David replied as they pulled up to Carter's restaurant.

As they went in and found a table for five, Jim pulled out the chair for Linda and Helen. Linda was impressed with Jim's manners, "Boy, we've got a gentleman in the crowd. Thank you, Jim," she said as she sat down. "Where are you from, Jim?" Linda asked.

"Greensboro, North Carolina originally. But I've been living in New York City for the last nine years."

"What brings you to Elon College?" She asked.

"I'm taking a course in history, in Miss Wilson's class. It's a continuing education course."

"That's great Jim," Linda said. "Do you work anywhere?"

"Yes, I work at Exum Textiles."

"Is that right? My mother worked for Exum Textiles."

"Is that right?" Jim said.

"Yes, she worked in the Asheville, North Carolina plant. She worked in the lab. Her name is Ellen Smith."

"Yes, I've been in that plant," James said.

"My mother said she knew Mr. Exum."

"How long has she worked there?" Jim asked.

"She's has been working there for over 20 years, about as long as I can remember. She loves working there. She said Mr. Exum was a nice man and he would always come by the lab and speak to everyone there when he was in the plant. Sometimes he would bring his little boy with him and the little boy would be wearing a suit and tie just like his dad. She said his dad was very proud of him. I understand his son now runs the business. They say he's only about 30 years old now and they say he's a very nice looking man, tall with black hair and brown eyes. And when he visits the plant, they say he dresses like he just stepped out of a magazine, his hair is always cut short and neat. The same length, every time they see him. And yes, he would always come by and speak to everyone, just like his dad did. Although he was a little less tall than his dad, but his good looks made up for that. They said all the women would talk about his good looks after he left."

"Do you know his son, Jim?" she asked.

"Let's say I'm getting to know him better," James said.

"She also said that a colored man is the president of the company now," Linda said.

James nodded, "Yes. His name is J.J. Washington."

It was Drew's turn to speak. "You mean the president of Exum Textiles is a colored man? I wonder how he got that job."

"Well, Drew, he has a degree in textiles from N.C. State University. I guess you could say he worked his way up. He started working there in the warehouse when he was a young boy. He did about every job there was to be done. He's a very smart man, and knows the textile business like the back of his hand," James said.

Linda chimed in, "mom said he was a really nice man, but young; around 30 years old."

David said, "Maybe you could put in a good word for Drew and I so we could get a job there after we graduate."

James nodded, "If that's what you want to do, I will do my best."

"That would help Drew and I get started in our own business," David agreed.

After eating their hamburgers and chatting more about their futures, Drew was ready to head for home. "Let's go back to our place and listen to some music," he said.

David sighed and nodded, "that sounds good to me."

As they prepared to leave, they heard a voice coming from the booth behind them. "Hey guys," the voice drawled. The trio turned to see Professor Stevens and Miss Wilson sitting together.

The guys smiled and nodded while Linda replied, "Hello Miss Wilson, Mr. Stevens.

Miss Wilson looked up at James and smiled, "And how are your feet, Jim?"

James nodded gently, "Just fine, thank you."

David grinned, "We've taught him how to dance and he's doing great!"

Sandra chuckled, "well, you guys be careful out there tonight."

"We're headed home," Drew assured with a smile.

As the group arrived at James' home, David turned to Helen and Linda and asked if they wanted to come in for a beer and maybe dance to some rhythm and blues. Linda and Helen looked at one another and shrugged.

"Sure, I guess we can stay for a while," said Linda.

They all went inside the house and Drew yelled ahead to David, "get all those beers out of the fridge; I'll put the records on."

James paused by his room. "Fellas, I think I'm headed to bed. My feet hurt a little and, at my age, I need the rest." He turned to the ladies, "Linda, Helen thank you so much for helping me with my dancing. I could not have done it without you two. You've been great but I'm going to call it a night." And then he finally turned to his roommates, "I'll see you guys in the morning."

"Sweet dreams," Linda said.

"You bet," James replied.

As James undressed, he couldn't get his mind off Miss Wilson. Seeing her at Carter's restaurant was great, but he didn't like seeing her with that professor. As he lay there, trying to fall asleep, his thoughts kept returning to her. *What a night*, he thought, reflecting on the whole evening. He had danced, drank beer and ate hamburgers at Carter's. He loved every minute of it. He had some fun in his life, but nothing like tonight.

Chapter 8

The next thing he knew, he was waking up to the sound of his shower running. Lying there, he listened to the water running, and wondered why David or Drew was in his shower. James rolled over on his side, watching the bathroom door to see who would be walking out. He finally heard the water stop and a few seconds later the door opened. White steam billowed out into his bedroom. Rather than David or Drew, out stepped a good-looking blonde wearing a towel around her waist. Her body was completely exposed from the waist up. It was Helen.

"Good morning, Jim," she said unabashedly.

"G-g-g-good morning, Helen," James stammered.

"Hope you don't mind me using your shower," Helen replied, "Linda was in the other one. Did I wake you up?"

"It was time to get up, anyway," Jim said trying to sound nonchalant despite the half-naked woman standing in his room. "By the way, what time is it?"

"About 11 o'clock," answered Helen.

"My God, I've never slept this late before!"

"Well, it is Sunday morning. You do know there's no school on Sunday," Helen said teasingly.

"Yeah, but I need to run over to the library and do a little research."

"Well, you could do some research on me, Jim. If you know what I mean."

"I know what you mean, but I'll have to take a rain check," said James.

"You've got one."

As soon as Helen walked out of the room, James got up and jumped into the shower. He then dressed and started out of his room. He could smell sausage frying in the kitchen. Drew called out, "Jim, I'm making sausage, grits and eggs. How do you like your eggs?"

"Over light," came the reply.

"Well, I only fix them one way," said Drew.

"How's that," asked James.

"Scrambled."

With a chuckle, Jim said, "That sounds good."

David walked in and asked, puzzled, "where's the girls?"

"They got dressed and left," answered Drew before adding, "How do you like your eggs, David?"

"You know how I like my eggs," replied David, "over light."

"That's what I thought," Drew mused, "scrambled."

David just smiled. "I've been eating those damned scrambled eggs for three years and always with sausage and grits. Drew when are you going to figure out that I don't like grits? They taste like sand!" David continued his complaining. "Damn, my head hurts," he said, rubbing his temples.

"Well, Dave, the first time I saw your head," Drew joked, "I knew you were going to have problems with it."

"Kiss my ass!"

Drew said, "Have some black coffee, fellas. It's on the stove."

James said, "I'm going over to the library to do a little studying."

"Not until you help us clean up this kitchen, old boy," said Drew.

Though he didn't let on, it was the first time in his life that James had washed dishes. On his way to the library, he stopped at a pay phone booth and called Grammy.

"How are you doing, Grammy?" he asked.

"I'm doing fine, James. And you?"

"I'm OK."

"How's school?"

"It's great, Grammy. I'm learning to dance."

"Oh Lord! I would love to see that," laughed Grammy.

"Well, you could say I'm a work in progress," laughed James. "Well, I just wanted to check in with you and see how you were doing. I'll see you in a couple weeks, Grammy. I love you."

"And I love you, too, James. Be careful."

"I'll see you later. I'm off to the library."

Chapter 9

It was a warm Sunday morning. Very few students were out walking. James could hear the church bells ringing in the distance. It was now 11 o'clock and church was beginning to start as he walked toward the library. He noticed Sandra was walking down the sidewalk at a fast pace as if she was late for church, but he could tell by her face that she was not in a good mood. James stopped her as they met each other going toward the library.

"Good Morning, Miss Wilson." James said.

"It's not a good morning, Jim." Miss Wilson said.

"What's wrong?"

"Well, I was up early and getting ready for church. As I went out to get into my car the right tire was flat. When I got the car jacked up, I took the wheel cover off and took two of the five lug nuts off. I thought I could have the tire changed in time to be at church on time, but the other three lug nuts were proving difficult to take off. So now I have to walk to church, and I'm going to be late!"

"I'd be glad to go up and finish changing your tire. I think I can get the lug nuts off." James said.

"You probably could, James. They were on too tight for me. It looks like I'm going to be too late for church anyway so let's go back to the house and change that tire." Sandra said.

On the way back, James asked Sandra if she had ever changed a tired before. "Oh yes," Sandra said. "I can change a tire if the lug nuts are not on too tight. My dad made sure that I could change a tire, just in case I was out somewhere by myself and had a flat. All girls should learn how to change a tire."

"I think you're right Miss Wilson." James replied.

As they arrived at Sandra's house, James could see that the car had been jacked up. The wheel cover had been taken off and the lug wrench was lying on the ground in front of the tire.

James loosened up the other three lug nuts and took the tire off. He then replaced it with a spare tire that Miss Wilson had put out. After snapping on the wheel cover, James turned to Miss Wilson. "Okay, you're ready to go." He said.

"Thank you so much, James. You came along just in time." Sandra said. She glanced at her watch. "It looks like church is just about over. I was going over to Sadie Mae's boarding house to have lunch after church. How about I treat you to lunch for changing my tire? It's all home cooked food, you'll love it!"

"It's been awhile since I've had a home cooked meal." James said.

"It's the best in town. Get in and I'll drive us." Sandra said as she started around the side of the car to get in. James followed her around to her door and reached for the door handle to open the door for her.

"Well it looks like we have a gentleman in the house." Sandra said as she stepped into the driver's seat.

James got in on the other side and Sandra pulled out of the driveway.

She turned left and headed toward town. James looked over at Sandra. He could not help but notice how young she looked. When she looked over at him with a big smile, her personality began to stand out and he liked what he saw. She had a down-to-earth attitude. Not the professor of history that he had been used to seeing. Now she seemed like a friend to him, and that's the way he liked it.

As Sandra started to pull into the parking lot, James noticed the three story building with windows all the way across the way across the front and from top to bottom. The building was painted white and had black shutters on either side of the windows. There were black double doors with a metal canopy painted black.

They appeared to be early as the gravel parking lot wasn't filled with cars. "Well nobody else is here yet, thank goodness. We can probably go right in and have a seat." Sandra said. James looked over the black canopy that read "Sadie Mae's Boarding House". Underneath it read in smaller letters, "Lunch for the public on Sunday only 12 to 2."

As James and Sandra entered the door, Sandra was met with open arms by Sadie Mae's owner. "Hey Sandra. How are you, honey?"

Sandra introduced James to Sadie Mae. She was a small lady who appeared to be in her mid-sixties. She had short black hair with a lot of gray, and was dressed nicely. She pulled Sandra off to the side and whispered into her ear with their backs turned to James.

"Where did you find him?" Sadie asked.

"He's one of my students." Sandra replied.

"Oh my, how do you get anything done with a thing like that watching you?" Sadie asked.

"It's not easy, but I do the best I can." Sandra said and they both laughed.

They both turned back to James. Sadie welcomed James to her boarding house. "Come right on in, Jim." She said as she walked them to the table. "You can have a seat anywhere you like." James pulled out a chair for Sandra to sit down, and walked to the other side to sit down in front of Sandra.

There was an older gentleman sitting in the chair to Sandra's left. Before James could sit down, the gentleman stood up and held out his hand. "I'm John Verton, but you can just call me John."

James took John's hand and shook it. "I'm James Andrews, but you can just call me Jim."

"It's nice to meet you, Jim." John replied. He was a big man who appeared to be in his mid-fifties. He had broad shoulders and a round barrel chest. James thought he could have been a weight-lifter. James noticed that he had a firm handshake as well, which meant good character.

"Are you from around this area, John?" James asked.

"No, I'm from around Pleasant Garden, northeast from here." John said.

"Let me introduce you to Sandra Wilson." James said and gestured his hand toward Sandra.

"It's nice to meet you, Sandra." John said. "Are you folks married?"

"Oh, no, I teach history up at the college." Sandra responded.

"I love history." John said. "Where are you from, Jim?"

"I'm originally from Greensboro." James said. "What do you do for a living, John?"

"I own a painting company. I started it when I got out of the service." John replied. "What do you do, Jim?"

"I work for Exum Textiles. They have a corporate office in New York City and I've been there for about nine years." James replied.

"That's a good place to work, Jim. I met Mr. Exum once while I was in Greensboro. He was a kind and generous man. Just look at what he's done for the area. He donated a lot to the schools around here as well as recreation areas. I remember one time I was in the shoe store in downtown Greensboro when a long black limousine pulled up in front of the school. The back door opened and out jumped out two little boys and a little girl. Mr. Exum got out right behind them with his top coat and his collar turned up. Mr. Exum walked over to the owner. 'I want you to fit these children with new shoes and send me the bill.'

"While he was standing there, he turned to me and introduced himself. 'Fit these boys with some shoes like John has on here. Are these good shoes, John?' He asked.

"Yes, since I make a living from painting, I spend a lot of time standing on ladders all day.' I replied.

"Well that's good enough for me.' He replied. 'Did you say you were a painter?'

"Yes sir, that's all I've done since I've gotten out of the service.'
I replied

"John, I'm going to need some painting done in about three
weeks. Would you be interested?' Mr. Exum asked.

"Why yes sir, I would.' I replied. He pulled out a pen and wrote
down his phone number on a piece of paper that was lying on the
counter.

"John, this is the number to the plant and those three numbers are
my extension numbers. Call me in about two weeks. I may have
some work for you.' He said good bye and waved to the kids as
he got back in his limousine.

"I looked down at those kids, and I knew their feet had to have
been freezing. Their shoes were worn out, and this had to be the
first new pair that they had had in a long time.

"After about two weeks I gave that number a call. His secretary
sent my call to him and he surprisingly remembered my name.
He told me that I could start the next Monday morning."

"It sounds like he had a big heart, John." Sandra said.

"Oh, that's not the only thing he did for me. I was in the process
of painting a hallway and two offices. After the first week, I had
it all done except for a little trim work. Everyday Mr. Exum
would come in to stop and shake my hand. He asked me how I
was feeling and would always compliment my work. He told me

to come to his office when I was finished and he would cut me a check on Monday. He had a way about himself that made you want to do a good job for him.

"That afternoon, I left to take my old pickup truck to the mechanic to get some work done. The mechanic had told me earlier in the week to just drop it off that night and he would have it done for me by Saturday morning. My home was about 5 miles up the road from the garage. When I got there, the mechanic wasn't in so I just left my keys on the floor board and walked out to the edge of the road to catch a ride home. It was about dusk and I had had a hard day, so I was ready to go home to get some rest."

Chapter 10

"I had only been walking for about 10 minutes when a black 1940 Ford pulled up beside me. It was a Ron Jackson, a gentleman that I had known before I went into the service. It had been the first time I had seen him since I had been home. I'd heard that he ran moonshine for a living, but I didn't know for sure. That particular day, I knew for sure he was running moonshine because as soon as I got in the front seat, there were cases of moonshine whiskey stacked to the top of the back seat.

"'How are you doing, John?' he asked.

"'I'm doing fine, Ron, and you?' I asked.

"'I'm doing fine, but I'll be doing better once I've unloaded my cargo. Do you still live in the same place, John?' He asked

"'Yep, same place. Just let me off in front of my house, and I would appreciate it.'

"I had hardly gotten the words out of my mouth when the red light came on right behind us. Needless to say, he took off like a bat out of hell. When we went by my house, it was a blur. That red light that was behind us could hardly be seen. As we started around the curve after he passed my house, there were two police cars facing us. He slammed on brakes, turned the wheel, and he did what I think they call a bootleg spin. He scared me to death.

He started driving in the opposite direction and passed the car that turned a red light on us in the first place.

"'John, when we turn up here on this little dirt road, I'm going to slow down. You'll need to jump out.' He said. I didn't say a word. I was ready to jump when he told me to. He turned on to that dirt road and they had just put fresh gravel on it. Needless to say, we spun around about twice and slid over in the ditch. He opened his door, jumped out and started running into the woods.

"My car door wouldn't open because it was jammed into the ditch, so I just sat there. I don't think I could have run anyway. I was scared to death! By then, the county deputy sheriff ran up to the car and pulled me out of the driver's side. He took me down to the county jail and charged me with all of the bootleg liquor. I was the only one they saw, so they locked me up in the county jail for hauling moonshine. Not having anyone to call, I just waited it out in the jail until Monday morning. I knew Mr. Exum would be in at around seven o'clock on Monday.

"The jailer let me make a call around 8:15 that morning, so I called Mr. Exum. When he answered the phone he said 'How are you doing this morning, John?'

"'Not too good,' I replied. 'I'm locked up down here in the county jail.'

"'What happened, John?' He asked.

"After telling him the story from beginning to end, he said 'Well, let me make a few phone calls, and I'll have someone down in the next hour to pick you up. We'll take you where you need to go.'

"Sure enough, within the hour, there was a gentleman down there and the jailer told me I could go. Needless to say, I picked up my truck and went over to the plant to finish the painting job for Mr. Exum. I thanked him for getting me out of jail.

"'Well John, you spent two years in the service for the government. I didn't think you needed to spend any more time than you had to.'

"He knew that if I had been found guilty, I would have gone to the federal penitentiary, not some little courthouse jail. After a week the sheriff came by and told me that my story had checked out. I didn't have to appear in court. That was a big relief, and I'll always remember the kindness Mr. Exum showed to me."

Sandra spoke up, "Speaking of bootleg liquor, I can remember when I was a little girl; my mom, dad, and I were sitting out on the front porch. In the distance we heard a siren coming up on our side of the mountain. Our house is about three quarters of a mile from the main road. We couldn't see the police car, but we heard the siren. The sun was going down over the mountain, and it had become dark all of a sudden. We heard an automobile coming down our driveway at a high rate of speed. They had the lights turned off, and you could hear the gravel land in the field as it rounded a curve. It came flying around to the front of our house and drove around to the back.

"I started to get up to run down the steps to see who it was, but my dad stopped me and told me to get back up on the porch. By this time, the siren had gone out of hearing distance. After a few minutes, a gentleman came walking around the side of the house to the front porch. He looked up at my dad and said 'How are you tonight, Mr. Wilson?' I didn't say a word as he walked up the steps to the porch. He took off his hat and greeted my mom. She offered him a glass of tea. They sat and chatted while he drank it.

"Well, it was nice visiting you folks, and Sandra, you have grown up to be a pretty young lady.' He said. Evidently he had met me when I was younger. He knew mom and dad for what sounded like a long time. As he got into the car and started backing out the drive way, I asked my dad who that man was.

"He's one of those Johnson boys that live down in North Wilkesboro.' He replied. After we finished our tea, we went back inside to get ready for bed. When we walked into the kitchen, there sat on our kitchen table, was a half-gallon jar of moonshine whiskey.

"Dad and mom never said a word. Dad just took the jar and put it in the cabinet. There was never a word mentioned about it inside our house.

"I think there is one out of every five families around Asheville that has a family member that has some kind of dealing with moonshine whiskey." Sandra said.

"Are you from Asheville?" John asked.

"Yes, I was born and raised in Asheville. I love that area." She replied.

"That is a beautiful area." John said.

"Some folks say it is God's country." James added

"Oh, have you been to Asheville, Jim?"

"Yes, I've been there a few times, but it has been several years." James said. He didn't bother to mention that he owned a plant located there with about 600 employees "I'm looking forward to going back."

"Well folks, it has been nice meeting you and talking, but it's time for me to move on. I've got to run a few errands." John said as he slid his chair back out from under the table. He shook hands with James and Sandra, and then turned to walk away.

"Well that was an interesting conversation. It seems as though Mr. Exum touched everybody's life that he had contact with." Sandra said.

"It sure seems that way." James replied.

Sadie Mae then walked up and said "What about some dessert?"

"Not for me." Sandra said. "I've had enough."

"That was a great lunch." James said. "It was very good. I haven't had turnip greens in a long time."

"Well, I'm glad you liked them Jim. You'll have to come back."

Sandra and James started to get up from the table when Sadie Mae motioned towards a table in the back corner of the room. It was a table for two, where an older couple sat who appeared to be in their late seventies.

"Today is their 50th wedding anniversary. They've been coming here for years." Sadie Mae said. James and Sandra noticed that the gentleman had his hand placed on top of hers as they carried on a conversation.

"They look as much in love today as they probably did 50 years ago. It's so sweet." Sandra said.

Chapter 11

As they walked up to the checkout station with Sadie Mae, James reached for his wallet.

"No, no, no." Sandra said. "This is my treat."

As they started to walk out, James opened the door for Sandra. She walked out and James said "Excuse me just a minute, Sandra." James stepped back inside and handed some money to Sadie Mae. He motioned his head toward the couple that was having their anniversary and thanked Sadie Mae again for lunch. He turned back around and caught back up with Sandra.

"What was that all about, Jim?" Sandra asked.

"I just thanked her again for the fine lunch." James replied.

As they started driving in the direction of Elon College, James said "I certainly have enjoyed my lunch with you Sandra. I really enjoyed the story you told about sitting on your front porch, when the moonshine hauler came up your driveway."

"Thank you, Jim. I have some great memories of living in that house. I enjoyed the lunch as well. I will see you in class in the morning, and don't be late." Sandra replied.

James stepped out of the car, and looked back at Sandra with a smile on his face. "I'm looking forward to it, Miss Wilson."

She smiled and drove off.

The next morning, James was up early, not taking time to eat Drew's breakfast that he had prepared for him. "See you this afternoon guys. I've got to be there a little early this morning." James said.

"We understand, Jimbo. Have a good one." Drew and David hollered from the kitchen as James went out the front door.

As he was walking fast up the sidewalk, he realized he was almost at a run. He stopped still and started talking to himself. "Slow down, James." He said as he began to walk slowly. "I know you're excited, but you don't have to act like a fool. You are 30. Act like you're 30. When you see Sandra, just act very casual, as if your heart was not bursting open to see her."

As James walked into the classroom, he walked in casually and didn't look over at Sandra.

"Just help me get to my seat without tripping all over myself." He thought. As James sat down, he looked up. Sandra was standing behind her desk. She had her head down, but her eyes were looking up at James. When their eyes met, Sandra looked away and then went to the blackboard to write out the page number for the lesson of the day.

For the next three days, James and Sandra would just smile at each other and say hi.

James knew there was something between them, but he had no idea what to do about it. Maybe it was just all in his head and she had no interest in him at all. The lunch they had together was maybe her being a nice person and just showing her appreciation for fixing her tire. "I'm sure she would do the same thing for anybody" he thought.

The next day James started out the door at the end of class when he heard Sandra say "Mr. Andrews." James turned around to face her. "Would you mind coming back for a few minutes?" She asked. James went back to his seat and sat down with a surprised look on his face.

After everyone had left the room, Sandra walked over to his desk. James stood up and Sandra put her right hand on his shoulder. "Jim, Sadie Mae called me because she has no way of getting in contact with you. She wanted me to tell you that the couple you bought lunch for on Sunday wanted to say thank you, and that they really appreciated it. That was a nice thing for you to do, Jim."

James just nodded his head and had no idea what to say.

It was now Friday, the last day of the week. Every time they would look at each other, they would just smile.

As James walked down the sidewalk, he thought about Sandra. It had been a good week getting to know her better, and letting her get to know him.

Friday and Saturday night went by fast. Linda and Drew had been out on dates both nights. The times that David and Drew were out listening to R&B, James was studying in his room. That gave him time to catch up on schoolwork and talk to J.J. concerning business matters. He gave Grammy a call to see how she was doing. It made for a quiet weekend.

Sunday morning, James was up and taking a shower. He could smell the coffee brewing as he walked into the kitchen. David was sitting at the table drinking his coffee.

"Good morning, David." James said.

"Good morning, Jim." He replied. "Come around and pour yourself a cup of coffee. Drew is still in bed and there's no telling what time he'll get up."

"I feel pretty good. I got some studying in and plenty of rest. I needed that. It was a quiet weekend." James said.

"That's because Drew wasn't here. That boy has to be doing something all the time. If he's not moving, he's sleeping." David said. "That dance contest coming up at Myrtle Beach has him

and Linda both occupied. Maybe that will give us both a break."
They both laughed.

"I never heard him come in last night. I'm sure it was this
morning sometime. He'll probably be up after lunch sometime."
David said.

"Well, I think I'm going over to the library to do a little more
studying." James said.

"I need to do the same thing, but I think I'm going to hang
around until sleeping beauty gets up and see what he wants to do
today." David said.

"I'll see you guys later today." James replied.

After spending an hour studying economics in Mexico, James
finally decided to leave the library. He walked down the
sidewalk and sat down on a bench overlooking the campus. The
big, confederate statue standing stood in the center of it all. As he
sat there looking at the beauty of the facility and the grounds, he
noticed the big oak tress whose leaves were changing colors in
preparation for the coming fall. It was a beautiful place to be on a
beautiful day. He felt blessed to be there and was enjoying the
quiet time. He glanced down the sidewalk and saw Miss. Wilson
walking toward him. She was dressed in jeans and tennis shoes
and holding about three books under each arm. Suddenly, James
felt that sick feeling growing in his stomach again.

"Good afternoon, Jim. How are you today?" asked Miss Wilson.

"I find it's such a nice day," replied James.

"It sure is. Mind if I have a seat and sit with you? Let's enjoy the beauty of this place. It is a beautiful place, isn't it, Jim? This is what made me want to stay here and teach," confessed Miss Wilson.

"Did you get your degree in Asheville?" Asked James.

"Yes, I got my teaching degree at the University of North Carolina at Asheville. After that, I came here to get my Master's in history. I just loved it so, I decided to stay. They offered me this teaching position and I have been here ever since, about six years," explained Miss Wilson. "What about you, Jim? What brings you here?"

"I just wanted to learn more, especially history," admitted James.

Nodding her head, Miss Wilson agreed, "Yes, history is a good subject.

"It's nice to know where you're going in life. But it's also equally important to know where you have been and history does that."

"You can say that again," Miss Wilson said with a slight chuckle.

In the distance, James could see Mr. Stevens walking hurriedly across the campus lawn.

"Is that your boyfriend, Mr. Stevens?" asked James, instantly regretting the question.

Ms. Wilson appeared not to mind too much, "Well, he's a friend. We've been dating for about a year."

"Is it serious?" James asked. He was furious with himself for prying but was unable to stop.

"Jim, you're getting personal," Miss Wilson chided with a half-smile.

"I know, I'm sorry," James said, looking down at the ground.

"That's OK, Jim.

"Miss Wilson, would you like to have a cup of coffee with me at the soda shop?"

"Well, I was going to the library... But I can go there later," said Miss Wilson, "Yes. I'll have a cup of coffee with you."

James and Miss Wilson got up from the bench and headed in the direction of the soda shop. Along the way, they continued their chat.

"So you work at Exum Textiles, James?"

"Yes, I guess you could say I do a little of everything."

"So... You just do whatever they tell you to?" asked Miss Wilson, sounding a little confused.

"Well, a lot of the time," replied James, wondering how he could evade her question without lying to her.

"I admire you for going back to college to further your education. It will help you move up the ladder," encouraged Miss Wilson.

"Maybe so," said James, looking for a way to change the subject.

"I'm familiar with Exum Textiles," continued Miss Wilson, "they have a plant in my hometown. Also, our next lesson in history is about textiles and how the industry got started. We'll be talking about the history of Exum Textiles. You know, they are the world's leading manufacturer of denim. Maybe you could learn something about the company you work for, Jim."

"That would be nice, Miss Wilson," Jim said as he held the door open for her.

They both sat down and ordered coffee.

"Do your parents teach?" asked James, relieved to be changing the subject.

"Well, my father was a car salesman, but my mother did teach in Asheville. Dad passed away about two years ago and mom is retired. If you pass the next test, I'll let you ride up with me to visit my mom," offered Miss Wilson.

"Boy, I would really love that, Miss Wilson," exclaimed James.

"From now on, Jim, when we are not in class, you can call me Sandra. My full name is Sandra Lynn Wilson."

"I'll do that," said Jim, trying to sound matter-of-fact.

"Do you have a car, Jim?" asked Sandra.

"Not now, but I need to buy one, soon."

"If you start saving your money up, maybe you can buy a car."

"Yes, I've got to start doing that; it's hard to get around walking everywhere. Especially if you have sore feet," James laughed.

Sandra laughed with him.

James continued, "I think maybe Drew, David and I may go in together and buy a car. Drew said his daddy mentioned to him that he may buy Drew a car. I don't know, but somehow we need to get a car. This walking everywhere is getting old."

After their coffee, James said, "I'll walk you back to the bench."

"You don't need to do that, Jim, but it sure is gentlemanly to offer," smiled Sandra.

After walking her back to the bench, James thanked her for having coffee with him, "maybe we can do it again sometime," said James.

"That would be fine," Sandra replied before James turned to walk away.

James took a deep breath and thought to himself; *that is the best looking woman I have ever seen and it feels so comfortable talking to her. I believe I could talk to her all day.*

Although they were at the soda shop for over an hour, it only seemed like 15 minutes. As he walked down the sidewalk to go back home, he felt light as a feather. His feet didn't hurt and he realized he was happier than he had ever felt in his life. In fact, work had not entered his mind in days.

Chapter 12

After three days of going to school and studying (and eating Drew's gravy and toast and sometimes sausage and scrambled eggs), the time had come to take the test that James had to pass in order to go to Asheville with Sandra.

The day before the test, James was up early. Drew had the gravy and toast ready. David just had toast. James was nervous. Although the test was about textiles, he knew he had to study hard to pass the test tomorrow.

He entered class and found a seat near the front. Miss Wilson walked to the chalkboard and spelled out, 'The History of Textiles.' After about 15 minutes of talking about pre-textiles, she started talking about the south, the War Between the States, the march that General Sherman made to the south and the burning of crops and cotton gins in Atlanta, Georgia. She discussed the path Sherman made North through the Carolinas and the surrender that General Johnson issued to Sherman in Raleigh, North Carolina and the surrender from General Lee to General Grant at Appomattox Courthouse which marked the official end to the Civil War.

In April 1865, the commodity of the south was cotton. It took approximately 15 to 20 years before the south could bring back its industrial use of cotton. In 1895, James Andrew Exum started the first cotton mill which produced denim wear for the working man. Now it was the largest manufacturer of denim in the world and has several locations in North Carolina and employs somewhere around 7,000 people throughout the state. With the success of his business, Mr. Exum shared this success with his community by donating money for schools, parks and hospitals to be built in areas where his plants where located. He was a very generous individual who cared about his employees. James Exum Jr. followed in his father's footsteps by finding ways to improve the product and making it a global business. Like his father, James Exum Jr. also cared about his employees by providing adequate pay, insurance and a good environment in which to work. He was well liked by his employees. About 9 years ago, Exum Jr. passed away and left his only son, James Andrew Exum III, the business. This made James Exum III the youngest owner and CEO of the largest textile and denim manufacturer in the world. Today, Exum III is about thirty-one years old. As reported by magazines and newspapers, he spends most of his time in New York City where his office is located and continues to follow in his grandfather and father's footsteps. He continues to work in research and development of new products and grows the global trade of denim products. Trade magazine reports say he is highly educated and speaks three languages. He was taught by his father at an early age about the textile business. It appears that he takes after his father by continuing to be generous to the areas in which the plants are located by providing to his employees. He has also donated money to schools, hospitals and colleges as well.

"So," Miss Wilson concluded, "I am sure we will hear of Mr. James Andrew Exum III in years to come, as well. This concludes our studies today on the history of textiles. I hope you have made notes. The test will be given in the morning, so study hard…" She paused for a moment and smiled, "class dismissed."

As James started out the door, Miss Wilson called him to the side.

"Well, Jim, did you learn anything today about your employer?"

"Yes, I did," James said, "and I'm going home to study for that test tomorrow so I can go to Asheville over the weekend."

Ms. Wilson just smiled and shook her head, "Have a good day, Jim."

As he was walking home, James thought to himself, *Boy if I fail this test, I might as well leave town.*

After class, James went home and put on some rhythm and blues music on the record player. He wrapped a belt around a doorknob and, holding one end of it, he began to shag. He was feeling good and had not had a beer. It was a good day. Later that afternoon, Drew and David walked in and asked him if he would like to go down to the Hole in the Wall and grab a beer.

"Why not?" said James, and off they started walking.

When they walked inside, the place was full of students. Linda and Helen were there, drinking a beer out on the deck. It was a beautiful evening, short-sleeved weather and most everyone was sitting outside. The three men sat at their table, drinking beer and talking. On the juke box, the song, 'Higher & Higher' by Jackie Wilson, played. Linda asked Drew for a dance and Helen asked James.

"You sure you want to dance with me," joked James.

"Sure," she said, pulling him out of his seat.

They went inside to dance and, after the song was over, Helen said to James, "you've really improved. Have you been practicing, Jim?"

"A little," he admitted.

"You can tell the song had a good rhythm to it. Anyone that has rhythm could dance to that song."

After a few more beers and a few more dances, Drew asked Linda and Helen if they would like to go back to his place and have a beer and listen to some records out on the back porch.

"Sounds good," the girls replied.

They all packed into Linda's car and drove back to the house. Sitting out on the back porch, the five of them drank beer and talked about going to Myrtle Beach to dance. Linda and Helen told David and Drew to let them know the next time they were going and they would try to go at the same time. As the evening grew dark, James decided to go to his room and put on a long-sleeved shirt. As he was taking off his shirt and rooting through his closet to find another, his door opened. In the doorway stood Helen.

With a sly grin, she asked, "do you mind if I use your bathroom, Jim?"

"That's fine," he said.

Helen walked behind Jim to the bathroom, but stopped. James felt her arms wrap around his waist, her hands moving up and caressing his chest. James turned around, but before he could say anything, Helen placed both her hands on either side of his face and kissed him on his lips. He stood, frozen, not knowing what to do or say in response to Helen's unexpected advances.

"Don't worry, I won't bite you, just having a little fun," purred Helen.

James asked, "How old are you?"

"I'm 20," she whispered.

"You're a little too young for me, honey."

"You're not an old man, Jim. You're young and very nice looking."

"Well, thank you for the compliment, Helen. But right now, I have another lady on my mind."

"I understand… Maybe another time and place."

"Maybe," replied James.

James threw on another shirt and they walked back out on the back porch.

With a knowing grin, David asked, "what have you two been up to?"

"Absolutely nothing," Helen replied.

James just grinned.

After a couple more beers, the girls decided they had to leave. David and Drew walked them to their car. James decided to go to bed. He hoped the extra sleep would prepare him for the test that awaited him the next day.

Thursday morning, James walked into class, feeling confident that he was going to pass the test. Miss Wilson greeted him at the door, "Have you been studying, Jim?"

"Every day, Ms. Wilson," he replied.

"I wish you luck."

"Thanks."

When everyone was seated Miss Wilson handed out the test. "You have one hour, students. Take your time and do the best you can. You can put your papers on my desk when you are finished and leave for the rest of the day. I will return them on Friday morning with your grade and we will review the subject."

Within 15 minutes, James had completed the test, but did not want to be the first person up to turn in his paper. So he sat there and waited until about half of the class had left before he turned his test in. As James was leaving the class, he placed it on the corner of Miss Wilson's desk. She looked up and they smiled at each other before he left.

The next morning, James was up early. He decided to pass on the gravy and toast that Drew had fixed. He couldn't wait to get to school. He felt like a five year old on Christmas morning. He took his time walking, just enjoying his surroundings in the cool morning air. It was a nice day.

When James entered the classroom, Miss Wilson was not there. On her desk were a stack of test papers, placed face down. Sorting through the stack, he found his paper and turned it over. There was a big red 'A' in the corner. He had passed. Attached to his paper there was a small envelope. Inside the envelope was a note that read;

'I will pick you up at nine in the morning. Bring one change of clothes just in case we spend the night at mom's. Have a good day, Sandra

P.S. Be sure to bring a jacket or a sweater and wear socks. '

James put the note in his pocket. When class was over, James looked over at Miss Wilson on his way out. She smiled and said, "Good job, Jim." He thanked her and kept walking. As he walked down the sidewalk, he thought, *I have a sweater but I don't have a jacket or pair of jeans. I'll have to go by TMS Menswear and pick me up a few things this afternoon.* On his way back to the house, he stopped by the Hole in the Wall to meet with David and Drew to have a beer. James told David and Drew that he would be leaving town in the morning for a day or two. He said he would be going with a friend to visit their mother and enjoy the scenery.

"Well," Drew said, "we're going to miss you Saturday night. They're going to have a good band here at the Hole in the Wall."

James replied, "Well, you two stay out of trouble and I will be back Saturday night or Sunday."

Chapter 13

The next morning, James was standing on the sidewalk in front of his house with a small suitcase by his side. He had on his new jeans and a sweater. He had even put on socks with his loafers. After a few minutes, Sandra showed up driving a 1965 red mustang. She said, "Just put the suitcase in the back seat, Jim."

James jumped in the front seat and Sandra drove off. James noticed Sandra had on jeans as well, but with tennis shoes. He smiled, "Good morning, Miss Wilson."

"You can call me Sandra, Jim. We've got three and a half hours of driving, so we might as well be on a first-name basis. I've never taken a man to visit my mother but I thought, you being new in town, it might do you some good."

"It will," he replied, "I really like your car."

"My dad bought it for me when I graduated from college. I don't have the heart to trade it and it's still a good car."

As they got on interstate 40 headed West, James looked over at Sandra and still could not believe how beautiful she was. She looked like a young girl with the way she fixed her hair and wearing her jeans and tennis shoes.

"Well, we've chosen a good time to go to Asheville, Jim," she smiled. "The leaves are beginning to turn and it is always beautiful this time of year. Have you ever been to Asheville?"

"It's been a long time, and I'm looking forward to it."

As they drove through Winston and Statesville, the mountains began to come into view and it was really pretty. As many times as James had been to Asheville, he had never seen it for what it is. He hadn't realized just how beautiful it was.

"When we get to Black Mountain, we will stop and have lunch. Is that OK with you, Jim?"

"That's fine," he replied.

"Did you let your mom and dad know that you would be leaving for the weekend?"

"No," James paused, "my mom passed away in childbirth with me, and my dad passed away about nine years ago. I live with my Grammy. She raised me, you might say."

"I'm sorry about your mom and dad, Jim." After a pause, she continued, "well, we're going to get some home-cooked meals this weekend.

"That would be great," he said, "I've gotten tired of Drew's gravy and toast and the beer and peanuts at the Hole in the Wall."

About that time, Sandra was pulling off the road, going down the ramp and turning right at Black Mountain.

"There's a little diner down here that serves pretty good food," Sandra said, "I think you will like it."

"I'm sure I will."

The car rolled onto a gravel parking lot. In front of the restaurant, there was a sign on the door which read, 'Granny's Home Cooking'. They parked the car and headed inside to find a booth.

Sandra looked over at Jim and said, "That's a nice looking sweater you have on." She reached over with her hand and slid her palm up and down his shoulder, feeling the fabric. "What type of fabric is that, Jim?" She asked, reaching to turn up the label to get a better idea. "My God, Jim, it's 100% Cashmere! Where did you get this?"

"It was given to me as a gift some time ago," he replied.

Sandra quirked a brow, "well someone thinks quite a lot of you, Jim. This sweater cost a lot of money."

James shrugged as the waitress handed them menus, "I guess." He paused to look over the offerings and asked, "what would you suggest, Sandra?"

"Well," she considered, "since I haven't had breakfast yet, I think I'll have some ham and eggs with grits."

"Boy that sounds good to me, just as long as there is no gravy with it."

They both laughed.

When they finished eating, they returned to the car. James walked to the driver's side and opened the door for Sandra. "Oh my," Sandra joked, "we have a gentleman here. Would you like to drive?"

"No, thank you," he replied, "you're doing just fine." James didn't want to tell her yet that he didn't know how to drive. He had always been chauffeured as a kid. When he lived in New York, he didn't want to drive and had no use for a driver's license so he used a chauffeur there, as well. After another forty-five minutes of driving they saw a sign welcoming them to Asheville.

"It won't be long now," Sandra said as they drove around Asheville, finally turning onto a single-lane road outside of town.

They entered into a rural countryside. As they drove on a winding road, James looked over the green pastures and the beautiful hillside with all the leaves in its many colors. They left the small road onto a gravel departure lined with a white fence and followed it up to a little house in the distance. It looked like a small English Tudor made of brick. The white fence continued on in front of the house and up the other side, making it look like a doll house. Sandra pulled up to a two-car garage and, as they came to a stop, the front door opened. A lady wearing an apron came out and, as Sandra got out of the car the lady came down towards her. The two women greeted one another with a big, long hug. As James joined them, Sandra turned back to her mother and said, "mom, this is Jim Andrews. He goes to school where I teach. He's a student in one of my classes."

"Hi, Jim, it's nice to meet you. You can call me Mrs. Wilson," Sandra's mother said.

"That will come easy," Jim smiled.

"Come on in, you two. I'm fixing Sandra's favorite meal," Mrs. Wilson said, holding open the door, "chicken and dumplings."

"You've got to be kidding," James laughed.

"Why is that?" Mrs. Wilson inquired.

"Because," James answered, "that's my favorite meal, too. I love chicken and dumplings and haven't had any in a while."

Mrs. Wilson replied, "Well this afternoon, you will be able to have plenty."

"That's great, Mom," Sandra said.

"Well," her mother said, "Ya'll sit down and rest a spell. I know you've got to be tired."

"Actually, Mom," Sandra interjected, "we feel pretty good."

"Well," her mother said, "take Jim out to the garage and show him around. That's where your dad hung out all the time."

Sandra smiled, "come on, Jim. I'll show you around the place."

As they went out the back door between the house and the garage, Sandra stopped and pointed towards a meadow. "Our property goes to the top of these ridges and back to the road and circles back around those meadows. We have about 200 acres. Dad raised corn on most of it." After a moment, Sandra continued on to the garage. "This is where dad spent most of his free time. He would come out here for hours and play his guitar. Often, some friends would come and play with him. They would play some good music," she said, "bluegrass music." As they went inside the garage, there sat a 1941 Chevrolet Business Coupe. The body was white and it had wide, white-wall tires. The coupe looked as though it had just rolled off the showroom floor. Inside and out, the car appeared brand-new. Over in the corner was a small pot-bellied woodstove with a big, black pot on top.

"Dad would come out in the mornings," explained Sandra, "and get the stove going. He'd put on a big pot of pinto beans and boil them all day 'til late in the afternoon. Then, he would invite his friends over and they would play music and eat beans well past midnight. Dad had a work bench on the back side of that wall where he hung car parts." Old oil signs hung on the wall and four straight-back wooden chairs surrounded the stove. "It was a great place for the guys to hang out. Dad loved this place."

"I can see why he did." James replied. "Does your mother ever think about selling this car? If she does, I would like to have the opportunity to buy it. I think it's absolutely beautiful."

"Dad would only get it out and drive it sometimes," Sandra went on, "Most times, he would drive it on Sunday. He bought it new. It was his pride and joy. Mom would always say, 'he loves that car better than he loves me.'"

About that time, Mrs. Wilson stuck her head out of the back door and called, "Come and get it! The chicken and dumplings are ready to eat!"

When they came through the back door, the smell of the dumplings permeated the air. A big bowl filled with dumplings was placed in the middle of the table. Heat waves from the piping hot dumplings wafted up from the bowl. Mrs. Wilson said, "Ya'll go wash up. I'll set the plates."

Ms. Wilson brought in another big bowl piled high with snap beans in one hand and a skillet of cornbread in the other.

Jim remarked, "I cannot remember when I have had a meal like this. It looks wonderful."

"I hope it tastes as good as it looks, Jim," laughed Mrs. Wilson.

As they ate, Ms. Wilson said, "You look like someone I've seen before, Jim, though I can't remember where…"

"Was he a good-looking man?" James joked.

Mrs. Wilson and Sandra laughed.

Eager to change the subject, James said, "I love that old car in the garage, and the garage looks as though your late husband is still using it."

"That's the exact way it was when he died and I decided to leave it just the way it is. I love that old car despite the fact that I'm sure he loved it more than me." Mrs. Wilson said.

"It's beautiful. If you ever decide you want to get rid of it, please let me know first. I'll take good care of it." James said.

"Well, it's not doing anybody any good just sitting in there…" Ms. Wilson considered, "I'll let you know if I decide to sell it after we eat the dumplings."

As James and Sandra were finishing their meal, Mrs. Wilson went to fetch a blackberry pie from the kitchen. When she came back, she sat the picture-perfect pastry on the table. "Do you like blackberry pie," she asked James.

"I can't remember the last time I ate blackberry pie," he replied, "but yes, I do love it."

"Well, I hope you like this one," said Mrs. Wilson.

James ate pie until he was full as a tick.

"Let's go out on the porch and sit in the swing," Sandra suggested, "it's beautiful this time of the evening."

"You kids go on out and I'll clean up," smiled Ms. Wilson.

Sandra volunteered to help, but her mother insisted that she go on and get out of her way. "But Mom!" Said Sandra, in mock protest.

"Ya'll go on. I'll be out later," insisted her mother.

Sandra and James sat together in the swing. James looked out over the meadow and at the distant layers of blue-gray mountain ridges. The sun was going down behind the mountains, throwing a golden light across the meadow. Every blade of grass seemed to glow from the warm, backlit sunset. The forest was radiant with autumn leaves in every hue in the spectrum; orange, ochre, red, maroon, yellow. They were all set against a foil of purple-blue shadows cast across the trees. The leaves sparkled in the late sun like morning dew drops on the ground. It was a glorious sight to see. The scenery seemed all the more spectacular because of his vantage point; sitting on a porch swing next to Sandra.

My heart is full and this a memory my mind will never forget, James thought.

The two rocked gently in the swing, feeling deeply satisfied and enjoying the mountain setting in all its glorious beauty. Finally, Ms. Wilson came out with three cups of coffee on a tray. Sitting the coffee down, she said, "Ya'll come on over here and have a cup of coffee with me. Are you going back tomorrow?"

Sandra stood to join her mother and replied, "We'll leave around lunchtime, Mom."

"OK," her mother answered, "I'll fix you and Jim a good lunch before you leave."

"That sounds good, Mrs. Wilson," James said as he helped himself to a cup of coffee.

"You can use the spare bedroom, Jim," Mrs. Wilson continued, "and I hope you sleep well tonight."

When they finished their coffee, Mrs. Wilson said, "I don't want to be rude, but I'm feeling a bit tired. I'm going to head to bed now, but ya'll stay up as long as you like."

"OK, Mrs. Wilson," James said, "Thank you very much for the chicken and dumplings and that incredible blackberry pie. It was too good."

For the next twenty or thirty minutes, Sandra and James just sat there quietly enjoying the scenery as the sun sank behind the last mountain ridge.

Finally, Sandra suggested, "We might as well go on in. Mom will have us up early."

They reluctantly got up and James opened the door for Sandra.

"Thank you, Jim," she said as she led him down the hall. She stopped at a room to her left and said, "This is your room, the bathroom is across the hall."

James thanked her as he paused to look down at her. Sandra rose up on her toes and kissed him on the cheek, "thanks for coming Jim." She smiled.

"You are most welcome, Sandra," James said, quietly. "It has been my pleasure.

As James walked into his room he thought, *well a kiss on the cheek is better than nothing right now. It's a start.*

Chapter 14

The next morning, Mrs. Wilson offered Jim a true country breakfast of salted ham, grits, red-eye gravy and homemade biscuits.

"You can't beat that for breakfast," grinned James.

After coffee, Sandra asked Jim if he would like to walk down to see the creek where she used to go swimming as a child. Jim agreed and the two set out. They walked down a small, crooked path near the tree line where they could hear the water gurgling as it ran across the rocks. After about fifteen minutes, she turned into the woods where a narrow deer path led them to the edge of the water. The water formed a small pond that had been dammed up by someone long ago to create a swimming hole. The small pond actually had a little, sandy beach surrounding it on all sides. Sandra pointed out that this is where she swam when she was a little girl. She said that neighbors and friends alike also came here for a swim. Over on the opposite side of the makeshift beach, there was a tree with a thick rope hanging down with big knots every few feet to make climbing easier.

"We had some great times down here," Sandra said wistfully, "A childhood that I will never forget."

As James sat, listening to her reminisce, he thought back to his own childhood. A childhood in which he never swam in a creek, never swung from a rope, never had friends over to play for an afternoon.

After a moment, Sandra looked over and caught a funny look on James' face. "You have a sad expression on your face. What's wrong?" She asked as she walked over and put her hands on his shoulders as if trying to comfort him. She looked up at him, questioningly, and he looked back at her with a mixture of sadness and envy in his eyes.

Without thinking it through, he bent down and placed his lips lightly on hers. She moved one hand from his shoulder to the back of his head. James put his arms around her and moved his hands up her back. He could feel every movement of her body and, for a moment, his mind went blank. He could no longer feel his body, except for his lips on hers. James held her a little closer, as she totally relaxed into his arms. His hand moved beneath her hair to caress the back of her head. The kiss had transformed from something light and tentative to something full of passion. It was a kiss that felt like it could easily last forever. She pulled away, slightly, to look up at his face. Silently, the two searched one another though neither was able to say a word. In his mind, James knew something was happening, but it was a feeling he had never experienced before.

Slowly, James reached down and took her hand. He pulled it to his mouth and touched his lips lightly to the back of her hand in a gentle kiss. They turned around and began to walk, hand in hand, back up the path toward the house.

Jim felt dazed by the experience, but he was also thinking about what he could possible tell Sandra about his childhood. How could he tell her about the fun he didn't have as a child? He wondered if she would like to hear how he sat behind a small desk behind his father's and did paperwork as early as six years old. Or, maybe she would like to hear how he listened to his father make deals over the phone all day. Or perhaps how his father tested him at the end of each day as to what he had learned about the textile business.

It was the first time James realized he had no childhood stories to offer. His dad had brought him up in the same manner as his grandfather brought up his father. The only thing the men in his family knew was textiles. Now, he realized it was all he knew.

He thought about his mother and how he was sure she had no life with his father. His father was a good man, very generous and loving to others; except his own family. A wave of hot resentment began to build form the depths of his psyche. There were no happy times in his childhood. How can I show Sandra a good time, he wondered, when I never had fun in my life other than what time I spent with J.J.?

When J.J. came home from college, James felt like his life was just beginning. But, at age 31, that now seemed a little late to begin a personal life. Again, he asked himself, *what experiences do I have that I can share with Sandra about my past like she shared about her past. Not a damned thing! Why would a woman want to spend time with a man who has only had half a life? A man who hasn't experienced life yet; who is starving for life beyond the textile business?*

Suddenly disgusted with his life and with his past, James decided now was not the time to begin a serious relationship until he found out just who he was. *Right now,* he thought, *I don't know what type of person I really am. I have no life to offer anyone.*

On the drive back home, few words were spoken. Some small talk, but mostly Sandra and Jim just stared at the road. At last, Sandra pulled up in front of the house to let James out. As he got out, he reached into the back seat to grab his suitcase. He looked over at Sandra and said, "I'm sorry."

"You have nothing to be sorry about, Jim."

"Yes I do," he paused for a moment, and then said, "Someday, I hope I can explain so you'll understand. I had the best time of my life. Thank you."

Sandra smiled, "I had a great time, too, Jim. You take care."

James closed the door and walked inside his house. No one was at home, so James went to his room and lay down on his bed, thinking over the weekend. He went over every word Sandra had said and replayed the kiss they shared by the creek. As he mulled over all that happened, the hurting in his stomach returned.

As James dozed off to sleep, he was awakened by laughter. He could hear David and Drew talking.

"Now it's my turn," David was saying.

"Well, wait a minute," Drew laughed, "Let me try it again."

"No, no, no! It's my turn" retorted David.

"OK, hold on a minute!" came the reply.

James decided to get up and go see what was going on. As he walked onto the porch, he saw David bent over. He was pulling his pants up from the front with his hand. Drew was standing to the side, holding a match to David's ass. About the time James reached the doorway, David passed gas and sent a blue streak of fire about 5 inches past David's hand. David watched his reflection in a mirror off to the side. David and Drew both fell down, laughing. James had never seen anything like it and could not help but laugh, too. All three just stood there, laughing like idiots.

"Hey! Jimbo! You want to try?" Drew hooted.

"Not today, Drew," James said.

"Well, boys, I'll tell ya'll, my grandma was the best at fartin'," Drew said, "She could put all of us to shame."

"What do you mean?" David asked when he could speak.

"Well," began Drew, "She would just fart and didn't know it."

James was puzzled, "How could she not know it?"

"She couldn't hear," Drew explained, "you had to yell at her to get her to hear anything. I remember one time, dad and I were listening to the Grand 'Ole Opry after supper one night when Grandma came walking through the den. She had this dress on with flowers on it and an apron tied around her waist. When she walked, her right foot turned and dad said it was because she was pigeon-toed. She had her little finger in her right ear, shaking it real fast and hocking…"

"Wait," David stopped him, laughing, "What's 'hocking'?"

"It's like you have an itch in your throat and you scratch it by hocking," Drew explained.

James and David looked at one another and laughed.

"I have no idea what the hell you're talking about, Drew," David said.

"Well, anyway," Drew continued, ignoring David. "She was walking through the living room, hocking and wrigglin' her little finger in her ear when she farted at the same time. Honest to God, it sounded like a bullfrog behind her. She acted like she never heard a thing. I looked at dad and he looked at me and we both just started laughing. It was a sight to see… And to hear! I tell ya', David, I think when old people fart; they just don't know when it's going to happen. It could be any time or place. And, if they do know it, they don't think anybody hears it so they just keep on walkin'. So I got it honest, David."

"Yes," David conceded, "but you can hear, you bastard!"

The three boys continued to laugh as they opened a beer.

Chapter 15

The next morning, James got up and got ready for class. Drew had breakfast ready.

James chuckled, "I think I am going to take a rain check this morning, Drew. I'm not hungry."

"Everybody is sick of your damned gravy, Drew," explained David groggily as he came into the kitchen behind James.

James shook his head, "I just feel a little nauseous this morning, Drew. That's all."

James was thinking about facing Sandra at class that morning. He had no idea what he was going to say to her. He knew his behavior must have seemed strange the previous day and he didn't know how he was going to make it right with her.

When James walked into class, there was a gentleman standing there. The man announced to the class that Ms. Wilson was taking the day off and he would be her substitute in class. James knew he could not just get up and leave class. He had to sit it out. It was a long hour. He had no idea what the man said during class, he couldn't even remember his name. His mind was on Sandra, wondering why she wasn't in class.

He felt compelled to go to her house and explain himself. As he hurried down Elm and made a turn onto Neeley, her house came into view. It was a small brick house with gray shutters. He knew at once Sandra was home because her red Mustang was sitting under the carport.

James started up the sidewalk, where Sandra had planted pansies along both sides. The shrubs in front had been recently trimmed and the lawn was neatly cut. James walked up the front porch to the door and rang the doorbell. Sandra opened the door and just looked at him without expression. She had on a green, heavy robe and bedroom slippers but no make-up. Her hair hung down over her shoulders, but James couldn't help but notice she was a natural beauty. James realized, after a moment, that he was staring. All he could manage to say was, "just give me five minutes."

Sandra turned around and left the door open for James. After a short hesitation, James followed her inside. She led him into the kitchen where she began to pour herself a cup of coffee. She looked up at James as he stood there, in silence, and asked him if he would like a cup as well.

"I'd love a cup," said James, "thank you."

There was a small round table in front of a bay window with bright yellow curtains behind it and plants sitting in front of it. Sandra nodded towards the table and said, "Sit down, Jim. We have to talk."

They both just sat there for a moment, looking down in their coffee cups. Finally, James opened his mouth to say something when Sandra interrupted him. "Jim," she began, "I owe you an apology. I don't know what happened… What got into me. All I know is you had an expression on your face. At that point in time, I could feel your pain. Don't ask me how, I just did. And when you reached down and kissed me… And yes," she assured, "I kissed you back… I don't remember much after that. It was something I had never experienced before. All I know is that I haven't been able to get it off my mind I just could not go in today and face you. All I can say, Jim, is 'I'm sorry'."

"Don't say you're sorry, Sandra," insisted James. "You gave me a memory that I will never forget on that creek bank. The way you look when you talk about your childhood and the fun times you had as a little girl at that swimming hole, and all the friends and family that you had there with you. It brought back memories of my childhood and mine was nothing like yours. I would love to have had a childhood like that, but I didn't. I didn't have a terrible childhood; I just never had the kind of fun with family and friends that you did. But I'm working on it. I'm having fun and making memories now so that in later years, I'll be able to tell my friends I had a good life. Maybe not as a child, but as a young man. As far as the kiss goes, I hope that it was something that we both will never forget. I know I won't." James was surprised at the tremendous relief he felt as he said it, he was glad to have it off his chest.

They both took a sip of coffee. Then, Sandra looked up at James and said, "Jim, there's something about you that seems strange. I don't know what it is. The way you carry yourself when you walk. The way you sit at your desk in class. Even the way you eat. It all seems like you're not comfortable or something. It looks like everything is all business with you."

James replied, "Sandra when I get where I don't do the things you just said anymore… Then, I will sit down with you and explain everything. I'm sure then you will understand. Give me a little more time," he pleaded, "I'm getting better." James stood and turned to her, "Don't give up on me. I do have deep feelings for you. That's all I'm going to say for now. I'll see you in class in the morning. By the way," he smiled, "you look good in that robe. It compliments your hair."

Sandra tried not to smile, and James left the house. As he walked back to his room, he felt better and hoped Sandra did, too. God, she looked so good without make-up. As he continued along Main Street, he looked into the window of the men's clothing store and saw a mannequin wearing a London Fog Coat. *I'm going to buy that for the football game next Saturday,* he thought. Elon was scheduled to play Appalachian State and Appalachian had won the last four games between Elon and Appalachian. He hoped maybe the tide would turn this Saturday. The coat made him realize all he had to wear in cool weather was cashmere sweaters, and he knew he would look out of place wearing cashmere. After making his purchase, he headed down the street and soon heard someone call out. "Hey! Jimbo!" It was David, crossing the street toward him. "Hold on," David said, "I'll walk with you."

James paused and waited. "How's it going, David?"

"I had to leave Drew's ass in class. He had to do some makeup work before he could leave. He'll be home in an hour or two. By the way you had a telephone call this morning after you left. Somebody named 'J.J.' said for you to call him when you can."

As soon as James got home, he went right to the phone and called J.J..

"Hey James," J.J. chuckled on the other line, "how is the college boy?"

"Just fine, J.J.," replied James, "How are things on your end?"

"Well, I just wanted to let you know I'm going to New York tomorrow. I want to check out a few things in the distribution center and see how things are going since you've been away. I want to see how those boys are doing in the research and development departments."

"That's good," mulled James, "how's Grammy doing?"

"She's fine. You might want to give her a call. She was fussing that you had not called her for the past three or four days. So, in other words, she's telling me to tell you to call her. She just wants to know that you're doing OK. You know how she is."

James smiled to himself, "I'll call her in a few minutes, J.J.."

Since David was nearby, James started to speak to J.J. in Spanish. James asked J.J. if he was given all the reports from New York that he needed. J.J. said he thought he had, but wanted to go up and make sure things were in order. Still speaking in Spanish, James asked J.J. to be sure to ask Jason for an update and review the shipping and receivables. James told J.J. he would get a better update later and J.J. knew that someone else must be nearby.

"I'll do that, James," J.J. assured, "by the way... Are you making headway with Miss Wilson?"

"Well," considered James, "let's just say I'm doing the best I can under the circumstances."

J.J. agreed, "I understand, James. Stay safe and I'll catch ya' later."

"OK, you too," replied James.

As soon as James put down the phone, David said, "Was that Spanish you were speaking?"

"Yes, it was."

"Where'd you learn that?" David admired.

"In school," answered James, "didn't you take Spanish in high school?"

"Yes, but I don't remember any of it. My dad made sure that I passed all my courses and one of them was Spanish. I just forgot everything… I guess if we run across anybody that speaks Spanish, you can be our interpreter." David smiled.

"I'd be glad to do that for you," James said, hoping David would soon change the subject.

"You wanna go down to the Hole in the Wall and grab a burger and a beer?" David asked, seeming to grant James' silent wish.

"That sounds good, David," replied James, relieved. "I'll leave a note for Drew. Let's go!"

After J.J. spoke to James on the phone, he flew the company plane to New York. When J.J. arrived at the corporate headquarters, he went straight to James' office. As he looked around the office, he noticed a picture of James with Grammy and a picture of him and James with their arms around each other's shoulders standing out by the fountain in the front yard, taken back when they were little boys. J.J. walked around and sat in James' chair. J.J. examined the room and couldn't help but notice how the office had been decorated; Similar to James' father's house in Greensboro. James had two paintings on the wall. One was a portrait of James' grandfather, the other of his father. J.J. stared at the oil painting of Mr. Exum and remembered how the old man would sit him on one leg and James on the other. He would tell the boys how they were going to run the business one day. He said that they would have to learn every day so they could learn the textile business inside and out. Mr. Exum was a hard man but he was the only father figure J.J. had ever known. J.J. supposed he loved Mr. Exum as a father, too.

J.J. got on the speaker phone, "Call the receptionist and ask her to call all the staff members to the conference room. Tell them that J.J. Washington wants to meet with them."

"Do you want me to do it now?" The receptionist asked.

"Yes, please" J.J. answered, then added, "and let me know if there is anyone who cannot attend."

In about half an hour, J.J. got up from the desk and looked in the small mirror that hung from the wall. He straightened his tie. J.J. was a striking individual. He had a light complexion and European features. He carried himself very business-like; in a way that commanded respect from those around him.

When it was time for the meeting to start, he walked into the plush conference room with its huge oriental carpet and tall windows overlooking the city. J.J. walked to the end of the oval table and greeted his staff along the way. Of the seventeen or so executives present, there were only four or five J.J. did not know personally.

J.J. spoke, "Good evening, gentlemen. Thank you for coming in on such a short notice." J.J. paused to look around the room. Everyone, except one man whom J.J. did not know, was in attendance. J.J. continued, "For those of you who do not know me… My name is J.J. Washington. I am the President of Exum Textiles, and acting CEO in James Exum's absence. I would like to take a moment to thank everyone for all the hard work they have been doing and for keeping me informed of the activities that take place here in New York. I just wanted to let you know you're doing a great job. James plans to be back in about four to six weeks so, until then, carry on. Continue to keep me informed, and I will continue to do the best I can until James returns. I plan to visit with each of you individually over the next two days. "Again," J.J. paused for one more look around the room, " thank you all for coming."

As people began to file from the room, J.J. remained for a few more moments shaking hands and greeting people. Then, he organized his papers, picked up his folder, and started down the hall back to James' office.

As he rounded the corner, there was a gentleman drinking from the water fountain. There was another man standing behind him. Immediately, J.J. recognized one of the men as the man who had not been paying attention in the previous meeting. As J.J. grew closer, he overheard the man saying, "I only take orders from Mr. Exum. Not this nigger!"

J.J. paused only a moment before tapping the man on the shoulder. As the man turned to face J.J., J.J. said, "You'll be taking one more order; you're fired. Don't bother going back to your office; I'd like you to leave the premises at once."

"Now, now!" The man sputtered, in an attempt to explain himself.

J.J. stopped him, "I said, now."

Finally, the man turned on his heel and walked away. J.J. turned to look at the other man. He looked back at J.J. and shook his head, "I'm sorry, Mr. Washington," he said, "I had no idea he was that type of person."

"Don't worry about it; we have that type down south, too. Just make sure he leaves the premises for me," J.J. said.

The gentleman nodded, "Yes, sir."

J.J. turned to leave.

After making his rounds and speaking with everyone J.J. went into the Shipping and Receiving Division Manager's office. Jason, the Manager, was a big man. His stomach billowed over his belt, and he could only tuck his shirt in the front. Although he didn't look like the 'executive' type, he was known for his effectiveness in this department. J.J. smiled and greeted Jason, "Jason," he said, "I need you to give me the printout of the last shipping and receiving report; as up-to-date as you have it. I need it to do some work on my way back home. I'll be leaving in two days." Jason nodded and pushed a button on the printer and it started after a couple of minutes. After it had finished its job, Jason folded the printout and handed it to J.J.. "This is the last report available," Jason said, "Have a good trip back."

J.J. thanked him. "I'll be talking with you soon, Jason," he said as he turned to leave.

J.J. still had to stop by James' condominium to be sure there were no problems on his way out of town. The high-rise was only two blocks away and J.J. decided to walk. As he reached the condominium, J.J. nodded to the bellman that stood at attention in the doorway. J.J. strode through the elegant lobby. It had a huge chandelier in the middle and a floor tiled in marble. Expensive oil paintings adorned the walls. A gentleman met J.J. at the elevator and asked for an I.D. J.J. showed him the door key with five numbers on it. The man nodded his assent and J.J. stepped on the elevator. He got off on the top floor, at the penthouse suite. He matched the numbers on the door to his key.

J.J. had only been to James' penthouse once 5 years ago when James had first purchased it. It was nothing more than empty space then. Now, there was a bar on the left side of the wall but it still looked as if the owner had just moved in. There were no pictures on the wall, no plants and no spare furnishings. The décor was modern and minimalist. J.J. moved to the bar and poured himself a Jack Daniels and coke, over ice. J.J. couldn't imagine James choosing this décor himself. There were a few books stacked on the coffee table. On top of the stack was a book titled, 'How to Win Friends and Influence People, by Dale Carnegie."

J.J. walked over to the big bay window overlooking the city. It had grown dark since J.J. arrived and the city was lit up with colorful lights. It was a beautiful sight. J.J. could imagine James standing here, looking out and feeling alone among all these people. J.J. turned around and walked towards the bedroom. He stood at the door and looked around. There was a king-sized bed with a huge dresser, but still no pictures on the walls of the bedroom. However, as J.J. walked closer to the bed, he noticed a small photo on the nightstand. It was a picture of Grammy holding James in her arms when he was a baby. In the picture, James was looking up at Grammy, and she looked down at him with a big smile on her face. He looked to have been about 1 year old. J.J. picked the photo up for a closer look. He could feel a lump in his throat as a wave of emotion swept over him. There was something about that picture. It and the lack of warmth in the apartment troubled J.J.. J.J. suddenly realized the loneliness that had haunted James his entire life.

J.J. tried to shake it off by looking around the apartment to see if everything was in order. He went over to the bar to rinse out his glass when a little typed note caught his eye. James had framed the note, which read: A man's word is his bond. Always tell the truth. Give a firm handshake and look a man straight in the eye when doing so. The note was signed by James' father.

J.J. turned and walked out, locking the door behind him.

Chapter 16

David and James had finished their beer and hamburger when Drew walked in. "Hey fellas," said Drew, "I'm sorry I'm late."

"What's up, Drew?" smiled David.

"Well," Drew began dramatically, "I didn't think I was ever going to get out of there. Thank God for Miss Wilson. If she hadn't shown up, I don't think I would have ever gotten out."

James felt as if someone had kicked him in the stomach at Drew's words.

"Two other guys and I were doing make up work when Miss Wilson walked in and whispered something to Mr. Stevens. He nodded his head and told us we could leave as long as we were sure to finish the work and have it ready to turn in by the morning. So, I left." He smiled, triumphantly.

James said, "I'm going to the bathroom, guys. I'll be back in a few minutes."

James just walked around in circles in the bathroom, wondering what Sandra had said to Mr. Stevens. He wondered why she was there. His mind was running 100 miles an hour.

He looked at his reflection in the mirror and thought, *what are you doing, James? Get a hold of yourself. You are not being rational. Just calm doing and everything will be OK.* He took a deep breath and walked back out to join David and Drew.

"You OK, Jim?" David inquired.

"Yes," James answered, "I'm fine. Are you fellows about ready to go?"

"Might as well," Drew laughed, "I still have make-up work to turn in tomorrow morning. Probably should go back and get started."

As they were walking up the sidewalk, headed back to their place, they saw Mr. Stevens and Sandra headed towards them. The two were walking side-by-side. Sandra had changed into dongle raised jeans and Mr. Stephens had his sweater off and the arms tied around his neck.

"I guess that's a good way to carry your sweater without holding it in your hands," James commented, but thought: *The lazy bastard.*

Drew said "Don't let them see us!"

The three young men crossed to the other side of the street just in time, but James kept his eye on Sandra. She and Mr. Stevens were headed into the soda shop.

Drew said, "It would be just my luck for him to see me coming from the Hole in the Wall and not doing my homework. I tell you boys, the way my luck goes, if I found the pot at the end of the rainbow and it would be filled with assholes."

David and James couldn't help but laugh. David said, "Drew where do you hear that crap?"

"I don't know," Drew said, "It just comes in my head. Let's cross back over."

James told David and Drew to go ahead; he was going to head up to the soda shop for a few.

"Well catch you later, Jim," Drew said.

By the time James reached the soda shop, it was about half full. The jukebox was playing and there was a lot of laughter and talking going on. James saw Sandra and Mr. Stevens sitting in a booth along the wall.

James headed to the booth, but before he could reach them, Helen and Linda stepped in front of him.

Helen jumped up and grabbed James around the neck. "Hey, Jimbo," she purred, "we had a great time at your place the other night. Where are Drew and David?"

"They're home studying," James replied.

"Thanks again for letting me use your shower, Jimbo," Helen smiled.

Jim looked over at the booth where Sandra and Mr. Stephens sat. Sandra was turned around, looking back at him. She had a look on her face that James didn't like seeing. *It seems as though I am having the kind of luck Drew was talking about,* James thought to himself. *The best thing I can do now is just leave.*

As James turned to walk out, Linda asked, "Are you going home, Jim? We're leaving, too. I'll give you a ride."

Linda and Helen left the soda shop with James. As they left, they turned the corner to Linda's car; Linda turned to Jim and asked, "Would you like to drive?"

"No, thank you," James replied, "I can't drive."

"What do you mean you can't drive," Linda laughed.

"Well," James began, "I never learned how to drive. One day, I guess I'd like to learn."

Linda said, "Well, it's easy and now is as good a time as any."

"What do you mean?"

"Well," Linda said, getting in the car, "we'll go over to that big parking lot behind the library and I'll teach you to drive. It's that easy."

"We'll see," James said cautiously.

As they started the car and headed out of the parking lot, Linda showed James how to work the clutch and gas pedals and how to switch gears. When they reached the lot behind the library, Linda switched places with James. They practiced driving around the lot. Each time James pulled off, the car died. After thirty minutes of this, James was finally able to make a smooth start and was even changing some gears. He was doing great for his first time driving. In another half hour, James was driving around flawlessly; stopping, starting and changing gears. It was easier than he had thought.

Finally, Linda said, "That's enough for tonight, Jim. Come on. We'll take you home."

As they pulled up in the driveway, James invited the girls in to have a beer with him and the guys.

"That sounds like a good idea," Helen said to James, and the girls went inside.

As James held the door open for the girls, he shouted, "Hey, it's me and the girls!"

David stuck his head around the corner and said, "Grab a beer from the fridge and come out on the porch."

Shag music was playing and Drew was singing along. He took Linda by the hand and started to dance. Helen turned and grabbed James' hand. James surprised David and Drew with how well he could dance now.

David hollered out, "Go, Jimbo!" as James danced.

After an hour or so of dancing, the girls said they had to go and do some studying. After a few more beers and a few more songs, the guys decided to turn in as well.

The next morning when James got up and came into the kitchen, the guys had already left. There was a box of cereal on the table with a note that said, "Test today. Had to leave early. Drew and David."

James left without eating. On his way out the door, he saw a pair of sunglasses on the coffee table. They were David's. *I'll just borrow those for an hour or two,* James thought to himself.

When he got to class, Sandra was sitting at her desk. James put on the glasses and walked in with his head moving back and forth a little bit like a chicken. He walked over to his seat and sat down and put his left leg out in the aisle and laid his head back. James looked over his glasses at Sandra and saw that she had her eyes half-closed and looked as though she was gritting her teeth at him. She got up and walked over to his desk, put her mouth close to his ear and said, "Did you have a hard time last night, Jimbo?"

James slid back up in his seat and Sandra walked back to her desk, shaking her head from side to side. When she sat down, she was grinning.

By the time class ended, James walked by her desk. "I was just trying to look relaxed for you," he explained. "Do you think I looked relaxed?"

Sandra said, "Yes, Jim."

"Well," James said, "if you think I look relaxed sitting down, you should see me eating. Don't even use a knife or fork, I'm so relaxed."

She looked at him and squeezed her eyes shut, "Jim," she said, "we need to talk. Come by the house around 8:00."

"I'll be there at 8:00. It may be longer because I'm going to be walking," he said, "relaxed."

"I'm going to relax you if you don't get out of here."

Chapter 17

At 8 o'clock, James rang Sandra's door bell. She opened the door and smirked at him, "Come on in, Jimbo."

James laughed as he followed her in.

"Would you like a beer or a cup of coffee?" Sandra offered.

"Beer would be great."

"I'm going to have a glass of wine."

"Oh," James decided, "a glass of wine would be fantastic."

Sandra looked at him, "do you like wine?"

"Very much so," James smiled.

Sandra smiled back, "I have red and white."

"I'll have what you're having."

Sandra nodded and poured two glasses of white wine and then motioned him to the den. There was a fire burning in the fireplace between two bookcases and a plaid sofa and wingback chair. A roll-top desk sat in the corner near a bay window. The only light in the room was coming from a light on a table between the sofa and chair. Everything was decorated tastefully.

James and Sandra sat on opposite ends of the sofa and Sandra turned to face James.

"Well," she began after a sip of wine, "tell me about the sunglasses and the way you were sitting in your seat in class. What was all that about?"

"Well," James began, sitting his glass down, "the last time I was here, you told me there was something strange about me. That there was something about the way I sat in my chair, and even walked. As if I were 'all business'. So," he explained, "I'm working on it."

"Well," Sandra laughed, "you don't have to go to extremes with it. Just... Relax."

"Like I said, I'm working on it."

Sandra looked at Jim, "What's this about 'Jimbo?'"

James chuckled, "Oh, you mean Helen."

"Yeah," Sandra said, "Helen."

"She's just a friend of David and Drew's. I met them at the Hole in the Wall, and they're teaching me how to dance."

"Well, just be sure that's all she's teaching you." Sandra smiled, "how about another glass of wine?"

"Yes, please"

As she was pouring the wine, Sandra said to James, "You know… She's a lot younger than you."

"Yes," James assured her, "I know." He paused, "Speaking of… What about you and Mr. Stephens? He looks about 10 years older than you?"

"He is," Sandra confirmed, "We've been seeing one another for about a year."

"Is it serious?"

Sandra considered as she sat back down, "I wouldn't say it's serious. He's a good person. He worked his way through college. He's earning his Doctoral degree now, and he works part-time tutoring kids to earn money. He's worked very hard to get where he is. He has continued to try to better himself."

"Well," Jim said, "He still looks too old for you.

About that time, Sandra sat her glass aside and slid onto the floor. She pointed her feet towards the fireplace, as if they were cold. James slid off, as well and slid up next to her, placing his right arm around her shoulders.

"Mmm," Sandra sighed, "that fire feels good."

James reached up with his free hand and switched off the light. Though it was beginning to die down, the fire cast a glow in the room. It was the only light around them. Their shadows danced on the walls around them.

That night, with the fire crackling and his arm around Sandra is a memory James will never forget.

James slowly moved to the side and, gently holding Sandra's shoulders, he eased her back onto the floor. He could see the outline of her face in the firelight. Her eyes were closed and James reached down and kissed her lightly on the lips. Then, he took her lower lip into his mouth and sucked on it to get the feel of it. He moved his lips to her cheek, then back to her mouth and then down the side of her neck, lightly kissing as he went. Slowly, he moved his lips back to hers and slid his left hand from her waistline up her side. His thumb traced the curves of her body as he stroked to her breast. He circled the curve of her breast with only his thumb and stopped only when he reached her nipple. Slowly, his thumb traced it and then trailed down the other side, sliding behind her neck. He could feel her body pressed to his, her hand moving up his shoulder. He stopped and raised up on one elbow.

Startled, Sandra opened her eyes and looked at him, "Jim, what's wrong?"

"I think you just poured wine down my back."

Sandra's eyes widened and she raised up. "Well," she surmised, "it's your fault. You made me forget what I was doing. Come on," she smiled, "let me clean you up."

As they walked into the kitchen, James said, "Just my luck but it probably saved us both.

"I guess you're right," Sandra agreed.

After she had cleaned up as much of the wine as she could, she said, "I think you'd better go home now, Jim. We both have class in the morning. I'll walk you to the door."

At the door, James reached down and kissed her on the lips. "I'll see you in the morning… Ms. Wilson."

"You ass," Sandra smirked.

As James walked down the sidewalk towards home, he couldn't help but think of the Doris Troy song, *'Just One Look'*. He sang to himself, *'That's all it took, just one look'*. James did a shuffle with his feet and continued along the sidewalk. He looked back in time to see Sandra looking out and him and shaking her head. She smiled at him.

Chapter 18

On the way back, while in the company plane, J.J. took the time to review the printouts Jason had given him. After an hour, J.J. realized something wasn't quite right. Now he knew why James had asked him for the printout in the first place. James must have also known the numbers just weren't adding up.

When J.J. went into his office in Greensboro, he told the secretary that he was not to be interrupted. He took the folder from his briefcase and spread the printouts on the conference table and continued to study them. Despite his instructions, the secretary came in a bit later. "J.J., there are two gentlemen out front. They would like to see you," she said, apologetically, "they insisted."

"I'm right in the middle of something, Miss. Johnson," J.J. replied.

"Yes, sir," she replied, and went back to the door.

On her way out, one of the gentlemen placed his hand on the door to keep it from closing. J.J. stood up as two neatly dressed gentlemen in sports coats and ties walked in.

"Mr. Washington," said the first man, "I'm Mr. Clark. This is my partner, Mr. McGuiness. We're with the FBI and we would like to have a few minutes of your time."

Mr. Clark looked back to J.J.'s secretary, "in private," he insisted.

J.J. excused Ms. Johnson and invited the men to have a seat. "What can I help you with?"

Agent Clark replied, "We're here to help you."

"How is that?" asked J.J..

"We have been monitoring your tractor trailers hauling goods from North Carolina to New York. We have had this company under surveillance for about six months. We believe there is some illegal activity going on. We've pinpointed it to your warehouses. The shipping and receiving in your plant's three locations… We're going to need your cooperation to complete our investigation."

J.J. considered the agent's words, "You have my cooperation, I'll give the owner and CEO a call and notify him."

"You mean Mr. Exum?"

"Yes."

Mr. Clark exchanged glances with his partner before turning back to J.J.. "We wish you wouldn't do that."

"Why not," J.J. asked.

"Well," Mr. Clark began, "your New York office knows he will be gone for a short time, and that's good. We feel like Mr. Exum's absence will make those complicit in the illegal transactions feel comfortable with what they're doing and that's what we want. We know where Mr. Exum is and we know what he has been doing."

"You haven't been spying on James, have you?" J.J. asked.

"When no one would give his whereabouts, we had to make sure he wasn't in harm's way," Mr. Clark confirmed. "We're dealing with some very serious and dangerous people and we felt we needed to ensure his safety. He's doing fine where he is. Our focal point, for now, is your transportation department and shipping and receiving, as well."

"It's strange that you came in this morning. I was just in New York yesterday."

"We know you were."

J.J. paused and looked at Mr. Clark a moment before continuing, "I just got some printouts from our distribution centers and noticed some things were not adding up. I was just going over them." He got up and led the men over to the conference table where the documents were laid out.

Agent Clark looked interested, "Have you had time to review them yet?"

"No," J.J. answered.

"Well, for now, Mr. Washington," Agent Clark said as he fingered the documents, "please don't say anything to anyone. And I mean anyone. Just let us continue our investigation until we get close to making some arrests. We will need your continued assistance. At that time, we will sit down with you and decide what course of action you will need to take internally to make this investigation a successful one." He stepped over to J.J. and handed him a business card, "here's my card," he said. "Keep it in your wallet and give us a call anytime; day or night. Again, do absolutely nothing for now. Don't make any changes that might arouse suspicion. Let things go just as they are going, don't question anyone. So far, we have everything under control. We'll be in touch."

J.J. stood and shook their hands and they left.

J.J. looked at the clock and thought to himself, *8:30. Maybe I can catch James before he leaves for class.* Then, he hesitated. *Maybe I should wait. James may be better off where he's at. Although, I hate keeping business matters from James, Elon is the safest place for him. I'll get him involved when the time comes, but for now I'm going to leave well enough alone. I'll just call to check in on him.*

Chapter 19

As James started out the door to class, the phone rang. He picked it up, thinking it was probably for Drew or David but the voice on the other end was J.J.'s.

"James? Is that you? It's me, J.J.. Just wanted to let you know I'm back in town and in the office this morning. I thought I'd try and catch you before you went to class. I just wanted to let you know I spent the day in New York with management and picked up the report you requested from Jason," J.J. said.

"Just put them somewhere safe," James said. "When I see you, I'll discuss them with you, but for now, just hold on to them."

"Will do," J.J. affirmed. "Well, I won't hold you from class. Just know I'm back in town if you need me."

"Thanks, J.J.. I'll talk to you later."

James headed out for class. On the sidewalk, Linda and Helen pulled up beside him and Helen held a book out the window towards him, "this is a driver's manual," she said. "You'll need to study before you can get your license. If you're not busy this afternoon, we can go over to the parking lot behind the library and you can drive some more. You just need a bit more practice and I think you'll be ready to take the test."

"That sounds great," James said.

"See you at 5:00 in the parking lot," Helen smiled.

"Thanks for the book," James said, "I'll study it tonight."

"See ya later," Helen smiled, "Jimbo."

James was 5 minutes late to class. When he walked in, everyone was in their seats.

"Good morning, Jim," said Miss Wilson, "glad you could make it."

James just grinned and took his seat. After class, he took his time getting out of his desk so he could speak with Sandra alone.

"The reason I was late," James said, "was Helen and Linda stopped me along the way to give me a driver's manual. I'm going to get my license."

"Well, it's about time, Jimbooo," Sandra said sarcastically.

"They are going to meet me in the parking lot behind the library at 5 o'clock to give me some lessons."

"Well, I hope it's just driving lessons, Jimbooooo."

"Well, I need to get my license so I can take my girlfriend for a drive, sometime."

"Oh," Sandra said, "do you have a girlfriend?"

"You better believe it," James said, winking at her as he walked out.

James was standing in the parking lot when Linda and Helen arrived with David and Drew. They all piled out of the car and told James to get in. James drove in circles and was getting pretty good changing gears. He practiced for about half an hour and all of them piled back into the car and headed to the Hole in the Wall to have a beer.

On the way there, Drew talked about how his father would buy him a car when he cut his hair, and not a day before. "Every time I go home, I have to listen to him give me hell about my hair being too long. So, one day I told him I didn't see what all the fuss was about. If he thought about it, Jesus had long hair."

"What did your dad say?" David asked.

Drew said, "He said, 'yes. And he walked everywhere he went'. So, I've never said anything about it since."

The jukebox was playing as they walked into the Hole in the Wall. There were only a few people there. Helen grabbed James' hand and pulled him to the dance floor. He made a turn and she ducked under his arm. It was the first turn he had pulled off. Helen seemed pleased and looked at James and nodded her head in encouragement of a job well done. When the song was over, they went and sat at the table.

"You've come a long way," Drew said.

James responded with a big grin.

The waitress came over and they ordered two pitchers of beer. Drew gave David a look and nodded his head towards the bar. David followed his gaze to a man standing at the end of the bar wearing a business suit.

"Look at those wing-tipped shoes," Drew said, "Who does that remind you of?"

"Jimbo," David replies without hesitation.

That drew James' attention to the man. He did look totally out of place. The waitress came back with the pitchers and Drew asked, "Who's the guy at the end of the bar?"

"I don't know," she said, "But he's not from around here. He's from up north."

"How do you know that?" David asked.

She said, "He doesn't say 'ya'll', he says, 'Y'uns'. He came in and asked for a mixed drink. He didn't know that we don't sell alcohol in bars in North Carolina."

"Probably works for a funeral home," Drew decided, "That's the only people who wear wing-tipped shoes."

David and James laughed. James noticed that the man turned and looked over at their table every once in a while. He knew then that something wasn't right. The man kept looking over at them as David, Drew and the girls continued to tell stories and joke. They quickly forgot about the man at the bar, but James was uncomfortable. Something about him just wasn't right.

When they finished the two pitchers of beer, they decided to go back home. James wanted to study the driver's manual and the girls had to study for some tests that were coming up. Outside, it was pouring rain. Drew told Linda he would go get the car and pull around, so she handed him the keys. James took one last look at the man at the bar. Drew pulled up and opened the passenger side door and they all jumped in. As they were pulling out, James looked back. The man with the wing-tipped shoes was standing at the door, watching them leave.

Drew spoke up, "Man, it's raining harder than a white horse pissing down a flat rock!"

As they stopped in front of the house, the boys jumped out of the car and ran for the front porch. The girls waved and pulled off just as David unlocked the door. Before they stepped inside, James looked back and saw a black sedan driving slowly by the house. It made uncomfortable. He didn't say anything to David or Drew about his suspicions.

"Time to hit the books," David said.

James went to his room and looked out the window. He saw the same vehicle going back up the road in front of the house. He closed the curtain. He tried studying for a while before turning in for the night but his thoughts returned to the man.

The next morning was cereal for breakfast again, and powdered milk. James had never had powdered milk before, but it wasn't that bad.

James left the house again, but there was no sign of last night's black sedan. As he walked, he let thoughts of it be replaced by his eagerness to see Sandra.

When he got to class, he found her at her usual place behind her desk. James sat down, and his eyes met hers. She was looking at him and James thought he saw passion. It was a look he hadn't seen before, but he liked it.

That afternoon, James decided he should go to the soda shop and wait on Sandra. He had something he needed to discuss with her and he knew she would come by the soda shop on her way home. He was on the sidewalk nearby when he saw Sandra walking down the steps of the building where she worked. He crossed over the street to meet her as she stepped onto the sidewalk.

"Sandra," he called out to her. "Do you have a few minutes to talk?"
"Sure," She said, "What about?"

"Well," He said, "I've got a little bit of a problem. I've been trying to learn how to drive, and I've been studying the driver's manual. I'd like to take the test sometime next week, but the only car I've ever driven is Linda's and that's a straight-drive transmission. I'd like to use an automatic to take the test and I was wondering if you'd let me use your car?"

"Have you driven on the road yet?"

"No. Not yet."

"Well," Sandra began, "tomorrow is Saturday. I'll come by your house about 9 o'clock and we can go out in the country and let you drive some on the road. Then, I'll let you know if you're ready to take the driver's test or not."

"I'd really appreciate it," James said. "I might even take you out one night after I get my license."

"We'll see how you drive first," Sandra smiled.

James was sitting on the steps the next morning when Sandra pulled up.

Sandra smiled, "How are you feeling this morning, Jim?" "Believe it or not, I'm nervous."

"I can understand that, but it's a great morning for a country drive!"

Sandra made two or three turns and crossed the interstate. After about 10 miles, they were in the rolling hills of Eastern Guilford County. Some of the trees still had their fall colors. In the distance, old barns dotted the meadows that lined the winding roads. Around every curve was something new. Further out into the countryside, Sandra found a place to pull off on the side of the road and she let James in the driver's seat. She instructed him to look back to make sure no other cars were coming. James put the car in drive and pulled off at her instruction. Sandra was impressed with just how well James was doing.

After ten or fifteen minutes, James began to feel more comfortable. As they approached a stop sign, he put his arm out the window and let it hang down beside the car to indicate that he was stopping. Then, he stuck his left arm out and turned it up in the air to sign that he was turning right. James did all the appropriate hand signals as were part of the test.

Sandra said, "You're doing a great job. I don't think you'll have a problem passing your test."

"Well," James replied, "an automatic does make a difference, although the straight-drive was fun."

"Did Helen show you how to drive, Jim?"

"Linda does most of the driving."

Sandra said, "Does Helen have a steady date now?"

"I don't think so. I don't see her with anybody."

"I think she has the hots for you, Jim."

"You think so?"

"Yes, and I think you know so, too."

James just laughed.

Sandra said, "Well, you better be careful, Jimbooooooo," mocking Helen.

They were getting close to Greensboro and James pulled over to let Sandra drive again. As they passed the welcome sign to Greensboro, Sandra said, "Jim, I want to take you somewhere and show you something."

She made a few turns along the outskirts of Greensboro. James did not know where she was going, but the roads seemed very familiar to him. Then, he saw his house in the distance. Sandra said, "Look, Jim. That's the home of James Andrew Exum. Isn't it beautiful?"

She turned down the road, leading to the house. There were dogwood trees on both sides. Sandra stopped about thirty feet before the gates. There was a gentleman in the guardhouse and James knew him as Mr. Sparks, who had worked for him for about thirty years. He would have lunch inside the house with Grammy every day. James had called him 'Mr. Sparks'.

The guardhouse had been installed when James' father began having problems with the union. Although the people in the plant voted against having a union, his father had continued to receive phone threats. Mr. Sparks came out of the guardhouse and Sandra waved at him. She stuck her head out the window and shouted that they were just admiring the house. Mr. Sparks just shook his head and went back into the guardhouse. James knew it was common for people to drive up the drive to get a look before turning around.

Sandra looked over at James. "Look at the beautiful water fountain and those beautiful white columns with the fancy carvings. And those pansies on both sides of the walkway are lovely."

Grammy always saw that fresh pansies were planted on both sides of the walkway leading up to the house each year. She loved pansies.

"Look at those big, wooden double doors with the stained glass. Aren't they beautiful?" Sandra continued on, "It's a huge house. I bet there's 10,000 square feet."

James smiled and thought, *9,000.* But he only nodded, and agreed with her. Truth be told, he had never noticed the beauty of the house before. She pointed out things that he never paid attention to and he just sat there, trying to see things from her eyes. It really was a pretty place.

"I bet it's beautiful in the winter, when it snows. I came one time at Christmas to see the Christmas lights, but there were no lights at all."

The only Christmas James had there was in the big dining room that Grammy would prepare. His father would give Grammy, J.J. and him one gift each. And that was his Christmas. James wanted to tell Sandra.

"I wonder if they are Jewish." Sandra mused. "I can imagine how it would look if someone would decorate it. I bet it would look just like a Christmas card!"

Sandra finally turned the car around and James looked back at the house in which he had spent his whole life. For the first time in his life, he took a good look at it. From Sandra's perspective, it was a beautiful place.

As they headed back down the drive to the main road, Sandra looked at James, "See what you can have if you apply yourself and work hard?"

"The only way I would have a place like that would be if it was left to me."

Sandra laughed and drove into town. "Greensboro's a nice town," She said, "They have everything here. Lots of shops… Sears and Roebuck have a big store here."

Back on the interstate, Sandra asked, "How do you like college, Jim?"

"I love it," he said.

"Are you going to sign up for another semester?"

"I don't know yet. I'll just have to see how it all works out. I'd like to, but I may have to go back to work."

"I understand," Sandra said.

As the welcome sign for Burlington came into view, Sandra said, "Do you have time to come by the house for a few minutes? I need to talk to you."

They pulled into the drive and entered the house. Sandra offered him a glass of wine and led him over to a table in front of the bay window and they had a seat. Sandra poured the wine into two glasses and gave James one.

She took a sip and looked at James as he looked back at her. She wore a serious expression and he knew what she had to say was probably not going to be something he wanted to hear. "You said earlier today that you would like to get your driver's license so you could ask me out, which would be great, I would enjoy going out with you, but we have one small problem. I don't know how it would look to the college to have a teacher dating one of her students."

"I guess you could say I'm a student. And, yes, you are my teacher. But I'm not a registered, full-time student. I'm only here for one semester and it's a continuing education course. And I'm 30 years old. It's not like you're taking advantage of a child."

"I know that, Jim, but I still don't know how they would take it. It's still a student and a teacher."

"Well, I only have 4 to 6 weeks left in the semester and, most likely, I won't sign up for another. As I said, I have to get back to work," said James.

"I understand," Sandra said, "But you know, I have more feelings for you than I should have. It hasn't been easy for me. It's hard for me, sometimes, to be teaching the class when you're there. I look at you and it breaks my concentration."

"Well, Sandra, I don't want to cause you any trouble with the faculty or cause you any problems teaching your class, but I have feelings for you, too. Probably more than you'll ever know."

"Well, at least we understand each other," Sandra said, "Now what do we do about it?"

"The only thing I know to do is make the best of things for now until the semester is over. At that time, we'll take a look at the situation and talk again. But I'm really going to miss spending time with you. It makes me happy."

"It makes me happy, too, Jim. But, to keep us both out of trouble, we just have to do the best we can until the semester is over."

James took the last sip of his wine and stood up. "Well, if it's OK with you, I'll just walk home from here. I need the time alone and the walk will do me good."

Sandra stood up. James put both hands on her shoulders and gave her a soft kiss on the lips. Without looking at her face, he turned towards the door and started to leave.

"Wait, Jim," Sandra said. She walked over and put both arms around his waist and laid her head on his chest and squeezed against him. Looking up at him, she said, "I'm sorry."

James put a hand on either side of her face, "Sandra, this is not the end. This is going to be the beginning. Understand?"

Sandra looked at him a moment, then nodded her head in acknowledgement.

James walked out. It was late afternoon now and he took his time walking home. He had a lot going through his mind and needed time to think about everything; Sandra, the business and where he was going in his life.

I'm only thinking about myself. What I'm doing has put Sandra's job in jeopardy, leaving my business and dumping it all on J.J. and not being truthful to anyone here. I'm just being selfish.

James walked until it was dark. The streetlights came on, and most of the stores were closed. Just a few students were left, walking up and down the sidewalk. For the first time in a long time, James felt alone. As he turned up the block to go to the house, a black sedan went down the street. He couldn't tell if it was the one he had seen last night as they were leaving the Hole in the Wall. At the moment, he had so much on his mind that he didn't care.

James walked into the house.

"Where the hell have you been?" David asked, "We've been worried about you."

"You didn't leave us a note," Drew added. "You're so pretty, Jim. Somebody could've kidnapped your ass."

James chuckled, "How you doin' Drew?"

"I'm hanging in, like a hair in a biscuit. Come on back and have a beer."

The beach music was already playing out on the back porch.

"Hey boys," David said, "We've got to move the clock back tonight."

"Hellfire," Drew exclaimed, "it's going to be dark by 5:30. That's not a lot of daylight, boys."

"I don't know why they just don't leave it alone," David agreed.

"At least it will be daylight on your way to school," James offered.

"Who in the hell wants to see going to school?" Drew asked, "I won't be able to see coming home. By the way, the girls are coming over tonight. Linda and I think Helen has the hots for you, Jim."

"I think I may be a little too old for her, Drew," James chuckled.

David was about to say something when there was a knock on the door.

"It's the girls," Drew said as he got up to open the door. "Grab a beer, girls, and come on back," he invited, "David and Jim are out on the porch."

When Helen walked out on the porch, the first thing she did was sit down in James' lap. James was in a rocking chair, so Helen set the chair rocking as she sat. Everyone started to laugh. James grabbed the chair with his right hand as his left held on to his beer. Helen took her foot and pushed against the floor, causing the chair to rock faster.

"We're rockin' and rollin' now!" Helen laughed.

"Be careful, Helen," David warned, "You could get Jim excited."

James laughed, but wasn't in the mood. After his conversation earlier that evening, he still had Sandra on his mind.

Helen took James' hand form the rocking chair and put it on her breast and began wriggling around on his lap, hollering, "I'm going to ride this cowboy!"

James pulled his hand away and got up out of the chair, standing Helen up with him. "Speaking of riding, Linda," James averted, "I'd like to try and get my license this week. Could I use your car?"

"Do you think you're ready?" Linda asked.

"I think I can pass it," Jim replied.

"Well, you can use it," Linda said, "Just let me know when."

"When could you drive me down?"

"I get out of class at 3:00 tomorrow. Do you think we could do it then?"

"I don't see why not," James said, "if you're ready then I'm ready."

"OK," Linda agreed, "I'll meet you at the house at 3:15."

"I'll be waiting on you."

After a few more beers and a little dancing, the girls said goodbye.

Chapter 20

The next morning, James arrived to class before anyone else arrived. Sandra looked up at him. She didn't look as if she felt good.

"Are you alright?" James asked.

"I didn't sleep at all," Sandra said, "I was up all night thinking about our conversation. I didn't like it."

"Neither did I," James said, "but it is probably the best thing for now. We'll work through this, Believe me."

As the other students began to arrive, James took his seat. As Sandra taught class, she walked around the room. Coming up beside James, she rested a hand on his shoulder. For James, it felt like a shock went through his body. As she continued to teach, she glanced at James with a solemn look on her face.

When class was over, James gave her a smile before leaving. He tried to make the smile more than just a smile. He hoped it quietly acknowledged the feelings between them.

At home, James brushed up on the driver's manual until Linda arrived. At 3:15 sharp, she pulled up in front of the house. James was waiting for her on the front porch.

Linda stuck her head out the window, "You ready?"

"Ready as I'll ever be," James said, getting in the car, "I'm about as nervous and excited as a virgin in a prison rodeo, as Drew would say."

Linda laughed, "Where he gets that stuff, I don't know, but it just keeps coming out of him!"

The DMV was a small brick building with gray double doors. James got out of the car and went in. Thirty minutes later, he came out with a smile on his face. He had been given the option to drive for 30 days with a learner's permit or to go ahead and take the test. If he didn't pass the test, he could always take it again in a month so, he opted to go ahead and give it a try.

Linda slid into the backseat, and James settled into the driver's seat. The examiner, a man in a gray uniform and gray derby hat, got in on the other side. James pulled out of the parking space and up the road he went, changing gears, Linda listened for scraping gears, but everything sounded good.

Fifteen minutes later, they pulled back into the parking space. The examiner told him to come inside and he would issue the license. Shortly, James emerged again with a license in his hand. He had never been so proud of himself. Out of all the tests he had taken (and there had been a lot of them), this test meant the most.

As he came up to Linda, he held up the license to show her he had passed. He didn't let her close enough to see his full name.

"Good job, Jim," Linda gushed, "I knew you could do it!"

"Well, I'm glad you did," James said, "I'm not sure I did. I knew I had to try, at least."

"Would you like to drive home?" Linda asked.

"I'd love to."

James slid into the driver's seat and off they went.

Back at the house, James thanked Linda again and she told him she would see him later that night.

James started into the house, then changed his mind. Instead, he decided to go see Sandra. He was eager to show her his new license. As he reached the soda shop, he saw Mr. Stephens and Sandra walking out the door, turning in the direction of her house. When he saw them together, James stopped, suddenly. A sick feeling was in his stomach. He decided to walk back home. He told himself he would show her his license some other time.

As he walked through the door, he shouted, "Hey guys! Where are you?"

"Back here!" David shouted back.

James joined David and Drew on the back porch and grinned, "guess what I got, fellas?" James pulled out his driver's license.

"Are you shittin' me?" Drew laughed.

"Nope. I passed the test just a while ago. I drove Linda's car. We're all celebrating tonight down at the Hole in the Wall. I invited the girls and drinks are on me."

"That's great!" Drew exclaimed. Then, "now, all we need is a car!"

"We've got a couple hours before we have to be there," James said.

David nodded, "Well, that gives me a couple hours to study. Lord knows I need it."

Drew got out his loafers and started to polish them, "Got to have these babies lookin' good."

A couple of hours later, James, David and Drew were on their way to the Hole in the Wall. It was a warm night. The three of them had polished their shoes and were wearing their dress pants with a nice crease down the front. They strolled down the street like three New York wise guys, not saying a word; just looking at the bright lights. When they heard the music, their hearts picked up the beat. They were ready to get it on. The night was young and they were in a mood for dancing and drinking.

Inside, the place was packed and the jukebox was loud. The smoke was thick in the air. Linda waited for them at the door. She grabbed James by the arm and pulled him toward a table where Helen was saving them seats. She was wearing a white mini-skirt with red black boots and a red sweater. Her hair was held back by a red bow.

"Guys, we're in for one hell of a night," Helen says, "Jim's buying!"

"You're looking good tonight, Helen," Drew said.

"Why thank you Drew," Helen smiled, "It's just something I threw on."

James couldn't help but agree that mini-skirt just stood out.

David said, "Damn, Helen, you look so good you might just get picked up tonight."

"I'm hoping so," Helen replied with a glance to James. He got the hint. As if on cue, a slow song came on the jukebox. Helen grabbed James by the hand, "Come on, Jimbo," she said, "let's dance to this one."

On the dance floor, Helen got real close to James and put her head on his shoulder. James could feel every curve when she moved her body.

David gave Drew a knowing look. "If Jim isn't careful," David said, "he's going to get lucky with Helen tonight."

"Well," Drew began, "She didn't teach him how to drive. But, I guarantee you there are some other things she can teach him."

When the song was over, Helen and James came back to the table. Sweat was running down the side of James' face.

Drew said to David, "My God, his face is as red as a fox's ass!"

James grabbed a cold glass of beer and drank nearly all of it before setting it back on the table. James gave Drew and David a big grin, and the two boys burst out laughing. They knew their boy had been bumping and grinding.

A second pitcher of beer was placed on the table. It wasn't long before all of them were on the dance floor. 'Stubborn Kind of Fella' by Marvin Gaye was playing, and everyone just had to dance to it.

A slow song came on, but before James could sit down, his hand was grabbed once again. This time by a good-looking girl he didn't know. She was tall and had dark hair. As she led him back out on the dance floor, James saw she had a Carolina blue sweater on that fit tight around her large breasts. She wore a dark blue pleated mini skirt that hugged her hips. White boots and a white scarf completed her outfit. She easily stood out from the crowd. As she slid her arms around James' neck, the two began to dance.

"Who is that girl?" Helen asked David and Drew.

"I don't know," Drew said, "But she stands out like a bastard child at a family reunion."

By now, the girl was getting a little too close to James for Helen's comfort. Helen didn't like it. She got out of her seat and walked over to where they were dancing. She tapped the girl on the shoulder, a request to cut in. The girl just looked at Helen and turned away, she wasn't giving up her place with James. Helen grabbed the girl by the arm and pulled it away from James' neck, then pushed the girl backwards. The girl shoved back with a vengeance and the next thing James knew, they were in the floor. All James could see was assholes and elbows.

James reached down to pick Helen off the floor when he was hit upside the head with a fist. He went to the floor. The next thing he knew, he was being pulled out the front door. A voice told him to wait there, but he had no time to figure out who was speaking to him. By the time he gained his senses, David, Drew, Linda and Helen were helping him to the car. David got him in the car.

Drew said, "Let's get the hell out of here. The law will be here any minute!"

The Police were pulling in as they were pulling out.

"Let's get Jim to the house," David said, "his nose is bleeding. Hold his head back so he won't get blood on everything."

When they got to the house, they helped James to the couch. "Sit still, Jim," Drew said, "We'll get you a towel."

"Put some ice in it," David instructed.

There was blood on Helen's white mini skirt. "What the hell got into you, Helen?" Drew asked.

"I wanted to cut in and she wouldn't let me," Helen explained. "She wouldn't move over, so I decided to move her out of the way."

"Who was it that hit Jim?" Drew pressed.

No one knew.

"How did you get out, Jim?" David asked.

"I don't know," James said, "when I came to, someone had me under the arms and was pulling me outside. The next thing I knew you guys were helping me to the car."

"Some guy had me by the collar," Drew added, "He started steering me toward the door and grabbed David on the way out. He told us to get you out of there and about that time, the girls showed up. He must have been a bouncer."

Helen came over and removed the towel from James' face. "Let me take a look," she said. As she moved the towel, a shocked look came across her face. "My God!" She breathed, "His eye is totally closed."

"I think we need to take you to the doctor and let them take a look at your eye," Linda said.

"No," James protested, "It will be fine by tomorrow. I'll just keep this cold towel on it tonight."

"You may want to stay home in the morning," David suggested, "And take care of that eye. It's going to look worse tomorrow."

"Hope not," James said.

"We hate to leave," Linda said at last, "but we need to get home and clean up and get the blood out of Helen's skirt."

"I'm sorry, Helen," James said.

"You have nothing to be sorry for, Jim," Helen sighed, "It was all my fault." She bent over and gave him a kiss on the cheek. "I'm sorry. I'll come check on you tomorrow."

"OK You girls be careful driving home," James said. Then, he turned to David and Drew, "If you guys don't mind, I think I am going to take a shower and head to bed."

"You do that, Jim," said Drew, "let me have the towel and I'll put some fresh ice in it."

After the shower, Drew brought the towel and fresh ice to James. "Hold this on your eye and we'll see you in the morning," he said.

James looked at himself in the mirror. His eye was totally closed. He also noticed just how long his hair had gotten. It was down over his ears now and was so long that just the bottom lobe of his ear was visible. He could run his hands through it and it would naturally fall back into place. It would feather back on the sides, which meant it was about time to have some of it cut off.

James didn't sleep well, but he slept late the next morning. He decided to stay in for the day and just sleep and rest. In the mirror he could see his eye and half his cheekbone were dark blue. James put on pajamas and grabbed a pillow off the bed and went into the den. He laid down on the couch and turned on the TV. A note was on the coffee table from Drew, saying he and David would check on him at lunch. James watched a little TV before falling asleep again on the sofa.

A knock on the door a few hours later woke him up. Feeling a little out of it, he stumbled to the door. There stood Sandra. James stepped back and Sandra stepped in.

"My God, Jim," Sandra said, "You don't look good. I heard you had a black eye, but I didn't realize it was this bad. Are you OK?" She asked, "Do you need me to take you to the doctor? What can I do to help?"

"Just come over here and sit down on the end of the couch. Just let me look at you," James said, "That will make me feel better." "I can do better than that, Jim." She bent down and kissed him on the forehead, then lightly on the lips.

"I feel better already," smiled James.

"Do you want to tell me what happened?" Asked Sandra.

"Well," James began, "I was bending over to help Helen off the floor and the next thing I knew a bouncer was pulling me off the floor."

"What was Helen doing on the floor?"

"I knew you were going to ask that," said James.

"Well, let's hear it."

"Well, a girl I didn't know asked me to dance and Helen tried to cut in but the girl ignored her. That's when all hell broke loose. The next thing I knew Helen and the girl were on the floor fighting. I reached down to help Helen up. That's when the lights went out."

"How does it feel to have girls fighting over you?" Sandra teased.

"Well, as you can tell," James said, "It doesn't feel too good."

"Well maybe it's time you started acting your age." Sandra said, "You're 30 years old and you're trying to act 21. You knew it was a school night. You should have been home studying."

"It was a special occasion," James insisted, "I invited everyone out for drinks. My treat."

"Oh," Sandra said, "So now you're a big time spender?"

"No, I took my driver's test yesterday and passed. As of today I can drive a vehicle."

"That's great Jim," Sandra said, "I thought you were going to use my car to take the driver's test?"

"I was going to ask you but Linda volunteered her car so I decided to try a straight drive and I passed. I was coming over to your house to tell you the good news when I saw you and Professor Stephens coming out of the soda shop headed toward your house. I didn't want to interrupt what you and the professor had going on."

"Yes," Sandra said, "I was going home and so was Professor Stephens. His house is only a block from mine and he was on his way home, as well."

"I didn't know that."

"Were you jealous?"

"I don't know what it was, but I know I didn't like it," James said.

"How do think it makes me feel when you go out dancing and have girls fighting over you?"

"Are you saying you're jealous?" Countered James.

"Let's just say it's not a pleasant thing to hear about. I'd rather see you do things that are going to help you be more successful in life, Jim. Not hanging out at bars and getting in fights. It's not what a professional does. He wouldn't put himself in that position. That's all I'm saying."

"Don't give up on me yet," James persuaded, "I'm a work in progress."

The door opened and in walked Drew. He paused, abruptly and looked at Sandra. "Well... Hey... Miss Wilson," He said as a smirk crept up one side of his face. "Thought I would drop by and check on Jim during my lunch break. See if he needed anything."

"That's nice of you, Drew," Sandra said, "The news is all over campus about the fight at the Hole in the Wall. When James didn't show up this morning, I thought I would drop by and check on my student."

"I'm glad you dropped in to check on him," Drew said, "It's nice to know someone in this house is being responsible."

James rolled his eyes, but Drew had a big smile on his face.

"Well," Sandra said, standing, "I have to get back to class." She turned to James, "I'll drop off your assignments and you can work on them here while you heal."

"I appreciate that, Ms. Wilson," said James, "Thank you for coming by and checking on me."

As Sandra left, Drew ran over to the window and peeked through the blinds. When she opened the door of her car to get in, Drew got a look at her knee as her dress moved up. "Lord, have mercy," he murmured, "that is one fine-looking woman."

"She is that," James smiled.

"I believe she likes you, Jimbo," Drew said as he turned away from the window at last.

"What makes you say that?"

"Just by the way she looks at you. So, do you need me to go to the drug store for anything?" Drew offered.

"No," answered James, "I've been taking aspirin and my eye feels better today."

"I'd feel better, too," Drew assured, "If I had Ms. Wilson checking up on me. Oh. By the way, the Hole in the Wall doesn't have a bouncer. No one knows who pulled you out the front door. The guy that grabbed me by the collar I didn't recognize him as being there."

"Well, I'm glad he was," James said, "I'd like to thank him. It could have been a lot worse than what it was had he not been there."

"The girls are doing fine," Drew continued, "Helen got the blood out of her skirt. They'll probably drop by this afternoon to see how you're doing." Drew stood and smiled, "I'm going back to school if you don't need anything else."

"I'll be OK. I'll see you this afternoon when you get in."

James took another nap. When he woke up, the phone was ringing. James reached over his head and took the receiver off the hook. "Hello," he said groggily.

"James," said the other party, "it's J.J.. I wanted to check on you and see how you were doing."

"Well," James said with a smile, "I'm hanging in like a hair on a biscuit, J.J.."

"What did you say?" Quizzed J.J.. "A hair in a biscuit?" He paused, and then laughed, "Man, you are picking up on some new lingo!"

James asked how Grammy was doing.

"Fine," J.J. said, "She was out working in her flowers the other day. She seems to be happy. She told me that you had been calling her regularly."

"I know how she worries. I try and call her every three days just to say hi. How's business?"

"You know it's getting close to the end of the year. Our guys are working on inventory to make sure all orders are filled by Christmas."

"That's good." James paused, then, "J.J.. I need a favor. There was a little accident last night. I was in a bar called the Hole in the Wall. It's a little local bar where all the kids hang out. There was a fight and I was responsible for some of the damage that was done. I'd like to see that it's paid for.... I just don't want to let them know where the money's coming from."

"I understand," J.J. assured, "I'll take care of it James."

As soon as J.J. hung up, J.J. made one more call. A voice on the other end confirmed, "This is Jack."

"Jack, this is J.J.. I just wanted to thank you for getting James out of the bar last night, and his friends, as well."

"You're welcome," Jack replied, "That's what you pay me for, J.J.. How is he?"

"I think he may be a little sore but otherwise fine. I've got one other thing I need you to do. Go by the Hole in the Wall, see how much damage was done and I'll see that it's taken care of."

"Will do," Jack replied, "I'll get back with you this afternoon."

"Thanks again, Jack. Keep up the good work. Just another month to go before this semester is over."

"No problem," Jack said.

J.J. hung up with Jack and placed a call to Agent Clark to check on the status of the investigation.

"I don't think it's going to be too much longer," said Agent Clark, "Our agent inside has given us some valuable information. I think in two or three weeks we'll need to get together and plan how things should come together. We need to coordinate things from your office. Be sure that Mr. Exum stays out of the way and that he does not go back to the New York office. We still need him out of there. I'll be in touch with you soon; we may also need to put an agent with you at that time. There is more going on than we first suspected. I'll cover everything with you when the time is right."

Chapter 21

Another knock at the door woke James. When he answered, before him stood Linda and Helen. He greeted them with "Come on in girls."

"We just wanted to check on you Jim. That eye looks like hell," Linda said.

"Well it feels better than it did last night." Jim replied.

Jim, I'm so sorry that I put you in that position. That bitch would not let me cut in." Helen said.

"I understand Helen, it's not a problem. I got to lie on the couch all day, I really needed the rest," Jim said, reassuring her.

Then Drew and David walked into the room.

"Hey, girls. How are you doing?" Drew asked.

Linda replied "We just wanted to stop in to say hello to Jim and see how he was doing."

"Would y'all like a beer?" David asked politely.

"I guess not. We've got to go home and study, since we didn't get any studying done last night," Helen replied.

As the two girls were leaving, Miss Wilson pulled up behind their car. "Hey, Miss Wilson, how are you?"

"I'm doing fine," Miss Wilson replied, "Just thought I would drop some books off for Jim to study while he was out."

The girls waved good-bye as Sandra walked in with the books under her arms. James greeted her at the door. "Hey, Miss Wilson, how are you?"

"Well I'm doing just fine. The real question is how you are." She replied.

"Well, other than the fact I can't see out of but one eye, half of my head is blue, and my head hurts; I'm doing just dandy."

Well, I have some good news for you, but I will have to tell you later." She said glancing nervously at David and Drew. "Study these books. Next Monday I will be giving a test, so you have six days to study."

"Yes ma'am." Jim said.

After a couple of days lying around the house, studying, and taking aspirin, James was feeling better. He could finally see, and the bruise on his eye had gone from a deep purple to a light blue with a little yellow around the edges. The white of his eyes were still red, but the swelling had gone down and his head didn't hurt. "So things are looking up." James said to himself, encouragingly.

Miss Wilson came by Thursday during lunch hour while Jim was the only one there. As she opened the door Jim called out to her "Come on in!"

"Are the guys in now?" She asked.

"They won't be back until this afternoon. Might I add, Miss Wilson, you sure look fine today."

"Well I must say you are looking better, Jim. And the news I was going to tell you about."

"Yes, what was the news you were going to tell me?" Jim asked.

"Well, I was talking to Mom about getting your driver's license for the first time, and she wanted me to tell you that she will sell you the 41 Chevrolet, if you still want it."

"Woo, yes I still want that car!" James said excitedly. "Tell her I will take good care of it and I'll come by and get it as soon as I can."

"She also told me that you didn't have to pay her all at one time," She added. "You can pay her a little bit every month."

"Well, I have a little bit saved up. What is she asking for it, Sandra?" James asked.

"She said to pay whatever you thought it was worth."

"Well I expect to pay full price for it. Whatever she wants, I will pay it."

"Now how are you going to get it?"

"I thought I would have Helen drive me."

"You are about to get the other side of your head blue." Joked Miss Wilson and James laughed. "Now you get well and we will look at going to Asheville maybe next weekend. How is that for you?"

"That would be great, Sandra. You can count on it! I will be ready to go. I'm so excited for my first car."

Sandra smiled at him. He was acting like a little kid on Christmas morning. She had never seen him so happy. James then reached for Sandra's face. He placed his hands gently on her cheeks and kissed her right on the lips.

Sandra said "My, Jim you are so happy."

"That is the best present I could buy myself. I'm looking forward to having that car and I will get to take my best girl on a date."

"Why, who is that Jim? Who is your best girl?" she said smiling.

"Helen." He replied.

"Just keep it up big boy.", Sandra quipped.

"Well I've got to go back to school; I just wanted to give you that information. I thought it would make you happy and help you forget about your eye." Sandra said.

"Thank you so much, Sandra. Please tell your mother I said thanks to her too." He said graciously.

That afternoon James described the '41 Chevy to Drew and David. He talked about the excellent condition, how it belonged to Sandra's father, and the details. It was white with white wall tires.

"When are you going to get it, Jim?" Drew asked.

"I'm going to get it in about a week or two. I've got to let my eye heal first. I don't want Miss. Wilson's mother seeing me look like this. As soon as it gets better, I'm going to Asheville to get that car."

"Well, we won't have to walk anymore." Drew said jokingly.

"Can we drive it sometime, Jim?" asked David.

"You can if you can treat it like your mother with tender love and care. She's a beauty.

"Is it a girl car?" Drew joked.

"Well," James replied "It's got a tag on the front that says 'Little Susie', so I guess it's a girl."

Jim walked back to his own room to put on some clothes. David turned to Drew and said "I've never seen Jim so happy."

"He's as happy as a kitten following a leaking cow." Drew said.

After taking a shower and changing clothes, James exited his room following the sound of the blues music playing out on the porch. When he stepped out on the porch he saw David sitting down with a beer.

David informed James that Linda had come by earlier to see Drew. They had a date at her house to practice dancing for a few competitions at Myrtle Beach in November. James had a suspicion that they just fancied each other, and was coming up with excuses to be together. "How long have you known Drew?" James asked David.

"We have been rooming together a little over three years. I met Drew the first week I came here. We discovered both of us always wanted to be an engineer. He had decided to be a mechanical engineer, while I wanted to be an electrical engineer. I will tell you something about Drew, and you're going to be surprised." David said.

"Nothing will surprise me about Drew."

"Well, you might be surprised he has a full four year scholarship paid for."

"Are you serious, David?" James said taken aback.

"He also has two patents on equipment that he redesigned himself."

"How would you know that?"

"I spent a Christmas with his family last year, and his father explained it to me. He said 'Drew had to get up every morning at four to go out and milk the cows. He figured out a way to redesign the machine so that it would be much easier and faster than the instruction manual. The only reason he did it was so he could sleep longer in the morning. He redesigned the whole system, and it worked. A veterinarian came by and asked him to draw it up for him the way that Drew had designed it.' His name was put on a patent and he's been getting royalty checks for it every so often. In the past three years his average in college is a 3.8. He doesn't even study half of the time."

"That does surprise me David. He doesn't seem like the type." James said.

"He's got a heart of gold, Jim." David replied. "The second year he and I were rooming together, my mother passed away. A neighbor called me at school to tell me about it. My dad works for the government in New London CT at a submarine base. He's gone about eighty percent of the time so no one could get in touch with him. Drew was determined to get me home, so we packed everything up and got a friend to drive us to the bus station. Drew paid for both tickets for us to get to Connecticut. Drew insisted that he should go. 'What kind of friend would I be to let you go by yourself? I'm not going to let you down.' And he hasn't to this day.

We arrived in Connecticut after two days. Mom's body was at the funeral home. Nothing had been done and I didn't know what to do. All I knew was that she wanted to be cremated and for her ashes to be spread along the banks of the inter harbor of the base, where the submarines came in. She loved that place. She would sit and wait for dad's submarine to come in. We sat there for hours playing at the water's edge. I was seven when she told me to spread her ashes there, and when I had told Drew, he made sure that's exactly what would happen.

Drew made all the funeral arrangements. He stood by me the whole time. When I received her ashes we went out on the bank to spread them. Afterwards we sat on a bench that I had sat down on so many times before, and I broke down crying. Drew stayed and supported me. Dad didn't even show up. I locked up the house, and left a note with my telephone number on the door. After that, Drew and I left for the college.

There's nothing I wouldn't do for Drew. That's why we decided to go into a business ourselves. We call it 'D and D, Mechanical and Electrical Engineering Company'. We decided we would do it here in Burlington. I don't know what I would have done without Drew. He's like the brother to me now. Ever since, I spend Christmas and Thanksgiving with his family.

He's got great parents. His dad said Drew has always been mechanically minded. When he was little his dad gave him a toolkit. An hour later, Drew took all the doorknobs off the doors and electrical plates off every wall in the den. Drew could tear up a steel ball.

He comes off as a good 'ole country boy, but he's very smart and if you have Drew as a friend, then he's your friend for life. He'll do anything for you if he likes you." His dad said.

James looked at David as David told the story about Drew, and thought about the relationship they have. He couldn't help but think of J.J. and what a great friend he's been to him. He considered J.J. to be the brother he never had, and how J.J. took care of him coming up through life. He thought about how maybe he hadn't appreciated the things J.J. had done for him. He realized he wouldn't know what he would have done without J.J. being there for him. J.J. runs the business, he takes care of Grammy, he handles the finances at the mansion, and he makes sure everyone is paid. Plus, he takes care of his marriage and household. James felt a little selfish, so he decided he was going to make it up to J.J. somehow, just because J.J. was always there for him.

James looked at David "You have a true friendship with Drew. I think you guys will have a great business. Not only are you friends, but you have total trust in each other, and that will take you a long way in running a business."

"Well thanks Jim," David replied. "Don't forget you're one of us now, and we're all going to look after each other. If you ever need anything from me and Drew, all you need to do is ask and we'll be there for you."

"Thanks, David. You guys can count on me to be there for you as well."

After having the discussion with David about Drew, James needed a long walk to do some thinking. He grabbed his jacket, and let David know he'd be back in about 45 minutes. It was a cool night, the streetlights had come on and there was still a lot of movement in the town. Students were bustling to the library and some students were hanging out on their porches.

James thought about the situation he was in, and what David had said about his friendship with Drew. He thought about everyone he had become acquainted with: Helen, Linda, Sandra, David, Drew, and even Sandra's mother. He felt like he hadn't been honest with them. He hadn't been totally truthful about himself towards them. He remembered his dad always telling him *'You are as good as your word. If a man's word is no good, then he's not a good man. Always tell the truth, James.'* He worried about what everyone would think of him, if they would still be friends with him.

"I've got to come clean to everybody," James said to himself. "But they all like me for the person I am. If Sandra loves me she'll love me for my personality not where I came from." As James walked into the intersection he decided to go to the Hole in the Wall across the street. He wanted to see if everything had been taken care of concerning the fights and the damage that had been done.

When he entered, he was greeted by the waitress that had waited them on the night of the fight. Her name was Beth. "James you look better tonight than the last time I saw you. You were on your back, that's what I had heard."

"I just wanted to come by and apologize for any problems or damages that may have occurred. I don't really know how it started." Jim said.

"Jim, all I know was there was a pole of people in the middle of the floor, and you were pulled out by somebody. All hell broke loose. There wasn't a whole lot of damage though. A few chairs, a couple tables, and the jukebox had been damaged. The next day, as we were cleaning up, a gentleman came in and said he was the father of one of the people in the fight. He said he would pay for damages if we didn't press charges. The owner said it was fine and the damages were about eight-hundred dollars. The man handed over fifteen hundred, and apologized for the incident."

"Do you know who it was?" James asked.

"No. It was probably a dad of a rich kid, who wanted to keep their kid out of trouble. So the owner just let it go. "

"Well, I'll pay for the drinks that we had. I wasn't able to pay you when I left, if you know what I mean." James said.

"I think I know what you mean. The money that the man paid the owner took care of it all. You don't owe us anything." Beth said.

"Well, I'm sorry that it happened. If there's anything I can do to help, I'll be glad to do it."

"There's nothing you can do, Jim. Everything is fine and you guys can come back anytime. You are all welcome."

James thanked Beth and headed home. On his way home, across the street, there was Bandit the three-legged beagle. He hadn't seen Bandit since he had first moved to town. "Well hey, Bandit." James said as he patted the dog's head. "How have you been buddy? It's been a long time since I've seen you. Where've you been keeping yourself?" Bandit licked James' hand. "You're a good boy, Bandit." James got up and kept on his path home. The dog hobbled along following James home.

When James looked back he realized Bandit was having a hard time, so he picked the dog up and set him on the porch. When he walked inside the house, Bandit just stepped right inside with him. James followed the sound of beach music to the back porch where David was sitting by himself drinking beer and listening to the radio. "Well, Jim, I see you brought Bandit home with you." David said.

"You know Bandit, David?" James asked.

"Everybody knows Bandit, Jim. He's been around longer than I have been here. Everybody on campus knows Bandit."

"Well, he just followed me home and came inside with me."

David looked down at Bandit. "Well, Bandit would you like to have a beer?" David got up to retrieve a big bowl, poured a can of beer in, and set it down in front of Bandit. The dog didn't leave a drop.

"Do you think it is okay to give a dog beer, David?" James asked cautiously.

"Well I don't know if it's good for them or not, but I know he likes it." David said.

As Bandit finished up his beer, James sat down on one of the rocking chairs. When Bandit finished he hobbled over to James and lied down at his feet. "Well Jim it looks like you have a buddy." David said.

Then Linda and Drew walked in. Bandit greeted them by jumping up. "Well hey there Bandit," Drew said. "How are you doing boy."

"So you know Bandit too?" James asked.

"Yep, Bandit is the college mascot. He belongs to everybody on campus. This is the first time I've seen him go into anyone's house."

"Well Jim brought him home, he's had a beer and apparently he's decided to have a nap." David said to Drew.

Drew looked at David and said "Y'all know... we had a dog back home that only had two front legs and no back legs. He had steel balls. Everyone in town called him sparky."

Linda and James fell over laughing. Even David started laughing. "Drew, you're a crazy son of a bitch. I have never seen anything like that." David said laughing.

"Will you get me a beer out of the refrigerator, David?" Drew asked.

"Get your own damn beer out of the fridge. You're not sparky. You've got two working legs." They all started laughing again.

"On that note, I think I'm going to leave." Linda said. Drew walked Linda to the front door, and Bandit followed behind them. He hopped between them and out the door. Drew reached down to Linda and kissed her gently on the lips.

James thought to himself "David is right, maybe they're more than just dance partners."

When Drew came back to the porch he said "Y'all, I think I'm going to bed. I am tired and about danced out."

"Oh, is that what they call it now? Dancing?" David joked.

Drew just smiled and walked toward his bedroom. James and David stayed up for another forty-five minutes until they decided to turn in.

The next morning, while James was starting his morning, he thought he would take his time and make sure Drew and David had time to leave the house. He needed to give J.J. a call to discuss a little business that had been on his mind. After the boys had left for class, James called the plant. Knowing that J.J. would be in his office early, James dialed the number directly to J.J.'s office. J.J. picked up the phone. "Good morning, J.J.." James said.

J.J. recognized the voice immediately. "Well good morning to you too, James. How is the college life?" J.J. said cheerfully.

"It's a different world out here, J.J.. I just wanted to thank you for taking care of the business down at the Hole in the Wall. They were pleased by the way it was handled. "

"No problem James. I'm glad to do it."

"J.J. have you had time to look over the inventory sheet that you got while you were in New York?"

"Yes I have. The numbers are not adding up. The numbers are off in two of our plants and the numbers in New York are showing less than what our production level is showing. Don't worry, though. I'm on top of it just give me a couple of weeks. I should be able to give you an answer."

"It may be that the inventory count in those two plants could be off. Someone may not have put it in the right figure. I don't understand how he could be wrong in two plants." James said.

"I've seen that as well, James. I agree with you, but give me a couple of weeks and we will sit down and discuss it."

"Okay, I'll talk to you in a few days. Take care." James said and he hung up the phone.

When J.J. put down the phone, he thought about how he didn't like withholding information from James. He also knew that it was for James' safety, and if this was the way it was going to be done; so be it.

Chapter 22

J.J. gave Detective Clark a call. "This is Detective Clark. Is this J.J.?" asked the voice on the other end of the line.

"Yes, this is J.J. Washington."

"I'm glad you called J.J.. I was going to give you a call in about 20 minutes. Do you have plans for lunch today?"

"There are no plans that I cannot change, Detective Clark."

"Good. I will pick you up around twelve o' clock today. I know where you park your car. When you leave, walk towards your car and I will pull up beside you. Then you can just get in."

"Okay. I'll leave my office at exactly twelve o' clock." J.J. said as he hung up the phone.

Later that day at noon, J.J. grabbed his briefcase. As he walked by the secretary he said "If anyone tries to get in contact with me, just tell them I'm in a meeting until this afternoon." The secretary just nodded and J.J. walked out the door.

When he walked into the parking lot, a black 1969 Ford Crown Victoria pulled along beside him. When the vehicle stopped, J.J. opened the door and vanished inside the car. Not a word was said inside the car until they got onto 29 headed north. Detective Clark began to speak:

"We are going to Danville, Virginia. There's a room set up for us at the Holiday Inn. There will be five other detectives waiting for our arrival. When we get there, we'll go over everything with you. I will give you whatever time you need from me. Is that okay?"

J.J. nodded as he looked at Detective Clark. He concluded that the detective was all business. He was tall, around his mid-forties. He had black hair that was turning gray, and he spoke with a New England accent. J.J. knew he could trust this detective with this investigation. About forty-five minutes later they pulled in at the Holiday Inn. They drove around back and parked, then got out of the car.

They entered in the side door of the motel which led them into a hallway. Detective Clark stopped at room one hundred. When he knocked on the door, a man wearing a white shirt with his sleeves rolled up and a loose tie around his neck opened the door. As they walked in, Detective Clark introduced J.J. to all of the other officers in the room who were dressed similarly as the man who opened the door.

Detective Clark pulled up a chair for J.J. and asked him to sit down. One officer pulled out a map of the whole east coast, another pulled down a white screen. One of the officers looked up at J.J.. "J.J., you are going to look at some slides of people and places. Some of them you've never seen, but I'm sure there's a few that you will recognize. When you recognize them, say 'stop'. We will stop the slide show and we'll discuss the individual.

This investigation has been going on for about a year. The more we've investigated the bigger the crime has gotten. We're dealing with some very hardened criminals. That's why we keep James Andrew Exum out of New York and out of the way."

Detective Clark spoke up and said "J.J. is keeping in touch with Mr. Exum and if anything changes concerning his activities that may jeopardize this investigation, he will let us know immediately."

The cop nodded his head and turned to J.J.. "That's good J.J.. The last thing we need is for him to get hurt during this investigation."

The officer then began the slide show. The first slide showed a tractor and a trailer backed up to a loading dock, and a young man was on a tow motor with a roll of denim taking it back to the trailer. J.J. did not recognize the young man. The next slide showed a man wearing a white shirt and a neck tie talking to the truck driver. "Stop" said J.J., and the detectives stopped the slide.

"That is Mr. Murphy. He is our shipping and receiving Forman on second shift in Asheville, North Carolina." J.J. said.

"What do you know about him?" The detectives asked.

"He has been with us for about three years. I know he's married and he doesn't have any children. I think he's from the Asheville area." J.J. said.

Detective Clark spoke up. "Well, let me tell you about the real Mr. Murphy. To start with, his name is not Murphy; his name is Ed Duncan. He was born and raised in Baltimore, Maryland, he then moved to New York about four years ago. He worked in a yarn manufacturing plant in the shipping department. He was there for about a year before moving to Asheville, North Carolina, and landed a job with Exum Textiles. His rap sheet includes robbery, forgery, embezzlement, and counterfeit money.

We think he is the only problem you have in this plant. The young boy driving the tow motor is doing what he's been told to do. He works out of your distribution center up there in New York. Each roll of denim is seventy-two meters long, thirty-six to forty-eight meters in diameter, and weighing about five-hundred pounds. The drive from Asheville to Greensboro is about three hours long." He then kept rolling the slides.

"Stop," J.J. said. "The gentleman in the white shirt and tie is the second shift supervisor over the shipping department. His name is Richard Keeler. He's been with the company for about two years."

"Well J.J.," Clark said. "He is the one we think is changing the number of rolls that are being placed in the back of the trailer. He is also the one that we think is providing the wrong information to your New York distribution center."

"Well that explains why the numbers of rolls and pounds aren't adding up at the end of the month."

The detective showed the next slide. It showed the Exum textile trailer backed into the warehouse in New York City's waterfront. "He's loading up in Asheville, North Carolina at about six thirty in the afternoon. Three hours later he pulls into the Greensboro plant, and after the trailer is completely loaded, he leaves the Greensboro plants and gets on 85 north. Around nine or ten hours of driving time, he pulls in a warehouse on the riverfront of New York City which puts him there at around seven thirty in the morning.

At the factory the rolls are put on an unrolling machine, and then counterfeit money is placed on the fabrics and rolled back up. They cut off the excess weight from the fabric and it's placed on a cargo freighter and shipped to Matamoros, Mexico to a workhouse. There it is unwound, stripped of the counterfeit money and distributed through Mexico to drug dealers. Then the process repeats and is hauled back across the border to an operation is Brownsville, Texas. These people are making money selling fake money into Mexico and your fabric in the US."

J.J. sat still and listened to the information being thrown at him as the slides changed. He knew this was more serious than just people stealing a few rolls of fabric. "Where do we go from here? What can we do as a company to fix this?" J.J. asked.

"We're going to have this set up where everything will take place at one time. We're going to make it so all of the people involved will be arrested at one time. We will have an agent in Asheville, North Carolina and the Greensboro plant. There will be several agents in New York City, where the money is being produced. Our goal is to make it so none of them can contact each other before we arrest anyone. This is going to take a lot of coordination with you and your fellows along with our agents to make this work out. We'll be getting in touch with you in a couple of weeks." Detective Clark said.

J.J. slowly stood up and thanked all of the detectives for all the hard work they were doing. "You will have full cooperation." he said while shaking each of their hands. J.J. and Detective Clark left the room.

As they drove back to Greensboro J.J. talked with the detective about his relationship with James. "I don't like the idea of not having James involved," He had said. "We've been together since we were kids. We've never kept anything from each other. I'm having a really hard time lying to him for the first time."

"I understand how you feel, but under the circumstances, it is definitely for the best that you keep the investigation away from James. The FBI director has already given strict orders to keep James away from the investigation to stay out of harm's way at all cost. When something like that comes from the director, we make damn sure we follow his orders."

J.J. understood what Detective Clark was saying, but he still had the uncomfortable feeling in his gut. J.J. was back in his office at four o' clock that afternoon.

Chapter 23

After James hung up the phone after his conversation with J.J., he grabbed his jacket and walked out the door. As he walked to class, he thought about leaving the business to J.J., knowing he was going to have to put in more hours of work to make sure everything was going right. The discussion he had with David about Sandra still lingered in his mind. If she was going to care anything about him, she had to know who he really was. The more he thought about it the more he felt like he had betrayed their trust. He knows Drew and David are truly his friends for the person he is, and not the name. He knew Sandra really cared about him.

James stopped and sat down on a bench although he knew he was late for class. He needed to get his thoughts straight. He thought about ways to handle his situation. He knew it wasn't going to be an easy thing to explain; especially to the people he cared the most about, and how he's been lying to them the whole time.

While James was getting his thoughts in order, Bandit came bounding up to him. James looked up and lifted the dog onto the bench beside him. He felt like Bandit would always be there for him no matter what. As James rubbed Bandit's head, it had begun to sprinkle rain although it was sunny outside. He thought about what his Granny would say when it was raining while the sun was shining. "Well I guess the Devil is beating his wife." She would say. James never understood what she meant by that.

He then realized he had never felt rain before. He had heard stories about being caught in the rain, it raining at a sporting event. James said to himself, "I've never been rained on in my life. I guess it's time that I got rained on. I'm just going to sit here in the rain just for the hell of it." James glanced down at

Bandit. He felt like the dog was giving him a look that made him feel like an idiot. He took off of his jacket and laid it on top of bandit. "Okay, just because I'm an idiot doesn't mean you have to be one too." He said laughing to himself.

Sandra saw James walking up the sidewalk through her classroom window. Later, she realized James had sat down when it started to rain. She looked back through her window and saw that he hadn't moved. She thought about going outside to see what was wrong. "Continue studying class, I'll be back in a few minutes."

Sandra walked down the hall and out the double wooden doors, stopping under the porch to look down at James on the bench. He was looking up at the rain as it fell on him. Pulling her sweater over her head, she walked down the steps and came to stop in front of him. Bandit stuck his head out from under James' jacket and looked at her pitifully.

"Bandit has sense enough to get out of the rain," Sandra said, "What are you doing here out in it?"

James returned her question with a smile, "This is the first time I've ever been rained on. It feels pretty good. I'm making a memory."

"Well, I think you need to get inside before you catch your death of cold."

James looked down where the rain was running down his arms. He reached down and bundles Bandit in his jacket. He stood and walked up the sidewalk with Sandra. At the steps he stopped and looked back over Sandra shoulder, "Look at the beautiful rainbow."

Sandra turned and looked. The rainbow had five beautiful colors stretching from one side of the campus to the other.

"Do you think there's a pot of gold at the end?" James asked Sandra.

"I would like to think so," Sandra replied.

As they made their way up the stairs, Sandra asked, "What are you going to do with Bandit?"

"I'm going to take him in with me," James answered.

"You can't take a dog into class," Sandra insisted.

"Why can't I? It's raining, Sandra!"

"It's against regulations to take animals inside of classrooms," Sandra explained.

"Sandra, this is Bandit. It he can't go in, then I'm not going in."

Sandra looked Jim square in the eyes as he stood there with a wet head and rain dripping off the side of his face. She could tell he meant business. "Well, it looks like bandits going to class today."

James started down the hallway, holding Bandit up to his face. "Well Bandit, you stuck with me in the rain when I needed you, and I'm going to stick with you when you need me. Maybe Miss Wilson has something to teach both of us."

Sandra laughed at them, "I've missed you, Jim. I'm glad to see you back in class."

"I'm glad to be back," Jim smiled, "Have you really missed me?"

"You know I have," Sandra smiled. She added, "And your face looks one hundred percent better."

"It feels a lot better too."

Sandra stopped James with a touch on his arm. "Before you go into class, how about you and Bandit go to the bathroom? Take some paper towels and wipe your face, comb your hair, wipe Bandit down, then come on in to class."

After drying himself and Bandit off, James walked into class carrying the dog. He sat the dog down in his lap. Everyone in class started laughing and calling Bandit's name. James laughed too. Bandit yelped from all the attention and excitement.

"Keep laughing," Sandra spoke up, "Bandit may just do a better job on next week's test if you all don't study this week."

Everyone calmed down and Sandra went on with class. She let class out a little bit early and most of the class stopped by James' desk and patted Bandit on the head.

"Jim," Sandra asked, "would you mind staying for a few more minutes?"

When they were alone, Sandra came over, giving Bandit an idle scratch as she spoke. "Would you like to drive up to Asheville Friday afternoon after class to pick up your car?"

"You better believe I would! I'm ready anytime you are."

"We'll leave right after class Friday and come back on Sunday," Sandra said, "I'll come by your place after class and pick you up. Be ready. But now, you and Bandit get out of here, go home and get dry. By the way, Bandit isn't invited."

James laughed as he left, Sandra watched them as they went and shaking her head from side to side. Outside, it had stopped raining, but he continued carrying Bandit until he reached the main sidewalk. Then he stripped his jacket off the dog and sat him down. Bandit sat back on his hind leg and looked up at him. "So long," Jim said, "I'll see you later."

Bandit turned and started hopping up the street, leaving James to go in the opposite direction. At home, no one was home. James went up to his room and got in a warm shower. After he finished and dressed, he opened the closet and pulled out a small suitcase where he had kept some things since he had first moved in. He set it on the bed and opened it up then unzipped an interior side pocket. He pulled a stack of money that he kept there for safe keeping and counted out ten, one hundred dollar bills to take with him to Asheville to pay for the car. Hearing the voices of Drew and David coming in the front door, he placed the money back in the suitcase and returned it to the closet.

James came down and called out, "Hey guys, what's happening?"

"I wouldn't come out here if I was you James," David called back from the screened in porch.

"Why not?" James shouted.

"Because Drew just floated an air biscuit."

"What's an air biscuit?" James opened the back door and stopped dead in his tracks before making a hasty retreat. "My goodness, what is that smell?"

Drew spoke up, "My air biscuit that David is making such a fuss about."

"I don't know why he would do that," James replied sarcastically, "But I'm going to get a beer and go into the den and watch some TV."

"Wait for me Jim," David called. "I'm coming with you. Drew can stay the hell out here."

Drew just laughed. A few minutes later, Drew joined the in the den, "Come on guys, let's go to the Hole in the Wall and get a hamburger."

It sounded like a good idea to James. The three left the house and started towards the Hole in the Wall. The sidewalk and the streets were still damp from the earlier shower. The streetlights had not come on yet, although it was dusk.

"I like this time of the day," David said, "Especially after a shower. The air smells fresh and the flowers perk up a little more. It just makes for a good afternoon."

"Me too," James said, then added, "Hey fellas, I'm leaving Friday afternoon with Miss Wilson. We're going to Asheville to pick up the '41 Chevy I told you about."

"I can't wait, Jim," Drew said, "We'll finally have a way to get around. Do you think we can use it to go to Myrtle Beach so Linda and I can enter that dance contest?"

"I don't see why not," Jim said.

David spoke up, "I thought you would be driving down with Linda."

"Well, she and Helen are riding down together in Linda's car and since Jim is going to have a car, I figure we can let you go too, David."

"Well that's mighty nice of you, Drew." All three started laughing.

"If you leave on Friday, when are you coming back," David asked.

"Sandra said we'll be coming back on Sunday," James answered.

"So that means you'll be spending three days with the most beautiful woman on campus," said David.

"That's what it looks like."

"I think she likes you as more than just a student, Jim." David observed.

"You think so?"

"I've seen the way she looks at you. When she was over at the house, the look she gave you was not the look she gave me and Drew. If you play your cards right, she might go out with you."

"You think so?" Jim said again.

"I think so. If you don't ask her out, you're a nut case," David said.

"Well, if I do, we'll have to keep it to ourselves."

"We'll keep it between the three of us," Drew interjected. "Nobody else will ever know. You have our word on it."

As soon as he said it, James knew he was sincere. The old philosophy said a man's word was his bond. That held true for Drew. "Well, that's good enough for me," James said.

When they entered the Hole in the Wall, Beth the waitress came over and escorted them to their usual table. "It's good to see you fellows back," Beth said, "We've missed you."

"Well, we thought we'd let the smoke clear," Drew said. "Jim said some man came by and took care of the damages."

"That's true. But you guys didn't cause any damage, so you had nothing to worry about."

"Well that's good to know," Drew said.

They stayed long enough to eat a hamburger and drink a beer, then headed back to the house. David said he had some homework to do and retired to his room. Drew went to listen to some beach music and practice for the dance contest. James started packing, getting ready some of his things for the next afternoon.

As he packed, James could feel himself start to get nervous and a little excited about being alone with Sandra for three days. On top of that, he was going to have his first car, a beautiful little white classic named Little Susie. It was going to be a great three day weekend.

Chapter 24

James was up early Friday morning. He couldn't wait to get started. He could smell sausage cooking, meaning Drew was in the kitchen. David was setting the table. "Morning Jim," David said.

"Morning David, Drew. It's going to be a big day fellas. I'm going to get Little Susie today."

"Drew and I were just talking about that," David said, "We can hardly wait until Sunday."

"How do you like your eggs James?" Drew asked as he was breaking eggs into the frying pan.

"Over medium."

"That's what I thought. Scrambled."

James and David laughed, the joke never getting old.

After breakfast and a little small talk, they all headed to class. During class, James kept stealing glances at Sandra and every once in a while, he caught her smiling at him as she shuffled papers on her desk. Afterward, James hurried home and finished packing. He was ready when she came by a few hours later, sitting on the front steps with his suitcase by his side. As he put his suitcase in the car, Sandra got out from the driver's seat. "You drive, Jim."

James sat his suitcase down and came back around and opened the passenger side door for her.

"You don't have to do that," Sandra said.

"Once a lady, always a lady," James replied. He ran back around and hopped in the driver's seat and drove off.

On the ramp to I-40 West, James said, "You must really trust me to let me drive your car on the interstate, Sandra. "

"You might as well practice on the way there. You've got to drive back by yourself."

James drove through Greensboro and Winston-Salem. "You managed driving through the big city very well, Jim. Now I think I can relax a little bit."

James laughed, "You didn't seem to be uptight to me."

"I just didn't know how it looked on the outside." They both laughed.

James relaxed as well, holding the wheel with only one hand now. His eyes kept going over to Sandra. "You sure do look mighty fine today Miss Wilson."

"Thank you, Jim, but flattery won't help you on your test Monday."

"I didn't think it would, but you can't blame a man for trying."

"Did you tell David and Drew where you were going this weekend?"

"I told them that you and I were going to your mother's house in Asheville to pick up the Chevy. They were as happy as I was when I told them your mother agreed to sell it to me. And Drew said I was the luckiest man in the world, to be able to spend three days with the best looking woman on campus. I agreed I was the luckiest man in the world to spend the weekend with you, but I didn't know about you being the best looking girl on campus."

Sandra reached over with her hand and patted him on the shoulder. "I just didn't want them to get the wrong idea. That's all."

James laughed. "I had a heart to heart talk with them, about how it could give some people the wrong impression. I told them I'd appreciate it if they kept it between me and them. They gave me their word, and that's good enough for me."

"That's good," Sandra said, "I like those two boys and they seem to get on good with each other."

"Well, I had a long talk with David the other day. Drew was out with Linda. I think their relationship is getting a little more serious than just dance partners. David thinks so too," James said.

"But anyway," he continued, "David was discussing how Drew looked out for him when his mother passed away. He went with him to Connecticut and looked after him and took control of the funeral arrangements for his mother. David's dad works for the submarine base in New London and wasn't there to handle things. Since then, he's been spending Christmas with Drew and his family the last few years. David says Drew is like a brother to him and there is nothing he would not do for Drew. So yes, David and Drew are very close."

"Sometimes I wish I had a sister or brother," Sandra said, "Being an only child sometimes is not a good thing."

"Yes, it has its disadvantages. I do have a best friend that I grew up with. From the time we were about three or four we were very close. He's like a big brother to me. He probably knows me better than anybody. I feel fortunate in having him for a friend."

"Do you ever see him or talk to him?" Sandra asked.

"Oh yes, we are in communication about every other day. He works for Exum as well. I would trust him with my life and there's not many people that can say that about someone."

"You can say that again," Sandra said. "What's his name?"

"I've always called him J.J." James said. "Are we going to stop and get anything to eat?"

"Well, we're near Black Mountain where we ate the last time," Sandra said.

"That sounds like a winner to me. Let's stop and get us a sandwich and something to drink."

It was beginning to get dark as he pulled off the interstate. The light was on in the parking lot and the neon sign was blinking "Granny's Home Cookin'". James stopped the car and got out and came around to open the door for Sandra. She already had the door open and was getting out.

"I was going to open the door for you," Jim said.

"I'll wait for you next time," Sandra smiled.

They started in. It had turned cold in the mountains. James reached over and put his arm around her shoulders. Her arms were folded. She took her left arm and put it around his lower part of his back and leaned into him. They ate a sandwich and drank a glass of iced tea. They left Granny's and continued west. After another 45 minutes of driving, they turned off the hard paved road onto the gravel road leading to Sandra's mom's house. It was eight o'clock. As James turned in the drive he looked across the meadow. There was a low haze of fog lingering over the meadow. Up the hillside where the house set, he could only see one light.

"Mom left the front porch light on for us," Sandra said.

James drove down into the valley and up the hill on the other side. As he pulled up beside the house, Sandra's mother came out on the front porch. Sandra got out and walked up the porch, giving her mother a hug. James considered how much Sandra looked like her mother. Both were about the same height, although her mother was a little heavier than Sandra. When James walked up, Mrs. Wilson turned and put her arms around James' neck and hugged him as well.

"How are you, Mrs. Wilson?" James asked.

"I'm doing fine. I guess you came to get Little Susie."

"Yes ma'am. I want to thank you so much for selling her to me. That's all I've had my mind on all week."

"Well, she's ready for you. I've signed the title. One of my husband's friends who works at the dealership downtown loaned me a 30 day dealer tag for you to use to drive back to Burlington. After you get your permanent tag, you'll need to mail this one back to me or bring it back to the dealership."

"It looks like you've gone through a lot of trouble to help me. I really do appreciate it. I'll pay you for all your trouble," James said.

"It was no trouble Jim. Just take care of her and enjoy her. My husband and I enjoyed that little car the whole time he had it. It brings back a lot of memories and I hope it does the same for you. Well, y'all come on in and let me fix y'all a glass of tea or coffee. I know it's been a long drive for you."

They went in and sat down at the kitchen table. Mrs. Wilson brought them their coffee. "Well Jim, how do you like college? I understand you are working on continuing education courses in Sandra's class."

"Yes ma'am. I'm thoroughly enjoying it. Sandra is a great teacher."

"Yes," Mrs. Wilson said, "I'm very proud of her. Sandra tells me you work for Exum textiles, up in the New York office."

"Yes ma'am. I've been there for about nine years."

"I have a lady friend, Miss Jenkins, coming over tomorrow and we're going downtown to do some shopping. She works in the payroll department over at the local Exum plant. I'll introduce you when she gets here. I'm sure she would like to meet someone from the New York office. "

James knew some people in the payroll department, but he could not remember a Miss Jenkins. He hoped she could not remember him. "Well I look forward to meeting her."

James watched Sandra and her mother talk. The way they looked at each other, he could see the love they had for one another. He could not remember a time his dad looked at him like that. He was a man of very little emotion. A man that demanded that his son do what was expected of him and to do it well. James thought that may be why he never expressed his feelings to anyone other than Grammy and J.J. He never maintained any friendships. One time, his Grammy told him, 'To have a friend, you must be a friend.' Now he was beginning to understand what she meant.

After more small talk and coffee, Mrs. Wilson said she was going to turn in since she had that big shopping trip with Miss

Jenkins tomorrow. Sandra got up and hugged her mother again. "Goodnight Mom, we'll see you in the morning."

"Goodnight honey. Jim, I've raised the window in your bedroom so you can get some of this mountain air. I hope you sleep well. Goodnight, kids."

"Thank you again, Mrs. Wilson," James said. "See you in the morning."

James and Sandra watched each other for a while after Mrs. Wilson left the room. "Come on," Sandra said, "I'll walk you up to your room."

At the bedroom door, Sandra said goodnight. The last time she walked him to his room, she had given him a kiss on the cheek. James decided this one was going to be different. He put a hand on each side of her face and leaned down, placing a kiss lightly on her lips. "Goodnight, Sandra."

Sandra stood there for a second or two just looking at him. Then she smiled, said goodnight one last time and walked away.

'I believe I could kiss her all the time,' James thought to himself. 'I think she's everything I have always wanted.'

James went into the bedroom. His bed cover had been turned down for him. As he lay in bed, he thought about the drive up; Sandra, putting her arm around him at Granny's Restaurant, the things she said to him, how she looked at him. He could feel her affection for him. He had never felt that from anyone ever before. She truly was everything he had ever wanted in a woman.

James was up early the next morning. When he turned on the bedside lamp, he could already smell something cooking which meant Mrs. Wilson was up and starting her day. He took his shower and got dressed but skipped shaving, resolving to keep his five o'clock shadow. It was the first time he could ever recall doing that. He hoped Mrs. Wilson didn't mind. When he arrived in the kitchen, only Mrs. Wilson was there.

"Good morning Jim, Mrs. Wilson said. "I hope you slept well. Cup of coffee?"

"I'd love one, Mrs. Wilson," James sat at the table and watched Mrs. Wilson roll biscuits on the kitchen table.

"You shouldn't have any trouble getting that car started, Jim," Mrs. Wilson said as she rolled. "I had a new battery installed and had all the fluids checked out in it. So it's ready to go whenever you are."

"Good morning Mom, Jim," Sandra said as she walked into the kitchen. She had on jeans and a long sleeved shirt that was three time her size, the sleeves of which were rolled up to her elbows. She wasn't wearing any makeup and her hair was combed naturally down her shoulders.

"How are you this morning, Sandra?" Jim asked.

"Fine, Jim. It looks like you forgot to pack your razors."

"No, I just thought I'd give my face a rest this morning."

Sandra smiled, "I thought I'd do the same. That's why I'm not wearing any makeup. After breakfast we'll pull the car out of the garage and get it cleaned up today so we can take it out for a ride."

"I'm looking forward to it," Jim said.

"You're going to find driving this car is different from driving my Mustang. Little Susie has no power steering, or power brakes and the starter is in the floor board. It may take you a little time to understand this car, but I think you will get the hang of it."

After breakfast and a few cups of coffee they headed out. In the sun, it was about seventy degrees, so they went ahead and got started. Sandra went into the side door of the garage and walked to the front. She reached down and pulled up the sliding door. "I'm going to pull it outside," Sandra said. "Then we'll wash it up and then you can drive it."

"Sounds good to me," James said.

Sandra walked around and got in the car while James waited outside. He watched her through the windshield as she started the car, revved the motor just a bit and slowly backed the car out of the garage.

James greeted her with a grin that went from ear to ear. He opened her door for her as she got out.

"What do you think of her, Jim?"

"She's a beauty," James said as he walked around the car. He admired the chrome bumpers, hubcaps and the perfect paint job.

Sandra walked up with two buckets of soapy water. "OK, here are a couple buckets of water and a wash towel. You wash this side, and I'll start on the other."

James grabbed a rag, dunked it in the water and began washing the right front fender.

"Whoa, Jim, Whoa!" Sandra exclaimed. "Start with the top, and then we'll do the hood and then the trunk. Then, the front and back fenders and side of the car. The wheels will be the last thing we do."

"Sounds like a plan," James said.

"You've never washed a car before, have you Jim?"

"Never had a car before."

After washing the car, drying it down and a little horse play with Sandra hosing James down with the water hose, they were ready to take it for a spin. James opened the passenger side door for Sandra before running to the other side and slid under the wheel.

"Turn the switch on, first, Jim," Sandra said, "and push the starter above the gas pedal. Make sure you put the car in neutral before you start it."

James followed Sandra's instructions and the car started right up. He put the car into first gear, let the clutch out slowly, and off they went. They pulled out of the driveway and onto the paved road, heading toward town. James pushed the car to 45 miles an hour as he looked over the long hood, enjoying the way the car was handling. It was a beautiful day with some fall colors left in the leaves.

Sandra watched James drive, studying the expression on his face. She had never seen him so happy. His hair had gotten long. So long that it was just over his ears and shirt collar. With the beard, he could pass as a rock star. She knew the feelings she had for him had gone way past 'like'. The more she was around him the more she wanted to be with him and when she wasn't with him, he was on her mind. She had never experienced that feeling with anyone before.

James, in turn, looked over at Sandra. He smiled as she gave him a wink and winked back. He could not get over just how beautiful she looked. Even with no make-up, and her hair down in her face, she was still stunning. It was a day to remember.

After driving around for an hour, they pulled back into the driveway. There was another car there in the driveway. Miss Jenkins, most likely. James got out of the car and noticed Sandra was still sitting in the passenger side, he knew she was expecting him to come around and open the door for her, but he started walking around towards the back door, instead.

"Hey, boy!" He heard Sandra holler.

James turned, and held out both arms, palms tilted up to the sky as if to say, 'what?'

"You get back here and open this door!"

"What's wrong with it?"

She shook her fist at him and he laughed. Walking back towards her side of the car, he said, "I was just kidding around with you."

"Well, you started this, so don't think you're going to stop now, *Jimbo*!"

Coming into the kitchen, they saw Mrs. Wilson and Miss Jenkins drinking iced tea.

"Little Susie drove great, Mrs. Wilson," James smiled, "I couldn't ask for a better car!"

Mrs. Wilson laughed, "Jim, this is Miss Jenkins. She is the lady I was telling you about that works in payroll."

"Well, hello, Miss Jenkins, I'm Jim Andrews."

"Nice to meet you, Jim. I was told that you work out of the New York office?" Miss Jenkins asked.

"Yes, ma'am, I do."

"Well, do you ever see that good-looking James Exum III?"

James laughed, "Yes, ma'am, I do."

"I'll tell you one thing, Jim. He is one good looking man. Every time he comes to the plant and makes his walk through, he comes into the payroll department just to say 'hi' to everyone and all the ladies just go nuts. You should see them patting themselves on the chest after he leaves. Some of them run to the window just to watch him walk out to his limousine. He looks like one of them movie stars, though he don't act like one. He seems shy and doesn't talk a whole lot, but he shakes most everybody's hand and smiles at them. After he leaves, everybody talks about his visit for the next couple of days. He really is a nice man, and young. He's not married, either. Least that's what I've been told. It would have to be a really lucky woman to catch that man!" Miss Jenkins purred. "So next time you see him, you tell him Miss Jenkins in payroll was asking about him."

"I certainly will, Miss Jenkins" James assured softly, "It was nice meeting you."

"Well, he sounds like the man for me," Sandra said with a smile.

Mrs. Wilson stood up, "Well, we better get going. We have several stores we want to visit."

Sandra and James said their goodbyes to Miss Jenkins. After she and Mrs. Wilson left, Sandra and James sat down for a glass of tea.

"To hear Miss Jenkins," Sandra said, "it sounds like Mr. Exum is quite the catch."

"Well, I don't think he's so good-looking," James replied. "He probably doesn't have a personal life. I know for a fact that he works 16 hour days and the only place you'll see him is work."

"Sounds like you're jealous."

"Why should I be jealous?" James held out both hands innocently, "just because I haven't shaved in two days and I've got hair down my back doesn't mean anything!"

Sandra burst out laughing and James joined her.

"Well, what's on the agenda for tonight, Sandra?"

"I have a surprise," Sandra confessed. "We're going out for dinner and then I'm going to take you somewhere I haven't been in a long while so you will need to shave and I'm going to trim some of that hair off of you before we leave."

"Well," James said, stroking his beard as he considered, "I do need a trim. It's been a while since I've had it cut."

"Well, I'm going to take a shower," Sandra said, "I'll see you out here in the kitchen around 6:30. That will give me a couple hours to get ready.

James watched her go, then got up and went to his bedroom. He was lying across his bed when he heard a knock on the door. When he opened it, there stood Sandra wearing a robe and brandishing a comb and pair of scissors.

"Come on, Jim," she said, "come to the kitchen and let me trim your hair before you shower."

"Well, let me put my shoes on."

"You don't need your shoes on for me to trim your hair, but you do need to take your shirt off."

James stepped back into the room and began to unbutton his shirt, taking it off with his back to Sandra. He draped it over the back of the straight-backed chair in his room. Sandra could not help but notice his narrow waistline and broad shoulders. She was a little surprised by his physique. It was very masculine and surprisingly, had a hairy chest.

"It looks like you've been working out, Jim," she said.

"Afraid not," Jim replied. "I just do fifty sit-ups and fifty push-ups every morning. That's it."

James followed her into the kitchen and sat down. Sandra draped a towel around his shoulders and began to comb and cut. The haircut took about twenty minutes. As James stood up and brushed stray hairs from his shoulder, he looked back at Sandra and said, "It sure does feel better."

"It looks better, too," she replied as she swept up hair from the floor.

James went to the bathroom and took his shower. Afterward, he dressed himself in a black pair of slacks and white long-sleeved shirt. The only sweater he had was the baby blue cashmere sweater he'd worn the first time he'd visited here with Sandra. He finished off his outfit with his oxblood loafers. Regarding himself in the mirror, he said out loud, 'this will have to do. It's all I brought with me.'

James was sitting at the kitchen table by the time Sandra was finished dressing. She walked in wearing a tan skirt a good five inches above the knee and a yellow turtleneck sweater and brown, low-cut high heeled shoes. James stood up. "Why, Sandra," he said as a smile crept over his features, "you look like a teenage girl, but still very distinguished."

"Thank you, Jim. You look nice, too. Especially with that cashmere sweater," Sandra admired.

"It will have to do," he answered, "it's the only sweater I have."

The back door swung open and Mrs. Wilson came in carrying bags from her shopping trip.

"Hi, kids," she said as she looked them both up and down, "you two sure look nice. And, Jim, you cut your hair! Did Sandra do that? She used to cut her daddy's hair when he needed it. It looks nice. Where are you two going tonight?"

"We're going to eat first, and then I have a surprise for Jim," Sandra replied.

"Well, there's no telling what you have cooked up for him," Sandra's mother said with a chuckle.

"I won't hurt him, Mom," Sandra joked, and both women laughed.

"Can we take little Susie?" James asked.

"Of course," Sandra said.

As they left, Sandra told her mom not to wait up. In a motherly tone, her mother told them to have a good time and to be safe.

At the car, Sandra waited for James to open her door. When she slid in, James couldn't help but notice how her skirt rode a little higher up. James slid into the driver side and had to remind himself that he needed to keep his eyes on the road. They drove for twenty minutes with Sandra giving him directions along the way. Finally, they came to a big Victorian house with a small sign outside that read, '1901 Vintage House Restaurant. Fine Dining.' James was familiar with this restaurant. When he visited the Asheville plant, he always stayed at the Grove Park Inn, a hotel built at the top of the mountains. Dignitaries from all over stayed there when they visited Asheville. The view from the hotel was extraordinary. When James stayed there, he always had dinner at this same restaurant. James knew that some of the waiters might recognize him but Sandra had booked reservations, and there was no going back.

What happens, happens, he said to himself.

James pulled little Susie under a canopy and a valet came out to the car and started to open the door. "That's OK," James said, "I'll park it. Just tell me where you want it."

The valet directed him to the end of the row but opened the door for Sandra first.

"I'll meet you in the parlor, James," Sandra said as she got out.

A few minutes later, James joined Sandra in the parlor. Sandra was waiting beside a gentleman in a suit holding a pair of menus. "Sorry about that, Sandra. I just didn't think he would know how to drive it, and I didn't want to take a chance on it."

Sandra smiled in understanding. The waiter inclined his head, "Would you like to be seated now, sir?"

They followed the maître d through the dining area. It was decorated elegantly. Oriental rugs were laid out throughout the dining room. A huge chandelier hung in the center of the room with its lights turned down low. Candles rested on every table. A huge rock fireplace covered one side of the wall with a natural fire burning inside. Another wall was made of a floor to ceiling window, overlooking the city of Asheville below. At the back side of the room, along the wall near the kitchen doors, was a table for two waiting for them. The maître d pulled Sandra's chair out for her as James settled into his chair.

"How do you like it?" Sandra asked when they were alone.

"It's very nice, and tasteful," James said, then added, "Do you eat here often?"

"You can count the times on one hand," Sandra admitted. "I just thought I would do something special for you tonight, to celebrate the new owner of Little Susie. I know dad would approve of you having her, and you showed me tonight that you're going to take good care of her by not letting anyone else drive her. And I'm going to pick up the check for dinner."

"I can't let you do that," James protested.

"Well, you have no say in it, Jim," Sandra grinned.

Giving up, James looked around the restaurant as Sandra skimmed her menu. He noticed two gentlemen talking with the maître d, who looked in his direction. He recognized both of the men. One was the owner. James quickly turned back around to face Sandra, who was opening her mouth to speak. But before she could finish her sentence, she was distracted by one of the men walking up to the table and looking directly at James.

"Sir, I'm sorry," the man began, "we seemed to have set you in the wrong location. Would you please come with me?"

Sandra looked at James in confusion, but James just looked blankly back at her as the man stepped behind Sandra to pull out her chair. She stood up and the man picked up their menus. "Please, follow me."

The man led them toward the rock fireplace. At the end of the fireplace there was a door size opening. He stepped back and waited for Sandra to go in. James had been inside this room on several occasions, when he wanted privacy and to be alone. Inside was a square table set for four, with candles already lit. The room sat out over the veranda on the bottom floor. When you were in there, you were actually sitting in front of the fireplace on the other side. The view was spectacular and very romantic. The gentleman pulled the chair out for Sandra once again and handed James the wine list.

"Wow…" Sandra whispered to James, "I've never sat out here before."

"You sure you've only eaten here four or five times?" James asked.

"Yes, I'm sure, Jim."

James smiled and reviewed the wine list. He saw several wines that he liked, but decided to let Sandra make the selections. He passed her the list, "You select the wine. You know what you like."

James had no sooner gotten the words out when the owner of the restaurant walked up carrying a bucket of ice with a bottle of wine in it. To James he said, "Please accept this sir, compliments of the house. We apologize for sitting you at the wrong table."

James gave the man a polite nod of his head. "Thank you, sir. We appreciate it."

Sandra looked at the owner with her mouth open, a look of surprise on her face. After he had left, Sandra leaned in to James again and whispered, "Jim, I think they have us mixed up with somebody else."

"Maybe so, but we got a free bottle of wine out of it."

Sandra laughed. "Yes, but we may get run off after they find out they've made a mistake."

"Well, let's order and eat fast then."

They ordered their meal and made some small talk while they ate. James watched Sandra while she talked, unable to get over how attractive she was. Her auburn hair was parted in the middle of her head and draped down the side of her face and down her back. When she smiled, her green eyes sparkled like the stars behind her in the distance. Her teeth looked like pearls in the candlelight. James couldn't escape his feelings for her. He could not explain how much he cared for her, but he knew there was no way he could ever be without her. 'If this is love,' he thought, 'I have a bad case of it.'

They sat and ate and drank wine and talked for an hour and a half. Finally, when the check came, James took the leather folder in his hand, but Sandra reached over and took it from him. "It's *my* treat."

"Sandra, please let me pay for this," James argued, "I owe you for all you've done for me."

"I'll let you pick up the next one, but tonight it's my turn." Sandra reached into her pocketbook and pulled out cash and slid it inside the folder. When they left the table, Sandra excused herself to freshen up and told him she would meet him in the parlor.

On his way to the parlor, the manager walked up to James and smiled. "Good to see you again, Mr. Exum. Was everything fine?"

"Everything was great," James told him, "I enjoyed it very much. And thank you again for the wine." He slipped some folded up money into the manager's hand, thanked him again and walked out. A few minutes later he pulled back up to the door in Little Susie. Sandra walked out and the valet opened her door for her.

As they drove out of the parking lot Sandra instructed him to head downtown and onto Tunnel Rd, then finally onto HWY 25. Finally, they came up on a parking lot on their right and James turned in. There were several cars already parked there and James could hear music coming from inside a white painted cinder block building at the back of the lot. A sign on the top of the building read, 'Patio Lounge.'

James looked at Sandra. She smiled back at him. "Well, you asked me one time if I could dance. You like dancing. So we're going in and we're going to do some dancing."

"You may not want to dance with me," James said, "The only people I've ever danced with have been Helen and Linda."

"Well tonight, Jim, you're going to dance with Sandra."

James heard rhythm and blues music coming from inside. His type of music. "Well, let's get to it."

Sandra reached into her pocketbook and pulled out a pair of shoes with no heels on them.

"Looks like you mean business," James said.

"Just can't dance in high heels, Jim," She replied.

James and Sandra went inside. They gave their money to a man at the front door and he stamped the back of their hands. The only lighting in the room was coming from the stage where the band was playing and little red bowls with candles burning on the tops of tables scattered throughout the room. A haze of smoke was in the air and James could make out a small dance area. There was a lot of talking and laughing going on. Everyone there seemed to know each other. Sandra took James by the hand, leading him through the crowd.

Halfway to the dance floor, James heard a woman's voice call out, "Sandra? Sandra Wilson!"

Sandra turned and looked and out of the crowd came two ladies who threw their arms around Sandra and hugged her.

"How are you doing, Sandra?" One of the girls asked.

"Come on over and sit with us," said the other. They each grabbed Sandra by a hand and lead her over to their table.

Sandra introduced James, "Jim, this is Pam and Iris. I went to high school with them, and to college with Iris."

They sat down to catch up, and found they had to speak loudly to be heard over the music. They talked for about 15 minutes, trying to get caught up on what one another had been doing for the past 8 years. Suddenly, James heard the band strike up his favorite song, 'Cry to Me' by Solomon Bunke. James grabbed Sandra's hand and said, smiling, "This is my favorite song to dance to."

"Well, let's dance," Sandra laughed.

As James got to the dance floor, he did what he had been taught to do. He stood beside Sandra and took her right hand in his left and slid his right arm around her waist. He took one step back and Sandra followed suit. Sandra turned to face him and pushed herself back a bit and they were in rhythm. In keeping time with the music, James found himself grinning from ear to ear. He was pleased to see that Sandra was a good dancer. As they danced, neither of them lost a beat. As the song came to an end, James pulled Sandra into him and, as she ducked beneath his arm, she smiled at him.

"You've caught on fast," Sandra admired.

"Where'd you learn to dance like that?" James asked, in return.

"Right here," Sandra answered, "at the Patio Lounge. This place has been here a long time."

The two returned to their seats where a waitress took Pam, Iris and Sandra's order for a glass of wine. James declined, explaining that he had to drive. James had no more than finished his explanation when a young man walked over to their table.

"Sandra Wilson," the man said with a smile, "How are you?"

Sandra looked up and returned the smile, "Roger!" She exclaimed. "How are you doing?" She turned to James and said, by way of explanation, "This is Roger, a classmate from college."

"Hey," Roger said, "how's about a dance? For old time's sake?"

Sandra looked at James for a moment, but James just nodded his head to say he was fine with it.

Sandra had just stood up when Pam smiled and said, "Come on, Jim! Dance with me!"

Pam led James out on the dance floor by the hand. In the lighting, James finally had a good look at Pam. She was lovely with short, dark hair and dark eyes. Her black mini skirt was well above the knee and her white shirt beneath a black sweater hugged her full-figure perfectly. However, James could not keep his eyes from following Sandra and Roger on the dance floor. Sandra laughed as she danced and seemed to be having a good time. After the song had ended, James and Pam walked from the dance floor. Pam casually laid her hand on James' shoulder and thanked him for the dance. Sandra and Roger walked back to the table, as well. Roger pulled Sandra's seat out and Sandra sat.

"Thanks for the dance, Roger," Sandra laughed.

"My pleasure, Sandra," Roger smiled, "it was good to see you again."

"Roger," Sandra said, "allow me to introduce my friend, Jim, to you."

James stood to shake Roger's hand, "Nice to meet you Roger."

"Same here, Jim," Roger shook James' hand before heading back to his seat.

James watched Roger stride back to his seat and, as he sat, noticed Iris had not yet danced with anyone. He paused. "Would you like to dance, Iris?"

Iris smiled, "Yes, I would, Jim." She said, "Thanks for asking."

Iris was also a good dancer, and an attractive girl and James could not help but notice how well they danced together. James glanced over at the table where Pam and Sandra sat, talking. Pam was looking at him and, before long, Sandra turned and look at him, as well. James wondered what that could be about as he heard the end of the song. James walked Iris back to her seat and pulled out her chair before returning to his seat between Sandra and Pam.

Pam looked to James and placed her hand lightly on James' leg, "Jim, you're a very good dancer."

"Thank you, Pam," said James, "I'm still learning."

About that time, the band began to play a slow song. Pam turned to James and said, "Would you like to dance again, Jim?"

James smiled, but said "I'm honored, Pam, but I save all the slow dances for Sandra."

Pam smiled and nodded.

James turned to Sandra and found her already standing up and ready to dance. Sandra wrapped both arms around James' neck and snuggled against his shoulder. In his ear, she said, "You know how to say the right things at the right time, Jim. And if she puts her hand on your leg one more time, I'm going to knock the hell out of that bitch."

James paused for a moment and pulled back to look at Sandra, a little shocked. It was the first time he'd heard Sandra curse.

As Sandra and James walked back to their table, Sandra sat down beside Pam, putting James on the outside and safely away from Pam. James smiled, knowingly and was a little happy to see Sandra showing signs of jealousy. Sandra made some small talk with Iris and Pam for a few more minutes before turning up her wine glass and, after downing the last bit, turned to James.

"Ready to go, Jim?" She asked.

"Whenever you are," James smiled.

Sandra turned back to Iris and Pam and said, "It was nice seeing you girls again, but we have to go."

As James and Sandra stood to leave, Iris reached over and shook James' hand. Pam gave Sandra a hug then walked around Sandra and hugged James, as well. Pam included a kiss on James' cheek for good measure. James cast a look to Sandra. He'd seen the look she was wearing before. It was the look Linda had been wearing that night at the Hole in the Wall before things got interesting.

James moved quickly away from Pam and laid both hands gently on Sandra's shoulders, turning and guiding her towards the door. Sandra didn't say a word until they were at the car. James opened her door and Sandra looked at him and said, incredulously, "Can you believe the nerve of that bitch?"

"She was just being friendly, Sandra."

"Yeah, she was being friendly, all right."

"Are you jealous?" James asked.

"No," Sandra countered, "A lady doesn't act like that. Especially to a friend, is all."

"Well," began James, "For a minute, there, I thought you were jealous." He looked at Sandra a moment before adding, "But, believe me, you have nothing to worry about."

Sandra slid a hand up James' face to caress his cheek, She looked at him a moment before kissing him on the lips. Sandra slid into the car. After walking around to the driver's side and getting in, he turned to her once more, "Well," he asked, "Where do we go from here?"

Sandra smiled softly and said, "I'm going to take you somewhere I've never taken anyone before. And after that, we'll go home. It's getting late. The place is close to my house, so just drive in that direction and I will tell you where to go."

As James drove, Sandra turned to look at him.

"I know she was coming on to you, Jim."

"Why do you say that, Sandra?" James asked with a laugh.

"When we were talking as you and Iris danced, Pam told me she had seen you someplace before. I asked her where, but she said she couldn't remember. She said you were a good-looking man with a great body and then asked me how serious I was with you."

"What did you tell her?"

"That's just between us girls, Jim."

As James turned into Sandra's driveway, Sandra said, "Right down here on the left. There's a little road that dad would drive his tractor on to get to the top of the mountain."

"Is it OK to drive Little Susie up there?" James asked.

"It'll be OK, James. The road is in pretty good shape."

As James drove along the winding, crooked road peppered with a low-lying fog, Little Susie slowly climbed the steep mountain. Finally, they reached the top. "Pull over here," Sandra said, pointing.

James pulled over and turned off the headlights. James walked around and opened the door for Sandra and the two walked to the edge of the mountain.

They stood there, James' arm around Sandra's shoulders and her arm securely around his waist. The scenery was absolutely breathtaking. You could see the whole city of Asheville from this point, bathed in bright moonlight. The stars above them sparkled like a handful of diamonds. It was as though the city was casting a double image, like mountains near a lake.

"It's absolutely beautiful up here, Sandra," James said, "I can see why you'd come here to spend time."

"This is where I came to spend time when dad passed away," Sandra said, "and when I had to make a decision to go to Appalachian or Western Carolina. This is where my decisions were made at.

James had his arm around Sandra when he felt her shiver. There was a breeze on top of the mountain and it was turning cooler. "Come on, Sandra. We can sit in the car as good as we can stand out here in the cold air."

They walked back to the car. Sandra wrapped both arms around herself as she climbed into the back seat. James climbed in behind her and pulled her close, wrapping both of his arms around her. "You feel so cold," James said.

"But you feel warm," Sandra replied.

James held Sandra in his arms and rubbed her back and arms to warm her up. He leaned down and kissed her on her cheek and when she looked up at him, on her lips, first a short one, then another longer one. He slid his lips to the side of her cheek and then down her neck. His kisses spread across her neck and then he moved his lips back to hers, lingering there as he lay her back in the seat. Their breathing became more rapid and the car windows began to fog up.

 Sandra reached down and began pulling up her sweater and James helped her pull it up over her head. He let it drop to the floorboard, and then pulled his sweater off. As he unbuttoned his shirt, Sandra reached back and unhooked her bra. Even in the dark of the car he could see the shape of Sandra's breast outlined in moonlight. She looked beautiful with her hair covering half of her face, her mouth slightly parted. James leaned down and pressed his lips against hers.

There was nothing to think about in James' mind, he was lost in the passion of Sandra's lips and her breast against his chest. He felt her hips rise up against his and he reached down and pulled the top of her panties down. Sandra raised her foot and free one leg from her panties. Holding himself over Sandra with one hand, James undid his belt and pushed his pants down below his knees with the other.

James took her in his arms, their lips tightly engaged. Sandra was breathing hard. When their lips parted, James could feel the air coming from her mouth into his. He was inhaling her breath and when he exhaled, Sandra breathed him in, their breaths and bodies becoming one.

Sandra felt as though she could not get enough of James, she just wanted to melt into him. She'd never felt this way before. She wanted him inside of her, body and soul.

James could feel Sandra's passion for him. He never wanted to let her go. He had very little experience with women, but with Sandra, everything felt so natural. He didn't need to calculate his movements. He knew now what the difference between having sex and making love was. There was no comparing the two.

Afterward, Sandra lie there, her legs tangled with James', her left arm lying across his chest. Her mind was just now coming to realize what had just happened. Feeling James beside her, her head on his shoulder, she felt emotions she had never experienced before. She knew now that the expression 'Sharing your love and being loved in return' would never come close to the actual experience.

James opened his eyes. Condensation was running down the back window, like rainwater, on the inside of the glass.

"Jim?" Sandra asked. When he didn't speak, she added, "Are you ok?"

"Yes," James said, "I just experienced something I didn't know existed."

"Well, just let me say that you're not in that boat by yourself," Sandra said. "I feel as though I could lay here for the rest of the night with you, but if mom happens to get up and we're not home, she'll worry."

Reluctantly, they sat up and got themselves in order. They got out of the back seat and slid into the front. James adjusted the steering wheel, turned the switch on and started to crank the car. The engine turned over twice and stopped.

"Come on, Little Susie, wake up" James said. As soon as he said it, Sandra and James looked at each other and laughed out loud. He tried it again, and this time, Little Susie started right up. They started back down the mountain and James glanced over at Sandra and said, "Now I know why your dad named his car Little Susie."

When they pulled into the front yard, the back porch light was on. "You think your mom is up?" James asked.

"No," Sandra said, "she left it on for us."

James got out of the car and went around to Sandra's door to help her out. He took her by the hand and leaned her back against the car, kissing her lightly on the lips. "Words cannot do justice to the evening I had with you tonight. My mind and my heart will never forget this evening with you. I did not know that the human mind, heart and body could experience such emotional, loving moments at the same time. It's something I never dreamed could be experienced by anyone, especially me."

"Those are the sweetest words I have ever heard anybody say, Jim," Sandra said. "I know you mean every word of it. Just let me say, my heart and body were just overcome. I had only you on my mind, holding you close to me. I could not restrain myself from loving you. If that scared you, I'm sorry. It was something that happened. I could not hold myself back, and I'm not sorry for it."

James put his arm around her shoulder and started walking her to the back door. "I hope you're not sorry."

"Don't worry, Jim, I'm not," Sandra said as she opened the back door and led him into the kitchen. She took him by the hand and led him down the hall to his bedroom door. There, she leaned into his ear and whispered, "See you in the morning, lover." Then, with a quick kiss on his lips, she turned and walked down the hall to her own room.

Chapter 25

The next morning, James was up early. He could hear Mrs. Wilson stirring around in the kitchen. He grabbed a quick shower and got dressed, then made his way downstairs where Mrs. Wilson was drinking coffee. "Would you like some, Jim?" she asked.

"I would love a cup," he replied.

Mrs. Wilson got up and poured him a cup of coffee and set it down in front of him. "Did you and Sandra have a good time last night?"

James told her about their date, the restaurant, the Patio Lounge and dancing, "Then Sandra took me out on top of the mountain to show me her favorite place, overlooking the city. It was beautiful up there."

"Well, I don't know how long she will have to go there," Mrs. Wilson said, "I understand Mr. Thomas has that mountain for sale. Has had it for sale now for about a month."

"Why is he selling it?" James asked.

"Well, the way I understand it, his children don't want it. The whole mountain is for sale. About 350 acres covers the whole mountain. It also has a lot of bottom land that goes down to the creek, and the creek follows the mountain. It really is a beautiful place. I haven't had the heart to tell Sandra, she's been going up there since she was a little girl."

"What is he asking for it?"

"I've heard he wants $500 an acre. I just hope that the person that buys it doesn't cut all the trees off of it, but I think the person that buys it will be buying it for the timber. If that's the case, it will be left in a mess." As she talked, Mrs. Wilson opened the pantry door and pulled out an ironing board. She set it up in the corner.

"Can I help you there, Mrs. Wilson?" James asked.

"No Jim, I've just got a couple of pieces of clothes I need to iron before Sandra leaves." She plugged in the iron and set it on the ironing board and picked up a piece of clothing that looked like Sandra's blouse. She spread it out on the ironing board. She picked up the iron and patted the hot surface with her fingers. "Not hot enough yet."

She turned and pick up a small glass of water off the table, took a sip, then picked up the iron with her right hand and spit a little of water on the hot surface of the iron. It made a whistling sound and James could see little beads of water running down the iron. Mrs. Wilson placed the iron on the blouse and started ironing.

James shook his head at Mrs. Wilson and stood up. "I'm going to go out and wash Little Susie. She got a little dirt on her last night driving up the mountain and I want to drive her home clean and shiny."

As James headed out, Sandra came into the kitchen and said good morning to her mother. "Is Jim still in bed?"

"Lord no, honey, he's been sitting here drinking coffee with me. He's gone outside to clean Little Susie. He told me it got dirty up on the mountain."

Sandra walked over to the kitchen window. "He's going to catch pneumonia."

"Leave the boy alone, Sandra. He loves that old car and boys will be boys."

"Well, I can see whose side you're on."

Mrs. Wilson laughed, "Why don't you take him a cup of coffee?"

"You're going to spoil him, Mom."

Sandra walked outside with two cups of coffee. James smiled at her when he saw her.

"Good morning Jim," Sandra said, "You're up mighty early."

"I couldn't sleep," Jim replied, "My heart was full."

Sandra smiled, "I'll fill your heart."

"You already have."

"You say the sweetest things that I have ever heard come out of a man's mouth." Sandra wrapped her arms around Jim's neck, still holding the cups of coffee, and kissed him on the cheek. She handed him his cup of coffee. "When you're done cleaning her up, come on inside. Mom is fixin' breakfast."

"I'll be in ten minutes. Fifteen minutes tops," James said. He watched her as she walked inside, her hips swaying in her blue jeans. She had that long sleeve shirt on that was four sizes too big. The shirt tail was hanging out and tied in a knot in the front. James thought she looked great in just about anything.

After putting the final touches on Little Susie, James walked into the kitchen where Sandra was sitting at the table talking to her mother.

"Breakfast will be ready in 15 minutes, Jim," Mrs. Wilson said, "Just as soon as I have these biscuits fixed."

James sat down at the table with Sandra and observed Mrs. Wilson as she rolled out the dough with an old wooden rolling pin. Next, she took a water glass and used the open end, pushing it down in the dough to cut the biscuits. He had never seen anyone make homemade biscuits before. After pressing out 10 biscuits, she took some lard from a can and spread it in the bottom of a pan. She lined them up in a pan and, taking the back of three fingers, knuckles down, she touched the top of a bowl of fried fat-back with her fingers and then touched each biscuit leaving just a little drop of grease on the top of each one. Then she set the tray of biscuits in the oven.

Once the biscuits were done, Mrs. Wilson set the table. Fried tenderloin, scrambled eggs and homemade biscuits. "Mrs. Wilson," James said, "I think this is the best breakfast I've ever had, those biscuits were fantastic."

"Well, I'll send the rest of them home with you," Mrs. Wilson said.

"I'm not going to turn down your generosity this time," James said.

"We'd better get ready and get on the road, Jim," Sandra said, "We've got a four hour drive. I'll follow you just to make sure nothing happens to Little Susie."

James packed his clothes and put them in the back seat of the car then gave Mrs. Wilson a hug and thanked her for her hospitality. He handed her a white envelope with the money inside. "Thank you again for selling me Little Susie," James said.

"You're Welcome, Jim," Mrs. Wilson smiled, "just be careful and don't hurt yourself in that car."

Sandra gave her mother a hug goodbye and they left down the long driveway to the main road. James looked back at Sandra's house. Mrs. Wilson was standing on the front porch, waving at them. Her left hand was shading her eyes form the sun. He gave her a wave back. She was truly a southern lady with all the hospitality that goes with it.

With the mountain in the background, surrounded by a Carolina blue sky, James drove and thought of the night he and Sandra had made love on top of that very mountain. It was a night he would never forget as long as there was breath in his body. On the interstate, James pushed the accelerator down and pushed Little Susie above 55 miles an hour. She was showing no strain. He reached over and turned the radio on and was surprised to hear the station was set on a rhythm and blues station coming out of Greensboro, North Carolina. The radio sounded great. It was very clear on top of those mountains. It seemed to make a difference in the sound. *Life is good,* James thought to himself.

James looked in the rearview at Sandra, who was sitting upright with both hands on the steering wheel. She looked totally uncomfortable. James slid down in the seat. The window was down and James held the steering wheel with his right hand as his left arm leaned out the window. He looked laid-back and carefree. He took his foot from the accelerator pedal and slowed down, letting Sandra pass him. As she pulled up beside him, she looked over where he sat with the air blowing through his hair. His head nodded in beat to the music on the radio. She narrowed her eyes at him and shook her fist at him. James busted out laughing and pulled himself back up in the seat. She fell back in behind him, grinning, but shaking her head. She thought to herself, *that man looks good in that car.*

When they pulled into the college town, Sandra waved at James and turned to go to her house; He waved back and continued on to his place. When he pulled up in front of the house, David and Drew were sitting on the front steps. They jumped from their seat and ran up to the car as he pulled up. David stuck his head through the driver's side window. Drew opened the passenger side door.

"It's absolutely beautiful," David said.

"Let me drive it!" Drew said.

James stepped out of the car and let Drew slide behind the wheel. David got in on the other side and the two of them pulled off with Little Susie. James walked up and sat down on the porch and waited for them to return. In a few minutes, Drew pulled up in front of the house and turned into the front yard where there was once a driveway, but which was now covered in grass. David and Drew got out and walked around the car, admiring it.

James said, "Her name is Little Susie."

"Can we drive Little Susie to Myrtle Beach so I can enter the contest?" Drew asked.

"I don't see why not," James said.

"Man," Drew beamed, "I'm looking forward to it. You, David, and I driving Little Susie to Myrtle Beach? Man, that's gonna be something."

"Well, let's go in and have a beer," David said.

"I could really use one," James replied.

David led James out to the screened porch, "come on back here and let me show you what Drew and I have made up for our new business." David returned with a black binder, "Drew and I have been over this several times. We think we have it all down.

Could you take a few minutes and look over it and tell us if you think we have it all down, or if you think something could be added."

David handed James the binder, which consisted of about 40 diagrams and notes. The front of the binder read, 'D&D Electrical and Mechanical Engineering Company'.

"I'm going out on the front porch while you read it," David said, "When you get through, call me."

James opened the binder and began to read. Forty-five minutes later, he called David back. "From what I have seen and read here," James said, "I think you and Drew have done a great job putting together a formula to start your own business successfully. I can't think of a thing I would do any different. Now, what is going to be your next move?"

"You've seen the figure of the money we need to get started. That's going to take some time to save up. So we're going to have to work for somebody until we have the amount we need to get started."

"Do you have any place in mind you want to work?" James asked.

"Well, that's where you come in, Jim. You know some people at Exum textiles, and we thought maybe you'd put in a good word for us," David said.

"I'll be glad to do that for you and Drew. Do you think I could keep this binder for a few days? I have someone I would like to let review it and it may take two or three days before I could get it back to you."

"Sure, Jim," David said, "Keep it as long as you like."

When David and James walked back to the front porch, they found Drew talking to the neighbors about Little Susie. Drew had the turtle shell raised, showing the insides of the trunk to the guys next door. He was as excited about the car as James was. James, still holding the black binder, walked out to the car.

"Hey fellas," James asked, "How do you like my car?"

"It's a great car, Jim," one of the guys said.

"Thanks, but if you'll excuse me, I've got to run an errand for David."

James started up Little Susie, backed out of the driveway and waved goodbye as he drove up Main Street. As James drove through town, students stopped along the sidewalk and gave him a thumb's up as they admired the Chevy. James felt good. He was proud of his car. It was a great afternoon. The sun was going down and shadows covered one side of the street, giving the car an extra shine as he cruised Main Street. As James crossed the railroad tracks, he threw up his hand at the Firemen sitting outside the station and they returned the gesture. As James drove out of town, he reflected on the first time he saw those houses in the back of a black limousine and just how much had happened in his life in such a short period of time. It had been a wonderful two and a half months. Now, it was payback time for the people who had done so much for him. He had to come clean with everyone who had given him their trust and confidence. It started with going to see J.J..

James turned onto the interstate and smoothed Little Susie out at 60 miles an hour. Thirty minutes later, he turned into the long driveway leading up to the mansion. Now, as he drove in, he looked at it from a different perspective. It really was a beautiful place. As he pulled up to the gate, Mr. Sparks came out, but didn't recognize James.

"Good afternoon, Mr. Sparks," James said.

Mr. Sparks looked at James, but said nothing for a few seconds. Then, realization set in. "James! I didn't recognize you with that long hair and 5 o'clock shadow! When did you learn how to drive? Is this your car?"

"Just recently, Mr. Sparks," James said, "And yes, it is. How do you like it?"

"Oh, it's a great lookin' car, James. You sure do look different than you do in the back of that limousine. I can't remember the last time I saw you without a white shirt and neck tie! Grammy'll be surprised to see you. Hang on and let me open the gate for you."

When the gate was opened, James drove around and parked near the back door, where J.J. always parked. As he started to get out, Grammy opened the back door and walked out holding what looked to be a dish towel. She had her apron on. She stopped and looked at James before she realized it was him driving up in that white car. "Why, James!" Grammy exclaimed, "When did you start driving? And when did you get that car?"

James just grinned as he walked toward her, "Give me a hug, Grammy!"

As James bent down to her, Grammy grabbed him around the neck with both arms and gave him a kiss on the cheek. Then, she stepped back to get a good look at him. "James you look so good! I liked to not have recognized you. With that long hair, and driving that car. And you look to have been out in the sun. You look good, baby!"

"Come on, Grammy," James smiled, "I'll take you for a ride!"

"I can't now, James," Grammy said, "I got food in the stove, Come on in and let me fix you a glass of tea."

James sat at the kitchen table and watched Grammy fix his tea. "Grammy," he said, "it looks like you're losing some weight."

"Well, I had to cut back on my sausages, country ham and gravy. You know all the good stuff. The doctor told me my blood pressure was too high and he wanted me to cut back on all that salt, so I've been watching it."

"Are you feeling all right, Grammy?" James asked.

"I feel pretty good, James, I'm just getting older and all that stuff just goes along with age."

"Why don't you let me get someone in here to help you, Grammy? You don't need to be doing all this work around here."

"The only thing I do is fix me and Mr. Sparks' lunch and work in my flowers. If I didn't do that, I don't know what I would do."

"I need to talk to J.J., Grammy. You think he may still be at work?"

"Well, he usually calls me every day just before he leaves and he hasn't called me yet so he's probably still at the office."

James picked up the phone and dialed J.J.'s direct line. J.J. picked up on the first ring. They spoke briefly and J.J. agreed to stop by the house when he was finished with work. When James finished the conversation, he took his tea and asked Grammy to tell J.J. to come up to the office when he arrived. As he ascended the winding staircase to the second floor, he stopped and looked into his father's bedroom. He remembered the day his dad had died. Grammy was at his bedside. J.J. and James flanked his either side. His father would not move his head, he would just turn his eyes toward James, then over to J.J. and then he would look at Grammy. He just kept doing that as his time grew near until, finally, he closed his eyes with a bit of a smile on his face. Grammy put both hands around his and he took one, last, big breath and passed away. James had gotten up off the bed and leaned over and kissed his father on the forehead. James' tears had fallen on his father's eyes, running down the side of his face. It made his father look as though he'd been crying, as well. J.J. put his left hand on the side of James' father's face as tears strolled down his own cheeks. Then, the two of then turned and walked from the room, leaving Grammy with James father.

James sighed and walked down the hall and opened the door to his father's office. Grammy had kept the office as though his father were still working in it. James sat down behind the large desk and swiveled in the chair, looking around the room. So many memories came rushing back to him. James could understand now why his father had pushed him so hard to learn the business at such a young age. From the time he was 18 until his father died, James had done all the work for the business because his father's eyes had failed him to the point he could not do the paperwork anymore. Talking on the phone had also become difficult for him. By midday, his father would be totally exhausted. J.J. was still in college during this time and could not help. James' father had known he was sick when James was still very young. That's why he started teaching James so early in life. Left to run the business and continuing school with tutors at night, it had been an 18 hour a day job for a long time. He thought now, if his father had not gotten sick when he was so young he might have had some type of childhood. But his father knew his time was running out and did what he had to in order to keep the family business running while keeping it within his family.

There was a tap on the door and J.J. walked in. James stood and greeted J.J. with a handshake and a shoulder bump.

"You're looking good, James," J.J. said. "You look like you've been outside a lot with that tan and long hair you really do look like one of those college guys. It's going to take me a little time to get used to it."

"How have you been?" James asked, "Are you getting everything out of New York that you need?"

"No problems there, James, everyone is doing what they are supposed to do."

"How are we doing with the inventory control that you and I discussed?"

"I'm doing some investigative work on that and hope to have it resolved within the next week or two," J.J. said.

"That's great. They're coming out with some new inventions; something called a 'computer' that works with a 'microprocessor'. One day, we'll be able to tie all of our plants and warehouses to one system and will be able to give an account for every yard of fabric we manufacture daily and will be able to show it on a computer screen.

"I've not heard of that, James, but that would be a great thing to have because we're getting ready to modify some of our machinery to run faster and produce more. It looks like we're going to have to add on to some of our plants to meet demand."

"That sounds great," James said, "You never know what they're going to make out of denim. Who knew that denim bell-bottom pants would take off like they did."

"Who knew we were going to land on the moon and Neil Armstrong was going to walk on it?"

"Can you believe it?" James smiled, "We're in an innovative time and if we don't keep up in our manufacturing and marketing strategies, we will be left behind. That's one reason why I'm here, J.J.. I need to talk to you about my two roommates, David and Drew. They'll be graduating soon. David, with an electrical engineering degree and Drew with a mechanical engineering degree. I understand that Drew already has patents on a milking machine he redesigned for his dad on their dairy farm. Both of them have good grades and I really think they can be an asset to our company and its future. They want to go into business together and are hoping to locate the business in Burlington. They are very close to one another, as close as brothers. They hope to work for a company until they save enough money to start their own business and then strike out on their own. I'd like you to take some time over these next few days, and review their business plans." James slid the binder over to J.J.. "Let me know what you think I'd like to see those guys get their start at Exum Textiles. I'd like to see them successful. They've helped me more than anyone could ever know and, now, it's time for me to return the favor."

J.J. nodded, "I'll look at the plans and go through the process just like we do everybody else. I'll see that they get a letter from Exum Textiles. With what we have coming up on the horizon, we need some good engineers on board. Rest assured, James, I'll take care of it."

J.J. didn't bother to tell James he'd had David and Drew both checked out before James had ever moved in with them.

"Well," James said as he stood, "I've got to get back. Walk me out to the car."

As the two walked down, Grammy was in the kitchen setting the table and waiting for them.

"Did you boys take care of business?" She asked.

"Yes, we did," they both answered at the same time.

"James," Grammy said, "your daddy would be so proud of you and J.J.."

"I think so, too, Grammy," James said. "Now give me a hug Grammy. I've got to go back to school. Now that I have this car, I want to come and see you more often."

"I would really love that," Grammy said, "I miss you so bad. You take care driving that car."

"I will Grammy. I love you. You take care of that high blood pressure."

As James and J.J. walked to the car, James asked J.J., "How is Grammy doing? I can see she's lost weight. She doesn't look too good to me."

"I talked to Dr. Nelson," J.J. said. "He's been her doctor for years. She threw a fit when I was going to get a specialist to look at her. She told me the only doctor she was going to was Dr. Nelson. She got real upset. She let me know right quick that was not going to happen."

"Is there anything I can do?" James asked.

"I don't think there is anything anybody can do. She's going to do it her way or no way at all."

"Yeah, I know. Just keep me informed on how she's doing. I'll try to come by more often. There's only a few more weeks left of classes and I'll be back in the routine again."

"By the way," J.J. asked, "How are things going with you and Miss Wilson? Is that going anywhere?"

"My feelings for her have gone way beyond anything I ever thought would happen. I'm totally in love with that woman. She makes every day for me a happy one. When I'm around her, I have a hard time keeping my hands off her. She makes me laugh. She's so funny and smart. I just love being around her."

"How does she feel about you?" J.J. asked.

"Well, we've had intimate moments. I know she loves me, but we have never come right out and said that to each other. The problem I have is, what is she going to do when she finds out that I'm James Andrew Axum and not just Jim Andrews. Every time I get up the nerve to tell her who I am, I just can't do it. I know I'm going to have to face the situation, I just don't know what her reaction is going to be. Is she going to accept it? Is she going to feel that I betrayed her trust; that I've been lying to her all along? I can't imagine what her reaction is going to be and it bother s me. And what about David and Drew? What is their opinion of me going to be when they find out? Are they ever going to trust me again? Those two guys and Sandra have given me all of their trust and I feel like I have betrayed them."

"Well, James," J.J. said, "They have to know the reason of why you did what you did. There is no way you could have gone down there as James Andrew Exum III, you would have had the press all over you and that would not have worked."

"I know that, J.J., but I don't know if they will understand. I am just going to handle it the best I can when the time comes."

"Well, if there is anything I can do you know you can call me."

"I've always been able to depend on you, J.J.," James smiled before asking, "How's your wife?"

"She just keeps on getting bigger and bigger," J.J. said, "We haven't got too much longer to go."

"Well, I'd better get back to Burlington. Keep me informed on anything you think I need to know."

As James drove off, he gave J.J. a long wave 'goodbye'. James knew there was one other thing he had to do, and that meant calling his lawyer of ten years. Brad handled all of his personal affairs and he would need to give him a call in the morning. As he drove, he thought about the next two weeks. Things would be coming to an end. The last two and a half months had been a wonderful experience. The time had given him some of what he had lost as a young man. He was not looking forward to it coming to an end. He would have to enjoy the time he had left before he had to go back to the real world. The memories he'd made would mean a great deal to him. Thanks to David, Sandra and Drew, they would be good ones.

At home, he parked the car and locked up Little Susie. On the front steps, Bandit was curled against the screen door. The dog raised his head and looked up at James, then hopped to one side as James opened the screen door, he followed James in. As James called for the guys, Bandit went hopping back to the screened-in porch. James grabbed a beer form the fridge and followed him and sat down in the rocker. Bandit curled at his feet. James reached down and gave Bandit a scrub on the head. James continued to sit and rock with Bandit at his feet, listening to music on the radio. He was beginning to realize that money and fame doesn't necessarily make a person happy, the love of a good woman, true friends and family were really what makes a person happy. He looked down at Bandit and said, "Yes, and a good dog and a cold beer, too."

The front door opened and David and Drew walked in. David was fussing at Drew, but Drew was laughing at David. As they came out on the porch David waved his arms about. "Dammit, Drew!" David said, "You could have waited 'til you got outside or you could have gone to the bathroom. There are a hundred things you could have done to embarrass the hell out of me."

"What happened?" James asked.

"You won't believe it, Jim," David said. "We decided to go down to the Hole in the Wall for a hamburger and beer. So, we're having a beer at the bar and Drew asked for a pickled boiled egg. Then he pulled a jar of pickled pig's feet over and asked the bartender for a couple of those. I could not believe a human being could eat such a thing! It looked like something you would see in a school lab for research or something from a freak show. So, the bartender laid two out on a napkin for Drew. Looked like they still had the toenails left on them! So, then Drew picked one up and started gnawing on it like an ear of corn. It was the damndest thing you'd ever seen Jim, I could not believe my eyes. He ate it like he loved it!"

"Well, some people like those pickled pig's feet, David," James said.

"You haven't heard the half of it," David continued. "About the time Drew finished his second pig foot, Linda and Helen walked in. Drew and I went over and sat down with them. Somebody put some money in the jukebox and we all started dancing. There were about four other couples on the dance floor when a slow song came on, so I danced with Helen and Linda danced with Drew. I looked over at Drew and Linda and Linda had her face buried in Drew's neck and Drew had this crazy look, with a smile on his face. I turned around, dancing with Helen so I wouldn't have to look at him. Honest to God, Jim. An odor came over the dance floor you would not believe. It was so bad Helen buried her face in my arm. As soon as I smelled it, I knew it was Drew. He had passed one of his 'air biscuits'. I turned Helen around to look at Drew, but there was nobody left on the floor but me and Helen. I know damned well everybody in there assumed I did it. When Helen and I walked off the floor, everybody in there was looking at me. I have never been so embarrassed in all my life!"

By the time David finished, James and Drew were both laughing hysterically.

"I think it was the pickled pigs' feet and that pickled egg that did it to me," Drew said. "The odor would gag a maggot, but I just couldn't help it."

"I just wish I hadn't turned my back on you, Drew," David said, "Me and poor Helen left out on the floor by ourselves. I was embarrassed for poor Helen. She told me that she thought you needed worming. I'll tell you one thing, I'll never forget this night. That smell and the embarrassment has been burned in my mind."

James and Drew burst out laughing again. When they calmed down, James said, "By the way, guys, I took your business plan to J.J. at Exum Textiles. He's going to review it in a couple of days and get back to you on it."

"Who is J.J.?" David asked.

"He's the President of the company," James said.

"You gave it to the President of the company? You know the President?"

"His name is Jonathan Jackson Washington," James said, "But everyone calls him J.J.."

"I thought you would probably give it to someone in personnel. I didn't know you knew the president. You've got more pull than I thought, Jim. Thank you so much. Do you think we have a chance of getting a job there?"

"I think so. He told me they were going to do some expanding and they may need a couple of engineers to help out with a few projects in the near future. So you may be hearing from him in a few days."

Bandit raised up and gave a big yawn and a stretch and started hopping towards the front door. James opened the door for bandit and took one more look at Little Susie before closing the door.

"Guys, I think I'm going to turn in for the night. I've got a big day ahead of me tomorrow."

Chapter 26

The next morning, as he came down for breakfast, James heard David and Drew in the kitchen.

"We owe him big-time," David was saying to Drew.

"You're not going to owe me anything," James said, "I was glad to help you fellas any way I can."

After breakfast, Drew and David left for school. After they had gone, James called his attorney. After a ten minute discussion, James ended the conversation with Brad's promise to follow up by that afternoon. After they hung up, James walked out the door and gave a quick look to Little Susie, sitting in the driveway.

Just as soon as I get out of school, Little Susie and me are going to take a ride, he thought to himself.

As James walked to class, he enjoyed the warm weather and watched the students as they walked along the sidewalk with their bell-bottom trousers flapping around their ankles. It was the latest style now. Some of the merchants were laughing and talking to one another as they prepared to open their stores. Everyone seemed to be happy and enjoying the morning. James was looking forward to seeing Sandra.

As he entered class, she was standing facing the blackboard. She had on a white skirt, white high heels and a black blouse with pearl earrings and a pearl necklace. She looked different than when she wore her jeans and her oversized shirts, but James thought she looked good in anything.

As James sat down, Sandra looked at her watch. The last of the students came in and Sandra began the class by saying, "I have to go to a meeting. I would like you to turn to the chapters I have written on the board. After reading those chapters, start studying for the test we are going to have Friday. If I am not back by the end of class, you may leave and I will see you in the morning." With that, she turned and walked out without giving James so much as a sign of acknowledgment that he was there. She never returned before the end of class. James knew there was something wrong, but didn't know what it may be. He thought he would find out before the end of the day.

At home, James looked over at Little Susie and who else was lying, curled up in front of the driver's door, but Bandit.

"You want to go for a ride in Little Susie, Bandit?" James asked as he walked over.

Bandit stood up on his three legs, looking up at James. James picked him up and laid him in the front seat. James started up Little Susie and headed up Main Street. Bandit put his two front paws on the arm rest and his third leg stood in the seat. Bandit looked out the window, barking at kids walking up and down the sidewalk. The kids called Bandit's name and he barked back at them as if to say, 'Look at me!' James cruised up Main Street at a slow speed to be sure that Bandit didn't fall over.

As James drove on through town, crossing the rail road tracks he sees the fire department on his left. It has two bays, one for the fire truck and the other for the rescue squad truck. The flagpole stood in the middle of the two bays with the American flag flying proudly above the station. The firemen stood hosing down the front drive. James made the quick decision to pull in and talk to the men for a moment. Once the car stopped, the men came to the passenger side window and patted bandit on the head. One opened the door, and let bandit down. The dog hopped through the front door of the fire department.

"Where's he going?" James said as he watched the dog hobble inside.

"Probably checking to see if there's something to eat, but we haven't put down his food yet." One fireman replied.

"Oh, so you feed him as well?"

"Oh yes. He sleeps here at night."

"Well, I wondered where he stayed at night." James said.

"He's been hanging around here for over five years." A fireman said.

"By the way, my name is Jim Andrews." James says as he holds out his hand.

"We know who you are, Jim." The fireman says returning the handshake. "Welcome to Elon." The men continued to chat until bandit returns from inside the station. He hops over the passenger side and waits to be let back into the car.

"Well, it looks like he wants to ride some more. I have to drive slowly because I'm afraid he'll fall over standing on one leg." James said.

"Hang on one second, let me get something." A fireman asked. The man ran inside quickly and came back carrying a yellow wooden Coca-Cola crate with a white towel inside. He laid the towel on the seat and set the crate on top of it. He then reached down and picked up bandit, setting him on top of the crate. Bandit sat down, and was able to see outside the window. James thought it was a perfect fit.

"Okay, Bandit let's go. I think this is going to work better for you, buddy." James shook the hands of the firemen and thanked them for Bandit's seat. As James backed out of the station, they all waved at Bandit as he barked back. James started back into town with Bandit holding his head out the wind. His ears were blowing in the breeze, he licked the sides of his lips as if he was eating air, and he greeted everyone with a bark.

James slowed down to cross the railroad tracks. The fire department siren went off, followed by Bandit's howling. It was about twelve o' clock and the students were changing classes or taking their lunch hour. They all pointed and laughed as Bandit howled with both paws on the window. James turned around and saw Sandra at the soda shop laughing with all of the other pedestrians. James face turned red with embarrassment, but he waved back.

James drove on, and pulled into the driveway. By this time, Bandit had stopped howling. James let Bandit out of the passenger side of the car. The dog hopped out and began heading towards the fire department. James grinned as he thought about how he must've looked. At least Sandra's attitude had changed since he had last seen her, thought James. The house phone rang, when James picked it up it was Sandra.

"Is this the fireman?" The voice said coming from the other line.

"Well, I'm glad I got a laugh out of you Sandra. You weren't laughing this morning."

"I know," Sandra said. "If you'll come up to the house this evening I will explain to you why I had that attitude."

"I'll see you later then, and you better stop laughing at me." James said.

"I'll see you, fireman." Sandra said giggling while hanging up the phone.

When James sat the phone down, David and Drew walked in. Both were laughing. "Hey Jim," Drew said. "Guess what David and I saw a while ago?"

"What was that, Drew?" asked James.

"We saw a one-man parade." They all started laughing. "There's nothing like seeing a guy driving through town with a three-legged dog howling like a siren outside of the window. You're the talk of the town, buddy."

David spoke up. "It was like it was meant to be with no cars on the road but yours. It was a sight to see, believe me." There was then a knock on the door. Drew opened the door revealing Linda and Helen. They were laughing as well.

"You should have seen Bandit running up the sidewalk. He was running so fast it almost looked like had six legs!" Helen said giggling.

"Well, Jim, you've made my day. I've never laughed so hard. I saw that car sitting in the driveway this morning. Is it yours?" Linda asked.

"Yes, it's mine. How do you like it?" Jim replied.

"I think it's beautiful. I've seen the sign on the front bumper saying 'Little Susie'." Linda said. "Well there was a song called Wake up Little Susie in 1957. Maybe that's where the name came from."

"Are you going to drive Little Susie to Myrtle Beach when we go down to dance in the contest?" Drew asked.

"Yes, sir," James replied. "I can't wait!"

"We only have one week to go, Drew." Linda said.

"I think we need to practice a little more, Linda." Drew said.

"Well just let me know." Linda replied.

"Well we've got to go. See you guys later." They said as they waved walking out the door.

David nodded. "We have to go back to class too. See you this afternoon. We'll go to the Hole in the Wall and have a beer."

"I'm meeting Sandra later. I'll come down after I talk to her." James replied.

"That sounds good. See you later." David said as he and Drew walked out the door.

The phone rang as James walked towards the back porch. When James picked up the phone it was Brad, his attorney.

"Hey, Brad. Do you have good news for me?" James asked.

"Yes, everything is in the workings. It will take a couple of days to get things worked out. The offer has been made, and he has accepted. The paperwork just needs to get done and I will get back with you when it's time to sign the papers."

"That's great news, Brad. Thank you for working so fast. It means a lot to me." James said. "Let me know as soon as you can, and I'll be up to signing the papers." He then hung up the phone and continued to the back porch. He listened to the radio which had rhythm and blues on. He began practicing his dance steps with the belt on the door. After a while, James realized it was about time to leave for Sandra's house.

As he walked down the sidewalk in the direction of Sandra's house, he passed a merchant who knew him by name. "Good afternoon, Jim. Did you leave your fire truck at home?"

"My siren ran off and left me." James replied, and they both laughed. As James kept on walking, people in the cars passing waved at him. He flicked up his hand in acknowledgement. After a while, Sandra's house was in sight. His heart and his feet picked up the pace, eager to see Sandra again.

When he arrived at her door, he knocked on the door. He could hear her yelling from inside. "Come on in Jim!" James slowly opened the door and stepped inside. He walked through the house into the kitchen. Sandra came out of the bedroom buttoning up her shirt after changing her clothes.

"Well, I see I am too late." James said.

"Well there is no fire here you can put out, fireman." Sandra said jokingly.

"Who knows? It's still early, Sandra."

"I think I've created a monster." Sandra said as they both laughed. "What would you like to drink? I have coffee, beer, or wine."

"What are you having?" James asked.

"I'm having wine." Sandra said.

"Then that's what I'll have."

"Well, have a seat." Sandra said waving her hand towards the table towards the bay window. James sat down as he watched Sandra pour the wine. His mind wandered back to the night on the mountain and how beautiful she was as she is now. She walked over and sat the glass in front of him, then sat down across from him. "Well, I must say I've had a very interesting day." She said.

"I knew something wasn't right with you this morning." James said.

"Yes, and I apologize for my actions. I had a lot on my mind.

"When I got home yesterday, Stephen called me. The first thing he asked me was if you drove daddy's car. I told him you had bought it from mom. He then asked me if you had spent the night with me up there. I told him we stayed with mom. I was angry with him for making a suggestive acquisition. He then said 'What would you think if the Chancellor heard about that?' I then told him where he could go, and I hung up the phone.

"When I got to school this morning there was a note in my mailbox from the Chancellor. He wanted to see me in his office as soon as I had my class organized. When you came in I was preparing my mind for the meeting with the Chancellor. All I was thinking about was what Stephen had said to him, and what he had heard. Needless to say, I was upset."

"What did he have to say?" Jim asked.

"It was quite a strange conversation, Jim.

"I walked into his secretary's office. I was calm, but I was ready to stand firm with him. I stepped in front of Ms. Smith's desk. Before I could say anything she pushed the button for the intercom and said 'Mr. Ross, Sandra is here.' She gave me a dirty look and nodded her head towards the door letting me know I could go in.

"When I walked into his office, he was standing behind his desk. 'Have a seat, Sandra.' He said. As I sat down, I noticed he had a folder lying on his desk. He started off by saying 'Do you know our policy about teachers and students?' Before I could answer him, the phone rang. Ms. Smith told him it was urgent, so he angrily answered the call.

"For the next few minutes he would periodically say 'yes, sir'. When he hung up the phone, he opened the folder, read through a few pages, and stopped to look at me. 'There's been a mistake, and I'm sorry for calling you in. Since you're here, would you like to be the on the building committee for the new library? The James Andrew Exum library.' He said apologetically.

"Well, I didn't know what to say. I was prepared to have an argument. I just knew Stephen had talked to him about you and I. Especially since he started off by asking me about the student and teacher policy. I think the person on the other end of that call changed his mind on discussing school policies. Someone may have explained the policy to him before he made an ass out of himself."

"What do you mean by that?" James asked.

"First of all, you are a continuing education student. Secondly, you are only taking one course in the school system. I went so far as to looking up your personal file, and I couldn't find one. It's like you don't exist here in the school system. The way I look at it, you are an adult continuing education. You are not a fulltime student, and you're not twenty two years old. Nobody is going to make me feel bad because I have an interest in a thirty year old man. You're taking one history class that I teach which is not justifiable for being reprimanded. What do you think Mr. Andrews?"

"Well do you have an interest in a thirty year old man?" James asked with a surprised look on his face, as if he didn't know what she was talking about.

Sandra looked at James with a surprised look on her face. She closed her eyes halfway, gritting her teeth and looking into James' eyes. She sat her glass of wine down, slowly got out of her seat, walked around the table, and kissed him. "Boy, you're asking for trouble." Sandra said and they both started laughing. James slid around his seat and Sandra sat in his lap. He wrapped his arms around her waist, and she rested her right arm around his neck.

"I'm not only thinking you're a great history teacher, I think you missed your calling. You would have made a great lawyer. You sure did convince me. You had all of your facts together and you presented it well." James said.

"Well I just think if you see something you want, sometimes you've got to fight for it." Sandra replied. James leaned in to kiss Sandra, only this one was more passionate. When the kiss ended, Sandra looked at James. "You make me happy when I am with you Jim. I don't want to give that up."

"That's the sweetest thing you've ever said to me." James said.

"Well I mean it. Don't let it go to your head either, fireman Jim." Sandra said. They both laughed together. "I've got to be at a meeting at 7:15," Sandra said as she stood up. "I think I'm going to be on the new Axum Library building committee."

"Oh, is that right?" James asked.

"Who knows, Jim? I may get to meet the young James Axum himself, and if he's as good looking as everybody says he is, I just may enjoy going to these meetings." Sandra said as she looked at James and winked.

"Why Sandra Wilson, are you trying to make me jealous?"

"No, Jim. I'm just kidding. Knowing him could look good on a resume someday. I think he would be somebody that would be interesting to talk to. I understand he's a very smart man, and I've heard he speaks three or four languages. I know where he lives as well." Sandra laughed. "Don't you worry, fireman Jim. I would take you any day over him."

"Well, I certainly hope so." James said holding his arms out "Just look at what you wouldn't have." They both laughed. "Well, I told Drew and David I would meet them at Hole in the Wall when I left here."

"Well do you want a ride there? It's on my way." Sandra asked.

"No, I think I'll just walk. I need the exercise." James replied.

"Well come and walk me to my car." Sandra said. As James opened the door, Sandra turned around and whispered in his ear "You have no idea how special you are to me, Jim." She then gave him a quick kiss and sit down in the car.

"That goes for me as well Sandra, dear." He closed the door and walked to the Hole in the Wall. When Sandra was out of sight, James decided to pay a visit to Stephen's house. He thought it was time to have a chat. Although he had never been to Stephen's house, Sandra had told him where he lived.

When James arrived, he rang the front door bell. He could see through the window that Stephen was coming to open the door. "Hello Jim," Stephen said answering the door looking to see if anyone was with James. "What are you doing out tonight?"

"I was wondering if you could spare me a few minutes of your time. I think we need to talk." James said.

"Well come on in, Jim. I think I know what you want to talk about." Stephen said as he walked through the house. James closed the door and followed Stephen. James noticed he was wearing black slippers, pinstripe pajama pants, and a white tee shirt. He walked into the den and turned the light on. There were books lying everywhere, and the room was cluttered. You could tell the man lived alone. He had two chairs, a sofa, a writing table, and a small TV in the corner. "You'll have to excuse this place, Jim. I'm doing some research on a book that I'm trying to write." Mr. Stephen said.

"Oh, you're writing a book?" James asked.

"I'm trying, Jim. It will be my first and it is taking more time than I had anticipated. So please excuse the mess." Stephen said as he moved a couple of books off of chairs for James to sit down. "Well, Jim. I'm guessing this is about Sandra."

"Yes and the discussion she had today with the Chancellor, Mr. Ross." Jim said.

"Oh, so he called her in this morning. I was expecting him to do that. I called Sandra last night to warn her about what might happen, but she got mad at me and told me to go to hell. I just tried to give her a call just before you got here, thinking she had time to cool off by now. I got no answer." Stephen said.

"No, she had a meeting to go to." James said.

"Well I wanted to explain to her when you and she were coming into town yesterday and she waved at you when she made her turn to go home. Mr. Ross and I were standing on the corner. He saw you and her come into town together. He asked me who was driving; I told him it was you. He asked if you were one of her students and I had to say yes.

"I knew when I saw you driving her dad's old car, that you two spent the night in Asheville together. When I was questioning her about where she'd been, I wasn't trying to interfere into her personal life. I was trying to figure out what she'd say before the Chancellor called her in. I guess it didn't go the right way, or I just didn't say it right. She let me know real quickly that it wasn't any of my business. I know when you piss her off; you will know where she stands on issues."

James chuckled a little bit. "You're right about that Mr. Stephens." I know you two have been close since you went to college together a few years back."

"I guess you could say that. I've been in love with Sandra for a long time, but she's always looked at me as a big brother. I was hoping someday she would change her perspective on me, but I don't think she'll change. She's fallen in love with you now, Jim. That night at Carter's restaurant with David, Drew, Linda and Helen I could just tell by the way she was looking at you. I could see in her eyes that she had more interest in you than just a student." Mr. Stephen said.

"Well, the last thing I wanted to do is cause any problems with you and Sandra's relationship. You're right though. She does look at you like a big brother. She's got a lot of respect for you. She's told me a lot about how you have worked hard to send yourself through school. She's encouraged me to do the same thing by watching what you've done with your life. She thinks the world of you and she's very proud of you." James said

"I'm proud of her too, Jim. There's one thing about it. You can't make someone love you if they don't.

"That's very true Mr. Stephens." James replied as he stood up from his chair. "Well, Mr. Stephens it's been a pleasure but I must be going. Thank you for taking the time to speak with me, and if there is anything I can do to help please let me know."

"I appreciate that Jim and please call me Ryan."

"Good night Ryan."

"Good night Jim."

As James made his way towards The Hole in The Wall to meet up with Drew and David, as he passed the house he noticed Drew and David sitting on the front porch.

"Hey Jim! We had a beer down at the Hole in The Wall, but the girls had to leave so we decided to come on back and wait on you." David said.

"That's ok, I'm tired anyway." James said. "Let's go inside and have a beer. I'm going to bed in a few minutes. It's been a long day."

"Me too." David and Drew said in unison.

"We saw Sandra ride by a while ago." Drew said.

"Yeah, she had to go to a meeting regarding the building of the new library." James replied. "They are supposed to break ground sometime next week."

"It's going to be a nice library from what I've been told. David said. It's going to be named the James Exum Library."

"Well, we will be gone by the time it's completed. Hopefully we will be working and making some money to start our own business, David." said Drew.

After drinking his beer and making some small talk with David and Drew, James went to bed.

The next morning James walked into the kitchen while Drew was making breakfast and David was sitting down at the table. "Good morning, fellows." James said.

"Good morning Jimbo." Drew said. "How do you like your eggs?"

"Make mine over light, Drew." James said though he knew Drew was going to make them scrambled anyway.

Drew set a bowl of grits on the table and raked some scrambled eggs onto James' plate. "Have some of those grits." He said. "The toast is on its way."

"When are you going to fix something I can eat with my eggs, Drew?" David asked.

Drew turned around and glared at David. "Look David. You are in the south. Here, we eat grits and gravy. You don't like gravy because that is the way your daddy fixed glue for your kites. You don't like grits because it feels like sand in your mouth. So until you learn to eat one or the other, you're going to just get eggs, you damn Yankee."

"Well you can kiss my ass, you damn Rebel." David said. They all burst out laughing.

After eating their breakfast, David and Drew put their plates in the sink and told James it was his turn to wash dishes. After he was done washing the dishes, he gave Brad a call to see how he was coming along with the legal documents.

James dialed the number that went straight to Brad's office.

"This is Brad." The voice said at the other end of the call.

"Good morning, Brad. This is James Axum."

"Good morning, James. How are you this morning?"

"Just wanted to give you a call and see how you were coming with the paperwork."

"James, I sent one of my assistants up to get the paperwork yesterday. He should have it in my office this morning. After I review it, I should have it ready for you to sign sometime today. I will give you a call when it's ready." Brad said.

"No, let me give you a call just before lunch, Brad," James said.

"That will fine, give me a call by 11:45."

James hung up and headed to class. In the classroom, Sandra was standing beside her desk. There were only two or three students in class.

"How did your meeting go, Miss Wilson?" James asked.

"It went fine. We're going to start breaking ground next week. Hopefully within about nine months we'll have it completed."

"I don't suppose that I will be around to see it built, since next week is the end of the semester and graduation for David and Drew after that," James said.

"Does this mean you're going back to New York after this semester?"

"I think I'm going to put in a transfer to the Greensboro plant."

"Do you think you can get that done?"

"Well, that's something we'll have to talk about," James said, "I don't want to discuss it right now."

James saw the expression on Sandra's face change, but there was no more time to talk. During class, every time he looked up at Sandra, she was looking at him. When she saw him looking at her, she closed her eyes and seemed to be gritting her teeth. She sort of smiled every time she did it. After class, James started out the door when Sandra motioned for him to come over to her desk. She handed him a folded piece of paper.

James left class and started down the walkway. He slipped the piece of paper out of his pocket and read it. In it, Sandra asked him to come by her house that night at six. He put the paper back into his pocket and continued walking home.

At home, he gave Brad a call. It was early, but Brad had the information for him. Brad asked if James wanted to come by and sign the papers.

"Do you have someone that can meet me halfway?" James asked.

"I'll send Ed down to meet you, he's one of my aides" Brad told him, "Just give me a time and place."

James arranged for Ed to meet him at a Holiday Inn off the interstate between Burlington and Greensboro at one o'clock. Brad told him that Ed would be in a Chevrolet. James would send Ed back with a check and the signed papers. James ended the conversation by asking that J.J. receive a copy of the papers to put on file.

James hung up the phone. He had about a half hour before he had to meet Ed, enough time that he could take a ride through town. He grabbed Bandit and started out to the car. He put Bandit in the passenger seat on top of the Coca-Cola crate and Bandit wagged his tail excitedly, ready to go. James gave him a pat on the head and climbed into the driver's seat and started the car up. Together they started into town, Bandit barking at everybody he passed. Everyone waved to Bandit as they drove by.

Passing over the railroad tracks, James looked at the gas hand on the dashboard. The car was running low so he pulled in at the local Sinclair services station. There were only two pumps, one regular and one high test. He pulled into one and the service attendant came out and started washing the windshields.

"How much gas do you want, sir?" The attendant asked.

James looked at the daily gas price. It was up to 34 cents a gallon. It just keeps going up, he thought to himself. "Fill it up," he said.

The attendant filled up the car, washed the windshields, checked the oil and patted Bandit on the head. James handed him three dollars and thanked him. "See you later Bandit," the attendant said, "you too sir." He gave them a salute and sent them on their way.

James pulled out and turned the car south and onto Highway 62. In the rural countryside, he passed meadows on both sides of the road. Farmhouses dotted the meadows in the distance with winding dirt roads leading up to them. It was a bright and sunny day, a good day for a drive through the countryside. Bandit sat up on his Coca-Cola crate with his head out the window, both ears flapping in the wind. His neck stretched out, his nose bobbing up and down. He reminded James of an old Pontiac hood ornament.

Eventually, James wound back towards the interstate and his meeting with Brad's aide. In the Holiday Inn parking lot he saw a young man leaning against a new white Chevrolet. James pulled about three cars over from it and went around and took Bandit out of the passenger seat. Bandit went over and to the grassy area near the cars to take care of his own business while James took care of his.

James walked over to the Chevrolet. "Is your name Ed?"

Ed looked James up and down; with his long hair, wearing no socks, and a three legged dog doing his business behind him. "Yes… and you are?"

"I'm James, Brad sent you with some papers for me to sign?"

Ed seemed to consider. "Would you mind waiting right here for a minute?"

"That's fine," James said. "I'll be right here." He went over and picked up Bandit and took him back to the car, placing him back on his Coca-Cola crate while they waited.

A few minutes later, Ed came out of the door of Holiday Inn. "Sir, would you mind coming inside for a moment? I have Brad on the phone and we would like to speak with you."

James followed Ed inside to a bank of pay phones. Ed handed James the receiver of one of them and James lifted it to his ear. "Yes?"

On the other end of the phone was Brad, "James is that you? Ed was telling me that someone driving an old car, with long hair, wearing khaki pants and loafers and carrying a three legged dog walked up claiming to be James Exum."

"Yes, it's me," James chuckled, "And he is exactly right, on all accounts."

"What in the hell is going on there, James? I told him you would be in a black limousine and I have him a magazine with your picture on it so he could make sure it was you. He said the picture doesn't look like you at all?"

"Well, I'll have to explain that to you later Brad, I don't really have time right now."

James hung up the phone and walked back outside with Ed. At the car Ed reached inside of his vehicle and pulled out the magazine Brad had given him. "I'm sorry for the inconvenience Mr. Exum, but this is who I was expecting when you pulled up."

Ed turned to the third page of the magazine and showed James a picture of himself standing behind a long conference table with his hands down on the desk. He was wearing a dark suit, with a gold necktie around his neck. His hair was cut severely short with a part on one side and his hair combed over the other side.

"Well, I can certainly understand your surprise," James said, "You did the right thing by verifying who I was. Don't worry about it. I'll give Brad a call later and explain everything to him."

Ed gave James the papers he was to sign. A few parting pleasantries later, James drove out of the parking lot with Bandit's head hanging out of the window. Driving into town across the now familiar railroad tracks, James felt sadness come over him. He knew these days were coming to an end and it made him feel melancholy.

Chapter 27

Pulling up in the front yard, James saw that the front door was open. David and Drew must have gotten home early. He gave Bandit a hand down onto the ground, and the dog began hopping off down the sidewalk toward the fire department. 'Must be feeding time,' James thought, 'Time for Bandit to make his rounds.'

James could hear the sound of music coming from the house as he went inside. Drew must be practicing again. Sure enough, when he looked in, Drew was holding David's left hand, practicing dance steps while David stood with his back to James. David had no clue they were being watched, but James knew that Drew was thoroughly enjoying holding David in this embarrassing position. As he walked through to the back porch James said, "Would you like me to hold his hand for a while David?"

David jerked his hand loose from Drew, sending Drew into a laughing fit. "Now wait a minute Jim," David complained, "The son of a bitch told me he couldn't hold the belt to the door knob and do this particular step, so that is what I was doing. Just trying to help him out."

"Would you hold my hand while I do some practicing?" James asked.

"Hell no, I'm not holding anybody's hand anymore."

James and Drew burst out laughing again.

"I'm just kidding with you David," James said.

"Let's get a beer Jim," Drew said, "and get one for Miss Harris here too."

James grabbed a few beers out of the refrigerator and passed them to Drew and David. All three of them walked out onto the back porch. When they sat down, Drew turned to James, "Well boys, know after this weekend, we'll be in Myrtle Beach."

"Well, the way I've got it figured out, we'll leave here around noon or maybe one on Friday. It will take about four hours to get there. By the time we get there and meet up with Linda and Helen, I'll have about two hours of practice with Linda before the contest starts at eight. They'll name the winner about eleven o'clock and after we get our prize money, we'll get in the car and drive back. That will get us back here around four in the morning. Graduation will start at one on Saturday so that will give us time to get back and take a nap before we have to get up and get dressed."

"Well it sounds like you have it all figured out Drew," James said, "But why don't we get a room and drive back the next morning early?"

"Mama and Dad are coming up for graduation and I want to get at least a few hours of sleep before they get here. I'm not about to pull up after driving all night and see them standing on the front porch waiting on me. Especially after drinking and dancing half the night and staying up the rest and driving home. I don't think we would look too good to them. But we can take turns driving. Two of us will be sleeping while one of us drives. That way, each of us can get some sleep while the other drives. That way, when we get here, we have time to clean up and get a nap," Drew reiterated.

"Well, the last thing I want is Miss Harris to see me crawling out of the back of little Susie half asleep," David said, "Lord only knows what she would think?"

"Well, I'll go along with whatever you guys want to do," James said.

"Well, that's the plan for now then. If something changes, we'll sit down and discuss it. So what do you guys want to do tonight?" Drew asked.

"I've got to study some before I do anything," David said.

"I'm going up to see Sandra at six," James said, "I don't know what time I'll be back. Afterward I'm planning on coming back and getting some sleep."

They finished their beers and talked awhile about the dance contest and the fun they were going to have in Myrtle Beach. Then James said, "Fella's I think I'll start walking to Sandra's house."

"Why don't you drive Little Susie?" David asked.

"Well, by now everyone knows who owns that car and I don't know how it would look sitting in Sandra's driveway. I don't want to start gossip."

"You're right. I don't think you could get by telling people she was tutoring you," David said. Drew started laughing.

James just grinned and headed out. The sun had gone down and as night came on the air had turned cool. James wondered if he should have grabbed a jacket or a sweater before he left. Winter was coming on, but James thought he was ready to see some cool weather.

Several students called out to him by his first name as he passed. Many asked where Bandit was. Some would ask why he wasn't in Little Susie. Everyone was so friendly. He would miss that if he went back to New York. The way he was feeling now, he thought if he did go back, it would only be for a short time and not to stay. The South was where he belonged. He enjoyed seeing the Carolina blue sky in the mornings and afternoons. One thing was sure, he wasn't going to give up on his relationship with Sandra.

As James passed the soda shop, he heard the sound of Elvis Presley coming from the jukebox whenever someone opened the door. The air around the shop smelled of cigarette smoke. All the students looked so happy. James hoped they could stay happy once they left college and entered the workplace and started taking on responsibilities.

He turned the corner and started up Neeley Road. Checking his wrist to see what time it was, he realized he didn't have on his watch. He stopped wearing his Rolex when he moved in with David and Drew. He knew it had to be close to six. He didn't mind being a little early, but he didn't want to get there late. His dad always told him that if you tell someone you will be there at a certain time; you make damn sure you are there on time. James walked up on the front porch and rang the doorbell.

The porch light came on and Sandra opened the door. "Come on in," she said, "I'll be just a minute. I've got to turn the stove down."

As she walked away, James noticed she was wearing jeans rolled up halfway to her knees and shoes that looked like bedroom slippers. A denim shirt hung out over her jeans. The shirt was two sizes too big but still looked good to him. She was definitely a country girl on the inside.

James followed her into the kitchen. Sandra took the pot holder and moved the frying pans to one side of the stove. The way she moved around the kitchen reminded him or her mother.

"Have a seat," Sandra said, "Can I pour you a cup of coffee or iced tea?"

"A cup of coffee would be good."

Sandra reached up into the cabinet, stretching up on her tiptoes to reach the cups. James watched her, feeling his passion for her stir. His face flushed with warmth. Sandra turned and sat the cup down in front of him and gave him a funny look.

"What are you smiling at?" she asked.

"You just do certain things that make me smile when I watch you. I can't help it."

"Well I guess that's a good thing." She turned and grabbed the coffee pot and poured his coffee. "I believe you drink it black."

"You would be right," James said.

"I thought I would fix you a home cooked meal tonight."

"Well there's nothing I like more than a home cooked meal."

"For someone who has an uptown attitude, you sure have a down home appetite," Sandra joked.

"I don't have an uptown attitude, do I?" James asked.

"Well, you act more down to earth now than you used to. It suits you better as far as I'm concerned. I've definitely seen a change in your personality. You even make me laugh sometimes," Sandra chided.

"But you always have integrity about yourself that I like," she continued, "you listen to people when they talk and you act like you really care about what they are saying. I think you have real feelings for other people. You're a true southern gentleman, Jim, and I like that about you."

"That's about the nicest think I have ever had anybody say to me, Sandra. Thank you."

"Well, don't let it go to your head, big boy," she joked. "By the way, Ryan and I had lunch together today in the teacher's lounge. I gave him the opportunity to explain himself. After listening to him, I think maybe I jumped the gun and hung up on him before he could explain himself fully. But anyway, we patched things up and I think things are going to be okay between us. I think he understands our relationship as well, especially after you and he had your little talk the other night," Sandra said.

"Well, I know that you two go back a long way together. After seeing you so upset with him, I knew I didn't want to feel like I'd come between your friendship. I know his friendship with you means a great deal to him. I think it does to you too so thought it was about time that he and I cleared the air. I think we had a real friendly talk and he does seem like a nice gentleman. I can see why you like him and why the two of you get along so well together. I just didn't want that relationship to end over a misunderstanding," James said.

"I think he wanted more out of our relationship than I could give. I really like Ryan, but I just wasn't in love with him. I like him a great deal. I respect him. He has worked hard to be where he is. I couldn't give him what he wanted from me. I began looking at him like a big brother and that's not what he wanted. We got that all cleared up today. We're just friends and he realizes that now. I appreciate you talking with him and he seems like he respects you more because of it," Sandra said.

"I'm just glad to have it all worked out and now everybody is in good standing," James said. "So Miss Wilson, what's for dinner?"

"Well at a high-end restaurant you could call it dinner, but a home cooked meal, you can call it supper. We're going to have some battered fried cube steak with gravy, some fried squash and onions and some speckled butter beans. And yes, before you ask, I'm fixing some homemade biscuits, just like Mom does," Sandra said.

"Well, if you can fix all of that just like you mama does, then I will be marrying you right after supper," James said.

"I guess mom was right, if you want a man's heart, fix him a good meal."

"You already have my heart, Miss Wilson," James said.

"Speaking of hearts, what is your plan after school? We only have about a week and a half to go before the semester is over."

"I think I'm going to work it out where I can stay down here. After this semester, I've really grown to love the area and the surrounding countryside and the people who live here," James said.

"Would there be any other reason why you would like to stay?"

"Well, since you ask, there is one other reason I would like to stay here," James said.

"Oh? What would that be?"

"Well, I don't know what I would do without Bandit," James said.

James had no more got the words out of his mouth when Sandra turned towards him holding a spatula in her right hand. She raised it over her head as she glared at him, narrowing her eyes and closing her lips real tight.

James stood up from the table and held his arms out as he walked towards her. He reached up and gently pulled her hand holding the spatula down and wrapped both of his arms around her as he looked into those beautiful narrowed eyes. "Well, maybe there is one other thing that would keep me here. A tall, good looking, green eyed history teacher."

Sandra laid her head on James' shoulder and squeezed him tight.

"I don't want to move to New York City, but if that is what it takes..."

Before she could finish her sentence, James spoke up, "That's not going to happen. You are a Southern lady and Southern ladies stay in the South, where they belong. That's the way I would like it. Don't you worry. I'm going to work it out."

"Oh!" Sandra exclaimed," I've got to turn the squash. You like to cause me to burn it, Jim."

"Well don't do that, I love squash and onions."

"How about you get the bowls out of the cabinet up there so I can put the squash in it before it burns up?"

James grabbed the bowls and sat them down on the counter. He watched Sandra rake the squash in it with the spatula. His heart filled up with love as quickly as the bowl filled with squash.

"How about you get the dishes out of the cabinet and set the table for me. The spoon, forks and knives are in that drawer," she jerked her head toward the kitchen drawer. "If you do that for me, I'll take care of the rest. We'll be eating in just a minute."

James set the table as Sandra asked. Everything seemed so natural and comfortable.

After Sandra placed the food on the table, she turned to open the oven to get the biscuits out. The doorbell rang and she looked over at James.

"Were you expecting someone?" James asked.

"No, I'm not expecting anyone."

"Would you like for me to go to the door?" James offered.

"No," Sandra replied, "I'll get it, Jim. Keep your seat."

As Sandra opened the door, there stood David and Drew.

"Hi boys," smiled Sandra. "Come on in."

"Is Jim here?" asked David as he stepped inside.

Sandra nodded, "He's in the kitchen. Go on in."

James stood as the boys came into the kitchen. "Hi, fellas."

"Guess what, Jim?" David asked as soon as he saw James. "Drew and I were sitting on the front porch when this big, long, black limousine pulled up in front of the house. A man got out wearing a black uniform and one of those chauffer hats and asked if it was the residence of David Clark and Drew Harris. I told him it was and he handed me this envelope. We had to let you know, Jim. We just couldn't wait for you to see it."

James had an idea what it was since it arrived with a chauffeur carrying it, but asked anyway, "What does it say, David?"

"Well," David began, "it is from the president of Exum Textiles. A Mr. J.J. Washington. He said he would like to meet with Drew and I this coming Friday at 4:00 at the corporate offices in Greensboro to discuss an offer to work for Exum Textiles as 'D and D Engineering'. He will have a limousine pick us up. He wants to discuss a deal to have us work with Exum, Jim!"

"That sounds great, David," Jim exclaimed, "Sounds like he's very interested in your proposal."

"I can't believe the president of Exum textiles would write us a personal letter," David continued to gush as he handed the letter to James to show him the personal signature.

Sandra reached over and took the letter from James' hand, "Do you mind if I read it, boys?"

"Please do," Drew smiled.

"Well," she said after a moment, "it looks like it's for real. I'm really happy for the both of you. This could really be a great opportunity!"

"Yeah," Drew said, "thanks to Jimbo. He took it to the personnel office for us. I wasn't expecting a reply so quickly."

Sandra looked impressed, "Jim how do you have so much pull with Exum Textiles to get these boys a direct reply from J.J. Washington?"

"Well," James responded, "Mr. Washington must have liked what he read in the proposal that was given to him. I just thought it was such a good proposal after I read it that I carried to the Exum Personnel Office personally."

"Do you know J.J. Washington personally?" Sandra asked.

"Yes," James replied, "I do. I've known him for a long while."

"That's great, Jim," Sandra replied, "maybe he'll put in a good word for you later on down the road if you try to get the transfer back to Greensboro."

"Well, I think he would work with me on that," James smiled.

Sandra placed the hot biscuits in a basket with a white and red checkered towel on top. James could see that David was watching her every move, admiring the biscuits as waves of heat wove up from the buttered, flaky crusts. Sandra also noticed Drew's gaze. "Hey you guys," Sandra began, "Why don't you let me get you a plate and stay for supper with us?"

"Oh no," Drew said, "We can't do that. We're sorry we've interrupted your and Jim's supper."

"Speak for yourself, Drew," David laughed. "I haven't seen a meal like this in God knows how long!"

Sandra and James laughed.

"Well," Sandra assured, "You are both more than welcome. We would love to have you eat with us tonight."

"Well," David replied, "When it comes to home cooked meals, I'm not bashful."

"The bathroom is down the hall," Sandra directed, "Go wash up and come on back and have a seat and we'll eat."

After David and Drew washed their hands and combed their hair, Sandra said the blessing. When she finished, she began passing everything to the right.

Drew could not stop talking about the upcoming interview. "Should we wear suits to meet with Mr. Washington?" He asked.

James nodded, "That's a good idea."

"Drew and I both have one suit each," David said, "we were going to wear it on graduation day. I think we could spare it for the interview as well."

David never stopped eating. He just kept looking back at Drew and smiling as he swallowed his food.

"Well, I'm just glad he didn't set the interview up for next Friday," David said at last.

"Why is that?" Sandra asked.

"Well," David began, "Drew, Jim and I are leaving for Myrtle Beach after lunch next Friday. Drew is going to be in a dance contest Friday night, he and Linda."

"Oh? Is that right?" Sandra smiled at Drew.

"Yes," Drew replied, "Linda and Helen are also coming down on Friday, but they are going to spend the night. Me, David and Jim are driving back after the dance Friday night so we can be here Saturday morning. Graduation is at 1 o'clock and Drew's mom and dad will be there, so we have to get back before they arrive."

"So, Helen and Linda are going to drive down by themselves?" Sandra asked.

David nodded, "But since they don't graduate until Sunday morning, they won't be coming back until sometime on Saturday. We're going down early enough that we can meet at Linda and Helen's room and practice a couple of hours before the dance starts, which is around 7:00."

As she listened to David, Sandra cut her eyes at James.

"We're going to leave early enough Friday so we can take our time and enjoy taking turns driving Little Susie," David grinned.

"Boy, I can't wait to get started!" Drew laughed.

By now, David was on his third serving of biscuits. "David, if you keep on eating, you're going to burst!" Drew warned.

"I can't help it's so good," David protested.

"Well," Drew countered, "you act as though you haven't eaten in six months."

"I haven't eaten anything like this in six months," said David.

"You just eat all you want, David," Sandra chuckled.

"Finish up!" Drew pressed David, "We've got to go. We have studying we need to do."

"Let me finish this last biscuit and we'll go," David promised.

After David finished his biscuit, he and Drew thanked Sandra for supper and headed home.

As soon as they left, Sandra turned to James and asked if he would like another cup of coffee.

"No thank you," James said, "but let me help you clear the table. And, if you'll wash the dishes, I'll dry."

"Well," Sandra smiled, "Aren't you considerate."

As they were clearing off the table and putting the dishes in the sink, Sandra turned to James and said, "That was nice of you to take that proposal to Mr. Washington at Exum Textiles for David and Drew."

"They both have excellent grades and they love what they're doing. This is something they have thought about for a long time. They put the proposal together and I thought it was excellent. I just think Exum Textiles would benefit from their talent and enthusiasm so I thought I would ask J.J. to review it and see what he thought about it. I know there will be some changes in the textile industry in the next couple years and it would be beneficial to have those guys working for us. But, it's entirely up to J.J. whether or not they're hired." James said.

"Well, it was nice of you to go to Mr. Washington and not just personnel. You went right to the top and that's impressive," Sandra said.

"It's like someone told me years ago. If you want something done, you start at the top and work your way down."

"Tell me about this trip to Myrtle Beach and the shagging contest and Linda and Helen staying in a motel room where you're going to meet them, Jimboooooooooo."

Somehow, James knew this subject would come up. He looked over at Sandra as she handed him the next dish to dry. "I found out today just before I came up here. Drew was telling me the plan before I left the house. About the motel situation with Linda and Helen, you heard about it the same time I did from Drew. I'm just going along for moral support for Drew and to give them a ride down there and back," James assured her.

"I think you're a big boy and you know how to conduct yourself as a gentleman around those young girls. That's the kind of trust I have in you. Although I think Helen has a crush on you and that's a situation you may have to deal with. And that's up to you, how you are going to handle it," Sandra said.

"The way I am going to handle that, Sandra, is I'm not going to put myself in that position where I have to handle anything. She already knows I'm not interested." James said.

"How does she know that, Jim?"

"She has already made a move on me."

Sandra stopped washing dishes and turned and looked at James. "Oh, she has, has she?"

James held up his hands. "When I first moved in with the guys I had only been there a couple of weeks when it happened and I put a stop to it right away without hurting her feelings. She hasn't made any other gestures since then."

"Well, I can understand that, Jim. You're a good looking man. I'm sure there are other young girls on campus that flirt with you, as well. I knew the first day you walked into my class you were going to be trouble. I couldn't keep my eyes off you. You look totally out of place in that classroom. I don't know what it was about you. The day you came to school with those blisters on your feet and when we were in the first aid room with you sitting up on that table. And when I finished working on your feet and you slid off that table in front of me and looked down into my eyes it did something to me. I'll never forget that," Sandra said.

"I recall both incidents well, and I will not forget them, either," James assured. "But, I think we've got to hold ourselves together until I've finished your class. We only have until the end of next week. Then, maybe we can have a real relationship out in the open. I think we're both still feeling a little uptight because of the situation we're in. It's like you said, both of us are adults and we should be able to show our feelings and not feel like we have to sneak around to do it. I'll be glad when next week is over and I get back from the beach. I'd like to take you out to dinner, there's a lot I need to talk to you about. After that, we can see which direction our relationship will go." He moved to hold her closer and smiled, "I am hoping it will continue the way that it is now," he said.

"I don't think you can say anything to me that will change the feelings I have for you, Jim," Sandra said, looking up at him. "So, I'm not going to worry about that part," she smiled as she turned away and handed him the last dish to dry.

As James put the last dish into the cabinet, he turned around and slipped both arms around Sandra's shoulders and pulled her close to his chest. He laid his head sideways on the top of her head and rocked her from side to side. He squeezed her tightly and kissed the top of her head as he whispered into her ear, "you have no idea what you have done for me, Sandra."

Sandra just held him tight. She did not want to let him go. She could hear his heart pounding in her ear as he took his right hand and stroked her hair. This was a moment he never wanted to forget. He could feel the passion and the love Sandra had for him. He just hoped after next week, after he explained to her who he was and why he had to do what he did that she would understand and forgive him for not being totally upfront and honest with her in the beginning. James laid a hand on the side of her shoulder as she looked up at him. He kissed her slowly on the lips as his hands slid up to cup her face. He peppered her face with five quick kisses; one for her forehead, one for each cheek, one for the tip of her nose and finally one for her lips. He looked into her eyes and said, "You have no idea what you do to me, Sandra Wilson."

Sandra opened her eyes and met his gaze. She just smiled as she laid her head back against his chest.

After holding him for a couple of minutes, Sandra pulled away a bit and looked up at him. "I can tell it's time for you to go, Jim," she said, smiling.

"I'm certainly glad you have control over yourself," James chucked, "Because I certainly don't have control over myself at the moment." He sighed, "I don't want to go, but I will because I know you're right."

"I'd love for you to stay, Jim," Sandra said, "but tonight is not the time."

"Well, I told the guys I'd be on in a little bit, anyway."

"Come on," said Sandra, "I'll walk you to the door."

As they got to the door, James reached down and gave Sandra a quick kiss on the lips and thanked her for dinner, "It was great," he smiled, "Your mother would be proud."

"I hope so," Sandra chuckled, "I will see you in class in the morning, Jim."

Jim started his walk home. As he opened the front door, he could hear David and Drew arguing. "What's going on, guys?" He asked.

"Well, David is arguing with me about the bowl of gravy Sandra had with dinner tonight," Drew began. "He is trying to tell me that it wasn't gravy. He is saying that it was a burn-a-sauce. He's refusing to say that he ate gravy and liked it. He's hard headed as a nail!" Drew sighed, "I can remember when my dad would say that I was hard-headed when he would ask me to do something a certain way. Well, naturally I would want to do it my way and it would be wrong. Then, my dad would say, 'Drew. Don't forget a hard head makes for a soft ass,' and I knew exactly what he meant by that." He looked back to David, "You ate gravy and you liked it and you won't even own up to it, you hard-headed Yankee, you!"

"If that was gravy Sandra made, I can eat it. It's good. That gravy you make will kill a fella. The first time I ate Drew's gravy I think it glued my insides together so bad I couldn't shit for two days." He turned to Drew, "I'm not ever going to eat your gravy again, Drew. You damned rebel, you!"

They all three burst out laughing.

"I'm going to bed on that one," James said.

Drew said, "I think I'm going to bed, too. I have to get up early so I can fix David a big bowl of gravy for breakfast in the morning."

"I don't think so," David called as he walked to his room, "Drew, you asshole!"

After two days of questioning James about J.J. Washington and what they could expect from the interview, Friday finally arrived. David and Drew sat on the porch steps, in their graduation suits, waiting for the chauffeured limousine that was to take them to Greensboro. David donned a dark blue suit and yellow tie, while Drew sported pin stripes and a light blue tie.

"You guys look real nice," James said, "Very professional. I think J. J. will be impressed with you."

"I'm so nervous, I don't know if I can talk with any intelligence," Drew laughed.

David said, "Hell, Drew. You can't talk with any intelligence when you ain't nervous!"

All three men burst out laughing.

"Look, Drew," James said reassuringly, "J.J. is a real nice person. He'll make you comfortable. He's real down-to-earth and easy to talk to. He won't come across as acting better than you, so just go up there and listen to what he has to say. Just be upfront with him and tell him what you guys are wanting to do about starting your own business and what you think you can do for the company if he hires you. If you guys will just be yourselves, you won't have any problems. I have a lot of confidence in you guys and I think you would be good for the company and do a good job. So just go up there and talk with him with that attitude." He paused and looked toward the road a moment. "Well, I think I'm going to walk down to the Hole in the Wall and have a beer, and I'll see you guys when you get back," James said. "You fellas enjoy your ride in the limousine."

"Are you going to leave us now, Jim?" Drew asked.

James chuckled, "You're on your own, Drew."

"Well," Drew scoffed, "you're one hell of a friend. With me standing here so nervous. I'm shaking like a dog shitting a cotton seed and you're just going to haul ass on us!"

"You don't need me, Drew," James laughed, "you'll be okay. Just take a deep breath and settle down. It's not the end of the world. It's just a job interview."

"Yeah, that's easy for you to say," Drew said, "you already have a damned job."

"I'll be here when you get back," James explained, "just settle down." He stepped off the porch and headed off.

Chapter 28

As James walked down the sidewalk, the black limousine passed him on its way to his house. James could not help but grin as Charles drove by. As James looked back over his shoulder, he saw David and Drew walking towards the car as it parked in front of the house. Charles stepped out to get their door for them. The two young men shook Charles' hand before crawling inside. James couldn't help but laugh, and kept walking . 'What a night it's going to be when those two get back home,' he thought to himself.

As the limousine traveled through town, students watched as the long, black car crawled along the streets. Although no one could see inside, David and Drew kept waving and grinning at the kids as they passed. Not much was said on the ride to the executive offices as the two continued to admire the leather interior. Every once in a while, they would just chuckle and look at one another in disbelief.

As they drove up to the executive offices, Charles stopped the limousine and rolled down the window to greet the guard stepping out from the gate house. "Mr. Harris and Mr. Clark to see Mr. Washington for a 4:30 appointment," Charles affirmed. The guard nodded, stepped back inside and consulted a clipboard. He checked off something and motioned Charles ahead with a wave of his hand. The gate opened ahead of them and Charles drove on ahead. He wound his way up a narrow paved drive with cement curbs. Tall Spruce pines lined the roadway. As the office came into view, Drew looked up at it through the window. It was almost 4 to 5 stories tall. It was brick with huge windows and a slate roof. David's eyes widened and

Drew shook his head in disbelief. It looked like a castle to them. When the car stopped, Charles stepped out to get their doors, but David and Drew had already pulled themselves from the car and were standing there, staring in amazement. Charles just shook his head and chuckled. "Gentlemen," he said, "I will return to pick you up after your interview."

David and Drew stood side by side and looked at the steps leading up to the front doors. David looked at Drew, whose mouth was hanging agape. David nudged him and they both started up the steps. There were two large lions carved of granite guarding the doors on either side. David laid a hand one of the large, ornate golden handles and tugged the 12 foot tall door open. The room on the other side of the doors looked like a museum. There were two huge chandeliers hanging from the ceiling above two camel back sofas surrounding a large cherry table in the center. Showcases lining the walls led to a desk at the far end. A young woman sat at the desk. She smiled and stood as David and Drew walked in. "Welcome to Exum Textiles," she said. "I assume you are Mr. Harris and Mr. Clark?"

David came back to reality, "Yes," he managed, "we are."

The lady smiled again and nodded, gesturing to the room around the room, "Please. Have a seat, or look around if you like. Mr. Washington will be with you shortly."

David and Drew walked around and gazed at the huge oil portraits along the wall while they waited. Soon, the elevator doors opened and a well-dressed black man smiled and walked over to them. He offered his hand and said, "Hello, Welcome to Exum. I'm J.J. Washington. How are you gentlemen?"

David and Drew were both surprised at how young J.J. was, and they had forgotten he was a colored man. His form was impressive and his manner charismatic. Both boys just stared and nodded their heads, they couldn't speak. J.J. smiled at them both and tucked a folder under one arm. "Shall we?" he offered, gesturing towards a side door off the main lobby.

Drew and David followed J.J. into the room. It was a large room, with a solid wood conference table to fit about 12 people. It was decorated very elegantly with large photographs of their textile mills, located in different parts of the Carolinas and one photo of the secondary corporate office in New York City. The entire room was padded with rich walnut siding and crown molding. The room gave the impression you were important, just being there.

As J.J. pulled out the chair at the far end, he motioned for David and Drew to have a seat. J. J. began by saying, "Fellows, I have a job proposal prepared line by line, explaining in detail everything we here at Exum Textiles are prepared to offer you. It includes terms of what we are willing to do in terms of assisting you in starting your own business, D&D Engineering, while also serving as employees of Exum Textiles." He spent the next half hour going over details of the offer. When he finished, he asked David and Drew what they thought.

David spoke up. "Mr. Washington, I think I can speak for Drew. The proposal you're offering is overwhelming. I would have never have expected this opportunity coming from anybody, especially from the world's largest denim and textile company…" After a moment's pause, he and Drew exchanged a glance and he continued with a grin. "You have my word, sir that we will work hard and do our best for this company."

J.J. nodded and smiled, "I know you will, David." He said, "That's why I'm making this offer. Now," he stood, "if you gentlemen will come with me, I would like to show you something."

J.J. led the boys back through the lobby to the hall at the opposite end. He opened two, large double-doors to reveal two huge work areas. "Gentlemen," he began, "These will be your offices. We will install all the materials you feel is necessary to do your job."

David and Drew were speechless. They simply could not believe someone would do so much for them.

J.J. said, "Do you think the size of the room would be adequate enough for what you want to do? To start your own business?"

David and Drew nodded quickly, "Yes sir," they said, "Very much, sir!"

"To be honest with you, Mr. Washington," David said, "I'm speechless."

"Well," J.J. chuckled, "I'm glad you like it. I think we will have a good working relationship."

Drew walked over to the window and looked out at the view. There was a huge lake with water shooting up from the center of it. It came down like a huge umbrella. It was spectacular.

"Well, fellows," J.J. continued, "I'll have Charles come back around to pick you up. I'm looking forward to working with you. I'll see you in two weeks after graduation." He paused to shake Drew and David's hands before disappearing behind the doors of what would be David and Drew's offices.

David and Drew stood at the windows and looked out. The sun was setting low in the west, throwing an orange glow over one side of the lake. Neither of them spoke.

After a few minutes, Charles pulled the limousine around front and the boys left their castle behind to slide back inside onto the leather interior of the Exum limousine.

Finally, Drew looked at David and said, quietly, "I can't believe what the hell is happening."

David smiled over at him, "Well, partner," he said, "It is happening."

As the limousine pulled down the highway, Drew said, "You know, I think we need to get out in front of the soda shop when we get back in town."

David laughed, "Drew, I think you're right. What an eye-opener that'll be, to see you and me getting out of this car dressed in these suits…" He smiled, "We'll have a lot of explaining to do."

"Yeah," Drew mused, "but we won't tell them a thing. We'll just keep 'em guessing."

The limousine pulled into town, just over the railroad tracks and right before the soda shop, David leaned up to the driver and asked, "Sir, would you mind stopping and letting us out in front of the soda shop?"

Charles spoke up, "Yes, sir. I would be happy to."

"That would be great," David replied as he sat back in the seat and grinned at Drew.

The driver circled around the confederate statue and headed back towards the shop. It was dark outside by now, and the street lights illuminated the limo, making it shine like crystal. There were already a few students standing outside the soda shop. It didn't take long for other students to begin to gather. It was clear they were all wondering just who was inside this limousine. This time, David and Drew remained inside the car until Charles came around to open their door. Drew stepped out first, and held his arms wide in the air as he walked up on the sidewalk. He said, loudly, "Ask not what you can do for your country, but what your country can do for you!" David climbed out behind David as the crowd burst out laughing.

David said to Drew, "you have it wrong, asshole, it's the other way around."

"Well," shrugged Drew, "it was close enough, half of them don't know the difference anyway."

Charles was laughing as he walked back around and got inside the limousine.

Students began to gather around David and Drew on the sidewalk. They gathered around them asking why they were in a limousine.

"I don't have time to explain now guys," David said "Maybe tomorrow."

"I can't wait to get home and talk to Jim" Drew said.

"I want him to go over the proposal with us." David replied.

"He's not going to believe what Mr. Washington offered us."

When they reached the front door, they could hear the music playing from the porch. Drew yelled out for James.

"I'm back here, follows!" James replied. James stood up from the rocking chair when Drew and David walked in.

"You're not going to believe what happened." David said.

"Well sit down and tell me all about it." James replied.

"Well first of all, that is one hell of a corporate office! We saw pictures of James Andrew Exum and his son. He was standing beside his dad, and he only looked to be about twelve years old.

He didn't look very happy either. J.J. stepped off the elevator and introduced himself. He didn't look like colored at first, he was light in color." David said.

"He looked young too," Drew said "He didn't look a day over thirty five."

"He's not." James said. "He's thirty three."

"He's pretty young to be a president of the company as big as Exum Textiles." David said.

"You can tell he's highly educated. He made us feel comfortable and he treated us like we were special." Drew said.

"Anyway, the offer he made us we could not turn down. He told us we could work for Exum Textiles as engineers for the first year and then he would work with us on starting our own business. He said we could use his offices for as long as we wanted to, providing that Exum Textiles came first. After that, we could do work for other companies if it doesn't interfere with the work we're doing for him." David said.

"It's a no lose situation." Drew added.

"Thank you so much for putting in a good word for us, Jim. I don't know what would have happened if you hadn't."

"I was glad to, boys. You're my best friends, and that's what friends are for." James replied.

"He wants us to work two weeks after graduation so we've got to figure out where we're going to live." David said.

"Guys I'll be leaving after we get back from Myrtle Beach, but I am willing to pay my part of the rent six months after I leave. By the time you go to work and draw a paycheck, you can just stay here. You'll just need a car to drive back and forth." James said.

"James, we can't ask you to pay rent and you're not staying here. That wouldn't be fair." David said.

"Well I'll be coming by sometimes to visit my favorite lady up the street." James replied.

"Oh I forgot about Sandra. That would be great! We could all stay together." Drew said. "Well, David, we must be doing something right because the man upstairs seems to be looking after us."

"You can say that again, Drew." David said.

"Now that we've got all that worked out, let's have a beer, listen to music, and celebrate!" James said.

A few hours later James told David and Drew that he was going to bed. "I'm going to Greensboro in the morning to visit a friend. I'll be back in the afternoon."

"Well, it's about my bed time too," Drew said. "I just don't think I can sleep. I'm so excited about everything."

"Have a couple more beers and I think you'll be able to go to sleep just fine." David said.

"I will as long as you'll have another one with me." Drew replied.

"I might as well. I'm not going to let you stay up in this house all by yourself. Goodnight, Jim. Thank you again for all you have done." David said.

The next morning, James was up early and got dressed. David and Drew had not gotten up yet. Not much activity was going on throughout the town. When he walked outside, there laid Bandit in front of driver's side door. "Well good morning, Bandit." James said. "I guess you want to go for a ride." James began his normal routine of letting Bandit in the car. As James pulled out of the driveway, Bandit stuck his head out of the window, ignoring the cool morning breeze. When James got to the interstate and turned down the ramp, Bandit pulled his head back inside and looked over at James. James reached over and patted Bandit on the head. "I'm going to introduce you to Grammy, and I know she's going to love you."

As James got into Greensboro, Bandit stuck his head back out of the window. James turned into the mansion and drove up to the guardhouse. When he arrived, Mr. Sparks came out with a big smile on his face. "Good morning, James." He said.

"Good morning, Mr. Sparks." James replied

"I see you have a buddy with you." Mr. Sparks said. "He's a fine looking beagle. I'm glad you came by this morning. I'm beginning to worry about Elizabeth. She hasn't been acting quite right."

"Why? What's going on?" James asked.

"Well, she walked out here the other day and told me to buzz her as soon as Mr. Exum comes in. Another day she told me to come up and have lunch with her. When I got there, the dining room was set up for four people, and when I asked her if she was expecting anyone else, she told me that those boys may be in any time now. I think it could be the medicine she's taking."

"Well Mr. Sparks, I'm planning on moving back in next Saturday. I'm having my clothes and things shipped down here from New York this coming week. I'll be here to look after her."

"That would be great, James. I'm looking forward to seeing you back here anyway. This place has not been the same since you left."

"I'm looking forward to coming back." James replied. "Well, I better drive on up and introduce Bandit to Grammy."

"Alright James, I'll open up the gate." Mr. Sparks said.

James drove around the side of the house and stopped at the back door. As James stepped out of the car, the back door opened and Grammy came running out. "Hey Grammy!" James said.

"You give me a hug, boy." Grammy demanded. James put both arms around Grammy and picked her up off of the ground. "Put me down, boy; before you hurt your back."

James set her down and noticed how frail she looked. He was surprised at the weight she has lost in the past couple of weeks. Bandit jumped out of the car. "Hey, I want you to meet Bandit." James said.

Grammy bent over and began to pet Bandit. "Well, where did you come from?" She asked. "We'll bring him inside and give him some water. What happened to his other leg?"

"I don't know. He had a missing leg the first time I saw him." James replied. As he entered the back door, he smelled sausage cooking.

"Have you had breakfast, James?" Grammy asked.

"Not yet." He replied.

"Well come on in. I have a pot of grits on and I'm fixing some sausage patties." Grammy said as she walked inside.

"Grammy, I don't think you're supposed to eat sausage." James said.

"The doctor said I could have one once in a while." She replied. As Grammy was getting some water for bandit, James looked on the stove. There was a frying pan with a sausage patty as big as a pancake cooking.

"My goodness, Grammy; that is the biggest sausage patty I have ever seen." James said.

"Well that's my sausage patty that the doctor said I could have one of." She replied.

"Well rather than fixing me a sausage patty, how about you give me some of yours. I think it's big enough that you could let me have some, and there would be plenty left for you." James said.

"I guess you could have a little bit of it." Grammy said as she sat a bowl of grits in front of James.

"How are you feeling?" He asked.

"I feel pretty good, James. I'm just getting old, that's all."

"Are you taking the medicine that the doctor gave you?"

"Yes, but I don't like taking it, James. It makes me feel right foolish sometimes." She said.

"Well you need to take it like the doctor said."

Grammy took a bowl out of the cabinet and filled it half way up with grits, then poured the sausage grease all over them. "You don't reckon that will make Bandit sick, eating all of that sausage grease?" James asked.

"No, it will make his coat shine." She replied. "I'm glad you have a dog now, Jim. You wanted one when you were a little boy, but your dad would always say you didn't have time to take care of a dog."

"Tell me something about Mom. Dad never talked about her around me." James asked.

"I know, James. I guess is just as good a time as any to tell you about your mother." She replied. "Your dad met her at a seminar he attended in Asheville, North Carolina at the Grove Park Inn. I don't know what she was doing there, but your dad said she lit up the room when she walked in. He knew she was the one for him, even though she was about ten years younger than him. She was a beautiful woman. Sometimes he would bring her over to the plant and introduce her to some of the people who worked there. She was a down to earth person. She always had a big smile on her face with her long brown hair and dark eyes. Your daddy loved her so.

"To make a long story short, your dad told me that she was the one for him after a week. She would always say that he swept her off of her feet. After a few months, she was pregnant with you. She was having problems from the beginning. Your dad asked for me to move in with them so I could look after her. After about five months a doctor took your dad outside and gave him the news. I saw your dad's head drop with sadness. He later told me that the doctor had said your mom would die within a week after childbirth. The doctor also couldn't guarantee that you would live. She had a fifty percent chance to live if she terminated the pregnancy. He asked me what he should do.

"I sat him down and I set my hand on his shoulder. I said 'I know you love her with all of your heart, but this will have to be her decision and you'll have to stand by it.' He stepped out and walked through the old family cemetery. I think he went to talk to his father about the whole mess. When he came back, I followed him up the stairs to the bedroom. He picked up her hand and held it to the side of his face. She knew what he was going to say. She told him that she was going to have her baby, no matter what. He tried to argue with her, but she wouldn't take back her decision. She then asked me to help take care of you. I said 'Honey, I will do that let hell or high water come.'

"Lord I wish we had the technology in 1938 that we do now. She may have been able to make it. I just hope she is satisfied with the job I have done."

James reached over and took Grammy's hand. "You've done a great job, Grammy." He said. "I know mom would be real pleased."

"I hope so, honey." She replied. "Now this is that hard part. Maybe this will help you understand your daddy a little bit more.

"The next couple of months weren't too bad, but the sixth month your dad paid a doctor just to stay at the house. We all took turns looking after her for about a week. Finally, the doctor said it was time for her to give birth. All he asked me to do was to hold her hand and wipe her head with a cold cloth.

"After half an hour, he delivered you. He handed you to me and said 'Elizabeth, clean him up and bring him back to his mother.' You were such a small baby because you were a month too early. Your mother could barely hold her eyes open, but when I laid you beside her she gave you the biggest smile. The doctor was still asking me for clean towels. She had discharged a lot of blood. I made several trips back to the kitchen to dump the water and to get more clean water. Finally the blood began to slow.

"The doctor went outside after a while and lit a cigarette. His sleeves were rolled up past his elbows. He looked at me and said 'Elizabeth, these next few days are going to be the hardest ones. I'm going to stay here and do the best I can, and I'm going to need your help all the way through this. I hope James can hold up. It's going to be extra hard on him.'

"The doctor was right. The next four days were the most emotional time of my life. The whole time, Ellen was awake. She wanted you lying on her chest, she would open up her top, and lay you between her breasts. She said she wanted to feel your heart beat. She would hold you until she went to sleep, and I would have to take you to change your diapers. The doctor kept changing the bandages, but he couldn't stop the bleeding. Your dad was always by her side, wiping her forehead with a cool cloth.

"She opened her eyes for the last time, and she laid you on her chest like she had done so many times before. She reached up and kissed your head, and when she laid her head back down closed her eyes for good. I picked you up and left the room. I could hear the doctor consoling your daddy. He stayed by her side until the funeral home came and got her. Your dad was going to go with them, but the doctor persuaded your father to stay behind. I changed the sheets of the bed and I cleaned up the room. Then I came in here and broke down crying. I cried until I heard J.J. in the other room, crying. I laid you on the bed and took J.J. out of his bed. He walked over to the side of yours just to look at you. He would then lie down beside you, and he went back to sleep. I just stood there looking at the both of you in tears and thought about how lucky I was.

"There was no one there when we buried her up on the hill. There was only me, the doctor, and your dad. He postponed the funeral for about three days to try to contact any of her family, but there was none to be found. After we buried her, your dad hired a detective to keep trying to find family who would miss her. The detective found nothing, and that always bothered your dad. After that, your dad threw himself into his work 16 to 20 hours a day. The only time I would see him is when I heard him going out the front door to the limousine that would take him to work.

"There were a couple of times that I got up to check on you and J.J.. When I looked into the room, your daddy would be sitting in the rocking chair holding you. I don't know how long he was in there or even how long he stayed. When you began walking, he would spend more time with you. He always said you looked like your mother, and it made him feel good to see the resemblance. He would watch you and J.J. as you played on the floor; it made him smile when J.J. never left your side. When J.J. started school, your father brought in all of those teachers. He said that it was a good time for a child to start learning. By the time you were 10, you could speak all of those foreign languages, and then you would teach them to J.J..

"You boys would have fun speaking to each other in foreign languages. Your daddy and I couldn't understand them, and you two would burst out laughing. When you were about 6, you wanted to go to school like J.J., but that was around the time people were sending death threats to your daddy. He set up a classroom off from his office. I knew it was hard on you, James, but it was for your own safety. By the time you were 13, you could help J.J. with his homework and he was in 12th grade. That's when your daddy started teaching you about the business. I told him that it was too much on you to have you learning everyday all day and night. He knew I was right, but he always said it had to be done.

"I later found out that he had been diagnosed with diabetes. It was getting to the point where he had a hard time walking up the steps to his office. He hired J.J. at the company to lift the heavy bales of cotton and sweep the floors. J.J. never complained, and after a while your dad would send him there to work on the machines. At supper, he would ask him what you learned that day. I think J.J. learned how to work every machine in that factory. By the time J.J. went to college, your father had him go to the best textile school in the state. There were only three colored kids accepted to NC State in 1953 and your dad made sure that J.J. was the fourth.

"He was very proud of the grades J.J. was getting in College, and he was proud of you for all of the degrees you had accomplished. I hadn't known it at the time, but I found out that your dad had made all the plans for where you two are in the business today. He got you two ready to run the business after he was gone. I'd say he did a pretty good job of it; just look at you two boys today."

Grammy stopped and got up to pour herself a cup of coffee.

"I think I'm going to take Bandit and walk up to the cemetery for a few minutes." James said.

"You go right ahead, baby. Take your time." She replied

James walked out the back door, and Bandit hopped right by his side as they headed up the brick walk way that lined each hedge that led up to the family cemetery. It was a small cemetery that was outlined by a black iron picket fence with a beautiful double door gate. There were only four grave sites that contained his grandmother, his grandfather, his mother, and his father. There was still plenty of room for others to be buried there. James stopped and viewed the cemetery. He was very pleased with the job Grammy had done keeping up with the cemetery. She had fresh cut flowers on all of the graves. In front of the gate, there was a cement bench with flower pots on each side that Grammy had planted her favorite flowers.

James sat down on a bench, picked up Bandit, and sat him down beside him. As he looked at each of the graves, James realized he had never felt as much emotion before. The only time he'd been there before, was on Father's Day and Mother's Day, but this time he looked at it from a new perspective. He could now feel the love that his mother must have had for him, and the love that his dad had for his mother. How a man's heart can accept a death of someone he loves so much, and then show love for his first born, James thought. How a heart shows sadness and happiness at the same time. He began to feel the sadness that his father had and the love that his mother had for him. Her love was unconditional. James could feel his face getting warm, and his throat tightening, making it hard for him to breathe.

Tears began to run down his face. James put both hands up to his face and began to cry out loud. Bandit stood up on one leg and put his front paws on James' shoulder, licking the side of his face. James picked up Bandit and held him while he cried. Bandit kept trying to lick his tears to take James' hurt and sorrow away. This was not something James had ever felt before. He finally felt the pain that he had pent up inside him after 30 years. After a while, James gained control of himself. This has been coming for a long time, James thought to himself.

James got up holding Bandit. He walked up to the gate, looked at his parent's tombstone and said in a low voice "Thank you so much. I love you with all of my heart." He turned, holding Bandit, and started walking back down the brick walkway to the house. When James walked back out into the opening he saw J.J.'s car sitting behind his.

James opened the back door and walked in. J.J. was sitting at the kitchen table. James sat Bandit down on the floor, walked around the table, grabbed J.J.'s hand, and pulled him in for a chest bump. "How are you, James?" J.J. asked with a big smile on his face.

"I'm just fine." James replied. "How are you holding up?"

J.J. looked down at Bandit, and then looked over at James' shoes. He noticed that James wasn't wearing any socks. J.J. started laughing "Well, I guess it's so." He said.

"What's that?" James asked.

"I got a call yesterday from Brad. He wanted me to check your signature on those papers that you had signed for him. He told me that he sent his assistant down for you to sign some papers, and that he had met you at the Holiday Inn on 85. He said his assistant called him and told him that some guy pulled up in an old car with a three-legged dog, wearing shoes with no socks claiming to be James Andrew Exum. He wanted to verify your signature on those papers. I told him that it was your signature, and the next thing he asked was what the hell was going on. I couldn't help but laugh at him." J.J. said. James couldn't help but laugh. "You definitely don't look like the same James. You look 10 years younger with that long hair and khaki pants. I think a lot of people would have a hard time recognizing you."

"Well they haven't so far." James said. "By the way, J.J., I really appreciate what you've done for David and Drew. I think the opportunity you gave them was a great idea."

"I really think those guys can be a big help to us, James. Drew is really creative when it comes to machinery and David is very detailed in his thinking. They make a good combination, and they will be good for this company." J.J. said.

"I think you're right, J.J.. We need young people with creative minds and believe me when I say, they do have creative minds. What those guys can come up with will amaze you." James said shaking his head smiling.

J.J. got up to leave after about an hour of small talk with James and Grammy.

"Hang on;" James said "I'll walk out with you to the car. I have to get back to Burlington as well." They both gave Grammy a hug and a kiss to say goodbye. "By the way, Grammy, I will be back next Saturday and I'm planning on staying a while with you before I go back to New York. You're going to have me hanging around for a while." James said.

"That's the best news I've heard in a long time, James. I am looking forward to having you back in this house, boy." Grammy said.

"It will be good to be back, Grammy. I'll see you next Saturday, so you take care until then. I love you!" James said as he reached down to pick up Bandit. Grammy patted Bandit on the head as they walked out the door.

As James and J.J. walked out to the car, James asked "What had the doctor said about Grammy? It looked like she had lost a lot of weight, and she's not looking well at all."

"I talked to the doctor on Friday," J.J. replied. "He said that he had been giving her medicine for high blood pressure, but every time he checked it, it was high. She's not taking her medicine, or she's not eating the right food. He also said he thinks there are other things wrong with Mama, but he won't be sure until the tests get back. They should be back next week, and then we'll know more."

"Well, like I told Grammy, after I get back from taking those boys down to Myrtle Beach, I think I'm going to move in here for a while. I can run the business from dad's office. I'll just have to install some equipment." James said.

"That will be great, James. It will be good to have you back home." J.J. said.

"It will be great to be back, J.J. I know now that this is where I belong. The business is a big part of my life but now I know there are other things in life besides business. It has taken me a long time to figure it out, and just let me say: J.J., thank you for giving me that opportunity." James said.

"It sounds like you may be in love, James." J.J. said.

"Sandra has opened my eyes to things, J.J. I don't know how to explain it to you."

"You don't have to, James. I understand completely." J.J. said. "Being in love is a good thing and I'm happy for you. Does Sandra know how you feel?"

"I know she does, but neither of us has come and told each other. We just know it." James said. "When I get back on Saturday, and I get packed up, I'm going to get Sandra. We're going to have lunch somewhere, and that's when I'm going to tell her the whole story about me. I just pray that she will understand the situation I was in, and why I didn't tell her everything about me."

"If she's the person I think she is, she will understand." J.J. said "By the way, when are you going to Myrtle Beach?"

"We're going to leave around lunch time next Friday and drive back that night after the contest. The next day, Drew and David are going to graduate around one o' clock." James said. "After the graduation, I'm packing up my stuff and I'm going to come home. I'll pay my share of the rent for the next six months, so the guys will have a place to live while they work. Who knows, I may go back just to hang out with those guys sometime. They're fun to be around, J.J."

"What do you think the guys are going to say once they figure out who you are?" J.J. asked.

"I think they'll get a big laugh out of it. Of course, I'll be cussed out by Drew." James laughed. "I'm having a hard time thinking of ways to tell them."

"Well James, it's been nice talking to you, and I'm glad to hear you say you're coming home. I've got a meeting at 1:30, though." J.J. said.

"Well don't let me hold you up, but give me a call when you hear about Grammy's test results." James said.

J.J. nodded, and James sat Bandit in the front seat of the car. He then climbed behind the wheel. As James pulled out of the driveway, J.J. started up his car and followed him down to the guardhouse. As James pulled off going towards the interstate, J.J. couldn't help but smile. He watched as the 41 Chevy headed up the road with Bandit's head sticking out, and James driving slowly like an old lady. J.J. turned left and headed toward 29 N toward Danville, Virginia. The meeting he was going to was going to be with the detectives Johnson and McGuiness. Johnson had called earlier that morning and asked that J.J. drive down to Danville to meet him at the Holiday Inn.

Chapter 29

J.J. had a feeling that the time was near to bring all of this to an end. This could be the final meeting before moving in and making the arrests. As J.J. pulled into the parking lot of the Holiday Inn, he noticed Detective Johnson's car parked in the parking lot. J.J. pulled into the first open parking space. He reached over, picked up his briefcase, opened the door, and headed to the breezeway where room 100 was. J.J. stopped at the door and took a deep breath before knocking on the door.

It opened instantly. "Come on in," Detective Johnson said. "You remember the Detective McGuiness?"

"Oh yes, and how are you doing, Detective McGuiness?" J.J. asked.

"Just fine, J.J.. Come around and have a seat. Would you like a coke or something?" Detective Clark said.

"No thank you. I'm fine for now, but I may need one later." J.J. said

"Well, let's get started." Detective Clark said as he walked up to the small blackboard. "Let me start with this: timing is going to mean everything. It starts with the Asheville plant. The driver of the tractor trailer usually pulls in at the loading dock around six o' clock after the supervisors and staffs have left for the day.

"The truck will be loaded with approximately 20 rolls of fabric. After he is loaded, he drives three hours to the Greensboro plant, which puts him there at around ten o' clock. The forklift driver will load about 15 more rolls, leaving space between the first load and the second load. That will take approximately an hour.

"The driver will pull out of the Greensboro plant around eleven o' clock and head to New York. He will only go through one weigh station. It has been fixed that he will just be waved through with no inspection. He always stops at Johnny's Truck Stop to have breakfast around six o' clock. That is about 10 miles south of New York City where he makes his delivery on the waterfront.

"When he stops, he always checks the locks on the trailer before going inside. When he goes inside to eat, that's when we'll take over. We have the key to the lock. We will open the door and eight agents will enter the trailer. They will place themselves in the space between the rolls of fabric that the forklift driver left for them in Greensboro. After locking the trailer back up, we will wait for the driver to return.

"He usually arrives around eight o' clock. After backing up to dock number three, he gets out and unlocks the doors on the trailer, then unhooks the trailer from the tractor. He knocks on the door three times to let the people inside know that the trailer is there and ready to be unloaded. He then leaves and drives back to the truck stop. There, he makes a phone call to Jason's office to let him know that the trailer is there and all went well. After the phone call, he will be placed under arrest by one of our agents who will be following him. By then, the trailer will be open from the inside of the facility. If all goes well, when all of those agents start pouring out of the back of the trailer, it will be a surprise so there will be no gunplay and the arrest can be made without anyone getting hurt. They then can gather the counterfeit money and plates at the same time.

"You and I will be at Jason's office to make the arrest. At the Asheville plant, our inside man will be making an arrest on your manager Mr. Ed Duncan. Our agent will be one block away from his house, standing by the phone booth in Asheville. As soon as he is notified by us, he will make the arrest. In Greensboro, another agent will be arresting Mr. Richard Keeltheer at his home at the same time. That way they won't be able to notify each other before we make the arrest.

"If all goes well, we can clean up all of this at one time. This operation will be called the Trojan Horses. We will set the command post up in James' office. That's where we'll make and receive our calls as we make the arrests to complete the operation.

"After all the arrests have been made, we will lock the trailer back up, call the Customs Department and the port authorities to pick up the trailer to deliver it to the freighter. That's going to take it down to Matamoros, Mexico, which is close to Brownsville, Texas. When it's there, we will have some of our agents, along with some federal aids and Mexican police. If it's handled the right way, we will be able to make the arrest of everybody involved. Even all the way down into Mexico. Do you have any questions, J.J.?" Detective Clark asked.

"When will we start this operation?" J.J. asked.

"The truck driver will be picking up the goods in Asheville North Carolina Tuesday afternoon, so we will begin the operation on Wednesday morning. You and I will need to get together Tuesday afternoon to go to New York City so we can be at your corporate office Wednesday morning to make the arrest on Jason.

"I hope the publicity will be a minimum, Detective Clark." J.J. said.

"It will be kept totally kept confidential. It will take two days for that freighter to get to Mexico, where it's going to be unloaded. It has got to be kept quiet until it takes place also. It also helps to keep James out of the way, and keep his whereabouts confidential." Detective Clark said.

"Where will you and I get together in New York?"

"I'm going to drive up on Tuesday and you are going to fly in."

"I will fly up on Wednesday morning. If you would like to go with me, you would be more than welcome." J.J. offered.

"Are you going to be flying commercial?" The detective asked.

"No. I'll be taking the company plane or James' jet."

"Does James have a jet?"

"Oh yes. This is his first jet. He uses it to take trips to Germany, Mexico, and Switzerland much faster."

"Well, I guess that you and I will be flying in James' jet to New York."

"Well I can fly up too." Agent McGuiness spoke up.

Before J.J. could say anything, Detective Clark interrupted. "No McGuiness, you're going to have to drive up with the other agents."

"I knew you were going to say that, Clark." Agent McGuiness said.

"I'm pulling rank on your buddy." Detective Clark said. He looked over at J.J.. "He knows he's in charge of the operation at the warehouse and the truck stop." He looked back over to McGuiness. "I'll tell you what, if all goes well, and we get everyone in custody, you can fly back with us."

"Well, that's fair enough." McGuiness replied. "It does beat driving back for eight hours. Maybe I can get home in time to have dinner with my wife and kids."

"That sounds good to me." Clark said. "Do you have any other questions?"

"What about James?" J.J. asked. "When can I tell him about this?"

"As far as I'm concerned, after we make the arrest of Jason and everything has been successful, you can tell him everything. For now, I want you to keep it quiet. We need to make sure these guys are behind bars. If either one of those fellows get loose, and get their hands on James, they will hold him hostage until the other is freed. We can't take that chance, so let James stay where he is until we know all of this is over." Clark said.

"Well he's leaving for Myrtle Beach on Friday with a couple of friends. He'll be back Saturday morning. Is that going to cause a problem?" J.J. asked.

"Nope, that will actually be good. He will be on the road most of the time which means he is moving." Detective Clark said.

"Okay, whatever you guys think. I will do whatever it takes to make this thing successful and to keep James out of harm's way." J.J. said. "The jet is in a hangar in Raleigh, North Carolina. I will get the pilot to pull it out and fly it to Greensboro Monday night. It will be ready Wednesday morning. We'll be at the LaGuardia airport by 5:30. If we leave around 4 I will have us a helicopter ready to transfer us over to the corporate office. We'll be waiting on Jason to arrive and he usually doesn't get in until about 8:30. The employees don't start coming in until 9. Hopefully that will give us enough time to do what we need to do before the employees arrive."

"That sounds great, J.J.. You're beginning to sound like a detective now." Detective Clark said.

"No thank you. I think I'm going to stick to my day job." J.J. said, and they all laughed.

"Okay. I will see you at the airport at four o'clock on Wednesday morning, J.J." Detective Clark said.

"I will have everything ready to go. See you then, Detective." J.J. said.

"Drive safe going back, J.J. See you later." Detective McGuiness said.

As J.J. got back on the highway headed toward Greensboro, he thought about all of the things the detectives had told him. He still didn't like the idea of not keeping James informed. For as long as he could remember, they had always been honest with each other. He was unsure what their relationship would be like after he finally tells James about everything. He just hoped that James would understand why he had to keep him out of it. Now he knew how James felt when he kept his identity from Sandra, David, and Drew. He knew why James did it, he just hoped that James would realize that he had done it for him and his safety.

Chapter 30

As James headed out of the driveway, he stuck his left arm out of the window and waved to J.J. as he turned. James then got on the interstate and drove back to Elon College. James looked over at Bandit and laughed. Bandit's head was sticking out the window waving up and down. James turned off of the interstate and headed toward the Village of Elon. He stopped at the fire department to drop off Bandit. He watched as the three-legged dog hobbled inside for his lunch.

James drove through town. When he was nearly at the house, he spotted Drew walking angrily down the sidewalk with a piece of paper in his hand. James pulled over and stopped beside him. "Can I give you a ride?" James asked.

"No thank you, James. I have a meeting with the Chancellor in about 10 minutes." Drew said.

"Well hold on, and I'll go with you." James said.

"You don't need to, James. I can handle this myself." Drew said.

"Well get in and let me drive you up to the parking lot." James said. As Drew walked around to the passenger side of the car, James asked, "Can I ask what the problem is, Drew?"

"Well David took this test and the teacher failed him because he missed one part of a two-part question. I'm saying he did not fail the test. The answer David gave was the correct answer and the teacher is wrong. I called a meeting with the Chancellor to clear everything up." Drew said.

"I'm surprised that the Chancellor would come in on a Saturday."

"He was in his office when I called, so he told me to come over while he was still there."

"Are you sure the answer is right, Drew?"

"Hell yes, I'm sure. I helped David study for this test, and I know damn well that answer is right." Drew said. James pulled into the parking lot and Drew stepped out of the car.

"Let me go in with you for moral support." James said.

"You can go in with me, James, but let me do all of the talking."

As Drew and James started walking down the hall, Drew stopped. There on the door with a big black, bold letters the word "Chancellors Office". Drew took a big breath, and knocked on the door lightly. "Come on in." said a voice from the other side of the door and the two boys walked in. A heavy set man with gray hair and a white mustache sat behind a large oak desk. He had on a white shirt with a bow tie.

"I'm Drew Harris," Drew said as he walked up to the Chancellor. "This is my friend and roommate, Jim."

"It's nice to meet you, Drew. I am Chancellor Marlowe. It's nice to see you fellows; I've seen you around the campus, have a seat. What can I help you with, Drew?"

"Well, sir," Drew started. "My other roommate David Clark, who is studying to be an engineer like myself, took a test on Friday and failed it. I reviewed the test when David showed it to me. There was a two part question that was counted half wrong. As I studied David's answer on the first part of the test, I'm confident that his answer is correct. I realize sir that on most tests, they require a direct answer, but the question that had been asked on the test does not require a direct answer. If the first part of the question was wrong, the second part would have to be wrong as well. The question could have been answered in one sentence, but David wanted to make sure he got it right so he put down more than what the question asked for; however, the answer was right."

The Chancellor asked to see the test. Drew got up and handed him the piece of paper in his hand. The Chancellor reviewed the test for a few minutes and got up to pull a book out of the bookshelf. He sat back down and started thumbing through some pages. He stopped at one and began reading to himself, occasionally looking back at the test.

"Well Drew, I think you have presented your friend's case well. It seems that what you have said is right, he could have answered it in one sentence, but he gave more than necessary. I can't fault him for that. The reason its marked wrong is that the teacher would have to go back and review several pages before finding out that David was right."

"Sir, I'm not trying to point any fingers at anybody. I know if I had been the teacher, I would have done the same thing too, but this test is the final test on the subject before we graduate. I didn't know whether it would cause any type of difficulty in David graduating."

James sat back and watched Drew as he presented his case. James saw a side of Drew that he has never seen before. Now he knew why David had said that Drew was a lot smarter than you would first think.

"Well Drew, I'm going to have this test re-examined by the professor, and I'm sure once I point it out to him he will correct the mistake. Then David will get a passing grade, and I want to thank you for bringing this to my attention. I will take care of it." The Chancellor said.

Drew stood up and shook his hand. James stepped forward and shook the Chancellor's hand as well. The Chancellor looked over to James, "It must be nice to have a friend that will step forth on your behalf and defend you. It was nice meeting the two of you."

James and Drew walked back out his office. They didn't say a word until they got into the car. "David is going to be really pleased with what you did for him." James said.

"Let's not say anything to him about it, Jim." Drew said.

"Why not, Drew?" James asked.

"He doesn't know that I have seen it. He asked me to pick it up on my way home from the library. When I got home, I opened it and I saw that he failed the test. I know I shouldn't have opened it, but I know it was the test I had helped him with. I just wanted to see what kind of grade he had gotten. I knew I had to do something about it because it was my fault that he failed the test. I was the one who coached him while he studied."

"It's your choice, Drew. It is fine with me." James said.

"David will be home in a little bit less than an hour. Just wait on him and we will all go to the Hole in the Wall. "

"That sounds good to me, Drew" James said.

As James and Drew drove home, they saw David walking down the sidewalk with a girl. "Pull up beside him." Drew said. James pulled up beside them and Drew stuck his head out of the window. "Do you guys need a ride home? My chauffeur, Jim here, will be glad to take you home."

"I'm just going to walk Malia home and I'll be home later." David replied.

The young lady standing beside David was tall with long dark brown hair and brown eyes. She was a very attractive young lady. "You guys just go on home. I'll be there in a little while." David said.

"Okay. Jim and I will be waiting on you. See you later!" Drew said. As they pulled back into the street Drew said "Man that girl looks finer than two new rear tractor tires. I've never seen her before."

"Neither have I, but David sure did have a big grin on his face." James said.

"Did he say that her name is Malia?" Drew asked.

"That's what I thought."

"What kind of name is that?" Drew asked.

"I'm sure we'll hear all about her when he gets home." James said as he pulled up into the driveway.

When they entered the house Drew said "I'll grab us a beer, Jim. Go on out and turn the radio on." As James sat down, Drew handed him a beer. "Well it looks like Linda and I will practice dancing starting Sunday night until we leave on Friday."

"I sure hope you and Linda do well." James said.

"Well first prize is $300, second is $200, and third is $100. I can use the money. There will be people from all over the south. It won't be easy being in the top three, so Linda and I need to practice hard and come up with a few new steps."

"Well I wish you luck."

"Thanks. We'll need it."

"I was really impressed with the way you handled yourself with the Chancellor." James said.

"Well that was one time I had to get down to business and be serious. A lot was riding on the Chancellor's decision and I couldn't let David down." Drew said.

"Well you certainly did a great job."

The front door opened and they could hear the refrigerator door open. David walked out and sat down looking at James and Drew. "What's up guys?" David asked with a big grin on his face.

"What's up', my ass! Tell us where you met Malia. How did you end up walking her home? I know you are too bashful just to walk up to her and ask her if you could walk her home." Drew said.

"You're right, Drew. I was standing in front of the library, talking to a couple of guys about the Vietnam War. I was telling them about my dad being in the Navy when Malia walked by. One of the guys motioned for her to come over. When she heard me say my dad was in the Navy, she told me that her dad was in the Marine Corp and he was stationed in Saigon. We stood there talking for a while, and when the other guys walked off, we started walking down the sidewalk talking about our dads. Her dad has been in the service for 20 years."

"How did she get the name Malia?" Drew asked.

"Her name is Malia Faulk. She was born in Hawaii."

"Her dad had been stationed in Hawaii when she was born. He had liked the name 'Malia', which translated to 'Mary' in English. She has two younger sisters named Avery and Sydney who were born in Draper, North Carolina." David said.

"Well that's understandable. It sure is a pretty name." Drew replied.

"She's having a really hard time about her dad being in the Marines. She said that sometimes she was afraid to tell people because they've all turned their nose up at her. A lot of people are against this war, and she was glad that she could talk to me about it. I told her that I understood. We get along really well and I feel like I've known her for a long time.

"I told her that I was going to join, but my dad would not hear of it. He even wrote a letter to the draft board letting them know that I was his son, and that I was going to college so they bypassed me for the draft. I know it made my mom happy. Why weren't you in the service, Drew?" David asked.

"I was drafted, but when I went to take the test and the physical, they turned me down because I had asthma when I was little." Drew said. "What about you, Jim? Why weren't you in the service?"

"I am ashamed to say fellows that I'm like David. My mother passed away when I was born and my father stopped any chance of me getting into the service because I was his only son. He needed me to be at home to run the business. I think he used his political pull to keep me out, I'm ashamed to say." James said.

"Well, with all the protests that are going on nowadays you don't know what to think about the war. All I know is that I have been told that when Uncle Sam calls, you go." Drew said.

"Well, anyway, boys. Tomorrow I'm going over to her place to listen to some records and just talk. I'm looking forward to it." David said.

"I would too, if I were you, David." Drew said. "Let's walk down to the Hole in the Wall to have another beer and a hamburger."

"Sounds good to me, let's go." David said.

After spending a couple of hours at the Hole in the Wall, eating a hamburger and drinking a few beers, they decided to start walking back to the house. As they got close, they could hear the music from the house beside of them. Someone from the house emerged and stepped out onto the porch.

"Hey! Drew, David, Jim, y'all come up here for a minute!" The man yelled.

"Hey, that's John Wiley. He lives in the house." Drew said to James and David. They all started walking up the sidewalk to see what John had to say.

"Go on in and head to the back of the house." John said.

As they walked in, they noticed the scattered beer cans, potato chips, and peanuts all over the floor. They watched as the girls that were there danced. John went into the kitchen and picked up a quart jar of moonshine whiskey. "Do you know what this is?" John asked.

"I sure do," Drew replied. "My dad keeps a jar of it all the time at the house."

"What is it?" David asked.

"It's homemade moonshine whiskey, David. It will knock you on your ass." Drew said.

"Drink it. It comes straight from the hills of north Wilkesboro, North Carolina." John said, handing them the glass. David picked it up and smelled it, and gave it to James.

"I think I'll pass on this, John." Drew said politely.

"I'll try it." David said. John handed the glass back to David.

"Just take a small taste of it." Drew said.

Carefully, David put it to his lips and took a sip. "Man you can tell that stuff will put you on your ass."

"I guess I'll taste it too." James said, reaching for it. He put the glass to his lips. "I can honestly say I have never tasted anything quite like it."

"No more, boys." Drew said. "Put the lid on it and let's go."

"What's the hurry, guys? Stay a bit longer and have some fun!" John said.

"We appreciate the offer, John but we all have things we've got to do tomorrow." Drew said.

John nodded. "I understand fellows. I wish you could stay. We'll try to keep the noise down for you.

James and David thanked John for the moonshine as they headed out the door. When they got home they settled down on their back porch where the music wasn't as loud.

"Let me tell you a story about moonshine whiskey and the preacher who used to visit mom and dad ever Saturday night." Drew said. "We called him Rev. Donaldson. He was a tall, slender man with red hair and no freckles. That man could preach a sermon, I tell you he had all the Baptists hollering. Some would even roll out in the middle of the isle and acted like they were going into a convulsion. Mom and dad said that he was the best preacher they had ever heard.

"He would always show up around seven o' clock knowing that my mom would have supper ready. He would stay after we all went to bed because the boxing matches would come on TV late Saturday night. We were one of the only families to have a TV. Dad would always tell the preacher to be careful, to turn the TV off before he leaves, and we all went to bed.

"After we ate we all went out on the porch and my parents would sit on the swing while the preacher would sit in the rocking chair. I would always lay out in the yard watching the stars. That was always the routine for a couple of Saturday's out of the month.

"One Saturday, dad got up and went inside. When he came back he was holding a quart of moonshine whiskey. They called it peach brandy. Dad offered the preacher some moonshine. 'No thank you, Mr. Harris,' he said. 'It's against my religion to drink whiskey.'

"'Well if you don't mind, preacher, I think I will have me a little drink.' My dad said. 'It keeps me from catching colds. I haven't had a cold in ten or fifteen years, thanks to this moonshine.' Dad took the lid off and took a drink right out of the jar.

"'Mr. Harris,' the preacher said. 'I can't drink whiskey because it's a sin, but I think it would be okay if I ate one of those peaches.' The preacher reached into the top of the jar and pulled out the first peach with his fingers. He started eating it like an apple.

"Well preacher Donaldson, you are welcome to stay up as long as you like. We all are going to bed. We've got to get up early to milk the cows before we come to church.' Dad said.

"'Well, thank you for supper and the peach.' The preacher said. 'I'll see you folks at church.'

"The next morning when dad opened the refrigerator, he noticed there wasn't a peach left in that jar of moonshine. He looked at me and laughed. 'Son, we're going to hear one hell of a sermon this morning.'

"By the end of the sermon preacher Donaldson had already taken off his coat, rolled up his sleeves, unbuttoned his shirt, and taken off his bowtie. He had sweat running down his face and his shirt collar was soaking wet. The preacher thanked everyone for coming and walked to the front to shake everyone's hand. Dad waited till everyone left before starting out of the church. Mom walked up to the preacher and praised him for his sermon. Then dad walked up and shook his hand. 'You preached a mighty fine sermon today preacher, but you made one little mistake. When you got to the part about David, you were supposed to say 'David took the jaw bone of an ass and slayed the lion.' He did not pick him up by his tail and kick the shit out of him'"

James choked on his beer and spit it out. David and Drew rolled out onto the floor and laughed hysterically.

"Drew, you're an asshole. You had me believing that." David said.

"You almost caused me to choke to death." James added.

"Well, I changed some of it, but most of it was true." Drew said. "That moonshine whiskey will drive you out of your mind. I know because mom said dad, Uncle Darrell, and his buddy would go out on the back porch to play music and drink moonshine. When we got up the next morning mom said she found him out in the pasture sitting Indian style mumbling some unknown tongue to a trash barrel that we burn trash in. After that night mom said she'd never allow any moonshine back in that house. To this day Dad can't remember what happened that night.

"So the reason why I don't want you guys to drink any of that whiskey is because I don't want to find one of you guys somewhere speaking an unknown tongue to a trash barrel." Drew said.

"Why, hell, Drew. Sometimes I think you are speaking some unknown tongue. I sure all hell can't understand you all of the time." David said.

"That's because you have a hard time comprehending, you damn Yankee." Drew said and the three of them laughed.

"I have had enough for tonight. I think I'm going to bed now. I'll see y'all in the morning." James said as he got up. He shook his head as he walked down the hall to his bedroom.

After taking a shower and getting dressed, James stepped out into the hall. He could smell Drew cooking breakfast. When James walked into the room Drew offered him some coffee and told him to sit down. David and Drew had their usual argument about grits, and then the phone rang. David got up and answered it.

"Good Morning Miss Wilson," He said. "I'm doing fine, thank you." There was a pause while David listened. "He's here. Hold on." David called James into the den and handed him the phone. "It's Miss Wilson." He whispered.

"Good morning Miss Wilson." James said.

"Good morning, Jim. Can you call me Sandra? We're not in school this morning." Sandra said. "What are you doing around eleven o' clock this morning?"

"I don't have any plans." He replied.

"Can you come by my house then? I am going to Sunday school, and I'm not going to stay for church. I should be home by the time you get there. I have something to tell you." She said.

"I will be there around eleven." He said.

"Well I'll see you then." She said and she hung up the phone.

When James walked back into the kitchen, David and Drew were looking at him. "Is everything okay?" David asked.

"I guess I'm going to see her later." James replied.

"Well, I'm going over to Malia's house around noon." David said. "I can't wait."

Drew turned around and raked the eggs into a bowl. "Well Linda is coming by and we're going to her place to work on some new dance steps. I guess we'll see each other back here late this afternoon." Drew said.

After eating breakfast, David took his turn to wash the dishes while James and Drew sat on the porch. They listened to the blues and drank their coffee.

"Well, boys, it's time for me to go. See you guys this afternoon." James said as he got up. When James walked out the door and to his car, there laid Bandit curled up in front of the driver's door. "Well, I guess you want to go for a ride this morning. Well, I don't see why not." Jim reached down, picked up bandit, and placed him in the front seat. Bandit hopped onto the Coca-Cola crate.

James backed out of the drive way and headed into town. James thought it was a fine day. He watched as the students hurried to church. In the distance he saw a lady walking on the sidewalk wearing a dark blue polka dot dress. He recognized her immediately as Sandra. As he got closer, he pulled up beside her and stopped. "Are you looking for a ride, good looking lady?" He said.

Sandra stopped, walked over to the car, and patted Bandit on the head. "Well I see you're out with you best friend." Sandra said.

"You know the old saying." James said. "A dog is a man's best friend. Come around here and get on this side." Sandra walked over to the driver's side as James got out and pulled the front seat forward.

"So you think I'm going to take the backseat to Bandit?" She asked.

"Well you know a dog is a man's best friend." He replied.

Sandra looked at him and closed her eyes. Sandra then took the front seat, pulled it back, and got into the driver's seat. She closed the door and said "I'll see you at my house." She shifted the gear and pulled off, leaving James in the middle of the road. Bandit barked at him, as his head was stuck out of the window. James laughed and started walking toward Sandra's house.

When he finally arrived, there sat Sandra on the first step with Bandit beside her. "I guess that will teach you. Never expect me to take a back seat to anyone. Not even Bandit." She said laughing.

"Well I guess you could say I will definitely know better next time." James said. He sat down the first step next to Bandit. "Boy, it's a fine Sunday morning." He said as he listened to the church bells ring in the distance. "I'm really going to miss this town. I believe it has been the best experience I have had in a long time."

"Well you definitely made lot of friends around here, Jim. I'm pretty sure they'll miss you too." She said.

"What are you going to do when school is out?"

"I'm going home to spend time with my mom." She said. "She called me Friday. You'll never guess what happened."

"What's that?" He asked.

"She got a registered letter from an attorney in Greensboro from a Brad Alston and Associates. It said a client of his, who remained anonymous, has purchased the Darrell Jones property that joins the property of Sandra Wilson. That is a total of 158 acres, and has been given the Wilson family exclusive rights to enjoy its habitat whenever they desire.

"Now I really appreciate having the rights to drive up to that mountain whenever I want to, but it puzzles me. Who would do that and what are they planning on doing with the property later? I looked up Brad Alston and Associates. It turns out, after talking to his secretary, that he's the personal attorney for James Andrew Exum and its foundation. I asked why he would want to buy that mountain. The secretary gave me his New York office number.

"When I called, the lady who answered transferred me to the person who organizes his itinerary. She said that he was on vacation in the Carolinas. She said the only thing she knew was that his jet was in the Raleigh/Durham airport. Jim, how would you like to have your own private jet?" Sandra said. James didn't say a word, he just smiled at her.

"Anyway, she couldn't give me a specific location, but he's somewhere in the Carolinas. He should be back in his office one day next week, so I'm going to call him and ask what his plans are for that property. I hope he's not planning on building a manufacturing plant there."

"Well I think you'll work it out." James said.

"Would you like a bowl of homemade vegetable beef soup?" She asked.

"That sounds really good to me, Sandra." He replied.

"Let's go on in, and I'll fix some crackling cornbread to go with it." She said as she stood up. "You just sit down over there at the table and I'll pour you a glass of tea. We can talk while I put this together."

"Speaking of putting things together," James said. "Yesterday while I was driving I saw Drew walking up the sidewalk. His facial expression showed that he had something serious on his mind. I stopped and asked him where he was going. He said that David had a failing grade on a test that Drew had helped him with. The professor only gave him half credit and thought that David's answer was right. He was on his way to meet with the Chancellor to prove that the professor was wrong. I decided I'd go with him.

"Drew introduced us to the Chancellor, and the Chancellor asked us to take a seat. Sandra, I had no idea of what to expect. The way Drew presented himself, and the way he spoke to the Chancellor, I almost didn't recognize him. He had the Chancellor totally convinced that he was right, by the time the meeting ended, the Chancellor assured him that the grade would be corrected. I was impressed, and I told him that David would be so happy when his grade was changed.

"Drew told me not to say anything. David hadn't seen the test and didn't know that he had failed. He didn't want David to know. What do you think about that, Sandra?"

"Jim, that doesn't surprise me at all. I'm going to tell you something that has to stay between you and me. Will you promise to give me your word?" Sandra asked.

"You have my word." He replied.

"About three weeks ago," Sandra started. "The committee decided to interview the college graduates of engineering for a job that is opening up next year for a new professor in that department. We started sorting by the students with the highest grade and the highest IQ. We finally got down to three of our students. We made sure that we didn't know their names so that a teacher would not be biased. We flipped the number one student's folder over. It was Drew Harris. His IQ is in the top 1% of the whole school.

"A week later, the personal board brought Drew in for an interview and offered him the job. He was going to start with a salary of a second year professor. Drew thanked them for the consideration, but he turned them down. He explained that he and David Clark had already begun to make plans to start their own business. They tried to convince him what an opportunity this would be. He didn't budge, and before he left he asked that the board keep this meeting confidential.

"Now, David's folder was also impressive. The difference between the two is that when Drew has an idea for a project, he goes to any length to accomplish what he's going after. On the other hand, David stops and values the weights. He eases into the situation. They are both good for each other. It's like they've adopted each other as brothers. I've never seen two young boys look after each other like those boys do."

"I'm really looking forward to seeing them at Exum Textiles. I'm confident that they'll be an asset to the company." James said.

"Would you like some more tea?" She asked. She sat the pitcher down and ran her fingers through James' hair. "I think it's time for another haircut." James turned around and patted his lap for her to sit on. "Have I told you lately just how good-looking you are?" She asked.

"Not lately, but I enjoy hearing you say it." He replied.

"I don't know who has changed the most, James. You or me, like I told you before, I knew the first time you walked into my class; I knew you were going to be trouble.

"I don't want to give you trouble, Sandra."

"You know what I mean. Don't sit there and act like you don't know what I'm talking about."

"My mother even said she has seen a change in me. She said I seemed to be happier and not so serious. She thinks it's because of you Jim." She stood up and shuffled her hands through his hair again.

"You almost made me burn my crackling cornbread." She said as she was taking it out of the oven. She turned it out of the big black frying pan onto a plate. Bandit hopped out from under the kitchen table. "You'll get your share, Bandit. Just hang on." Sandra said.

"Well, it won't be long now." James said. As she reached up into the cabinet, James couldn't help but notice her standing on her tiptoes barefooted. She's smart, but country all the way through, James thought. Sandra took out three bowls and a coffee cup to dip the stew out of the big steel pot.

"I'm going to give Bandit a bowl first, with a little bit of cornbread mixed in. Maybe it will be cool by the time we eat." Sandra said. Bandit was standing by her side wagging his tail. "Just hang on, Bandit, let it cool down first." She put a bowl in front of James and another across the table for herself, along with two sauces for the cornbread. She cut the cornbread in pie shapes and sat it in the center of the table. "Help yourself, James." She said as she sat down a bowl for Bandit. The dog started eating the stew before the bowl had even reached the floor. "Well at least I know Bandit likes it, even if you don't, Jim."

"Well it sure looks and smells good." James said. As Sandra took James' hand to say a blessing, they could hear Bandit lapping up his bowl of stew as it was being pushed around on the floor.

"When do you think was the last time he was fed?" Sandra asked when she was done giving her blessing.

"Evidently your stew is good or it's been awhile since he's eaten." James said.

"I like to think it was because it was really good."

"Well, I'm sure it is." James said as Sandra glared at him.

"Keep it up big boy, and yours is going back into the pot."

"I know it's good, Sandra."

"How do you know?" She asked. "You haven't even tasted it yet."

"I'm just going by the way Bandit ate his." After eating his bowl of stew and his two slices of cornbread, he said "Let me just say, Sandra, that on behalf of Bandit and myself that this is the best stew I believe I have ever eaten. That crackling cornbread was fantastic. I'm impressed."

"You don't have to overdo it, Jim. It was just soup and cornbread." She said.

"It was really good, Sandra; with all joking aside."

"Well thank you. I'm glad you liked it."

"What do you say we take Little Susie and ride out into the country? It's such a nice day." James said.

"I would enjoy that." She said. "Let me change my clothes first." After Sandra changed into jeans and a turtleneck, she walked back into the kitchen.

"You sure are a fine looking woman." James said as he stood up.

"Like I've said before, Jim, you know when to say the right things at the right time." She walked over the sink, picked up a piece of cornbread that was left on her plate, and fed it to Bandit. "Well, let's get going." She said.

Chapter 31

As they got into the car, Sandra sat Bandit on top of the Coca-Cola crate and closed the door. "I'll give Bandit the window, but you'll have to watch your elbows when you change gears, if you know what I mean."

"Do I have to?" James asked when a big grin on his face.

"Yes, you have to." She replied and smiled back.

After pulling away from Sandra's house, they headed toward S. Highway 62 and Bandit barked at everyone they passed.

"I've never seen a dog enjoy riding more than Bandit. I think you've spoiled him." Sandra said.

"He's my buddy, alright."

They headed toward the two-lane road, out into the countryside. It was a winding road that split beautiful farmland. On each side, they were passing hayfields with farmhouses as they went off into the distance.

"It really is a beautiful day," Sandra said. "The sky is so blue and the way the wind is blowing the straw, it looks like the ocean."

"This is what I call a good Sunday afternoon." James said.

"Oh, look at the pumpkin field!" Sandra exclaimed. "Let's stop on the way back and get one. It has a sign that says they are for sale. I will make you the best pumpkin pie you have ever eaten."

"That sounds good to me." James said.

After driving for a while, and not having much to say, Bandit got a little bit antsy. "I think we need to stop and pull over for a few minutes, James." Sandra said. James pulled off onto the grass along the road, stopping in front of a huge field or corn. It had just been cut and bound into bundles that stood upright. There was a white fence on the east side of a gravel road that led to a small farmhouse in the distance.

As James got out, Sandra walked around and helped Bandit out of the car. He started sniffing around the ground, hopping along in the tall grass that grew along the road. Bandit had not gotten about fifteen feet, when a rabbit jumped up and darted across the field with Bandit right behind it. "My God, look at that three-legged dog run." James said.

"Can you believe that dog can run like that, with just three legs?" Sandra said.

"Well he is a beagle," James said. "That's what he does; run, rabbit, run."

The rabbit made a big circle in the field. You could see the rabbit come up and out of the grass occasionally, with Bandit behind him with his head bouncing up and down. The rabbit headed toward the road where Bandit had jumped him.

James knew that the rabbit was going to run across the road and Bandit was not going to stop chasing him. He looked up and down the road to check if there were any vehicles coming. As he looked, he saw a big flatbed truck filled with bales of straw coming over the hill. "Stay here." He said as he took off running up the road to stop the truck. Sandra hollered at Bandit and started running down the road to stop Bandit from crossing the road. James stood in the middle of the street waving to signal the truck driver to stop.

As the truck came down the hill, the truck driver tried to slow down. The back wheels slid as it went by James. The truck had gotten to where Sandra was standing, the tires still sliding. The rabbit dashed underneath the truck and came out the other side. Bandit tried to slow down, but only having one leg, he was unable to slow down in time. The truck had almost stopped when Bandit ran into the side of the back tire, knocking him under the back of the truck, and he rolled behind the truck.

James was there by the time Bandit had crashed. Bandit was lying on the side of the road, blood coming from his mouth, his legs moving, and his eyes wide open as James bent down. When the truck driver came running back from the truck he was having a hard time speaking English.

"How is he? I tried to stop! I'm sorry!" The truck driver said in broken English. James reached down and picked up Bandit. To save time, he began speaking Spanish to the truck driver. He told the driver that it was not his fault, and that he had done the best he could by trying to stop. Sandra was standing behind James, as he spoke. She could not believe how fluently James could speak Spanish, so much so that she had almost forgotten that Bandit was hurt.

The driver pulled out a business card from his wallet and handed it to James. He had told him that this was the veterinarian that looked after his livestock. James took the card and thanked the driver. Holding Bandit, James and Sandra turned around to run to the car. Sandra jumped in first and James handed Bandit to her as he got in.

"Jim, let's go up to that house on the hill." Sandra said. "I'm sure they will have a phone."

"I sure hope so." James replied.

Bandit started to try and get up out of Sandra's arms. Sandra let him sit up in her lap and lick her hand. "He seems to be feeling better," Sandra said. "How badly do you think he's hurt?"

"I don't know." James said "The truck didn't hit him, he ran into the tire."

Sandra looked at Bandit's mouth. "It looks like he cut his mouth."

"Well if we're lucky, it's not internal." James said.

As they pulled around to the back porch of the house, James jumped out of the car and hurried to the door. When he knocked on the door, an elderly gentleman answered it. He was wearing a white long-sleeved shirt and overalls.

"Good afternoon, Sir. My name is Jim. My dog just got hit by a truck and I was wondering if I could use your phone to call a veterinarian." James said.

"You sure can." The elderly man said. "Where is the dog?"

"He's out in the car."

"Well bring him in, and I'll have a look at him."

"Yes sir." James said. He turned around and walked back to the car. He picked up Bandit out of Sandra's lap. "Come on in Sandra. The man wants to see Bandit."

 As they walked up on the back porch, the elderly gentleman led them to the kitchen. He took the tablecloth off of the kitchen table. "Here, set him down on the table." James laid Bandit across the table. "My God, it knocked his leg off!" The man said.

"Oh, no sir, he was already missing a leg." James said. Bandit's mouth had stopped bleeding, and he seemed to be doing okay. The man started rubbing Bandit down his back and pressing into his back bone. As he rubbed his hands through the rest of Bandit's body, the dog never made a sound.

"It seems as though he's okay." The man said. "There are no broken bones." He lifted Bandit's head and opened the dog's mouth. "It looks like there's just a cut on the inside of his mouth. I think he'll be alright. You can call the vet tomorrow and have him check him out, but he looks good to me."

James stuck out his right hand, "Thank you sir, for letting us in and checking out our dog for us."

As the gentleman shook James' hand he said "My name is Calvin Ross. I've been around animals all of my life here on the farm. I've had dogs, cats, goats, horses, and cows. I've seen all types of injuries on this farm, so I know a little bit about animal injuries." He looked and Sandra and then shook her hand. "I'm guessing this is your wife, Jim?" He asked.

Before James could reply Sandra spoke up "No, Mr. Ross. I'm not his wife. My name is Sandra Wilson."

"Well I think he would be making a big mistake to let a pretty thing like you get away."

"Well, thank you sir. I think you're right." She said laughing as she looked over at James.

"It's nice to see two young people in love these days. I wish you both well. Next time y'all are over this way, just stop in. The old lady would be glad to meet you folks. She's up at the church with a few of her buddies. They're up there quilting, and she'll be home before dark."

"Well thank you again." James said as he started out the back door with Bandit in his arms. When they got to the car, Sandra got in first and James handed her Bandit. As they started down the gravel driveway, they waved back at Mr. Ross who was standing in the doorway.

"He was a really nice man. It's nice to know that people like that are still around." James said. When they approached the end of the driveway, Sandra asked James to stop the car and turn off the engine. "What's wrong?" James asked.

"You and I have to talk." Sandra said sternly.

"This sounds serious." James said.

"It is to me." Sandra said as she put Bandit back on his Coca-Cola crate. "I've got two questions for you."

"Okay. Ask away."

"First, how long have you been speaking Spanish? You spoke it so fluently, that it tells me that you use it quite often."

"Well, I've been speaking Spanish since I was about ten or eleven years old. The reason I speak it so well is because I speak to my customers in Mexico quite often. It makes my job easier to deal with customers when I'm able to speak their language. It's really not a big deal, Sandra."

"It just surprised me. Just when I think I'm beginning to know you, you do something like that. Then I begin thinking that I don't know you as well as I think I do, and that bothers me. Sometimes you get excited over small things that I take for granted every day. Then I think that you haven't been around much. The first day you walked into my class, you acted like you were scared to death. You looked around observing everything as if you had never been in a classroom before. I know you are a smart man, but there's just something about you that I can't figure out."

"Just don't give up on me." James said. "Now what's your next question?"

"Well back there at the house, Mr. Ross said we look like two people in love. Do you think we look like we're in love?"

"I don't know what people look like when they are in love." James said. Sandra closed her eyes and shut her mouth in a tight line. "Okay, so you want to know if we look like two people in love." James said as Sandra sat up and turned to look at him directly in the eyes.

"Sandra, I want you to listen to every word I am about to say to you. Whatever happens in the future, I want you to know this." James said and he took a deep breath. "The first time I saw you, a feeling came over me that I have never experienced in my life. When I'm with you, I can't take my eyes off of you. When I'm not with you, I can't stop thinking about you. You make me laugh, you make me happy. You are everything that a man could want in a woman. I have never been with a woman that makes me as happy as you do.

"I am thirty years old and I have never been in love before. If all of the feeling I have for you is love, then I love you with all of my heart. I'm glad some people can see it in my face." James finished. Tears were running down Sandra's face. She opened her mouth to speak, but she couldn't find the words. She reached over and put her arms around James' neck, and kissed his left cheek.

They sat there like that for a few minutes, just holding each other. Sandra wanted to tell James how she felt, but her throat was so tight, she could hardly swallow. Without saying a word, Sandra sat up in her seat and gave James a signal to start driving. She picked Bandit back up, sat him in her lap, and rubbed him as she stared out the window, not saying a word.

The car was silent all the way back to Sandra's house. James pulled up into the driveway. He got out first; Sandra picked up

Bandit and slid out behind James. By now Sandra had gathered her composure. "Can you come in for a few minutes, James? I've got something to say to you." Sandra handed Bandit to James and unlocked the door. When they got inside, she poured Bandit a bowl of water and sat it on the ground. She then motioned James to come and sit at the kitchen table with her. Sandra sat directly across from James, and he was not sure if this was going to be good or bad. James sat his hand on the table, and Sandra put her hand on top of his.

"When I was in high school, I had a boyfriend." Sandra said. "When he broke up with me, it broke my heart. I refused to go anywhere. Mom and dad were worried about me. When my dad would walk in the door he would say 'Hey baby, how are you today?' Naturally, I always told him I was fine. He said 'Honey, I know you are hurting, but you will get over it. It's something that all teenagers go through. You may fall in love a few more times before you find your true love. This love that you had for your boyfriend, its puppy love, but it still hurts, I know.'

"I didn't understand what dad meant when he said all of those things to me. I was about 17, and I thought I knew all there was to learn. I had no idea what my dad was talking about. The day you walked into my class and the first time I saw you, I could hardly speak. I remember having a hard time teaching the class because I couldn't take my eyes off of you.

"That night we were in Asheville, out at the Patio Lounge and my girlfriend was coming on to you, I came close to showing the Wilson in me that night. Believe me, that is not a pretty sight."

James started laughing. "I bet so." He said.

Sandra started speaking again. "What I'm trying to say is that I don't think, and I don't believe, but I know for a fact that I've been in love with you since the first time you walked into my class. So where do we go from here? School will be out next Friday."

"Well like I told you the other day, I've made arrangements to move back to Greensboro and work out of the corporate office. That will give us all the opportunity we want to be together." James said.

"I'm glad it's all out in the open. We know how we feel about each other, and there's no doubt in my mind anymore."

"Just keep in mind what I told you earlier. That is exactly the way I feel, and I want you to save me a date for next Saturday. I think I will be able to clear up any suspicions that you may have about me." James said.

"What do you mean by that?"

"You'll just have to wait for next Saturday. It will be a surprise for you."

"Well at this point, I am a happy woman, and nothing you say is going to change my mind about you. I feel like I'm in this relationship for the long haul, and I hope you are too."

"You can count on it." James said as he stood up. He took Sandra by the hand, and pulled her up out of her seat. He put both hands on her face and lightly kissed her lips. He looked into her eyes "I love you Sandra Wilson and you can count on that."

"I love you too James. You can count on that." Sandra replied as they embraced each other. Sandra looked at the clock. "I've got to change clothes. I've got to go back to church tonight."

"I'll take Bandit and take him to the vet in the morning." James said.

"No," Sandra said. "Let me look after him through the night, and you can pick him up in the morning."

"Well this will be the first day I'll miss a class since I nearly got my head knocked off at the Hole in the Wall." James said.

"This time it will be for a good cause."

"I'll come by early and pick him up at around 7:30" James walked over and patted Bandit on the head. He was lying on the mat in front of the kitchen sink. "See you in the morning, big boy." James turned and walked out the back door, giving Sandra a wink as he left.

As James pulled up into his driveway and climbed the steps to the front door, he could hear music coming from the back of the house. When he walked onto the porch, Drew was sitting in a rocking chair. "How was practice, Drew?" James asked.

"I tell you what, Jim, Linda has worn me out. That girl could dance all night long. We picked up a few new dance steps, and we have them down pat. She is one hell of a dancing woman, and good looking, I might add." Drew said.

James could tell by the way Drew was talking, that he had feelings for her more than just a dance partner. "Well if she dances as well as she looks, she's a good dancer." James said.

"You can say that again, Jim." Drew said. "Have you heard from David?"

"No, I just left Sandra's house. This is the first time I've been back since 11 this morning."

"Well when he left, you could smell English Leather shaving lotion from a mile away. He had those bell bottom pants on.

Those pants were flopping so fast, I think he cleaned the side walk all the way over to her house."

"So he was in a hurry." James said.

"Well, maybe he'll be home in a bit and he can give us a rundown on how it went with Malia." Drew said.

James then took a few minutes to explain everything that had happened with Bandit that day. He said he wouldn't be going to class and that he was going to take Bandit to the vet.

"Do you think he's going to be okay, Jim?" Drew asked.

"Yes, he seems fine. I'm just going to make sure." James replied.

The front door opened and David came in whistling as he walked to the back porch. He stopped in the door way and smiled as he put both hands against the frame.

"By God, he looks like a possum grinning like that." Drew said.

"Well, come on and tell us about it." James said.

"I'll tell you what, boys. She is one fine lady, but she has one problem that I've got to get used to." David said.

"What's that?" Drew asked.

"She loves country music. Her favorite singers are Conway Twitty, Loretta Lynn, and Elvis Presley. Now Elvis is fine, but the other two are going to take some time to get used to. She wanted to learn how to dance to beach music. I tried to teach her, but you can't dance to country music." David said. "So it looks like I'm going to have to start liking country music, and I'm willing to do that just to spend time with her."

"David, I cannot see you sitting around listening to Conway Twitty." Drew said.

"Well I'm going to do what it takes to be around her." David said.

"All I can say, David, is that you seem happier than I've seen you in a long time." James added.

After making small talk for a few hours, James stood up and declared he was ready to go to sleep, and Drew decided he would stay up with David.

Chapter 32

The next morning, James was up early. When he got to Sandra's house at 7:30, there was note on the door. It read 'James, I had to go to school early this morning to attend a meeting before class. Bandit slept beside the bed on the floor all night. He showed no sign of any problem this morning. I fed him and took him out. He's been blocked off inside the kitchen. Give me a call to let me know what the vet had to say. I love you. Sandra.'

James could not help but smile when he read the note. He folded it up and put in his pocket. It was his first letter with the words 'I love you' on it. When James opened the door, Bandit was standing there waiting for him. He picked Bandit up and took him to his car. James pulled out the business card from his wallet and read the address. He headed towards Burlington to Dr. Wright's Veterinarian Hospital.

When James pulled up in the parking lot, he picked Bandit up and started walking inside. When James walked in the building, there were two young ladies working at the desk. One turned around, looked at Bandit, and then looked back at James. "I can't believe it! It's Lucky!" She said as she reached over the counter and took Bandit out of James' arms. "How've you been doing, boy?" She asked as Bandit tried to lick her all over the face. The lady looked up at James and asked "Where did you find Lucky?"

"Well it's more like he found me." James replied. "I'm a student at Elon College, and that's where Bandit's home is. He belongs to the community, but he lives at the fire department in Elon."

The veterinarian stepped out from the back. He was a tall man with black hair, and a dark complexion. He looked to be in his early 40's, and he was a very distinguished looking man. He heard all of the commotion out front and came to check to see what was going on. He walked over and patted Bandit on the head. "Well, if it isn't Lucky." The man said. Bandit started to lick his hands. "Where did you find him?" He asked. Then James repeated his story to the veterinarian. "Well it's been a long time since we've seen him. I'm Dr. Wright, by the way."

"How do you know Bandit, Dr. Wright?" James asked.

"Well two young boys brought him in one day. They said that he had jumped out of a box car while the train was still moving and it snapped his leg in half. There was only a small piece of skin holding it on and he had lost a lot of blood. He was unconscious when he was brought in, so I went ahead and took the leg off. I managed to stop the bleeding and used the excess skin to sow him up. We cared for him for about two months. He got where he could get around pretty well. Everybody here named him Lucky, and one day he just disappeared. We sure did miss him. Why is he here today?" Dr. Wright asked.

After explaining to the doctor what had happened, they carried him to the back and gave him an x-ray. "Well it looks like he's in good shape." The doctor said. "No broken bones. He looks like he's been well-fed and he's been taken care of."

"Well, like I said, the whole community takes care of him." James said. "How much do I owe you?"

"You don't owe me anything for Lucky." Dr. Wright said.

"Well, Dr. Wright, this is what I'm going to do," James said. "I'm going to give you my name, phone number, and address. I'm going to give the firemen your address and ask that they bring him here. Please take care of him, and send me the bill no matter what the cost. I'm going to ask the firemen to bring him here for regular check-ups. This dog means a lot to me even though he's the community's dog. I'm going to be leaving town soon, and I want to make sure that he is taken care of."

"We'd be glad to do that for you. Just give the girls your information, and I'll take care of it." Dr. Wright said.

After James filled out the information, the girls handed Bandit back to James. James thanked them for their help and the information they gave to him about Bandit. As James was driving back to Elon, Bandit seemed to be acting like his old self. His paws were hanging out of the window, and he barked to everyone as they passed. James stopped at the fire department. The firemen came walking out and picked Bandit up out of the car. He sat Bandit down and the dog started hopping inside. They had been worried about Bandit, and after James explained the accident to them, he gave Dr. Wright's business card to one of the men. He told them that Friday would be his last day and that he had made arrangements with Dr. Wright.

The firemen thanked James, and told him that they would be glad to see that Bandit would be taken care of. They hoped that James would come back and visit with them the next time he was in the area.

James pulled out from the fire department and waved back to the firemen. As James crossed over the railroad tracks he looked over at the little garage where it all began. When he drove back home, he reminisced about all the places he had been. He remembered the soda shop, where he had his first vanilla coke. He remembered the TM Clothing Store where he bought his first pair of khaki pants and banlon shirts. He remembered Edward's Shoe Store where he bought his first pair of loafers. In the distance he could see the bulldozers clearing the land near the old library for the new addition.

James knew the time was coming near that he would be leaving this place where he'd had the happiest memories of his life and it made him feel sad. He also knew a happier life would be beginning with Sandra, David, and Drew. He knew this would be his home away from home.

When James arrived at his house, he opened the front door to hear the phone was ringing. "This is Jim." He said.

"Well how are you, Jim?" Sandra's voice said on the other end.

"Well, how are you today, Miss. Wilson?" He asked. They both laughed.

"I just wanted to know how Bandit checked out. I saw you headed home, but I couldn't see Bandit with you."

"He checked out fine. I let him off at the fire department. I think he was glad to be back, and all the firemen had been worried about him. I explained everything to them, and said that Bandit was fine."

"Well I guess I should get back to class. I also have a meeting this afternoon concerning the new library. I probably won't be able to talk to you until tomorrow morning. I've missed you so much today."

"I've missed you too, Sandra. I enjoyed our time together yesterday. I hope you have a good day and I'll see you in the morning." James said.

"Okay, you do the same." Sandra replied. Then she lowered her voice. "I love you." she whispered.

"I love you, too." James replied.

After hanging up the phone, James walked out onto the back porch, sat in the rocking chair, and thought. That had been the first time a woman had told him that she loved him, and truly meant it. He sat on the porch for a while with the radio on when the front door abruptly opened.

"Jim?" David's voice called from inside the house.

"I'm in here, David." James called.

As David walked out onto the back porch, he was a little out of breath. "What's up, David?" James asked.

"I'm going to grab a quick shower and then I'm going over to Malia's house. I left Drew talking to Linda outside of the classroom. I think he's going over to her house tonight to practice some new dance steps. I think he's practicing something other than dance steps, if you know what I mean." David said.

A few minutes later, James could hear the shower running and David's voice echoing from the bathroom. Later, David stepped into the doorway." How do I look?" David asked. He had on black slacks, a maroon sweater with a white button down collar, and a long sleeved shirt on.

"Man, it's obvious you dress to impress." James replied.

"You can say that again."

"Would you like me to drive you to her house?"

"No thanks, Jim. I think I'll walk over to her house. It may give me chance to calm down. I don't want to act too excited about seeing her."

"I understand, David." James said. "Are you guys going out anywhere tonight?"

"No, but I think I will hear a lot of Conway Twitty and Loretta Lynn. When I'm looking at her, though, I never hear the songs."

"Well if you need me, I'll be hanging around. I think I'm going to stay in tonight."

"Okay, see you later Jim." David said as he walked out.

A few minutes later, the phone started ringing again. James picked up the phone "This is Jim."

"James?" The voice said on the other end. James recognized it immediately.

"J.J., how are you?" He asked.

"The question is, James, how are you?" J.J. asked.

"I'm doing fine."

"Are you ready to get back to work?"

"I must say, J.J., I am ready to get back to work. Thanks to you, I've had the best experience of my life. I've definitely learned there's more to life than just working 18 hours a day."

"That's great, James." J.J. said. "There are a couple of things I need to run by you. Can you talk?"

"Yes."

"James, I would like for you and I to have this conversation in French for confidential reasons."

"That's fine." James said.

"You're going to have to speak slowly though. I'm a little rusty at it. It's been awhile." J.J. said.

"Would you rather speak Spanish, J.J.?"

"No, French is fine."

"Okay. Let's do it. It reminds me from when we were little kids." James said.

"I wanted to know if it would be problem if I used your jet on Wednesday." J.J. asked.

"Absolutely not, J.J.," James said. "You're welcome to it anytime you want. Is there a problem?"

"James, trust me when I say I can't discuss it now over the phone. I will explain everything to you when I see you." J.J. replied.

"Do I need to come up and see you now?" James asked.

"No, stay right where you are. There's nothing you can do right now. Just trust me." J.J. said.

"You know you have my total trust." James replied.

"Good. This is what I'd like for you to do, James. I understand that you are taking Drew and David to Myrtle Beach on Friday. You'll be back on Saturday, right?"

"Yes."

"You're going to have dinner with Sandra Saturday night, right?"

"That's right." James said.

"Well I want you to stick to that plan. You and I can talk on Sunday. Will that be okay with you, James?"

"That would be fine, J.J.." James said. "Does this have anything to do with Grammy?"

"No, but this is what I've done concerning mom. She's not eating right and she's not taking her medication like she should. I've asked Mr. Carter to keep a close check on her and stay in the house as much as he can.

"I got Miss Alston, the company nurse, to go over and stay with her to make sure she's taking her medicine on time and to keep her away from those pancake sausages she's been making. She's known Miss Alston for years, so she doesn't have a problem with her being over there. So everything has been taken care of and I should be back by Wednesday afternoon." J.J. said.

"Well that's great J.J.. I don't know what I would do without you. Thank you so much for all that you do."

"Everything has been taken care of, so you just go ahead and enjoy this last week and I'm looking forward to having you back, buddy."

"It's going to be nice to be back in the old house with you and Grammy. I'll call you before I leave on Friday." James said.

"By the way," J.J. said, "There have been a couple of reporters asking for you. I've been telling them you are taking an extended vacation. Of course, they want to know where, and one of them already knows your jet is in a hangar in Raleigh. I'm going to have Roy fly it to Greensboro early on Wednesday morning to pick me up. When I get back from New York I'm going to have it back in Greensboro. To tell you the truth, James, I didn't think you could pull this off for three months."

"I guess you could say I've just been lucky J.J., and it's been one of the best three months of my life."

"Well, you have a good week. I'll talk to you later, James."

"By the way, J.J., you did a great job speaking French. I'm impressed." James said.

"You did a good job teaching me." J.J. replied.

They said their goodbyes and hung up the phone. James grabbed a beer out of the refrigerator and went back to the porch to sit on his rocking chair. He thought about the conversation he had with J.J.. He knew something serious was going on in the company business that J.J. could not discuss, but he also knew that if J.J. needed him, he would let him know. James thought it must be pretty serious if J.J. wanted to speak in French. He was also happy that Miss Alston was going to be looking after Granny; it was a relief off of his shoulders.

Chapter 33

James heard the sound of the front door opening. Linda walked out onto the patio first. "Hey James, how are you doing?" She asked.

"I'm doing fine, Linda. How are you?" James asked.

"I'm doing great. We had to come by and get Drew's dance shoes. We're going over to my place to practice some new dance steps." Linda said.

Drew walked up behind Linda with the shoes in his left hand and his right arm around her shoulder. Linda took her right hand and put it up on Drew's arm. James could tell that their friendship had ended and a relationship had begun. He could see the affection on both of their faces.

"I may be getting in late." Drew said.

"I understand." James said. He looked at Linda who had a big smile on her face.

"Are you going out tonight?" Drew asked.

"No, I think I'm going to stay here and listen to some music before I go to bed. Tomorrow is the last day and I want to be at my best."

"Okay then." Drew said. "We're out of here. If you're up when I get in, I'll see you tonight."

James was up earlier than usual. He could hear one of the guys taking a shower. James put on his tan khakis and his white long sleeved shirt. He thought he would wear Sandra's favorite sweater, the baby blue cashmere that she liked so much. It would be his last day and he wanted to look his best. James stepped out into the hallway and headed toward the kitchen where Drew sat eating a bowl of cereal.

"I don't feel like fixing breakfast this morning, Jim." Drew said. "Grab yourself a bowl and make yourself some cereal."

James shook his head. "For some reason I'm not hungry this morning. I think I'll take my time and just walk on to class."

"Okay. I'll see you this afternoon, Jim."

As James walked out the front door, he looked at Little Susie parked in the driveway. Frost was on the windshield and James thought to himself that it was a little cooler than it normally is. He then walked down the steps onto the sidewalk

James was about the only person who was out and about at that time in the morning although it was daylight and the sun was shining. His breath gave out a little white mist of air. As James crossed over to the other side of the road on to the campus grounds, there was a tree branch on his left that had fallen out of one of the oak trees. There were a couple of red birds pecking at it, trying to eat the insects that may have been hidden beneath the bark. As the frost was beginning to melt, it looked like diamonds had been scattered all over the ground.

Some students were beginning to arrive at the school. As some took shortcuts across the grass, they were leaving footprints across the frost. James continued walking on the sidewalk and up the steps. When he looked down, he noticed he was not wearing any socks. He criticized himself as he opened the tall wooden doors and walked down the hall to enter his classroom. No one was there, not even Sandra. James walked over to the window and watched as all of the students crossed the streets. They were laughing and James thought that they were having the best times of their lives and they didn't even know it. James leaned sideways against the window with his arms folded in front of him.

As Sandra started into her class, she noticed her classroom door had been left open. She walked up to the door and stopped as she watched James look out the window. She could only see one side of his face and his black hair was still wet from his morning shower. It looked as if he just ran his fingers through his hair rather than use a comb. The way the sunlight shone through the window, it made a perfect side profile of his face. Sandra thought he could pose for a magazine. She thought he was a very handsome man, and she took a deep breath before she entered the room.

"Well good morning, Jim." She said. "What a pleasant surprise, and I love that sweater on you."

"Oh, I just thought I would throw this old thing on since it was so cold outside." James said.

"I bet you did." They laughed together.

"I thought I would just come in early and soak up my surroundings on the way here. It's such a beautiful town. I'm going to miss it."

"There are a lot of people around here that will miss you too. I hope you won't become a stranger here."

"Are you saying you'd like to see more of me?" James asked. Sandra closed her eyes and gritted her teeth, and James knew what that look meant. The students started coming into class.

"You can come by the house tonight around 6. I have a staff meeting and I won't be home till about 5:30." Sandra said.

"Sure, I'll be there at 6." James said.

As class began, Sandra informed the students that their final semester grade would be posted outside her door. She then gave a farewell speech to the class and advised them that they would be getting their letters in the mail on Friday concerning the graduation ceremony. After about 45 minutes, she dismissed the class and wished them well.

As James walked down the sidewalk, a lot of the students were running toward the soda shop. As they ran, some stopped and said good morning to him. Some were still calling him the fireman and asking him where Bandit was. James then realized that he and Bandit had become the talk of the town.

"Hey, Jim," A voice called from behind him. When James turned around, Drew and David were running across campus grounds towards him. "Hold on a minute!" They said as they caught up to him. "Well, it's all over boys." Drew said.

"You can say that again." David said.

"You guys want to go down to the Hole in the Wall and have a few beers while we eat?" Drew asked.

"I bet that place is going to be packed tonight." David said.

"I've got to meet Sandra at her house at 6. So I will be able to be there around 7. By the way, hold the tab for me. This one is on me tonight, and you're welcome to invite your girls." James said.

"You're on, moneybags!" David said. "I'm bringing Malia."

"I'm going to go home and take a nap. I didn't get into bed until about 1:30 this morning." Drew said.

Later, the guys left for the Hole in the Wall while James left for Sandra's house. James pulled up in her driveway right on time. He walked up to the side door and knocked on the door. When Sandra opened the door she was holding a glass of wine. "Come on in, Jim. Want a glass of wine?"

"That sounds good." James said. "Give me whatever you're having."

Sandra was still wearing her clothes she had worn that day. Her shoes were kicked off and she was walking around the house barefooted. "How was your day?" Sandra asked.

"It was okay. The guys were excited about the last day. Drew didn't get in until late last night, so he took a nap. David and I sat around and talked business. He really has a good business sense. I think those guys will be fine at Exum Textiles, and they're excited about working there. The only thing that Drew has on his mind is the dance competition at Myrtle Beach. How was your day?" James asked.

"Busy. I had a lot of filing to do to make preparations for the graduation. Then I had a quick staff meeting about the library. By the way, I was told today that two men were over there inquiring about James Andrew Exum."

"Is that right?"

"Yes. They wanted to know if he'd be at the college since they started breaking ground on the library. The Dean told them that he wasn't here, but he may be here at the Grand Opening. That's about nine months away. They kept questioning him. When the Dean didn't give them the information they wanted they turned around and walked out. They seemed strange to the Dean."

"It must have been some reporters." James said.

"Well it could have been. They must've been from up north because they had a northern accent." Sandra said. "Would you like a sandwich?"

"No thank you. I promised the boys I would meet them down at the Hole in the Wall to celebrate their last day."

"Well that's nice. Be sure you stay out of trouble. You remember what happened last time, don't you?"

"Oh yes. That won't happen again." James said.

"I'm going in the den, propping my feet up, and having myself a glass of wine. I'll probably be going to bed early. I've got to go to work in the morning. It will be Monday by the time I'll have any time off. If you want to come by tomorrow, we can go out and have a sandwich somewhere." Sandra said.

"That sounds good to me. I'll meet you here tomorrow afternoon. I'm going to go on down to the Hole in the Wall and have a beer. I'll see you tomorrow."

As James stood up to leave, Sandra sat down her glass of wine and put her arms around James. She laid her head against his chest while James held her tight. "I love you, Jim." She whispered.

"I love you too," James replied. He lifted her chin up and kissed her lightly on the lips. "And don't you forget that, Sandra Wilson."

As James walked outside and got inside his car, Sandra was standing at the door waving at him. When he pulled out of the driveway he thought about how Sandra had said that she loved him. He hoped that she would still love him after she found out that he was really James Andrew Exum. As he turned the corner and headed toward the Hole in the Wall, he could see the glare of the lights in the distance. Drew was right, the place was packed. When James finally found a parking spot, he could hear the music playing from inside. It sounded like the jukebox had been turned all the way up. A lot of laughing and talking was coming from the inside.

All James could think about was what Sandra had said to him. James thought that he should be home with Sandra instead of being here, but he promised the guys and the drinks were on him. As James opened the door, a gray haze covered the room with smoke. James started making his way through the crowd and Beth stepped in front of him with a tray of beer bottles. "Follow me, Jim," she said.

James followed right behind her as she maneuvered herself through the crowd. Beth led him to the table where David and Drew were sitting. Drew pushed David with his elbow, and everyone slid down one seat. Drew reached down and set up a chair that had been folded underneath the table. "Hey, buddy! You made it!" Drew said.

"This is Malia." David said as he leaned back in his seat. Malia stuck out her hand to shake James' hand.

"I've heard a lot about you, Jim. It's nice to meet you." Malia said.

James shook her hand. "It's nice to meet you too, Malia. I've heard a lot about you as well." He said. There was no use in trying to make conversation. It was too loud and crowded. Beth sat a beer in front of James, and then he felt two hands on his shoulders. When he looked up, he saw Helen. "Hey, Helen, how are you?" He asked.

"I'm fine. How are you doing, handsome?" She replied.

"I'm doing well."

"Are you going to dance with me tonight?" Helen asked.

"If there's room out there, I'll dance with you." James replied.

"We'll make room when the right song comes on."

Linda then reached over and patted James hand. "Hey Linda," James said.

"There's so much damn smoke in here. I can hardly see you." Linda said. "I'm glad you could make it."

"Thank you." James replied.

After a couple of hours of drinking beer, Linda and Drew became a little cuddlier. David only danced with Malia when there was a slow song on. Helen and James danced to a couple of songs by The Tams.

James sat down, sipped on his beer, and watched Drew and Linda dance. After a few minutes, someone tapped him on the shoulder. When James looked up, he saw it was John Wiley, the guy who lived next door.

"Hey Jim," John said as he held out his hand.

"Hey John," James said as he took John's hand.

John pulled James up and whispered into James' ear. "That guy standing over near the jukebox with the white t-shirt was the guy who kicked you in the head when you were pulled out of here."

"How do you know that was him?" James asked.

"I know the two guys he's talking with. I was over there when he told the guys that the last time he was here, there was a fight and he kicked some guy's head. He said that this is the first time he's been back since the fight. He's been out of college for about 4 years, but I don't know what his real name is. I know that everyone calls him Bull because he played football for Elon. He was the defensive tackle, and a pretty good one I understand. I was told he was a bad ass." John said.

James looked over in the direction of the guy. He could see why he was a defensive tackle. He was a pretty good sized young man. The t-shirt he had on showed off his muscles, and he could tell that the guy like to show off. "I think I'll go over and ask him for an apology." James said.

"Jim, I don't think I would go over there, now that he's had a few beers. He gets mean as hell when he's drinking, and you can bet your ass he's not going to apologize to you."

"We'll see."

As James walked through the crowd, Drew watched James walk up to Bull. He knew the look on James' face, and that this wasn't going to be a good meeting. Drew stopped dancing and walked over to David. He tapped David on the shoulder and motioned for him to come with Drew. David never questioned Drew, so he got up and started walking with him towards James' direction.

James tapped Bull on the shoulder. James lifted his voice towards Bull's ear to make sure he could hear over the music. "I understand that a few weeks ago, you kicked a man in the head while he was down on the floor. Is that right?" James asked.

"Who's asking?" Bull asked as all of his friends watched.

"The guy who you kicked in the head. I'm here for an apology."

"Well you're going to have to wait a long time before you get an apology from me." Bull said.

Drew and David walked up and listened. "Why don't you come with me outside so I can hear your apology?" James said.

"I'll come outside with you, but this time I'm not going to kick your head, I'm going to kick your ass." Bull replied.

As James started walking towards the front door, Drew put his hand on James' shoulder. "Jim, don't go out there. This guy is one mean son of a bitch." Drew said.

"It seems like I've heard that before." James replied.

"If you're going, David and I are going with you." Drew said.

"Fine you can go, but you can't get involved. This is between me and him."

Bull, his two friends, Drew, David, and James headed for the front door. Everybody inside seemed to know what was going to happen, so everyone followed them to the front door. When they got outside, Bull turned around and said "Okay, pretty boy. Are you ready to get your ass kicked again?"

"All of this could be avoided if you would just apologize to me." James replied.

"The only apology you're going to get is my fist upside your head." Bull said as people formed a circle around them. Bull made a quick swing at James' head with his right fist. James blocked the swing by throwing up his left arm, simultaneously taking his right hand and grabbing Bull by the throat, squeezing his windpipe. Bull's eyes become big, his mouth gaped open, and his face contorted in plain.

Bull gradually went down on his knees with his mouth open and looking directly at James. "Do you apologize?" James asked as he looked down. Bull nodded his head as best as he could.

"That's all I wanted, Bull. Apology accepted." James said as he let go of Bull's throat. Bull fell forward clutching his throat. James reached down to help him up onto his feet. "Take him to his car. He'll be alright in a few minutes." James said as he turned towards the bar.

Drew ran up beside James. "What did you do to him?"

"I got his attention, is all." James said.

"That is the damnedest thing that I have ever seen." Drew said. "Where did you learn how to do that?"

"It's a long story. I'll tell you all about it sometime." James said. As he walked inside, Beth was standing at the door.

"I'm glad you put that son of a bitch in his place." Beth said. "That has been coming for a long time."

"I'd like to apologize. I didn't mean to cause a scene and disrupt everyone." James said.

"That's okay, Jim. A lot of people around here are glad to see it happen. He's bullied just about everyone who has come into this bar, so maybe this will teach him a lesson."

"Let me pay the check for Drew, David, and their girls." When James finished paying, he walked up to the bar with David and Drew. Linda, Helen, and Malia walked up to them.

"What happened out there, Drew?" Linda asked.

"Oh, Jim took the Bull by the throat and put him on his knees. That's the best way to describe it." Drew said.

"Girls, I apologize for the disruption. I didn't mean to cause a disturbance." James said. He turned to Drew and David, "You guys stay and have a good time. I'm going to head home. I think I've caused enough trouble for tonight."

As James headed for the door, Drew turned to David. "I didn't think Jim had it in him. I've never seen anybody move so fast."

"He just acts easy-going. I've never seen him become mad or upset." David said.

"He didn't act mad when he grabbed Bull by the throat. After Bull tried to throw a sucker punch, he was so calm about it."

"I wonder where he learned that stuff."

"I don't know, but it works."

When James got home, he went straight to his room. He could still smell cigarette smoke in his clothes. After taking a shower, he laid down on his bed thinking about the altercation he had with Bull.

He was not proud of what he had done; he had never been in a situation where he had to be physical before. He knew it could have been avoided if he would have stayed in his seat, and hadn't approached Bull. He had forgotten about the kick in the head from Bull, but he thought it was the fact that Bull was bragging about it that had made him upset. He thought it was his pride. His dad had always tried to teach him that it took a better man to walk away from a fight.

On the other hand, he had seen to it that he was the one who was defending himself. He had taken self-defense classes in case he was put into that situation. It doesn't take a smart person to do what he had done, which bothered him the most.

Chapter 34

J.J. pulled up to the Greensboro Airport Wednesday morning at 4 am. There was very little activity going on and the fog had not lifted. It was cold enough that J.J. had to put on a light-weight leather jacket. After locking his car, J.J. turned around to see a dark figure in front of him. "Good morning…" The voice hesitated, "J.J." It was Detective Clark's voice coming from the figure. He was wearing a trench coat with his hat on.

"Damn, Clark. You scared the shit out of me, sneaking up on me like that." J.J. said. Clark started laughing. "I've never seen you with all of that get up on. You look like Dick Tracey." J.J. said.

"You look like Warren Beatty with that black jacket and black slacks." Clark said laughing.

As they walked onto the tarmac, a golf cart pulled up beside them with Roy the pilot driving. "Get in." He said. "I'll give you a lift."

"Thanks, Roy." J.J. said. "This is Mr. Clark."

"How are you doing, Roy?" Clark said.

"I'll be better after we get above this fog and level off in some clear sky." Roy replied.

"My God, I thought it was going to be a small jet. I didn't think it was going to be this big." Clark said as they pulled up to the plane.

"James only goes first class, Clark." J.J. said.

"It's beautiful." Clark said as they got off of the golf cart. The plane was solid white with the Exum coat-of-arms painted on the door and tail fin. The steps of the plane were down and ready for boarding.

"Let's go, fellows." Roy said. "It's time to get going."

As J.J. and Clark boarded the plane, Clark stopped and viewed the interior. It has a sofa and recliner with a mahogany oval table in the center, all done in tan leather. In the back was a full bed with a built-in desk and wing-back chair.

"Fellas, have a seat and buckle up. After we level off, you can unfasten your seat belts." Roy said.

Clark sat in the recliner and buckled up. J.J. sat on the edge of the sofa and buckled his as well. In just a few minutes, the plane had broken through the clouds and leveled off into the dark blue sky.

After a few minutes, Roy came walking back. "Mr. Clark, J.J., there is some wine, soft drinks and other beverages over here if you care for anything." He opened a cabinet door near the entrance way going toward the back of the plane.

"Who the hell is flying the plane?" Clark asked.

Roy grinned, "It's on automatic pilot, Mr. Clark."

"What kind of plane is this?" Mr. Clark asked in astonishment.

"It's a Grumman G159 manufactured in Bethany, New York. They just finished it about 3 months ago. James has had it on order for about a year." Roy replied.

"I don't want anything to drink now," Clark chuckled, "but if things go well in New York, I'll have two or three hard drinks on the flight back."

.J.J looked over at Clark, "and I'll have two or three with you!"

Clark looked around the plane. "I'll tell you one thing, J.J. Mr. Exum knows how to go first class."

"That's the way he is when it comes to business. Everything he does is top-notch. I think that's why we're so successful. James is always looking to the future and ways to stay ahead in the textile industry."

"What's he doing going to Elon College? Is he teaching down there or what?"

"Well," J.J. replied, "Let's just say he is trying to catch up on some of the past he missed growing up. Don't forget, he won't be 31 until May."

"Only 31?" Clark asked, "Well he must have a good head on his shoulders."

Roy stepped through the door again, "Ok, fellas buckle up. We'll be landing in about ten minutes."

"Now, buddy, that's fast." Clark said. "We've only been in the air about an hour."

As the plane landed, J.J. looked out the window and saw a passenger helicopter sitting near the hangar where they were headed. "Well, it looks like our second ride is ready."

Roy taxied the plane into the hangar and opened the door. The steps folded out for J.J. and Clark's decent. The pilot stood in the hangar wearing a jumpsuit. "This way, Mr. Jackson," he said as he shook J.J.'s hand.

In what seemed like minutes, the helicopter landed downtown on top of the professional building. J.J. led Clark to an elevator and pushed the button to the 82nd floor.

"How many offices does James have on the floor?" Clark asked.

"We have the whole 82nd floor. I think there are a total of 53 offices on that floor." J.J. replied.

The elevator doors opened right into the main lobby of Exum Textiles.

They walked down the hall and J.J. took out his keys to open the glass door labeled 'James Exum, President and CEO' in gold leaf script.

"My God, what an office," Clark exclaimed. "Look at the view of the city. Isn't that a sight?"

As Clark looked around, he picked up a small picture from James' desk. In the photo, James and J.J. stood with their arms around a black lady who stood smiling in the center.

"That's me and James," J.J. explained, "He was about 16, I was about 19. It was my first year in college and I was home for the weekend and mom just had to have a picture of the both of us together. My mom is the only mother James knows. She raised the both of us."

"Well now I know why you two are so close." Mr. Clark said.

"He's like a younger brother to me. That's why I'm doing this without his knowledge. Besides, if he got hurt in any way, the first thing my mother would want to know is where I was and why didn't I help." J.J. sat the picture back down and led Clark out into the hall. "Jason's office is right down here on the left. He's usually here at about 8:30."

"He may decide to be in a little earlier this morning." Clark said.

"You're probably right," agreed J.J.

J.J. and Clark walked down the hall. J.J. took out his master key to open Jason's office door but when he placed the key in the lock, it would not turn. He tried again. The key was supposed to unlock every door on this floor.

"I think he's changed the lock," J.J. surmised.

"He probably has," Clark said.

"Well it's only about 7:15. We'll go back to James' office and wait. It's still early."

Back in James' office, Clark asked "What's the distance from his office door to his desk?"

"Probably about 20 to 30 feet."

"Okay," decided Clark, "This is what we've got to do. After he comes in and goes to his office, we'll wait until we hear the phone ring. That should be the truck driver calling to tell him that all has gone well. After he hangs up, we'll give him a minute and then we will walk up to the door, knock and open the door. If the door is locked, that's fine. When he opens the door, I will step in with you and make the arrest. If the door opens when you turn the knob, then go in and I will wait outside for a few seconds. I want to give him time to settle down. He's going to be surprised to see you anyway this early in the morning. After he's over the initial shock, and you have time to be at his desk, then I'll enter and make the arrest. The point is I don't want both of us to walk in at the same time if the door is unlocked. After the phone call, he's probably going to be a little bit jumpy and I don't want to have to cross 20 or 30 feet of floor before I can reach his desk. Just those 20 feet could give him time to pull a weapon or do something stupid before I get to him."

A few minutes later, they heard the elevator door open. J.J. reached up and turned the lamp off. They could see a shadow as Jason walked past the office door. Then they heard him open his own office door and close it. Quietly, they opened the door leaving out of James' office and made their way to Jason's office. They stood there a few minutes until they heard the phone ring. Then, they could hear Jason pick up the phone. He said "That's good," waited a few moments and hung up.

Clark glanced down at his watch. By this time, the arrests were being made at the warehouses in Greensboro and Asheville. It was time to make their move.

J.J. knocked on the door and turned the knob. It opened. As J.J. walked in, Jason stood up from behind the desk. "What in the world are you doing here so early, J.J.?" Jason asked.

"Just had some things I needed to go over with you first thing." J.J. replied.

Jason sat back down in his leather recliner. "Have a seat," he said, motioning his right hand towards the chair in front of his desk.

Just then, Clark walked in and strode up to Jason's desk. Jason looked up with a puzzled expression on his face. "Who are you?" he demanded.

"Jason Harard?" Clark asked.

"Yes?"

"I am Special Agent Clark with the Federal Bureau of Investigation. You are under arrest for the embezzlement of textile fabrics from Exum Textile companies in Asheville and Greensboro, North Carolina." He reached down and took Jason by his right arm. "Put both hands on the desk and step back. Spread your legs." Clark commanded.

Jason stepped back and places both hands on his desk. Clark began to search his upper body for weapons. He moved down Jason's legs to his ankles, patting him for any concealed weapons. Suddenly, Jason took his right hand and opened the top right hand desk drawer and pulled out a pistol.

When J.J. saw the pistol in Jason's hand, he dove over the desk and grabbed the gun with both hands causing Jason to fall backwards over Clark. J.J. held on to the weapon, refusing to let it go. As Jason struggled to get loose, the gun went off. The bullet struck a trash can and then ricocheted off a metal filing cabinet.

As J.J. and Jason wrestled with the gun, Clark pulled out his own weapon and put it to Jason's head. "Let go of that damn gun or I'm going to blow your damn head off!"

Jason immediately stopped struggling. Clark laid Jason on the floor on his stomach. J.J. took the gun from his hands as Clark handcuffed him.

"You have the right to remain silent," began Clark. "Anything you say or do will be used against you in the court of law. Do you understand these rights as I have stated to you?"

"Yes." Panted Jason, "and I want my damn attorney right now."

J.J. followed as agent Clark walked Jason down the hall by his arm. They could hear the phone ringing in James' office. J.J.

opened the door and Clark sat Jason down in the chair. Clark picked up the phone and answered, "This is Agent Clark."

"Clark, this is Thompson in Greensboro. Everything went well here, our man is in custody. The same is true for Asheville. All is secure down south."

"That's good news," Clark said, "I'll talk to you later."

Clark hung up the phone and looked over at J.J.. "Now if I could just hear from the guys at the warehouse."

He had no more than gotten the words out of his mouth when the phone rang. It was Hank, telling him the truck driver had been arrested at the phone booth. They had him in custody and were on their way to the Police Station. As J.J. sat in the chair, keeping his eye on Jason, he looked down at the floor and noticed there was blood. He held up his hands to see where it was coming from. He turned his hands over and saw blood dripping from his left index finger and raised his hand. There were two small holes in his leather jacket. Clark, who had just hung up the phone, had noticed them as well and instructed him to his jacket off so he could have a look.

J.J. stood and took his jacket off; his shirt sleeve was soaked with blood. Clark took him by the hand and rolled his sleeve up. There was a one inch gash in his left arm.

"Looks like the bullet just grazed you." Clark said.

J.J. took out his handkerchief and pressed it against the wound to stop the bleeding. "I think you'll be okay." Clark said. "It's just a flesh wound."

"I didn't even feel it; I just saw the blood on the floor."

"You have a lot of adrenaline flowing."

Fifteen minutes went by with J.J. and Clark staring at the phone while J.J. held his handkerchief on the wound. Finally, the phone rang. It was McGuiness.

"It's about damned time, you had me worried," Clark said.

"Well, when we came off the truck, they scattered like rats." McGuiness replied. "We had to run two of them down the alley. I just got back and I'm still out of breath, but we hit pay dirt. We have the counterfeit money… Everything we need to wrap this deal up. I've also called the shipyard to pick up this container and get it to the freighter to get it down to Atamoros. I just hope they have as good of luck down there as we've had up here."

"So do I," Clark agreed. "As soon as you wrap up things there, meet me at the Exum corporate offices."

Clark hung up the phone, "Well, J.J., it looks like everything has gone as planned; except you getting shot in the arm. Do you want me to take you over to the hospital and have the doctor take a look at it?"

"No, it stopped bleeding. I'll take care of it when I get home."

"Well, the city detective is on his way over to pick up Jason. As soon as that's done, we'll take a break."

Chapter 35

It was 8:45 when James stepped out of the shower. He could hear David and Drew talking in the kitchen. After he was dressed, he went down to the kitchen where they were having coffee. When he walked in, Drew said "Well if it ain't Gorgeous George!"

"Who's Gorgeous George?" James asked.

"He's a famous wrestler," Drew replied. "He used a sleeper hold on everybody. He could put them on their knees and put them to sleep, just like you did to Bull."

"Well I didn't mean to put him to sleep, I just took the air out of him." James chuckled.

"Well, it was the damndest thing I ever saw." Drew laughed. "It looked like a wrestling move to me. I almost came out of my shoes when you did that. Where did you learn to do that?"

"It's a long story," James answered. "I'll tell you about it some other time."

"The coffee is in the pot," David said, "help yourself."

"I could sure use a cup of coffee this morning." James said. "I'm not proud of what took place last night, fellas. I could have handled it better than what I did."

"He kicked you in the head for no reason," David said, "and then he was down there bragging about it. I say he had it coming"

"Well that type of action doesn't prove anything. I've always been told it takes a better man to walk away from something like that. I let my pride get in the way and wasn't thinking clearly. And a smart person could have handled it better than I did."

There was a knock at the door.

"Who could that be, this time of morning?" Drew wondered aloud.

"It's 9:30, Drew. It's time for everybody to be up." David said as he headed to the door.

As David opened up the door, there stood Sandra wearing blue jeans and a turtle-neck sweater. David could tell she wasn't in a good mood. She had a serious look on her face.

"He's in the kitchen having coffee," David said.

James met her in the hallway, still sipping his coffee. "Good morning, sunshine." He said.

Sandra just looked him up and down. "Well I see your eyes aren't blue and closed like last time. What got in to you, Jim?"

"News travels fast, doesn't it?" James quipped.

"I was leaving a meeting this morning when two students stopped and told me all about it," Sandra said. "I didn't know what to expect. It seems to me you would have learned your lesson the first go around."

"I have to admit it wasn't smart of me," James said. "But I think pride and beer got in the way of rational thinking."

"So you're okay? He didn't hit you?" Sandra asked. "I know that young man. He was a defensive tackle for Elon, they called him 'Bull' because he's so big and strong. He would just run over people like a raging bull."

"Well he didn't act like a raging bull last night," Drew commented. "He acted like a little baby calf when Jim got through with him."

"Did you hit him?" Sandra asked.

"No, I didn't throw a single punch." James assured her.

"Are you telling me there wasn't a fight?" Sandra asked.

"I'm just saying there wasn't much to it." James said.

Sandra just gave him a puzzled look. "Well, at least you didn't get hurt this time."

"Oh," James grinned. "Were you worried about me?"

Sandra narrowed her eyes and bit down on her bottom lip.

"Okay, okay, okay!" James laughed, putting his hands on her shoulders reassuringly. "So what are you up to this fine Wednesday morning?" James asked, trying to change the subject.

"I've got to go down to Burlington to pick up a few groceries at A&P," she said. "Then go by the drugstore to pick up a few things. Would you like to ride with me? We won't be gone but a couple of hours."

James grabbed his jacket. Sandra turned down his collar for him. "Want me to drive?" James asked when they got out to her car."

"No, I'll drive." Sandra said. "I know where I want to go and I know my way around Burlington better than you do. You just sit over there and look handsome."

Sandra pulled out and headed back through the town on Highway 70 into Burlington. James noticed all the other students loading things into their parent's cars. Some were carrying televisions, some carried cinderblocks they used to sit their bed on in each hand.

"Have you ever been to Burlington, Jim?" Sandra asked.

"This will be my first time."

"You mean in the three months you've been here, you've never been to Burlington?"

"I've never had a reason to come down here before" He said. "I've always been headed in the opposite direction, into Greensboro."

Sandra drove over a small incline then put on the brakes. There was a Burlington city Police car with blue lights flashing and a policeman standing outside the car detouring traffic off Highway 70.

"Wonder what's going on?" Sandra asked.

"Pull up close and ask him." James suggested.

Sandra pulled up next to him and asked what was going on.

"We have a lot of folks marching in honor of Dr. Martin Luther King Jr.," The officer said. "They want the city to name a road after him. The city council is meeting tonight so they are all marching towards the city hall to encourage them to vote to name a certain highway in his honor."

They could see that the road was full of people both black and white, all walking towards the town with their arms locked together singing slogans that Sandra and James were too far away to understand.

"Thank you, officer." Sandra said as she followed the detour around the march.

"I sure hope the city council votes to name the street after Mr. King." Sandra said. "Lord knows he paid the ultimate sacrifice. April 4th, 1968 will be a date that no one should forget."

"Well now I won't" James said. "It was a sad day. As I think back, Bobby Kennedy was killed June 5th, just about two months after Dr. King. I just wonder what those two people might have accomplished by working together to bring change and solidarity. I definitely believe we would be living in a better age, but now we'll never know.

"Yes, I believe they could have done great things for this country." Sandra said. "There's no doubt about it."

"Sandra pulled up to a stop sign and turned left down Main Street. James was impressed by the cleanliness of the town. It was a typical southern town with a small train station that looked as though it had just been painted bright red. A local bank stood across the street and people casually window shopped along the street. There was a hardware store beside the bank that sold all types of garden tools. Across the street was Zack's Hot Dog Joint. There was a painted picture on the window of a foot long hotdog, and underneath was a sign that announced 'Serving Burlington since 1952'.

"You know," James said. "Just riding around through this town gives you a good feeling. It's pretty easy to get down on America with what's going on in Vietnam and with all the Civil Rights struggles, but after seeing this town it gives you hope that in time, things will be just fine."

"I'll be glad when it's over," Sandra agreed, "and things can settle down."

As James pushed round the cart, it brought back memories of when Grammy would take him to the store with her. She also let him push the cart and he would watch her as she picked up fruit and smelled it before putting it in the cart, or how she would pick up a snap bean and snap it three or four times before she put it into a paper bag. As James thought back, he looked over where

Sandra smelled a cantaloupe before putting it in the cart. He couldn't help but smile. They didn't talk much as they shopped. Sandra was reading labels and checking prices, sometimes shaking her head before putting the item back on the shelf. In the checkout line, Sandra walked up beside James and put her left arm around his right one as if she planned to escort him through the line. She gave him a big smile and leaned into him, putting her head on his shoulder. James put his arm around her shoulder and pulled her tight into his side.

As they left the store, Sandra said, "How about you take the groceries and put them in the backseat and I will meet you at the drugstore across the street?"

James put the groceries in the backseat and walked across the street. Inside, the first thing he saw was a magazine rack. On one there was a headline in big, capital letters which read, "Have You Seen This Man?" Underneath the caption was a picture of James Exum wearing a necktie. James picked it up and thumbed through the pages until he got to the article. It began with a picture of J.J. sitting behind his desk. The article quoted J.J. saying that James had taken a vacation for the first time and was doing fine. The reporter asked when James planned to return to work.

"When he feels like he's ready to return to work." J.J. responded, "You guys need to give him a break. He needs time for himself. He's been working 16 hour days for about 9 years. I think he deserves some time off."

As James read on, Sandra walked up beside him. "Are you reading one of those tabloids?" Sandra asked, "You can't pay attention to that stuff. They will say anything in those papers."

James folded the paper up and sat it back on the rack backwards and started walk off. Sandra looked back and reached over to turn it front facing. "Oh, Jim, you're not paying any attention!" She started walking towards the front door without ever looking at the tabloid.

They got to the car and headed out of town. James thought to himself how tired he was of keeping his identity secret. It didn't seem right to keep doing it and he could hardly wait until Saturday when he could finally explain to Sandra over dinner. He hoped she wouldn't go off the deep end.

As they drove back into Elon, James noticed Sandra didn't have much to say, "Are you okay, Sandra?" He asked, "You haven't said much since we left Burlington."

"I've just got a lot on my mind, Jim." Sandra answered, "By the way I won't be able to see you off Friday morning when you and the fellas go to Myrtle Beach. I forgot I have a doctor appointment Thursday morning in Asheville. It's an annual checkup, so I thought I would leave after lunch today and spend the night at mom's house so I can be at my appointment in the morning. I'm going to spend the Thursday and Friday with mom and drive back Saturday morning so I'll see you when you get back from the beach and we'll plan on dinner Saturday night."

Sandra pulled to the curb in front of James' house. "Would you like me to go home and unload the groceries for you?" James asked.

"No, it's not that many. I'm going to unload them and then head to Asheville. I'll see you sometime Saturday."

"Can I have a kiss before you go?"

"It's not the place, Jim." Sandra said as she reached over and put her hand on top of his, "Everyone knows this car. Just know that I love you."

"I love you, too," James said, "Be careful driving to Asheville. I'll look forward to seeing you Saturday."

James watched Sandra slowly pull off and stood there for a few minutes watching her as she drove towards town. He saw her looking back at him in the rear view mirror as she drove away. James knew something had gone wrong. Sandra's attitude had changed sometime during their trip and he wondered if it was something he had said, or if she had seen him on the cover of that magazine. His mind wandered in every direction as he walked inside. He went to the back of the house and sat in his rocker, going over everything in his mind that had been said that day. He didn't like the way the day had ended.

Chapter 36

About that time, the New York City detective arrived to pick up Jason and Agent McGuiness walked in.

"It's been one hell of a day." Clark said.

"I'm so glad it is over," Agreed McGuiness.

"It will be when we finish up down in Brownsville. We still need to keep this under wraps until everything down there has been completed. It's important that we keep this out of the press until everything is 100% complete." Clark reminded them.

"All the paperwork had been done downtown," McGuiness said, "And they know what to do with Jason."

"James' secretary will be here anytime now," J.J. warned. "Let me have 10 minutes with her before we get on our way back down south. I want to let her know everything is okay and that all this must be kept confidential. So if you guys want to go into the break room and have a cup of coffee, I'll be with you soon."

J.J. came back about thirty minutes later. "Everything's been taken care of fellas and the helicopter is on its way back to pick us back up."

When they got back to the airport, Roy was waiting for them. "I see we have an extra riding back with us," Roy said as J.J., Clark, and McGuiness settled into their seats.

"He deserves this ride back." J.J. said.

"Man, this is one hell of an airplane," McGuiness exclaimed, "I gotta meet this Mr. Exum!"

"When all of this is over and James is back working, I'll invite you fellas back up to the mansion and we can have dinner and drinks. You can meet him then." He said with a smile.

After about an hour into their flight, Roy stepped out. "You may want to drink those down fast. I've been told by the Greensboro control towers that we're headed into a severe thunderstorm. I've been given clearance to fly above it, but it might get a little rocky so finish your drinks and hold on tight."

As they finished their drinks, they noticed the rev of the engine and the feeling of the plane elevating to a higher altitude before leveling off after a few minutes. As the turbulence smoothed out, Roy stepped out of the cockpit to give them an update.

"We'll be alright for the time being but the storm is over Greensboro and Winston Salem. We're going to circle the area for a little while and try and wait this out. Roy informed them. You guys relax and I'll let you guys know shortly."

Twenty minutes passed, Roy stepped out of the cockpit.

"Fellas, this is what we're up against. This storm is covering the whole triad and mother nature is flexing her muscles." Roy quipped. "Anywhere we try to land is going to be tough, but we have waited this out as long as we can. We are running low on fuel and will only have one shot at this."

"You know best Roy." J.J. replied.

"We have one try, so I'm going to go at it blind using the manual controls and the guidance system. With the help of the tower we will get out of this in one piece." Roy explained.

"Are you shitting me"? McGuinness asked.

"The first try has to be the right one, so let's all have a drink." Roy replied. "Then will get this underway."

Roy picked up the bottle of Jack Daniels and took the glass out of McGuinness's hand. He poured himself a shot, downed all of it at one time, and handed the glass back to McGuinness. McGuinness looked up at Roy, he was a tall and slender man about 35 years old with a ruddy complexion. A veteran pilot, he was the guy you wanted in this situation. The look on his face didn't give any of them confidence. All they could do was hope for the best.

As the sound of the engine backed down a bit and the front of the plane tilted down, black clouds started passing the windows. Then the rain came, the plane was rocking back and forth for what seemed like hours. J.J. could see Roy pulling on the yoke, turning knobs, and looking down at the blue circle on the panel trying to keep the plane level as the plane kept descending. Looking out the window all you could see were white clouds, and hear the rain as the plane seemed to be going slower. J.J. could see Roy trying to look out. He was talking on the radio as the force of the plane got lower and lower.

A few seconds later the plane's tires hit the runway. J.J. was watching Roy, he looked as if he had both feet on the brakes as he leaned back in his seat. As the plane ran down the runway, J.J. could see the dim lights from the facilities that ran along the runway. J.J. thought to himself, "We're on the ground, now if we can just stop this thing before we run off the end of the runway."

As the plane came to a stop, J.J. and Clark took a deep breath and smiled at one another.

Clark said, "Well, that was one hell of an experience."

"You can say that again, Clark." replied J.J..

Clark looked over at McGuinness who looked white as a ghost. "Did that scare you McGuinness?"

McGuinness looked straight into Clark's eyes and replied, "No, it didn't scare me Clark. I had to shit anyway."

Everybody busted out laughing, Roy included.

After pulling the plane into the hangar, J.J., Clark, and McGuiness stepped out into the hangar, stretching their legs. "Man that was one hell of a ride." McGuiness said.

"I'm just glad we had a great pilot on hand." Clark said. Roy pulled a golf cart around for the guys to get in to be taken to their cars.

As Roy began to drive away, J.J. stopped him. "Roy, I just wanted to say thank you for a great job piloting that plane. Now I know why James selected you to be his pilot. You're a great pilot and thank you again for your help."

"You're welcome, J.J.. That's what James pays me for. I'm just doing my job." Roy said.

Clark and McGuiness shook Roy's hand to thank him for his piloting. "It took one hell of a pilot." McGuiness said.

"Well thank you guys. I do appreciate it. I hope the next ride is a lot more pleasant for you." Roy said.

Clark looked over at J.J. who was sitting beside of him in the golf cart. "As soon as I get the word from Mexico, I will give you a call and tell you the results. I should know by Friday night or Saturday morning."

"That would be great, Clark. James will be coming home Saturday afternoon and I plan on sitting him down to tell him the whole story. I'm hoping he won't get too upset with me for not keeping him informed about what has been going on."

"Well you've got to tell him that it was our suggestion to keep it a secret. It could have put him in jeopardy. If he had gotten hurt, J. Hoover would have our ass. You be sure to tell him that it was our idea. We're still not out of the woods yet, I just hope they do a good job down in Mexico." Clark said.

"Me too," J.J. said as he shook McGuiness and Clark's hands. As J.J. turned around to walk away, Clark put his hand on J.J.'s shoulder.

"J.J., I just wanted to thank you for your help with this case. It could not have been done without your cooperation, and I thank you for the way you handled yourself with Jason. It was a brave act and it saved both of our lives. I owe you one. Take care of that arm when you get home." Clark said.

"I will." J.J. replied.

As J.J. got into his car, he thought he would go by the mansion and check on Grammy. He could clean up his arm and change shirts before going home. It had been a long time, he thought. He almost got shot and almost crashed in a plane, all in one day. Being the president of Exum Textiles was a piece of cake, he thought.

Chapter 37

After listening to rhythm blues while thinking about Sandra, Drew and David opened the front door. "Hey Jim, we've been over to the practice field, watching Elon practice. We're going to eat a sandwich and go back over there for a while. Do you want to go back with us?" David said.

"Sure, I'll go with you." James said.

"They're looking good this year. They are playing Appalachian State Friday night. They could win this game." Drew said.

"Well if they do it'll be the first time. They have lost to Appalachian in the last four games that they've played with them." David said.

After eating a ham sandwich, all three started walking toward the practice field. As they got closer, they could hear the coaches giving directions over the voice horn. James was surprised at the amount of people that were in the stands watching the practice game. It seemed like everybody out there were wearing sweaters and light-weight jackets. A lot of them were wearing Elon jackets. It was almost as if it wasn't a practice game, but a real game. Drew, David, and James stepped up to the third bleacher to have a seat.

As James watched them practice, he turned his attention to the folks in the other bleachers. Suddenly he noticed an individual who was in the front row, looking back at him. It was Bull with his Elon jersey. For a while they stared at each other until Bull stood up and started walking down the front bleachers with his two friends following him. James sat still and watched them make their way towards him.

Bull stopped in front of James. "Can you come down and meet me behind the bleachers for a minute, James." Bull asked.

"Sure, I'll be right there, Bull." James replied.

As James stood up, David and Drew stood up with him. James turned around to look at them. "Hey guys, I know what you're doing, and I thank you, but I don't want you guys to get involved."

"But he has two of his buddies with him James." Drew said.

"I know, but it will be okay. You guys just stay here." James said.

"If you think we're going to just sit here while you go around there with three guys by yourself, then you're out of your mind." David said.

"You can say that again, David." Drew said. "Let's go." They passed James and walked down the bleachers.

James shook his head and started walking behind them as they turned the corner behind the bleachers. There Bull stood with his two friends. Bull stepped in front of James. "Last night you made me apologize to you for kicking your head while you were down on the floor." Bull said. "Today I want to apologize to you. Not because you're making me do it, but because I want to. The night I kicked you I was drinking. I didn't know who I was kicking, and at the time it really didn't make a difference who. I just wanted to say that I'm sorry." Bull stuck out his hand for James to shake.

James reached for Bull's hand and shook it. "I'm sorry too. I hope I didn't hurt you." James said.

"The only thing that was hurt was my pride and how stupid I've been, Jim. I hope that we can be friends." Bull said."

There's nothing I would like better than that, Bull."

As they walked back to their seat, Bull walked beside James. When James turned to sit in the bleachers, Bull patted him on the back and said "See you later, buddy."

Drew turned to James as they sat down. "I believe you taught him a lesson, Jim. That's the damnedest thing."

"That's the last thing I thought would happen." Drew said.

After a few hours of watching the practice, they all decided to go back to the house. Drew went over to Linda's and Dave went to Malia's.

After Drew and David left the house, James decided to watch TV. Later he went to bed. It had been a long day and he couldn't get Sandra off of his mind.

Chapter 38

As Mr. Sparks opened the gates J.J. drove through, and pulled around back. As he went in Miss Alston was sitting at the kitchen table. "Hey Miss Alston, how is it going?"

"It has been a bit of a rough day. Your mom is laying down now. I think she will sleep through the night."

"Well that is good!" J.J. said.

"She has been walking the floor most of the day, and at times she doesn't know who I am. Finally I got her take her medicine and she went to bed." Miss Alton said.

"I will get the doctor to come over tomorrow and check on her. Right now I am going to wash up, borrow some of James' clothes and have a cup of coffee."

About 15 minutes later J.J. comes down stairs and walks into the kitchen. Ms. Alston hands J.J. a cup of coffee. "J.J., it doesn't look good, I don't think there is anything else we can do, but keep her comfortable."

"Well you have my number. Call me anytime you need me. I can be there in about 10 minutes."

"I've already told Mr. Sparks. He said he was going to stay late, and be back early in the morning around 5 am."

"He's been good about calling and checking on me. He walks up here to check on us as well."

"Yes. Mr. Sparks is like part of the family. Well, while she's asleep, I'm going home and I'll be back in the morning." J.J. said.

"That's fine." She said as she opened the door for him to leave.

At 8:30 the next morning, J.J. showed up at the back door and knocked lightly. Miss Alston opened the door. "Come on in, J.J.."

"How did it go last night?" J.J. asked.

"She was up one time for a couple of hours, but she went back to sleep around 4:30 this morning. She's sleeping right now." Miss Alston said.

"I called the doctor before I left the house. He said he would be here around 9. I thought I would wait around until he got here. Sit down and I'll pour you a cup of coffee." J.J. said.

"That sounds good to me." Miss Alston said. "How is Sally doing?"

"Well she just keeps getting bigger and bigger. She's a little over 6 months now." J.J. said.

"You and Sally are going to be such good parents, J.J.."

"We're going to do our best."

"Have you heard from James?"

"Yes. He'll be moving back in Saturday night. He wants to spend some time with mom and spend some more time here in Greensboro. I will be glad to have him back home." J.J. said.

Then there was a slight knock on the door. "It's the Doctor." J.J. said as he got up and opened the door. "Good morning Dr. Gray. Thank you so much for coming by this morning."

"I thought I would come in before I make my rounds over at the hospital." Dr. Gray said.

"Come with me, Dr. Gray. She's upstairs."

They entered the bedroom where Elizabeth was lying, sleeping on her side. The doctor pulled out his stethoscope and listened to her heart. He then checked her pulse without waking her up. He motioned for J.J. and Miss Alston to come back downstairs. As they walked into the kitchen, Miss Alston sat an empty coffee cup down and poured Dr. Gray a cup of coffee.

"Thank you Miss Alston. I needed that." Dr. Gray said. He then looked at J.J.. "Elizabeth, as you know, has high blood pressure and I've done everything I know how to try to get it to come down. Your mother has worn herself out and her heart is not strong. I gave her pills for her heart, but she is refusing to take them. From the state that she's in now, she could live a week or a year. I've done all that I can do. It's in God's hands now. The only thing I can tell you is to keep her comfortable and don't let her do any strenuous work. I will stop by and check on her this afternoon."

"I could put her in the hospital, but personally, being here with Miss Alston and your daily check-ups is better than what they will do at the hospital." Dr. Gray said.

"So just keep giving her the medicine. Try to get her to eat and rest." Dr. Gray said as he took his last sip of coffee. He stood up and shook J.J.'s hand. "J.J., you have done all that you can do and Miss Alston is doing a fine job with her. I will see you guys this afternoon." He said as he left.

"Well Miss Alston, I've got to get back to the office, and get some things worked out that took place in New York yesterday. I should be back by lunch. If mom wakes up and you have any problems, you can call me."

"That's fine J.J.. She'll be okay, I'll be here. I'll see that she takes her medicine and gets her rest."

Chapter 39

James was up early. He could smell the coffee brewing in the kitchen. As he walked into the kitchen, Drew was sitting at the table drinking his coffee. "Good morning, Jim." Drew said.

"Good morning, Drew. How are you this morning?" James asked.

"I didn't sleep too well. I was thinking about leaving in the morning for Myrtle Beach. I don't know where I will place. All I know is that Linda and I have worked hard on doing a good job. If we're in the top five I will feel good about it." Drew said.

"I'm confident that you will do well, Drew."

"We'll know tomorrow night." Drew said.

"David is still in bed." James said.

"He didn't come home until late last night. He was with Malia until about 1 o' clock this morning."

"Well I'm going to clean up Little Susie and go fill her up with gas to get her ready for our trip. I may go see Bandit today as well. I think I'll take him with me. It may be a while before I have that opportunity again."

"I'm going to take some clothes to Linda's house. I'm going to get her to press them for me, and give my shoes a good shining."

"I'm going to get a bucket and start cleaning up the car."

"There's some dishwashing detergent under the sink that you can use. I'll be out in a few minutes and give you a hand." Drew said.

"It won't take me that long. I just wanted her to look good on the way down to the beach."

"I understand."

"When I go to get gas, I'll give you a ride to Linda's if you need one." James said.

"That's fine, but for now I'm just going to sit here and drink my coffee while I wait for sleeping beauty to wake up. My stomach feels a little upset. I guess it's because of my nerves knowing that the deadline is here."

"Just settle down and you'll be okay." James said as he grabbed the box of dishwashing detergent and headed out the door.

James pulled Little Susie up closer to the house so the hose could reach. As he started washing the top of the car with soapy water, he couldn't help but think about Sandra and how she taught him how to wash a car. She told him to start up at the top and work his way down. He smiled. He had a degree from Harvard, Princeton, and doctorate in textiles and he could speak three different languages but he didn't know how to wash a car.

James thought back to when he left Sandra's house yesterday. She had seemed a little depressed, and he knew that something had to have gone wrong.

He was squatting down washing the wheels when he felt something touch his back. When he turned around, Bandit was sitting behind him. "Well hey, Bandit. You just knew I was going to take a ride today, didn't you?" James said as he patted Bandit's head. "I'll be done in a few minutes. Just hang on for a little while and we'll take off."

After drying the car, James opened the passenger door. Bandit tried to get in by himself, but with a little help from James, he was sitting on his Coca-Cola crate in no time. Since it was an unusually warm day, James left the windows down for Bandit. James pulled out of the driveway and headed into town. The sidewalks were fairly empty because all of the students had left. As James crossed the red railroad tracks, the service station came into view. When he pulled up to a gas pump, an attendant walked up to the passenger side and patted Bandit on the head.

"Hey Bandit, are you out for a ride today, buddy?" The attendant said. "What can I do for you today, sir?" He said when he looked up at James.

"Just fill her up." James said.

"Man I sure do like this car; it's the first one I've seen in a long time. They don't make them like this anymore. I've seen you come by before."

James thanked the attendant and pulled out. He drove home slowly to enjoy the day. When he pulled up in front of the house, David was sitting on the front steps. David got up and met James at the car. "Linda came by and picked up Drew." David said.

"Do you want to get in and ride around with me for a little while?" James asked.

"Sure. Let me get in the back so Bandit can have shot gun." David said.

"I thought we would ride out in the country and enjoy the scenery." James said.

"There's some pretty scenery out in the country."

James adjusted the rearview mirror so he could see David as he talked. "Are you going home for a few days, David?"

"No. There's nobody there. I haven't heard from dad in the last two or three weeks, but I'm used to that. It used to aggravate my mom so much. I'm sure I can't call him where he's at anyway. Ever since the Vietnam War, my dad has been gone most of the time. I'm going home with Drew and his parents. I guess you could say they've adopted me as their family. Drew insisted that we get back here and get to work. We have a lot to do to get ready for Exum Textiles. I'm so excited about it. Mr. Washington really gave us a good deal."

"I think we're lucky to have you and Drew." James said.

"I can't wait to get started." David said.

"How are you and Malia getting along?" James asked.

"We're just fine. She is one fine southern lady." David replied. "I think Linda and Drew have gone past dance partners. I think they really love each other and Linda is good for Drew."

After a while, James turned around headed back for Elon. "We better head back and rest up for the ride in the morning. You guys have to get things ready for graduation on Saturday."

"It's going to be full day on Saturday, especially after driving back from Myrtle Beach all night."

"It's going to make for a long day on Saturday." James said.

"You can say that again, Jim."

When they got home, James pulled into the drive way and let out Bandit who started hopping down the sidewalk. "I'm going in and start getting ready for leaving in the morning. I'll lay out all of my things for graduation so when we get back, I can just jump right into them. I'll probably need to lay Drew's out as well. Then I'm going over to Malia's house for a little while. I'll be back by nine, but there's no telling when Drew will be back."

"Sandra went to her mother's house in Asheville, and she won't back until after we leave. I think I'm going to go to the library to catch up on a little reading." After a couple of hours, James came home and David had already left for Malia's house. James sat down and started watching the news on TV when the phone rang.

"Hey, handsome," Sandra's voice said when James picked up the phone.

"I'm so glad you called. I've been worried about you." James said.

"Why?" Sandra asked.

"When you left yesterday it appeared you weren't feeling too well."

"Well I'm fine now."

"How was your doctor's visit?" James asked.

"He said I was fine and that I'm in good health." She replied. "I just wanted to call you and say goodbye before you leave in the morning. My mom just told me to say that she says hello."

"You tell her that I said hi and I'm looking forward to seeing her again." James said.

"I'll tell her that. I'll see you on Saturday for that special dinner that you promised me. I'm looking forward to it."

"So am I, and Sandra I love you with all of my heart."

"You have no idea how much I needed to hear you say that. I love you too. You guys be careful going down to Myrtle Beach tomorrow. I love you, bye."

Chapter 40

Later that afternoon, J.J. pulled up to the gate and Mr. Carter came out of the guardhouse. "Hey, J.J.," Mr. Carter said.

"How's it going, Mr. Carter?" J.J. asked.

"I just got back from up at the house and your mother is sitting at the kitchen table having a glass of tea with Miss Alston. She's talking with a clear head. I don't understand it."

J.J. pulled around the house, walked up to the back door, and started to knock. When he looked through the window he could see Miss Alston waving at him to come inside.

J.J. stepped inside. "Hey son, how are you doing?" Grammy asked.

"I'm doing fine, mom. How are you?" J.J. asked.

"I'm doing just fine. Would you like a glass of tea?" Grammy asked as she started to get up from the table.

"I'll get it Elizabeth; you just keep your seat." Miss Alston said.

As Miss Alston got up, J.J. took a seat next to his mother. He noticed that she didn't have her white apron on, and he hadn't seen her with it off since he was a little boy. He could tell things were not right by the expression on her face.

Miss Alston sat a glass of tea in front of J.J. and took a seat herself. "I've asked Dr. Gray to come by today and check your blood pressure." J.J. said after taking a sip of his tea.

"I don't know why you would do that, J.J.. My blood pressure is fine." Grammy replied.

"It may be, but I want to be sure." J.J. said.

"You and James worry too much about me. I'm fine." After a while there was a knock on the door. It was Dr. Gray with his satchel in his hand.

Miss Alston opened the door for him. When he stepped in he asked "How are you Elizabeth?"

"I'm doing fine, Dr. Gray. What brings you over?" Grammy asked

"I was in the neighborhood and J.J. asked that I come by to check on you. I told him I would." Dr. Gray replied.

"Those boys worry too much about me. I'm doing fine." Grammy said.

Dr. Gray pulled out a chair and sat in front of Elizabeth. He took out his stethoscope and listened to her heart. He then wrapped her arm with the blood pressure apparatus. After he finished, he put his tools back in his satchel. "Are you taking your medicine like you're supposed to, Elizabeth?" He asked.

"Yes I am." She said with a disgusted look on her face.

"Are you eating better?"

"Yes I am." She said with a sharp tone.

Dr. Gray shook his head. He knew that she was only saying what he wanted to hear. "Well I'm glad to hear that, Elizabeth. Keep it up." Dr. Gray said as he stood up from his seat. "I've got a patient across town that I need to see. I'm going to leave you alone for now, Elizabeth."

"Well you need to see somebody who is sick. I'm not sick." Grammy said.

"J.J. and I just want to be sure." He replied.

"Well y'all worry too much. I'm not going until the Lord says so, and no doctor is going to change that."

"You're right, Elizabeth." Dr. Gray said with a chuckle.

J.J. walked Dr. Gray out. Dr. Gray turned to J.J. when he reached his car. "Her heart rate is not normal; her blood pressure is high, but not as high as it was this morning. Just tell Miss Alston to give her the medicine on time. Make sure she doesn't do anything that is straining, and we'll have to see what happens."

"I understand. I really appreciate you coming to see my mom." J.J. replied.

"It's no problem, J.J.. I just wish there was a way I could make her better, but she has a good point."

"What do you mean?"

"She's not going until the good Lord comes and gets her. She's right about that."

Chapter 41

When James woke up, he heard David and Drew in the kitchen. As he walked out into the hall David greeted him. "Good morning, Jim."

"We're all packed and everything has been put in the car. We're ready to go when you are." Drew said.

"You guys must have gotten up really early." James said.

"I haven't had a wink of sleep. I've been going to the bathroom almost every hour all night. I guess I'm just too excited. I've been waiting for this for a long time." Drew said. "David and I had a bowl of cereal."

"I think I'll have a rain check on the cereal and I'll just make myself a cup of coffee." James said.

"I thought we'd go down early and have some time to check things out before we meet the girls at the Pied Piper Motel. It's not far from downtown. They aren't going to be there before two o' clock." David said.

"That'll give us time to look around." Drew said.

"That sounds good. I've never been to Myrtle Beach." James said.

"You've never been to Myrtle Beach?" Drew said surprised. "That's where we went every year for our vacation."

"Don't feel bad, Jim. I had never been until I started going with Drew and his family." David said.

"Where did you go on vacation?" Drew asked.

"I just worked all the time, Drew. I never had time to go on vacation. I'm looking forward to it. Let's get started." James said. As he started walking out the door, Drew stopped.

"Hold on just a minute." Drew said as he ran back into the house.

"What's wrong?" David asked.

"Just hold on." After a few minutes, Drew walked out and locked the door behind him. He walked to the car where David and James were waiting for him. Drew held up a roll of toilet paper. "I figured I'd take this along. My stomach has been so upset; I believe I could shit through a keyhole at 30 paces."

James and David started laughing. "Drew, you're something else." David said. "I think I want to get into the back seat so you can have the front, just in case you have to get out quickly."

"Thanks, David. James you need to pull over quickly when I say. I only brought one change of clothes and I don't want to have to use those until it's time for the contest." Drew said.

"I understand, Drew."

They all laughed as they piled into the car. James backed out of the driveway and headed up through town. "Boys, we're lucky to have such a pretty day to drive in. It feels like 70 degrees." James said.

"That's great. That's one good thing about living in the south. I love the weather." David said.

They drove through town and turned down the ramp towards Graham, North Carolina to get on Highway 87 toward Sanford. Little Susie was purring like a kitten with rhythm blues playing on the radio. David and Drew were singing along, snapping their fingers. 'It's a good day.' James thought as he looked out the windshield over the hood where the morning sun reflected off of it. 'Little Susie had never looked better than she does now, and most of all, I'm a happy man.'

After a couple of hours and a few pit stops for Drew, they drove past the Fayetteville, North Carolina sign.

As they drove through Fayetteville, there was a historical sign posted on the side of the road. It read "The Home of Fort Bragg." A military base in 1919 named after the Confederate General by the name of Braxton Bragg. The home of the 82nd Air Borne Division, population 67,000.

"That's what I would have liked to be; a paratrooper." Drew said.

"Yeah I can see you now, Drew. You're jumping out of the back of an airplane holding a roll of toilet paper."

"Don't make me laugh, David. You're going to cause me to shit my britches." Drew said.

David was bent over laughing in the front seat.

James closed his eyes and shook his head as he laughed quietly. As they drove out of town, a convoy of jeeps and trucks passed on the left side. "Well we'll be in Whiteville in about 45 minutes. If you can hold on, Drew, we'll get out and take a break to stretch our legs." James said.

As they entered the town of Whiteville, James pulled into a service station. When James parked at a gas pump, an attendant walked out. "Fill her up, please." James said.

As David, James, and Drew stood around inside drinking Coke. James watched the attendant as he washed the windshield and checked the oil. When the attendant came back inside, he said "Sir that is a really nice looking car. I'd love to have one like it."

"Thank you, young man. I appreciate it." James replied as he sat down the empty Coke bottle into a wooden crate. He paid the young man for the gas, and turned to the boys. "You guys ready to go to Myrtle Beach?"

James pulled onto the highway from Whiteville towards South Carolina. After driving for about 20 minutes David said. "Boy, there are plenty of flat lands and pine trees in this area."

"It's what they call the Long Leaf Pine in North Carolina. That's how the state got its nick name 'The Tar heel State'."

"How is that?" David asked.

"In the early colony years, they would cut down the pine trees, put them in a pile, and burn them up until the rosin ran out. They would use that to patch the bottoms of wooden boats to prevent shipworms from damaging the hull. A lot of British ships and English navy used it. As the rosin was burning, it would turn black and it would get on the bottom of their shoes.

"Back in the Civil War, a North Carolina confederates brigade kept the union soldiers at bay. Supposedly when Robert E Lee was looking at the battle, he said 'look at those Carolina boys. They're sticking like they have tar on their heels.' That's why it's called the Tar Heel State" James said.

"Well I'll be damned. I always wondered where that name came from." Drew said.

"Well it won't be long now boys. We just entered the great state of South Carolina." James said.

After about 45 minutes, a sign that read 'Myrtle Beach: 6 miles' appeared. "When we get there, turn on Ocean Boulevard, Jim. That will take us right by the bowery where the contest is going

to be. Find a parking spot and we'll walk around a little bit."
Drew said.

As James pulled on to Ocean Boulevard and headed down the
street, he was surprised at the amount of people there were this
time of year. "Why are all of these people here?" James asked.

"Well a lot of them are here because of the dance contest. Most
of the people are here from North and South Carolina, and then
you have the older people. They like to come here in the winter
because it isn't as crowded." Drew said.

James continued driving slowly through town. There were a lot
of people with shorts and t-shirts. As they walked down the
sidewalk, they were all laughing, talking, and holding hands.
You could hear music coming out of the restaurants and bars. As
he continued driving, there was a small amusement park on the
right side of the road. You could hear the people screaming on
the roller coaster, the pipe organ playing high pitched notes, and
the smell of cotton candy was in the air.

When James spotted a parking spot, he quickly wheeled in.
"Let's stop right here," James said. "I want to look at the
amusement park."

"It's mostly for kids, Jim." David said.

"I know, but I want to check it out for a few minutes." James
replied.

"You go ahead and take your time. We'll meet you at the
Bowery." Drew said.

"Okay, guys. I'll be back in a little while." James said. As they
all got out of the car, David and Drew started walking back up
the sidewalk to where the Bowery is located.

James stopped at the entrance of the amusement park and let the scenery soak in. He looked down and noticed that he was standing on sawdust. The rides and colored lights changed colors as they rotated in circles. The sounds he was hearing, he had never heard before. He began a slow walk through the park. As he walked, he could smell the popcorn and fried onions. There were stuffed animals hanging everywhere, and there was laughter as little kids picked small rubber ducks out of a tub of water. There were kids walking around with bright red candy apples. The carousel was spinning with brightly painted ponies with small children riding on their backs and holding on to the shiny steel pole with the multicolored lights going in a circle with the parents riding beside them with a look of joy on their faces. As he exited the amusement park, he looked back and his heart was racing as if he had just gotten off the roller coaster himself. He wished he had experienced this as a child. 'I will experience this one day through the eyes of my children,' he thought.

Chapter 42

As James started walking up the sidewalk, he met David and Drew who were walking toward him. They had been to the Bowery and they were on their way back. "Did you see what you wanted to, Drew?" James asked.

"Yep, the competition starts at 8 o'clock and we must be here at 7:30 to get signed up." Drew said.

"We will need to leave the motor lodge around seven. What time is it?" David asked.

"It's about 3:30." James said.

"Let's start heading to the motel. It's on the left side of 17 going out of Myrtle Beach. You can't miss it." Drew said. It wasn't long before they pulled up in front of the Pied Piper Motor Lodge. "Here it is, boys." Drew said.

As they got out of the car, they heard a voice calling out from the second floor. It was Linda and Helen leaning over a black railing. "Hey guys, come up here! Go around to the side and walk up the stairs to room 209." Linda called.

When David, Drew, and James reached the room, the door was open. "How do you like the room?" Helen asked.

"It's great, Helen. There are two double beds, a dresser, and a TV. You can't beat it." David said.

"We've got to be there at 7:30 to sign up, Linda." Drew said.

"Drew, you guys go down stairs to the restaurant and have a cup of coffee. Helen and I will take a shower and get dressed. Afterwards we'll come down and you can come up to take a shower. We'll all go out to eat before going over to the Bowery. Drew, you need to settle down. You're making me nervous. It's just a dance contest, it's not the coming of the Lord, so calm down and everything will be alright." Linda said.

Drew took a deep breath as he looked at Linda. He turned to David. "Let's go downstairs and get a beer, David. Come on Jim." Drew said as he walked out the door and down the stairs. "Can you believe she said that?" Drew said.

"Said what?" David asked.

"'It's not the coming of the Lord.' That was mean. She's the kind that would turn the heat up in a wax museum." Drew said.

"She's right, Drew. Calm down. Just go over there and dance. It's all about having a good time." David said.

As they walked into the lobby, Drew walked up to the clerk and asked where the bar was. The Clerk directed them down the hall and to the left. Drew opened the door to the bar. It was small, and the only light was at the pool table. There were only about six tables, and a ballgame was on a TV that was mounted on the wall behind the bar.

"Let's have a seat at one of the tables, guys." Drew said. By the time they reached the table, the bar maid walked over.

"Hi, guys. What can I get you?" She asked.

"Three Budweiser's," David said. When she left, David looked over at Drew. "Look at me, Drew." David said. "I know you've been looking forward to this and you have worked hard. You put in a lot of practice. Yes, it's a dance contest, but when it's over we're going home.

"Tomorrow we are graduating, and then we're going to concentrate on starting our business at Exum Textiles. Those are the things that we have to be looking forward to, and tomorrow no one will care whether you won or lost. The only thing you need to think about it going out on that dance floor with Linda and have a good time. For now, just sit back and enjoy your beer." David said.

The waitress brought over three Budweiser's and sat them down on the table. James gave her a five dollar bill and told her to keep the change. David looked up at James. "Did you just give her a five dollar bill for three beers?"

"Yes." James said.

"And you told her to keep the change?"

"Yes."

"The tip was more than what the beers cost, Jim."

"I know, David, but your speech just inspired me to have a good time. Money isn't everything, you know." James said.

"I know, but you can't do anything without it." David said. He rose up his beer. "To good friends," All three raised their bottles and tapped them against each other. "Are you okay, Drew?"

"Yeah, I guess I did lose sight of what was really important. Linda was right. It's not the coming of the Lord." Drew said.

"Yeah, if that were going to happen, then you would have a reason to be nervous." David said.

"Kiss my ass, David." Drew replied. James and David laughed at Drew. A few minutes later, Linda and Helen walked in.

"I might've known y'all would be at a bar." Linda said. She had on black slacks, and a long sleeved shirt tucked in, accentuating her slim figure. Her blonde hair was combed straight back into a ponytail with a black ribbon tied around it that hung down her back.

"Wow, you look great, Linda." Drew said.

She walked over and laid her hands on each side of Drew's shoulders. "I'm sorry for being a smartass with you, Drew. I could tell you were about to have a meltdown, and I just wanted you to calm down."

"Well, I deserved it." Drew said.

Linda moved her hands up to the sides of his face and kissed him quickly on the lips. You could see Drew's face getting red, even in the dark. "Now go up and take a shower. I'll be here waiting on you." Linda said.

On Drew's way out, he passed Helen. He directed her to the table where everyone was sitting. She had on jeans with the legs tucked into her black boots, her dark hair flowed midway down her back, and a red turtleneck sweater. "Hey guys, how's it going?" She asked as she walked over.

"Well you gals are going to turn heads in there." David said.

"It's going to be fine now. I think Drew has settled down. They got him straightened out." James said.

After about an hour, Drew walked back inside the bar. He was wearing black slacks, a long sleeved black shirt, and his black dancing shoes with no heels. The creases in his pants were razor sharp along with his long sleeved black shirt.

"If you don't win the dance contest, you should win the contest of best looking couple on the dance floor." James said.

"You can say that again." David said.

"Finish your beers and let's go. I'm getting a little hungry." Drew said.

James left a couple of dollars on the table for a tip as they all walked out. As they all got into their cars Linda said, "We'll follow you guys."

"Hey, let's get something fast and light on the stomach. I haven't been feeling too good." Drew said.

"That's fine with me, Drew." Linda said.

They got into the car and pulled out of the parking lot. They turned on Ocean Boulevard. As they got closer to town, Drew saw a sign that read 'Jake's Diner, Curb Service'. "That looks good to me." He said. "What about you guys?"

"That's fine, Drew." James said.

As James pulled in, and parked between the white lines, Linda pulled up beside him. "What do you think about everybody ordering something quick so we can get going?" Drew asked Linda.

"That's fine."

After everybody ordered hotdogs and a coke, they stayed for about 20 minutes. They pulled out of the parking lot and headed down Ocean Boulevard to the Bowery. "That was a good hotdog; I've never had one with mayonnaise, slaw, and chili." James said.

"Usually I have onions on mine, not slaw." Drew said.

"How did you order hotdogs in New York, James?" David asked.

"You only have two choices; sauerkraut or pickled relish." James said.

"I can't imagine eating a hotdog with sauerkraut on it." Drew said.

"It's different, but that's what a lot of people get on their hotdog up north." James said.

As they got closer, parking spaces were beginning to get hard to find. "Pull over in this parking lot, Jim." Drew said. "We'll just have to walk from here."

James pulled the car into a parking spot and Linda pulled in beside him. Drew quickly got out and opened the door for Linda. "Well it's time to get this show on the road." Drew said. As they walked down the sidewalk, they stopped behind a line of people leading to the main entrance. "Is this the line for the dance contest?" Drew asked the person in front of him.

"Yes, but if you're entering the contest, you need to go around to this line. There's another line on the other side for participants." The person replied.

Drew looked around and said to James and David. "Well, boys, this is where I leave you." Drew and Linda stepped out of line.

"We'll see you inside, Drew. Everything is going to be alright." David said.

Drew and Linda walked away into the crowd. You could hear the music playing from the inside. The lights had been turned on outside the Bowery. The Marquis overhead the Bowery had been lit up 'Dance Contest Tonight. Come To See The Best From The North And South'.

David looked at James and said "This thing seems bigger than what I thought."

"Yes. I didn't think it was going to be a big deal." James replied.

"Now I'm getting nervous." David said.

"Well I hope your stomach doesn't get as upset as Drew's." James said.

"I wish you hadn't said that. I'll be worried the rest of the night now." David said.

Helen started laughing. "As much as those two have practiced, I'm sure they'll finish in the top 10. I've seen them practice, and they have their steps down perfect." She said.

Slowly, the line moved up. When they finally got to the door, there was a man at the window who passed out the tickets. "That'll be two dollars a person." He said. As David reached into his pocket, James stepped in front of him and handed the man a ten dollar bill. The man handed James his change and three tickets.

"You don't have to do this, Jim." David said. "I have the money."

"I know, but this is our last night out together before graduation, so this is my treat." James said as he handed Helen and David their ticket.

When David, Helen, and James walked in there was a lazy haze of smoke across the room. The floor was about the size of a basketball court with hardwood floors. There were tables and chairs outlining the dance floor. People filled the tables as they drank beer and smoked. There was a medium sized bar, and people stood shoulder to shoulder on all four walls. There were three spot lights shining down on the crowd moving around the room.

James, Helen, and David maneuvered their way through the crowd to find a good spot. "Man, I had no idea this thing was going to be as big as it is." David said.

Before long, Drew and Linda walked up. "I've been looking for y'all." Drew said.

"We just walked in, Drew. There was a long line outside." David yelled so Drew could hear him over the crowd.

"Can you believe this crowd?" Drew said.

"It's bigger than I thought it would be. Are you nervous?" David asked.

"Right now, I'm shaking like a dog trying to shit a peach seed. I think when we get started, I'll settle down." Drew said.

David handed Drew a rag to wipe the sweat off of his face. "You're going to be just fine, Drew. Enjoy yourself." James said.

"Hey, look at what number they gave me." Drew said as he turned around and showed them the tag number. "Number 43; that's Richard Petty's number. If I can just finish where he does when he's racing, I'll be okay."

A couple of minutes passed and the background music stopped. A voice came on over the loudspeaker. "Can I have your attention, please?" The voice said and the crowd quieted down to a whisper. "Ladies, and Gentlemen, we have 110 couples that are going to participate in this contest. There will only be 20 couple dancing at a time. There will be five judges who will select the best five competitors out of the 20. We will continue this method until we get down to the last five couples. At that time, we will choose the first, second and third place.

"At this time we would like to call the first 20 contestants. We will play three songs and the end of the third song we will call out the top five. The rest may go sit down."

After all the contestants got into position, the music began playing, and they all began to dance. The spotlights moved across the contestants, occasionally stopping on a particular couple to give them a quick review. The crowds would cheer, meaning a particular move had been a good one.

After playing two more additional songs, the judges walked out on the floor and laid their hand on the shoulders of the winners. They would then point them to step outside the dance floor.

Another 20 couples entered the dance floor. David looked over at James and took a deep breath. "I don't think my nerves can take much more of this." David said.

"Those top five they chose were good, but I don't know if they were showing all they've got. They might be saving some for the next round." Helen said.

"Well if that's all they've got, then I feel a lot better about Drew and Linda's chances." James said.

When the last song stopped playing, the judges repeated the same process as before. Drew and Linda were up next in the next group of 20 couples. Drew and Linda walked out onto the dance floor and got into position. When they music started, Drew and Linda stepped backwards. Linda turned into Drew, with Drew's hand behind her back. He gave her a push back in front of him.

David looked over at James and Helen. "They're too stiff. They aren't in their rhythm." David said. David walked off making his way down to where Linda and Drew could see him. As Drew made a turn pulling Linda under his arm, he saw David standing on the sidelines. As soon as he caught eye contact, David made a motion with both index finders to his mouth. He pushed up the sides of his lips, indicating a smile, and to loosen up.

Drew immediately looked at Linda and smiled. He bent over just a little bit and started moving his hips. Linda noticed what Drew was doing and immediately settled down. She began to dance in rhythm with Drew. After a few moves, David knew they were on their game; he started walking back to where James and Helen were standing.

When the first song ended, the second one started playing Smokey Robinson's, 'I Can't Help Myself'. That was one of Drew's favorite songs. As they got started on this song, Linda and Drew were in sync. Not only were they dancing well, but they were enjoying it.

After the third song, the judges walked out. Drew and Linda was the first couple chosen out of the five. As they walked to the side, James, David, and Helen gave each other a thumb's up. "I think they're going to be okay, now." David said.

"Yup, I think they're going to be fine now." Helen agreed.

"All thanks to you, David." James said.

An hour passed, and the top five contestants had been chosen. The announcer came over the loud speaker. "Folks, we have chosen 25 couples. We're going to put all 25 couples on the floor. We're going to choose 10 out of the 25 couples, this go round. Then we will choose the final three out of the 10. So would the 25 couples step onto the dance floor?"

As they all walked out, they got a standing ovation from the crowd.

The first song was 'I Heard it Through the Grapevine' by Marvin Gaye. By now, the crowd had really gotten into it. There was more smoke in the air and more beers had been drunk. As the spotlight moved all over the floor, the crowd was applauding. Drew and Linda were doing the steps they had practiced. They were both in sync, their moves were perfect and in rhythm with the song.

At the end of the third song, the crowd whistled and yelled. The spotlight followed the judges out to the floor. They chose the following numbers: 12, 33, 43, 54, 16, 23, 39, 22, 27, and 9. Out of those 10 couples, the first, second, and third place would be chosen.

A voice came over the loud speaker. "Folks, we're going to take a 20 minute break and give our contestants time to rest up for the finals."

"I'm going over to get us a beer. I'll be back in a few minutes." David said.

Drew and Linda walked up as Helen and James waited. "Hey guys." Linda said.

Helen started hugging Linda and telling her what a great job they were doing.

"Where's David, Jim?" Drew asked.

"He's gone to get a beer." James said as he handed Drew a rag to wipe his face with. "You guys are doing great."

"If David hadn't come over and loosened me up a little bit, we probably wouldn't have made it out of the first round. I was

scared shitless until I saw his ugly face, and it woke me up."
Drew said. "Jim, there's going to be such a crowd leaving here
when this is over. Linda and I will ride back together and we'll
just meet you guys back at the motel. I'll get my things and we'll
leave from there to go home. It's going to be later than I thought,
though. We won't have time to stop except for maybe gas. We'll
be lucky to be back by 5 or 6 o'clock in the morning. Tell David
what the plan is, and we'll see you guys back at the motel when
this is over."

"I'll do that, Drew. Now you get back out there and win this
thing!" James said.

"Jim I already feel like a winner, to be in the top 10. Anything
else is gravy." Drew said. "We better get back. They'll be calling
us in a few minutes."

Drew walked away with Linda with his hands on her waist.

Helen looked at James. "You know they really have the hots for
each other, don't they?"

"I didn't know for sure until tonight. You can see it in both of
them. David has been telling me all along that there was more to
them than just practicing and dancing." James replied.

"You can say that again. I know Linda loves Drew to death."
Helen said.

A voice came over the loud speaker again. "Contestants please
take the floor." All contestants walked out onto the floor. They
spread themselves on the floor to give them plenty of space to
dance. The first song was 'Riding for a Fall' by The Tams.

David walked up with three beers. As he turned towards the
dance floor, Linda and Drew were just getting started.

"Now you're really going to see some dancing, fellows." Helen said.

The crowd was cheering them on. Drew and Linda started making some turns, and had done certain dance steps that they had never seen before. James and David turned to look at each other with a surprised look on their faces.

Drew and Linda were now giving it their all. They did what they call a belly roll, went into a double turn, and did it all without looking like an exhibitionist. It all looked natural.

"That boy can dance." David said.

The next two songs, Linda and Drew did an outstanding job. They did steps that no one had ever seen before, and when it was all over the crowd went nuts. Spotlights were all over the floor. After a few minutes, the crowd settled down. The judges walked onto the dance floor and laid their hands on the couple's shoulders. Drew and Linda had won second place.

The crowd cheered as the top five contestants stood next to each other.

"Ladies and Gentlemen, it's been a great night. The best dancers from the Carolinas are here." The voice on the loudspeaker said. "All five contestants will receive trophies. The first place prize is $500. The second place prize is $300. Lastly, the third place prize is $200. Let's give all of the contestants a big hand, Ladies and Gentlemen. Thank you all for coming tonight; drive safely as you go home."

After telling David that Drew was going to ride back to the motel with Linda, they hustled their way through the crowd. When they got out onto the sidewalk, they hastily walked to where Little Susie was parked. As James pulled out of the parking lot, Linda was driving up the highway. She paused to let James pull out. Linda fell in behind James and they drove towards Highway 17 to the motel.

After pulling into the motel parking lot, they all got out of their cars. James, Helen, and David congratulated Linda and Drew for their second place win. "Well the last song they played just didn't have enough get up where I could make up the steps that I wanted to. It was a really low-key dance. We came in second and got a $300 check." Drew said.

"I think you guys did great, Drew." James said.

"The guy that won was from Draper, North Carolina. His name was Ken Atkins, and he was a really good dancer. I didn't mind losing to him. He was a really nice guy; he even wished us luck when we went out on the floor." Drew said.

"It sounds like the guy has class." David said.

"Here, Linda. You keep the check and let me have your room key. I'm going to get my change of clothes and we can get out of here. We've got a 5 and a half hour drive back home." Drew said. Linda handed him the key and he started jogging up the steps to the room.

"Well, Helen, I guess we'll go on up and get ready for bed. We're going to have to get up early in the morning and head home. We want to get ahead of as much traffic as possible. We don't want to miss seeing you and Drew graduate, David." Linda said.

After a couple of minutes, Drew came running down the steps, holding a plastic bag with his clothes in it. "You could have just put those on a hanger." Linda said.

"I didn't have time for that." Drew said as he opened the car door and threw the plastic bag into the back seat. Drew walked over to Linda. "Take care of that $300, babe. We're going to have a party after graduation."

"Well give me a kiss before you go." Linda said. Drew looked at James and David. He then gave her a kiss on the cheek. "I think you can do better than that." She said. Drew then kissed her lightly on the lips. He walked around to the passenger side of the car. David climbed into the back seat from James side, and James climbed into the driver's seat. As they drove out of the parking lot, they stuck their arms out of the window to wave goodbye to Helen and Linda.

James looked up into the sky. It was a dark night, and no stars were out. The trees on the side of the road swerved a little bit back and forth. "It looks like we could be running in to some rain, boys." James said.

"Man, I hope not. It's going to take us long enough as it is." Drew said.

"If we get back by six AM, we'll be okay." David said.

"Well it's 12:45 now, so that gives us five hours to get home. We should be okay, and it will give us a couple of hours to sleep after we get there." Drew said.

"Well, I'm not sleepy, so I'll drive the first couple of hours. You and David can take over after that for the next two hours." James said.

"That's fine with me." David sad. "I'm going to lie down back here and try to take a nap. Then I'll take over for a couple of hours. Drew can have the last leg in."

"That sounds good to me, David." As Drew slid over in the corner of the front seat and closed his eyes. James looked over at Drew, and could tell that he was tired from all the excitement that he had today.

Nearly an hour had passed and James reached over to turn on the radio on its lowest setting. He could hear David snoring in the backseat, and Drew was breathing heavily. Both of them were fast asleep.

James looked over the hood of Little Susie. The headlights were on bright and there was a light sprinkle of rain. The black tar pavement on the road had gotten shiny. The bright yellow line on the road was the only thing that stood out. There was no moon or stars. It was quiet other than the faint sound of the radio and the purr of the engine. The silence gave him time to think about the next couple of days. He thought about moving back into the mansion with Grammy, getting back into the textile business, and his dinner with Sandra. 'I just hope she understands the circumstances why I was not totally honest with her.' James thought.

James turned onto Highway 87, just outside of Fayetteville, North Carolina. He had made it about half of the trip before becoming tired. He needed to rest up a little bit for what he had coming in the next couple of hours.

James pulled into a service station and filled up Little Susie with gas. James walked inside the service station and went to the bathroom. When he came out, he noticed David standing outside the car, looking up at the sky. "Did you get any sleep, David?" James asked.

"Yes, I did. I feel a lot better." David replied. He looked up into the sky as the misty rain covered his face. David took his hands and wiped them all over his face as if he were washing it with the rain and ran his fingers through his sandy hair. "Boy this cool mist will wake you up." He said as he took his hands and wiped them over his face again. "I'll drive for the next couple hours. We'll let Drew sleep for another couple of hours." James crawled into the backseat. "I used Drew's plastic bag full of clothes as a pillow. It's not great, but it helps."

James stretched out as best as he could and took David's advice for a pillow. David felt refreshed as he climbed into the driver's seat. He put Little Susie into first gear and gradually pulled out of the service station. As he got onto the highway, he shifted gears and leveled Little Susie at 55 miles an hour. After feeling comfortable with David's driving, James drifted off to sleep.

After driving for a couple of hours, David had driven through Sanford and on his way to Pittsboro which was only 30 minutes away. David looked over at Drew. He was leaning up against the door and in a deep sleep. He decided he would drive to Pittsboro before waking Drew up.

When he drove into Pittsboro, he looked down at his watch. It was 4:45, and he looked for a place to pull over. After driving down the road for about two miles, he came to a stop sign. He slowly applied the brakes and looked back into the rearview mirror. When he looked back at the road, all he could see were bright headlights coming towards him. It blinded him, so he put his arm over his eyes to keep the glare from the oncoming vehicle out of his eyes.

As David covered his eyes from the glare, a tractor-trailer struck the left front fender mashing it in toward the driver's seat and knocking the vehicle down an embankment. The tractor-trailer came to a stop in the middle of the road on the other side of the street. The driver from the car behind them, and the truck driver ran down the bank to give assistance. When they got there, both doors had been knocked open. David was lying in the road face down, and Drew was lying on his side. James hung halfway in the car with his upper body hanging out. His head and shoulders were on the ground while his legs were still in the back floorboards of the car. The driver of the car behind them pulled James out from under the vehicle, and away from the car.

The car was smoking and the driver could smell the gas. He directed the truck driver to assist him in putting this one in the back of his car. There was only room for one. Then they both carried David and Drew up the bank to lay them down. "Use your radio and call for help." He said. "I'm going to take this one to Duke Hospital and that is where I'd like these two to go as well."

He then took off driving at a high rate of speed. He sped through Chapel Hill and into the parking lot of the emergency entrance of Duke Hospital. He ran inside and demanded assistance to help him get James out of his car. As they loaded James onto a gurney and wheeled him down the hall, the man went to a pay phone. After he dialed the number, it rang a couple of times and then someone answered.

"This is J.J.." The voice on the other line said.

"J.J., this is Jack. I'm at the emergency room at Duke Hospital. James has been in a serious car accident. You need to get down here as quickly as possible. It doesn't look good for him or the other two guys."

"I'm on my way, Jack." J.J. said as he hung up the phone. It was nearly 6 am, and he was already dressed.

J.J. ran out the door, leaving no explanation for his wife who was still in bed. He jumped into the car and sped to interstate 85. J.J.

thought of James and how young he was. He quietly said a prayer to God as he drove.

Within 45 minutes, J.J. was pulling up to the emergency entrance at Duke. There was an ambulance outside with its emergency lights on. When J.J. came inside, everybody was moving quickly. He was rushing to the front desk when Jack walked up and turned J.J. around.

"How is he, Jack?" J.J. asked.

"He was unconscious when we brought him in. He wasn't bleeding anywhere, but one side of his head is swollen pretty badly. When we got him here, his pulse was slow and he was having hard time breathing, but they put a tube in his throat. They've taken him down the hall." Jack said.

Chapter 43

Linda and Helen were not able to sleep because of the noise outside. They decided to leave earlier than they had planned. After getting up, taking a shower, and packing the car, they headed towards Burlington in the misty rain. They drove for about 3 hours and only stopped once for gas.

After passing Fayetteville, North Carolina, a voice interrupted the music on the radio. "There has been an accident south of Pittsboro and traffic is backed up on the north lane. Expect a delay." The announcer said. "The accident involved a tractor trailer that struck an old classic car. The truck driver was not injured but the three individuals in the old car were taken to Duke Hospital with severe injuries."

Linda and Helen looked at each other. "It's them, Helen. I know it." Linda said.

"Head toward the Apex exit, we can bypass the traffic that way. Then go to Cary and from there we can head to Durham." Helen replied. Linda turned off of 87 to Highway 401.

At about 8 am, the phone rang at Sandra's house. When Sandra answered the phone, her mother's voice was on the other end. "Sandra?" Her mother said in a frantic tone.

"Hey, mom, what's wrong?" Sandra asked, concerned.

"Are you looking at the news on TV?"

"No, I'm just getting ready to go to school. There's a graduation today."

"I was watching the news this morning. There's been an accident outside of Pittsboro. A vehicle has been hit by a tractor trailer and three of the occupants in the vehicle are seriously injured. They showed a picture of the car, and it looks like your daddy's. It had the small plate on the front bumper that said 'Little Susie'!" Sandra's mom said.

"Hang on, mom, I'll call you right back." Sandra said. She hung up the phone and ran to her car. She drove to James' house to see if the car was in the driveway. As she made her way down Main Street, the guys' house was coming into sight. The car was not in the driveway, and without thinking Sandra made a U-turn in the middle of the road. She got onto the interstate and headed toward Durham.

Sandra looked at her watch. She could be there in about 40 minutes. Her heart was pounding. "This can't be happening now." She thought as she passed cars on the interstate.

J.J. walked over to the admissions desk. "Hello, I'm J.J. Washington and I'm here to see James Andrew Exum. He just arrived about an hour and a half ago."

"Yes, Mr. Washington, we've been trying to call your office but with no success. Let me see if I can get the doctor." The woman said.

After a few minutes, a doctor walked out into the hall. He had his mask hanging down under his chin and he was dressed in his scrubs. He looked to have been in his mid-forties and his hair was graying around the temples. The doctor walked up and held out his hand.

"I'm Dr. Enso. Step back here for a few minutes so we can talk." He led J.J. into his office. There was a desk with two chairs sitting in the front. The doctor walked behind the desk and took a seat.

J.J. began to feel sick to his stomach; he didn't think it looked good.

"May I call you J.J.?" The doctor asked.

"Yes, you can."

"Is he the James Andrew Exum that I think he is?"

"He's the owner and CEO of Exum Textile."

"I thought so." The doctor said. "J.J., from what I can tell now, he has a brain concussion. This means his brain has been bruised. He has possibly three broken ribs, and his right lung has been punctured. Right now, we have him on a ventilator to pump air into his lungs. His brain is swelling, so right now he's in a coma, which could cause damage onto his brain. Right now, we cannot say he's going to have brain damage. Some cases are more severe than others. Let's just hope for the best with this one. We're currently trying to get his heart beating properly, and we're having a hard time doing that. It's going to be a wait and see thing for the next couple of hours." He said. "The longer he lives, the better his chances."

"Doctor, do all you can, and if there's any other doctor out there that can help us, just give me his name. I can have him here quickly." J.J. said.

"That's comforting to know, but for right now I don't know if there's anybody who can help. If there's any change, I will come and get you. There's a room down the hall where you and immediate family can stay while he's in intensive care."

"What is the likely hood of him making it, Doctor?" J.J. asked.

"Right now, I'd say 40%. We're doing all we can do, but we're still in the stages of learning about these situations."

"Thank you, Doctor. By the way, I expect the press to be here soon. I would appreciate it, if you would tell the staff not to reveal any type of information concerning his condition. It will be very important that no information is given out and for other reasons that I can't go into right now. I'm going to have a guard placed at his door twenty-four hours a day and the only people that will be able to go in his room are the doctors and care assistance. No one else can go in there without my permission. I would appreciate it if you could work with me on this, Dr. Enso." J.J. said.

"You have my support 100%. I will notify the staff immediately to keep all information confidential." Dr. Enso replied.

"How are the other two boys doing?" J.J. asked.

"I don't know, J.J.. We've just wheeled them into the other emergency room."

"The same goes for the other two boys. If there is any other doctor that can help, let me know."

David and Drew had been placed in a room next to the adjoining emergency room where James was. They could hear the commotion going on in the next room. Although the doors were closed, there was a bright light coming from under the door. The only light in the room was coming from an x-ray panel.

Not long after, a ward walked in. "Boys, Dr. Thompson will be with you in just a moment. He's scrubbing up now." She said. She stood between two gurneys as she started checking their pulse.

David looked over at Drew. "I sure hope Jim is going to be okay, Drew."

"He'll probably be okay, David."

"I'll be back in just a minute, boys." The nurse said as she walked out.

Both boys lay there, with their faces pointing directly at the ceiling and their eyes closed. "How are you feeling?" David asked.

"I could be better." Drew replied.

"I'm sorry, Drew."

Drew opened his eyes and looked over at David. "Sorry for what, David? You have absolutely nothing to be sorry for. How are you feeling?"

David turned his head sideways and looked at Drew. "My head sure does hurt."

"David, the first time I saw your head, I knew you were going to have a problem with it." Drew said. A big grin spread across David's face, as he turned his head to look back up towards the ceiling. Drew noticed blood slowly trickling out of David's ear. He was about to call for the nurse when David began to breathe harder and his chest expanded bigger. Drew reached over and put his left hand on David's shoulder. David took his left hand and reached over his chest to put it on top of Drew's hand that was on his shoulder

Still holding a smile on his face, with his sandy light hair feathered back over the top of his ear, he took one more deep breath and his left hand relaxed and slid off of Drew's hand down to his side. Then his chest was still. Drew slid the leg that wasn't injured off the gurney and laid both hands on David's shoulders.

"David?" He asked as he shook David's shoulders. "Open your eyes, David." He said as he kept shaking. When David never moved, Drew yelled. "David, open your eyes. Don't screw with me. You can't leave me now. Help! Please, Doctor, help!"

The doctor and the nurse ran back in. They grabbed the gurney and pulled David into the next room. Drew tried to follow, but the nurse stopped him and made him lay back down.

When J.J. went back into the lobby he spoke to Jack. "Will you please go back to my house and explain to my wife what happened? Could you also drive to the mansion and tell Mr. Carter what happened. Be sure that no one goes through those gates but you and I. Tell him to go tell Miss Alston, but not mom. Make sure she doesn't listen to the radio or watch the television. After that, come back here and we're going to stay here for as long as it takes."

Jack nodded and said good bye. J.J. watched through the glass doors as the reporters began to gather outside and were setting up cameras and holding up microphones. As he observed the circus that was taking place outside, he spotted a red mustang come flying into the parking lot. The woman jumped out without closing the door. As she opened the doors she went right past J.J. and to the receptionist desk.

"Excuse me, what room is James Andrews in?" She asked.

"I'm sorry, miss. We don't have a James Andrews here." The receptionist replied.

"He was brought in this morning with two other boys. They had been in a car accident." The woman said.

J.J. walked up behind her and put his hand around her arm. "Are you Miss Wilson?" J.J. asked.

"Yes, I am." She replied.

"Would you mind coming with me?" J.J. asked as he began leading her away from the desk.

"Who are you?" Sandra asked.

"I'm J.J. Washington."

"Oh. You're James' supervisor. What room is he in?" She asked.

"Come with me for a moment and we'll talk."

"I want to see him first."

"You will, but come with me first." J.J. said as he led her down the hall to the empty room at the end.

As they walked in, there was a sofa, two recliners, and a small table off to the side. J.J. sat her down on the sofa and pulled out one of the chairs from the table to sit down. Sandra slid herself up to the edge of the sofa and held her hands between her legs, staring J.J. in the face.

"Sandra, what I'm about to tell you is important and I need you to stay calm and be strong because I'm going to need your help." J.J. started.

Tears began welling in Sandra's eyes. "What's wrong, J.J.?"

"He's not doing well, Sandra. He has a punctured lung, and he was struck hard on the head. Right now he is comatose because of the brain swelling. The doctor has told me that James has a 40% chance of living."

Sandra slid off the couch and onto her knees. She put both hands over her face and began to cry profusely. J.J. let her cry it out for a little while. Suddenly she looked up and began stuttering her words. "This can't happen, J.J.." She paused. "He's going to be a father." She then began to cry again.

J.J. didn't know what to say. He took a deep breath and stood up, pulling Sandra to her feet as she continued crying with J.J.'s hand on her shoulder. J.J. took a handkerchief out of his back pocket and handed it to Sandra. "I will get you a cup of water." He said as he walked out of the room. Sandra sat back down on the sofa, and wiped her eyes.

J.J. decided that this was not the time to tell Sandra who James really was. He decided he would tell her when she calmed down.

The door opened and Dr. Enso walked inside. After seeing Sandra on the sofa, he asked J.J. if they could speak for a moment. J.J. didn't like the look on Dr. Enso's face, and he began to shake.

J.J. stepped outside the door and the doctor began to speak. "I have two things that I need to cover with you. One of the other boys, I believe his name is David."

"Yes. David and Drew are their names." J.J. said.

"Well, I hate to tell you this, J.J.. We lost David. We think a blood clot ran to his heart."

"Oh no," J.J. said.

"The other boy is having a really hard time dealing with it. We may need some help with him. He has a broken collar bone, a broken ankle, and he's bruised all over. He's going to be fine, we just need him to calm down. There are also two young ladies up front who are insisting to see them. I'm going to leave the decision up to you."

J.J. looked down the hallway. He could see Linda and Helen standing beside the receptionist desk. J.J. walked down the hallway and greeted them. "Ladies, are you here to see Drew and David?" He asked.

"Yes we are." Linda said.

"Let me introduce myself." J.J. said. "I'm J.J. Washington."

Before J.J. could say another word, Linda interrupted. "Are you the man who gave the guys the job at Exum Textiles?"

"Yes. Yes I am."

"Drew has talked so much about you. He was so happy that he and David are coming to work for you." Linda said.

"Ladies, would you mind coming with me?" J.J. asked.

Helen and Linda looked at each other with a puzzled expression. They followed J.J. down the hallway. As J.J. opened the door, they saw Sandra sitting on the sofa. It was obvious that she had been crying. They ran over and started hugging her. They were all three crying now. After a few minutes, they began to calm down a little. Sandra told Linda and Helen James' status, and they began to console her.

J.J. knew what he was about to tell them was going to make them upset again. From what James had told him, Linda and Drew were really close. Maybe Linda could go in and calm Drew down.

"Linda," J.J. started. Linda looked up at J.J.. "Drew has a broken collarbone, a broken ankle, and he's bruised pretty badly. In time, he's going to be okay."

"Oh, thank God!" She said as she held both hands to her face and began to cry.

"Linda, look at me." J.J. said in a firm voice. Linda looked back up at J.J. with tears running down her face and her eyes now swollen. "Drew needs your help, and you need to be strong and hold in as much emotion as you can for Drew's sake."

"What's happened?" She asked.

"While Drew and David were lying on the gurney, and before they were taken into the emergency room, David passed away. Drew was with him when he died, and they can't calm Drew down. You'll need to go in and try to calm him down so they can give him a sedative to repair the damage to his collarbone." J.J. said.

"Oh, God, not David, that will kill Drew." She replied. She leaped up and ran to the door.

"Hold it, Linda. I will take you to him." J.J. said.

Linda nodded without saying a word. She followed J.J. into the hall and down to the first door open across the hall.

Two nurses and a doctor were standing around Drew, trying to console him. Drew was sitting up on the side of the gurney. All he was saying was "I want him back," He said. "I want him back now." Crying and waving his arms around in the air. Every time someone tried to lay their hands on him, he would pull away. "I want David. I need him back." He would shout and continued waving his arms to keep anyone from getting close to him.

J.J. stood at the door and Linda slowly walked over to the gurney. The two nurses moved aside and Drew threw his arms around Linda's waist. He laid his head against her chest and cried because his heart was completely broken. Linda laid the side of her face on top of his head as they both started crying profusely. "He's gone, Linda. He's gone… Oh God…"

"Drew, I need you to please lay down so the doctors can help you, and I will stay right here with you." She said soothingly.

Drew leaned over on his right shoulder and looked up at Linda. "I can't see doing anything without David." He said.

"I know, I know. We will do the best we can. Now lay down so the doctor can check you out." She replied.

The doctor gave Drew his shot, and Drew's breathing began to calm down. He looked up at Linda with a small grin on his face as he gradually closed his eyes to fall asleep.

Dr. Enso looked at Linda. "Thank you so much, young lady for helping us. Now maybe we can set that collar bone." He said as the nurses wheeled Drew into another room. Linda began to follow them out. "Miss, if you don't mind, wait in here for us. He's not going to wake up anytime soon and when he does I will come and get you."

"I'll be waiting right here." She said.

"Thank you, young lady." He said as he walked into the room where Drew had been taken.

J.J. walked over to Linda. "Are you going to be okay, Linda?" He asked.

Linda looked up at J.J. with tears streaming down her face. "J.J., Drew loved David like a brother. I don't know if Drew will ever get over this."

"Just stay in here. I'm going to go check on the other two ladies." J.J. said as he walked out into the hallway.

As J.J. entered the room, Helen stood up and walked up to him. "J.J., what are we going to do about Drew's mom and dad? I'm sure they're at the house."

"Hold on, let me get Jack." He replied.

J.J. stepped back out into the hall and walked towards the lobby. The lobby was filled with reporters. Jack saw J.J. coming down the hall and walked up to him. "Jack, I need your help.

"Drew's parents are at their house in Elon. I'm sure they haven't heard about the accident yet. Could you go up there and explain to them what has happened. Let them know that Drew is going to be fine, and ask them to follow you back here. In the meantime, I'm going to call my secretary and ask her to book us five rooms up at the Holiday Inn. I'm sure we're going to need them before this is over."

Jack nodded and began to walk away. "Hey, Jack." He heard J.J. say behind him.

"Yes?"

"One of those rooms is for you. Notify anyone you need to, so they can know where you are." J.J. said. Jack nodded his head and walked towards the lobby doors.

When J.J. went back to the room, he explained to Helen what he had done. "Does he know where the guys live?" She asked.

"Oh yeah, he knows where they live." J.J. said. Before he could say anything else, Dr. Enso entered the room. His mask was down under his chin, and he looked grim. Sandra raised her head and looked at Dr. Enso.

"I'm sorry J.J.," He said hesitantly. "But we've lost James."

J.J. collapsed into a nearby chair, Helen buried her face into her hands, and Sandra dropped to the floor. As soon as the words came out of the Doctor's mouth, the door opened and another doctor poked his head in. "Dr. Enso, come quick. He's breathing again." He said in a frantic tone.

Dr. Enso followed the young doctor as he pulled up his surgical mask and followed him out of the room. J.J., still in shock, managed to help Sandra back onto the sofa. He sat beside her, and she leaned against his shoulder. No one said a word for a very long time. Finally, Sandra sat up. "I want to see him J.J.. I want to see him now. I want to let him know that I am here. I want to be there when he breathes his last breath."

J.J. turned to look at Sandra. Her eyes were bloodshot and swollen, but she did not have a single tear in her eye. He knew that she meant every word that she had said. J.J. stood up and went to the door. "You will get your wish. I'll be right back." He said as he walked out the door.

About ten minutes later, Dr. Enso and J.J. stepped back into the room. "Miss Wilson, I'm going to let you go in, but let me warn you about what you're going to see. I don't want you to be shocked when you see him."

Dr. Enso explained that there were going to be many machines and many tubes attached to James. J.J. looked at Sandra- it was as if she had become another person. She took a deep breath, stood upright and nodded to show that she understood. "Let's go doctor." She said as she followed the Dr. Enso out of the room and into the operating room. She could see his feet with a sheet pulled over him. There were two nurses on each side of the bed.

As she got closer, she could see his head was wrapped up in a bandage. There was a machine sitting beside his bed making a sucking noise. She could see bags hanging on a metal post with tubes running down to his arm. There was a bandage wrapped around his throat with a clear tube running into it.

Sandra walked over to the right side of the bed, next to the nurse monitoring his heart. She listened to the blips of noise from his heartbeat. She knew that it wasn't a regular heartbeat. She took one of his hands into hers and kissed the tips of his fingers. His hand seemed cold to the touch, and his face was swollen. Her eyes began to glaze over with tears. She sat on the bed, and caressed his hand.

J.J. walked back into the room, and Helen was sitting on the table. "How are you feeling, Helen?" He asked.

"I'm feeling better now that I know that Sandra is with Jim and Linda is with Drew." She said.

"Helen, I need your help."

"Just name it. I'll do it." She replied.

"Here is Sandra's car key. I'm sure her house key is on it." J.J. said. "I have a white 69 Chrysler station wagon. Here are the keys. You need to go to Sandra's house and get her some things to stay overnight. I need you to do that for you and Linda as well.

"When you go outside, take the side exit and bypass the reporters. When you get back, you can go to the Holiday Inn, and just tell them that you want two of the rooms under the name of J.J. Washington. You can put your things in one room, and

Sandra's in the other. When you come back here, pull as close to the side exit as you can." J.J. said. He handed her his keys. "Can you do that for me?"

"I will be back as soon as I can." She replied.

"Helen, take your time and be careful. We don't need another accident."

"You can say that again." She said as she took the keys from J.J.'s hand and walked out of the door.

J.J. picked up the phone sitting beside the sofa, and called the front desk. "Receptionist office," The voice said.

"Yes, Ma'am, this is J.J. Washington. I would like to know if any members of David Keller's family have been notified of his death."

"Yes sir. His father's number was in his wallet. We called the submarine base in Connecticut. When I called the number, they said his father would be out at sea for at least 30 more days. When I told them about his son's death they said they would have a commanding officer call me. I'm waiting on his call right now." She said.

"Would you please let me know what they're planning on doing, and see if I can be of any assistance?" J.J. asked.

"I certainly will, Mr. Washington. "

"Thank you ma'am, I appreciate it."

A couple of hours later, Jack walked in with Drew's parents and introduced them to J.J.. J.J. could see the resemblance of Drew in Mr. Harris. He was tall with dark hair and a ruddy complexion. Mrs. Harris was a small woman.

"It's nice to meet you folks. I'm sorry it is under these circumstances that we had to meet, but Drew is going to be fine. He's having a hard time coping with David's passing." J.J. said.

"They've been really close for four years. We were close to David, and it's going to be hard on the whole family." Mrs. Harris said.

Linda walked in and walked over to Mrs. Harris before J.J. could introduce her. "Drew is going to be physically fine, but getting over David is going to the hardest part." Linda said.

"Do you think we can go in and see him now?" Mrs. Harris asked.

"I don't see why not. He's sleeping. The doctors gave him enough medicine to knock out a horse. I'll take you to his room" Linda said.

Dr. Enso walked in before they could go out. "Dr. Enso, this is Drew Harris' parents. Would it be okay if they go in there for a few minutes?" Linda asked.

"Yes, of course." Dr. Enso said. He then explained Drew's condition and what to expect when they see him. Mr. and Mrs. Harris nodded, and then followed Linda out into the hall.

"We just heard from the commanding officer. They're going to send a military helicopter to pick up David and then bring him back to Connecticut. His father will then make arrangements from there." Dr. Enso said to J.J..

"How is James?" J.J. asked.

"Well, I have some good news. James doesn't have a punctured lung after all. The rib did some damage to the lung, but it is not punctured. His heart has also become steady, so that's a big improvement. Maybe that young lady holding his hand had something to do with his improvements. Who knows?" Dr. Enso said.

Around eight o' clock that night, Helen walked in. "Everything has been taken care of, J.J.. Here are the keys to the hotel rooms." She said.

J.J. took the keys and handed one to Jack. "Drew's parents are here, and in the hospital room with him. When you get the chance, tell them everything has been taken care of and that they can stay for as long as they'd like with no expense to them. This is all on me." J.J. said.

J.J., Helen, and Jack then waited for any updates concerning their friends. "I'm going to grab this chair and go out and sit by the door." Jack said. J.J. looked at the clock. It was nearly 9 pm and Sandra had not emerged from James' room for nearly 10 hours. He had to figure out a way to tell Sandra the truth about James before she found out from the media. He hoped that she wouldn't be mad at James, but be mad at him for not telling her before now.

J.J. walked out into the hallway, where Jack was seated. "I'm going to try to get Sandra to take a ride with me. I think it's time that I explain James' situation."

"I wondered when and how you were going to do that, boss." Jack said.

"It's not going to be easy, Jack. The girl is going through a hard enough time without having this bombshell dropped on her. I have to do it tonight, though before she finds out in the morning." J.J. said. "There will be more reporters gathering outside."

When J.J. walked into James' room, there was a nurse monitoring his heartbeat. Sandra was sitting in a chair beside James' bed holding his hand. J.J. walked over to her, touched her shoulder, and motioned for her to follow him out into the hallway. She nodded and followed him.

"Sandra, it is imperative that you go with me for a couple hours. There are some things I need to talk with you about concerning James." J.J. said.

"Can't you just tell me here?" Sandra asked.

"I could, but I think you'll understand better if you go with me." He said. Sandra looked into J.J.'s eyes as he was not asking, but pleading for her to go with him.

"Okay, J.J.. Let me go back inside and tell him that I'll be back in a minute." She said.

"Do you think he knows you're gone?" J.J. asked.

"If he does, I want him to know that I'll be back." She replied.

"I'll meet you in the hallway; I need to make a phone call first." J.J. said. He walked down the hallway to the pay phone and dialed the mansion.

"Exum residence, this is Miss Alston."

"Miss Alston, this is J.J.."

"Hey, J.J. how is James?" Miss Alston asked.

"Well he doesn't have a punctured lung and his heart seems have a regular heartbeat now." J.J. said.

"What can I do for you, J.J.?"

"I'll be there in about an hour, and I'm bringing James' girlfriend with me. There's a lot that I need to explain to her, and I think that doing it there is the best way to do it."

"That's fine, J.J.. Elizabeth has gone to bed because she was feeling tired. I was about to go to bed myself."

"Is Mr. Carter on the gate tonight?"

"No, he went home early after the reporters left. He said he'd be back early in the morning for when the reporters do return."

"Well, that's good. I have a key to open the gate and I'll use the front door, so I don't wake Momma up. How is she feeling?" J.J. asked.

"She seems to be doing okay." Miss Alston said. "She just gets tired easily."

"I understand. Do you have the number at the hospital so you can reach me?"

"Yes, I have it right here beside the phone. I'll call you if there's any kind of change with Elizabeth." Miss Alston said reassuringly.

"Thank you, Miss Alston."

"You're welcome, J.J.. I'll turn the porch light on and the gate lights on for you."

"Thank you Miss Alston. I appreciate it. I'll check in with you tomorrow." J.J. said and hung up the phone. When J.J. turned around, Sandra was waiting behind him.

"I told Helen that you and I were going somewhere and that we'd be back later." Sandra said.

J.J. quickly led Sandra through a side door and into his car to avoid the reporters. As he pulled out into the city street of Durham he headed towards the interstate under the bridge and headed towards Greensboro. J.J. glanced over at Sandra as he drove.

"I've rented you a motel room at the Holiday Inn. I also got a room for Linda and Helen, as well as Drew's parents. I hope you don't mind, but I gave Helen the keys to your house so she could get some things for you. I know you won't be going anywhere anytime soon, so that room can be a room away from home as long as you need it." J.J. said.

"I really appreciate that. I'm not going anywhere until James is on his feet. I'm confident that he is going to get better. I think he knows I'm there with him." Sandra replied.

J.J. passed Burlington, and kept on the highway towards Greensboro. "Where are you going, J.J.?" Sandra asked.

"Well the things I'm going to tell you now, are the things that Jim was going to tell you over dinner this evening." J.J. said.

"He told you that we were going to dinner?" Sandra asked.

"Yes, and he was concerned." J.J. said.

"What in the world would he be concerned about?"

"That is what this little trip is all about, Sandra. I think I can explain it better this way." J.J. said.

J.J. merged off of the highway and into Greensboro, making turns towards the outskirts of the city. As he made his final turn into the mansion drive way, Sandra knew exactly where she was. "Why this is Mr. Exum's house. J.J. do you know him well enough that you can just drive to his home at this time of night?"

"Oh, yes I do." J.J. said. He pulled up to the gate and stopped the car. Sandra noticed that the light on the front porch was on. She could see the huge white columns lined across the front porch and the steps leading up to it. The fountain in the front was lit up and the circle driveway around it was visible.

J.J. unlocked the iron gate and pushed open one side of the gate so that he could drive through. After closing the gate, he pulled around the circle and stopped in front of the steps. He opened the door for Sandra and she stepped out of the car. "I knew this house was big, but I didn't know it was this big." She said in awe.

J.J. took Sandra by the arm and led her into the house. "Do they know we're coming, J.J.?" She asked.

"Yep," He said as he started unlocking the door with his key.

"You have a key to this place?" She asked.

"Yep," He replied as he opened the door for her to walk in. She gave him a look as if she wasn't sure whether she should go in. J.J. just smiled and waved her forward.

Sandra's jaw dropped when she saw the living room. There was a huge winding staircase made out of mahogany, two foot crown molding, a rock fire place, and two tan leather sofas with oriental carpets decorating floor. The oil paintings on the walls were exquisite and highly valuable. There was a huge chandelier hanging in the middle of the room. J.J. eased his hand under her arm and led her toward the staircase. Sandra just stared at the paintings in awe.

J.J. led her into an office where James had worked with his father. "Whose office is this?" Sandra asked.

"Well right now it is James Andrew Exum's office. Before that it was his father's." J.J. replied.

"Does he let you bring people up here?" She asked. J.J. just smiled and walked across the room.

"Do you see all of those hundreds of books up there, Sandra?" J.J. asked and Sandra nodded. "James has read most of them."

J.J. then pointed her to a small room attached to the office. Sandra looked inside and saw a small desk with a blackboard. "This is where James went to school six days a week. He had three tutors come in everyday and work with him from 8 am to 3 pm. When his father got home, he would work with his father until about 7 o'clock at night." J.J. said.

"When did he have time to play and do other things that other children do?" Sandra asked.

"He didn't. The only time he got to play was with the nurses' son who was black. The nurse looked after the James' mother until James' mother passed away. The little black boy was the only person he had to play with."

"It's almost as if he was in a prison." Sandra said.

"Yes, maybe to you. He was the son of a very wealthy man, who had been threatened by the Union on several occasions. In order to protect his son, he kept him in the house. He put up a brick wall in the front with a guard gate to protect his only son. When James was 21, his father passed away with diabetes. James then owned the biggest denim company in the world.

"James took over the textile company when he was 21. He has doubled the size of the company in 8 years with a corporate office in New York. His distribution center sent denim all over the world. He never had a social life. All James knew was business. He put in 16 hours a day every day.

"One day, on his way to Greensboro, his limousine had car trouble and the driver pulled over into a small town. As they worked on the car and he fell in love with the town. Everyone seemed friendly. He watched as the kids walked around with books underneath their arms and how happy they all appeared to be.

"After the limousine was fixed, he came here to his office and called the president of the company to meet with him here. He told the president that he wanted to learn social skills and be able to interact with everyday people. He desired to attend a private school and be just like one of the other students. They decided he should attend for a semester. Sandra, the small town was Elon."

Sandra stared back at J.J. with wide eyes. She walked backwards with her arms across the front of her stomach. She sat down in a chair beside the bay window and looked back at J.J.. She was speechless as she shook her head from side to side. He squatted down in front of her, looking at her in the face.

"Are you telling me that my Jim is James Andrew Exum?" Sandra asked.

"That is what I'm trying to tell you. He was going to tell you at dinner tonight. He's been worried sick about it because he didn't know how you were going to take it. He didn't want you to think he had betrayed your trust. If all those reporters had known where he was, that campus would've been a circus. He could never have been able to meet you, Drew or David. He's also been concerned about how they would feel when his identity became known and would they feel that he betrayed their trust.

"Those three months that he's spent there have been the best three months of his life. He got to be a normal person for the first time and he loved it. He loves you." J.J. said. He stood up and walked over to the desk. He picked up an envelope and handed it to Sandra.

"What's this?" She asked "It's addressed to him."

"It's okay. I'm giving you permission to open it." J.J. said.

She opened the flap and pulled out several pieces of folded paper. It was a deed of trust. As she slid one page to the side to view the next piece of paper, which was a map drawn out on it; it said '156 acres, joining the acreage, of the Wilson family paid for in full.' It was deeded to Sandra L Wilson. "That's the mountain beside my house." Sandra said.

"It's yours now." J.J. said. Sandra burst out crying and looked up at J.J..

"He knew it was my favorite place in the world to go. I was worried that somebody was going to buy it." She said.

"You don't have to worry about it anymore. It's yours." J.J. said.

"Now I know why all the reporters were showing up at the hospital." Sandra said.

"I wanted to tell you tonight because by morning it would be all over the TV and radio. I wanted you to hear it from me." He said.

"Well J.J., I'm glad you did. I can now appreciate his reasoning. He could not have done otherwise the things he did with David or Drew. I can see why he kept his identity a secret." She replied. "Boy is my mother going to be surprised. As a matter of fact, a lot of people are going to be surprised. He'll always be my Jim to me." Sandra said.

"I think that's the way he wanted it." J.J. said. "Let's head back and hope to have some good news."

As they got back into the car, Sandra looked at J.J.. "Jim and I drove up here one time. We sat in front of the gates because the guard wouldn't let us in. I wanted to show him how beautiful this house was. I pointed out some things that I thought were beautiful, and he didn't say a word. I think when he gets better; I'm going to kick his ass."

J.J. couldn't help but laugh. He turned back onto the interstate and headed back towards Durham. Sandra didn't have much to say on the way back. J.J. could tell that she had a lot on her mind.

Suddenly Sandra looked back at J.J.. "It all makes sense now. The first day he walked into my class he acted like I did the first time I went to New York City. I was in awe of all the skyscrapers. Jim basically did the same thing. He looked like he had never seen a classroom before."

"That's because he hadn't." J.J. said.

"I couldn't believe he didn't have his driver's license either." She said. "I had to show him how to wash a car. I guess that's one reason why I fell in love with him. He was so humble and every time he did something simple, he acted like a 4 year old on Christmas morning. He always was concerned with other people's problems. He listened and he was willing to help any way he could."

"He has a big heart." J.J. said.

"Yes. Everything he does, he does with sincerity. You can't help but like somebody like that." Sandra said.

"I think that's why he gets so much attention. The things he does aren't for recognition, but it's what he feels is the right thing to do. He's 100% trust worthy." J.J. said.

"When I think about it, he never talked much about himself. When I asked him something he would always say that he'd explain later or change the subject." Sandra said thoughtfully.

"Like I said, not being totally upfront and honest was worrying him to death. He wanted to know that you and everyone else liked him for him. I'm sure you proved to him that you love him for the person he is."

They were quiet for a while. When J.J. turned off the highway and towards Duke Hospital, Sandra spoke up. "J.J. I wanted to thank you so much. Now every question I had about him is clear. I know why he got to upset sometimes, and why he's so forgiving to other people's needs."

When they turned into the hospital, there were still reporters outside with their microphones and cameras. J.J. pulled around to the side door again and parked. "I'm not telling you what to do, but for right now I wouldn't say anything to the reporters. We will wait until James gets better. Don't tell them anything about your relationship with James." J.J. said. "If they find out that you're his girlfriend, the next thing they're going to find out is your medical condition. If you want to be able to tell James anything personal, then I would advise you not to say anything personal to them concerning your relationship.

"I know you're right, J.J.. That's exactly what I'll do. Does Jim know the kind of friend you are to him?" Sandra asked.

"Yes he does." J.J. replied. "I know what kind of friend he is to me."

Sandra and J.J. got of the car. They then walked inside the hospital and into the waiting room. Helen and Linda were sitting on the sofa. Linda stood up. "They've taken the ventilator off of James and they say his heart is regulated." Linda said.

"Oh, that's great news." Sandra said as she turned around and walked to the room where James was located.

J.J. looked down at Linda and Helen. "Well, I guess it's time that I tell you ladies something. Just have a seat and I'll explain everything." J.J. told the girls the story of James, and why he kept his identity a secret.

"I knew something was different about him." Linda said when J.J. finished. "I just couldn't put my finger on it. Now it all makes sense."

"Damn, I tried to seduce him." Helen said. "He wouldn't go for it. Thank God, I thought it was me."

J.J. grinned and shook his head. "James thinks a lot of you girls. He won't forget the things you've done for him over the past three months. You've shown him that you are true friends and that means a lot to James."

The girls then began to analyze James' odd behavior. J.J. sat and listened until the phone rang in the waiting room. "Hello?" J.J. asked when he picked up the phone.

"Is this Mr. Washington?" The voice asked.

"Yes, it is."

"Mr. Washington, there are two gentlemen out front that would like to speak to you."

"Are they reporters?"

"No, they say they're with the FBI. They said their names were Mr. Clark and Mr. McGuiness."

"Oh, yes. Send them up." J.J. said and put the phone down. He got up and opened the door. Agents Clark and McGuiness were walking down the hall towards him. J.J. met them at the door and shook their hands. "Hey, fellas; how's it going?" J.J. asked.

"Better than you right now, J.J.. How is he?" Agent Clark asked.

"He's improving. They've taken him off of the ventilator and he doesn't have a punctured lung. He's still in a coma though, and his head is swollen." J.J. said.

"Who is that sitting out by the door?" Agent McGuiness asked.

"He's a private investigator that I hired a couple of months ago. I hired him to make sure everything was okay with James down at the college."

"Well, we called your office and found out you were down here. We wanted to come and tell you personally that everything went well in Brownsville, Texas. They made all of the arrests at the warehouse. You can say we have a clean house down there and in New York as well." Agent McGuiness said.

"We know it's late but we just wanted to come and say hello to you. We're sorry about James and we hope he'll get along okay. If you need anything, just let us know." Agent Clark said.

"Agent Clark, you and McGuiness have been a big help. I really do appreciate you guys coming down to tell me that; especially at this time of night. It takes a load off of my mind. Now I won't have to worry about somebody coming up here to finish the job off. Now poor Jack can take a break and go home. The doctors say that if it hadn't been for Jack, James wouldn't have made it here in time." J.J. said.

"Well thank God for that." Agent Clark said.

"Well, we better go J.J.. It's nearly midnight and you guys need some rest. We've got to drive up to New York in the morning. Let us know how James is getting along." Agent McGuiness said and shook J.J.'s hand.

The two agents then walked back down the hallway and left the hospital.

J.J. walked into James' room and Sandra was sitting beside his bed holding his hand like she was before. He looked over at the machine that monitored his heart. It seemed like his heart beats were stronger than before. His head was still wrapped up in bandages and there were tubes still connected to him. Sandra was asleep, so J.J. went to go check on Drew.

When J.J. walked into Drew's room, Mr. and Mrs. Harris were sitting in chairs watching Drew sleep. It looked like Drew had half of his body in a cast. His right arm was in a sling and he was wearing a neck brace. His right ankle was lying on a pillow with the cast covering his foot and half of his leg.

"Mr. and Mrs. Harris, did Linda tell you that I have a room for you at the Holiday Inn for you to stay?" J.J. asked.

"Yes, she did, Mr. Washington. We really appreciate it." Mrs. Harris said.

"You're most welcome. If there's anything else I can do, just let me know." J.J. said.

"We certainly will. Thank you again."

J.J. turned and walked back out the door back towards the visitor's room.

"Well J.J., I guess all we can do now is sit and wait." Linda said.

"I'm going to let Jack go and get a good night's sleep." J.J. said. "That man needs a break. He hasn't slept in two days."

J.J. walked into the hallway. He could see Jack standing at the door with his arms folded. Jack was a very intimidating man. He stood about 6 foot four, weighed 270 pounds and all muscle, he looked about 40 years old, with dark black hair. Although close shaved, he still looks like he has a day's growth of beard. J.J. had known Jack for about 5 years, and Jack had done many private jobs for the company.

"How are you doing, Jack?" J.J. asked.

"Just fine J.J.." Jack replied.

"I resolved the problem that I had earlier. I don't think you need to stand guard at the door anymore. Right now, all we have to worry about is James getting better. I've got one last thing that I need you to do for me." J.J. said.

"Just name it."

"I need to know where they took James' car." J.J. said.

"I can find it for you."

"Well, find the car and find someone to restore it. I want that car to be the exact same way it was before the accident."

"I know a guy who can do it in Greensboro. He'll fix it like the day it was manufactured." Jack said.

"That's what I want. You can start on that tomorrow after getting a good night's sleep." J.J. said.

"I'll get on it first thing in the morning."

"Thank you, Jack. I won't forget the help you've given us through all of this. Thank God you were following them back home." J.J. said.

"No problem." Jack replied. "I'm just doing my job."

J.J. shook Jack's hand. "Go get a good night's sleep and let me know what's going on after you set everything up."

"What are you going to do about those reporters outside?" Jack asked.

"Tomorrow, Dr. Enso and I are going to answer some questions. Let's hope that will satisfy them enough so that things can calm down around here. Right now we just need to make it through the night." J.J. said.

"I know what you mean. I'll give you a call as soon as I find out something about the car." Jack said. He then turned and walked out of the hospital.

Chapter 44

It was Sunday morning, eight days had passed since the accident and Linda was pushing Drew around in a wheel chair. He still had his neck brace on and his arm was in a sling. Linda knocked on the door of the visitor's room. Helen answered it and smiled. "Well hey Drew!" Helen said as she stepped aside.

J.J. stood up. "Glad to see you up and moving around, Drew." J.J. said.

"I just wanted to know if I could go in and see Jim." Drew said.

"I don't see why not. Let me step inside and see what's going on in there first." J.J. said.

As J.J. opened the door and peeked in, Sandra was reading a book out loud to James. "Hey, Sandra" He said. Sandra closed the book and turned to J.J.. "Drew is outside. He wanted to come in and see James."

"Great! Tell him to come on in." Sandra said.

J.J. stepped aside and held the door while Linda wheeled Drew into the room. She pushed Drew around to James' bedside. James was lying on his back with a bed sheet folded down neatly over his waist. His head bandages had been taken off and his hair was combed straight back.

Sandra stood up from her chair and laid the book on an end table. "Drew, how are you feeling this morning?" She asked.

"I've felt better, Miss Wilson." He replied.

"I understand Drew." She said. "Your mom and dad can come in if they'd like."

"Mom and Dad went back early this morning." Drew said. "They wanted me to go with them, but I told them that I wasn't going anywhere until Jim can leave with me. I can't leave him now. I know he wouldn't leave me and I know David wouldn't leave him here. We have an understanding between the three of us and I'm sticking to it." Drew rolled up closer to James' bed. "I'll be checking on you every day until we get out of here. You take it easy until tomorrow when I'll be back."

Drew backed up and looked at Linda. He couldn't speak anymore. Tears were rolling down his face. Linda looked at Sandra and J.J.; her eyes were watering as she pushed Drew toward the door.

J.J. held the door for Linda and Drew. "Has Linda told Drew who James really is?" J.J. asked.

"Yes, and I will tell you his exact words. He said 'I do not give a damn about who he is to anyone else or what title he had in a textile business.' To me, he's always going to be Jim, his and David's roommate." She replied.

"Has the doctor been in this morning?"

"Yes. He was here early this morning. He made a comment about how the swelling had gone down. The nurse and I are rolling him on his side every two hours. When I gave him a shave, his eyelids were moving a little bit. When the doctor comes back, I'm going to talk to him about it."

"Is there anything I can do to help you in here before I leave?" J.J. asked.

"No, everything is taken care of. I washed his hair and shaved him. He's had a bath, so I'm just going to wait for him to wake up and keep reading to him until he does." J.J. turned and started walking towards to door. "Have the reporters left yet?" Sandra called behind him.

"After we had the conference there's only been one or two hanging around. I've been keeping them up to date on what's going on, and they've been showing enough respect that they haven't been bothering anybody." J.J. replied.

Five more days had passed with no significant improvements with James. Sandra sat beside James reading to him and holding his hand. In midsentence, she thought she felt a finger move. She looked up from the book and looked at James' eyes. They were closed, but they still seemed to be moving underneath his eyelids. She then looked down at their hands, and saw James' finger raised slightly over the others. She dropped her book and called for the nurse.

When the nurse reached the room, Sandra was hysterical. "He's moving his finger! Look at his eyelids!" She said.

The nurse observed the scene and went to the other room to find the doctor. Sandra laid her face next to James. "It's going to be okay Jim. I'm right here." She said.

When the doctor stepped in, he politely asked her if she would mind stepping out of the room for a few minutes. He said he would come and get her after he finished checking James out.

James heard a voice he had heard hundreds of times before, every morning of his life.

"James, wake up honey. It's time to wake up now." He heard. He felt the sensation of someone pinching his cheeks. Grammy would always do that to him before waking him up. James opened his eyes and looked over to the side of the bed. Grammy sat beside him with her white apron on and gray hair pulled back into a bun. "Now don't make me pinch that cheek again. It's time that you wake up, young man."

"Yes ma'am. Can I just lay here for five more minutes?" James asked.

"Five more minutes is fine, but then I want you to wake up." Grammy replied.

"Yes ma'am."

Chapter 45

Sandra was waiting for about an hour until Dr. Enso came out of James' room. J.J., Sandra and Helen stood up as he walked out.

"Well, he's awake and doing well. He was disoriented at first, but I explained to him what had happened. He wanted to know about his two buddies. I didn't know what to tell him about David, but he kept insisting on their condition. When I told him about David, he took it hard, but it showed me that he can accept trauma. Even at this early stage of waking up from a coma." The doctor said.

"Can I go in and see him, doctor?" Sandra asked.

"I think one at a time will be okay for short periods of time. He may talk a little slow."

J.J. looked at Sandra. "You go on in and cheer him up, if you know what I mean."

"Do you think I should?" She asked.

"I don't know anything better to cheer him up, than to tell him that he's going to be a father." J.J. replied.

When Sandra walked in, the bed had been raised so that James was sitting straight up. She stopped at the foot of the bed and looked at him. James just smiled and winked at her. She ran around the side and sat on the bed. Carefully, she laid down across his chest with her head leaning against his face. James put his arms around her, and could feel her tears running down the side of her face.

"I'm sorry, honey." James said.

"Don't say anything, Jim. Just hold me for a minute." She said. Sandra raised her head and looked him in the eye. "Sometimes you don't know how much you love someone until something like this happens. I don't think I could bear it if I lost you."

"Sandra, there's something I want to say and I hope you give me the time to say it." James stopped and hesitated. "I'm not sure how I should start off telling you."

"You don't have to tell me anything. J.J. explained everything to me from the beginning. I understand why you hid your identity, especially after seeing all of the reporters here. There's no way you could have attended Elon College if they were always surrounding you." She said.

"No, that's not what I was going to say." James said.

"Oh, I'm sorry. Take your time." She replied.

"Well, I've never done this before, and I don't really know the protocol. I'm just going to come right out and say it. Will you marry me?" James asked.

Sandra looked up at James with a puzzled look on her face. It was the last thing she expected him to say, and she couldn't speak. She picked his hand up and kissed it with tears running down her cheeks.

"I take that as a yes?" James asked.

Sandra nodded her head and kissed his lips. Holding her right hand under her throat it was shaking as she patted herself on the chest. "That was the last thing I expected to come from your mouth. Yes, yes I will marry you. I love you."

"Well, you have made me the happiest man, and I will do my best to make you happy." James said.

Sandra reached down off of the bed and picked up the book that she had dropped on the floor. "Well, Mr. Exum, while you're laying here doing nothing, this is something you and I can both read." She said as she held the book up to read the title of the book: 'Staying Healthy During a Pregnancy'.

James looked up from the book and back up at Sandra with a serious look on his face.

"You're going to be a daddy." Sandra said.

A big smile came across James' face and his eyes began to water. He suddenly felt emotions that he had never felt before, and he embraced Sandra in a tight hug. "When did you find out?" James asked.

"I found out Thursday when I went to have my regular checkup. I was going to tell you Saturday night over dinner."

"I'm so sorry for what you've gone through these past two weeks." James said. "I can't imagine how hard it's been for you."

"Well, right now my main focus is getting you well so you can help me with this baby." Sandra said.

"Oh, I'm looking forward to that." James said.

As Sandra was about to leave to let J.J. spend time with James, Dr. Enso walked in. "Okay, I hate to break this up but we need to run some tests on James, and we have some real food for James to try. We've also set up some physical therapy for you, James." Dr. Enso said. "Sandra, would you mind telling J.J. that it may be late this afternoon before he can come in and see James?"

Sandra nodded. As she left the room, she blew James a kiss and mouthed "I love you." James looked back at her and smiled.

When Sandra walked back into the waiting room, she was excited. "J.J., he proposed to me before I even told him I was pregnant. I thought he was going to talk about his past, but I don't care about that stuff. He'll always be the man I know and love."

"Well congratulations, Sandra." J.J. said. "I'm happy for the both of you, and I know you have made James a happy man."

A few hours later, Dr. Enso walked into the waiting room. "We gave him a mild sedative so he can relax a little. We still have a heart monitor on him, and we'd like to observe him over night to see how he's feeling in the morning. If everything goes well, we're going to move him out of intensive care. J.J., you can see him in the morning." Dr. Enso said.

"That's good. We just want what's best for him." J.J. said.

After the doctor left, J.J. turned to the two girls. "Well, Ladies I'm going to check on my wife. I'll be back first thing in the morning. I'd advise you girls to get a good night's rest as well."

"Are you kidding me J.J.? I'm going to drive back to Elon and call my mom. I have to tell her I'm getting married, and I'm going to call everyone else I know. I may just have to call people I don't know." Sandra said as she laughed. "I'm going to spend the night in my bed tonight, and get up early to come back here." She looked over at Helen. "Would you like to go with me?"

"I'd love to Sandra, but I thought I would go over to the motel to spend some time with Linda and Drew. I want to try and cheer them up a little bit with the news about the marriage proposal." Helen said.

"Well, just be careful, Sandra." J.J. said. "I'll see you guys in the morning."

Chapter 46

Early the next morning, J.J. walked into the hospital and to the waiting room. When he opened the door, Sandra was sitting on the sofa.

"I thought you were going home to call your friends and get a good night's sleep?" J.J. asked.

"Well, I did, but when I got in the bed I couldn't sleep. My mind was racing and I couldn't get Jim off of my mind. I got up, took a shower, and drove back here. I just feel better when I'm closer to him." Sandra replied.

Later that morning, Dr. Enso walked in. "Good morning, Sandra. J.J., he's done really well. He slept well and he ate a good breakfast this morning. We've gone ahead and moved him out of intensive care. We're going to keep him here a few more days for physical therapy and then he can go home."

"Thank you, doctor for all that you've done for us. We'll never forget you." J.J. said.

"Thank you and Mr. Exum for being so generous to this hospital. I'm so glad that we could have been so helpful to you." Dr. Enso replied and shook J.J.'s hand.

"I'm going down to see James, Dr. Enso. Thank you again, and I'll be talking to you later." J.J. said.

After the doctor left, J.J. turned to Sandra. "I need about 45 minutes with him alone, and then you can spend the rest of the day with him."

"I'll be right here." Sandra replied.

As J.J. walked down the hall to room 201, he gave a light knock on the door and opened it halfway. James was sitting up on the side of the bed, and he turned around to look at J.J..

"Come on in, J.J.." James said.

When J.J. walked around the bed, James stood up and they embraced each other in a hug. "Man, it's good to see you well." J.J. said.

"It's good to be back in the living world." James replied.

"For a while I thought I was going to lose you. I know one woman that is glad we didn't." J.J. said.

"Can you believe it, J.J.? I'm going to be a husband and a father. I can't wait to get out of here." James replied.

"There are a lot of people who can't wait for you to get out of here, James."

"How did you get in here without Grammy, J.J.? Did she go back home?" James asked.

"What do you mean?"

"I don't think she spent the night here. I thought maybe she would be back this morning."

"When did you see her James?" J.J. asked.

"She woke me up, J.J.."

"What do you mean she woke you up?"

"Well, she pinched me on the cheek, just like she used to. Do you remember that?" James asked.

"Oh, yes, I remember that." J.J. replied.

"Well, she pinched my cheek and told me it's time to wake up. When I looked over at her she had on her big white apron. She said that if I didn't get up soon that she was going to pinch me again."

J.J. looked at James with wide eyes. He couldn't believe what he was hearing. "You must have been dreaming, James."

"No, I wasn't dreaming." James said. J.J. was speechless. "What's wrong, J.J.? I can tell that something is wrong by the expression on your face."

"I wasn't going to tell you today. I was going to wait a couple of days for you to get better." J.J. said.

"What were you going to tell me?" James asked.

"Mom passed away three days after your accident. She went very peacefully in her sleep. Her heart just gave out. We buried her on that Friday. I didn't know this but Brad showed up at the funeral with a piece of paper. It was your Dad's will requesting that she be buried beside him. I hope that's okay with you." J.J. said.

"I would not have it any other way, J.J.. That's where I would have buried her." James said. "I don't understand. She was right beside me, plain as day."

"James, you know how mom was. I don't doubt that she wasn't here. I think she's always going to be looking over you and me." J.J. said.

Tears welled in James' eyes. "Did she know I was in an accident?"

"That's what's so strange. I never told her because I didn't want her to be upset. You know she would have tried to come up here

while she was sick, and I wouldn't have been able to stop her."
J.J. said.

"All I can say, J.J., is that you didn't stop her because she was
right here beside me. She's the reason why I woke up. God bless
her. I'm going to miss her; the house will never be the same."

"If mom is looking down on us, I'm sure there is nothing more
that she would like than to see than you happily married with the
patter of your children's feet running around that house."

James looked at J.J. and smiled. "I think you're probably right,
J.J.. I would have liked my kids to know her though."

"I know what you mean. I'm not three months away from having
my first child and I know how you feel." J.J. said.

"I'm sorry, J.J.. I can't imagine what you've been through the
past couple of weeks. God knows what would have happened if
you weren't here to take care of these problems. I think dad knew
you would." James said and hugged J.J. again. "Thank you so
much, J.J.."

The two stood together with tears streaming down their faces.
They knew that there was a bond between them that could never
be broken.

After a few minutes J.J. said "There's a little lady who can't wait
to be with you. I can tell her to come in now, if you'd like."

"Sure. I need a little bit of cheering up." James said.

"I'll be back later in the day. If there's anything else we need to
talk about, we can talk about it then." J.J. said.

"That's fine J.J.. There are some things we need to talk about,
but I'll wait until later." James said.

"Well I'm going to get your new fiancé." J.J. said as he walked out of the room. James nodded with a smile.

When Sandra walked in, James was still sitting on the side of the bed. She walked in and sat down beside him. "I've been thinking." She said.

"What have you been thinking about?" James asked.

"Have you thought about where you want to get married?" She asked.

"Anywhere you want is just fine with me." James said.

"Well, you know the mountain that you bought me?" Sandra asked.

James' eyes widened. "So you know you have a mountain?"

"*We* have a mountain. I think that's where we should be married. I just want a simple wedding with just our close friends. Mom can give me away, and it can be in the late afternoon when the sun is setting in the west. We could all go back to my mom's for dinner afterwards. What do you think?" Sandra asked.

"That sounds great to me. The best moments of my life were on that mountain." James said and winked at Sandra. She glared back at him. "No, I really mean it though." James said. He put both hands on her shoulders and pulled her close to him.

"Men, they're all alike." Sandra said.

Around that time, there was a knock on the door. As it opened, Linda wheeled Drew in. "Well hey buddy!" James said.

"How are you today?" Drew asked.

"Well, I'm awake. Thank God." James replied.

"You can say that again." Drew said. "I've got a question for you.

"I've received a call from David's dad. He said that he had David cremated and asked if we could spread his ashes where his mother's ashes were spread. He said he'd appreciate us both spreading his ashes, and that he'd be willing to give us transportation."

"Drew, it would be my honor for me to go up with you and do that. We'll fly up as soon as I get out of the hospital." James said.

"Well good. He said David's ashes are at the funeral home. He left them there in case we wouldn't be able to be there. He might be out at sea, and he said he might not be back in time." Drew said.

Chapter 47

Four more days of intense physical therapy had passed before
James was ready to go. At 9 AM Friday morning, James walked
into the waiting room where J.J., Sandra, Linda, Helen, and
Drew had been waiting. He had on black slacks, a turtle neck, a
leather jacket, and his hair was combed straight back. "I'm ready
to go, guys." He said.

"My God, he's beautiful." Helen whispered to Sandra.

'Yes, he is." Sandra whispered back.

"Is everything set up, J.J.?" James asked.

"Yep, the limousine is at the side entrance. Roy is standing by at
the Raleigh Durham airport. He'll be landing in New London,
Connecticut at the Groton Army airfield." J.J. replied.

"Is that a government airstrip?" James asked.

"No. It was turned over to the city in 1946 for public use." J.J.
said. "Now when you get to New London, there will be a
limousine waiting on you and Drew. The driver will have
David's ashes, and he'll know where the park is. Drew will
decide where the ashes will be spread. After that is over, the
driver will bring you back to the airport where Roy will fly you
back to Greensboro."

"Well, as usual, you have thought of everything. What in the
world would I do without you?" James said.

James walked over to Sandra and kissed her lips. "I'm going to
come to your house when we get back. Then we can make plans

for our wedding. I want to get married fast before you change your mind about me."

"I'll be waiting on you." Sandra said.

James turned around and grabbed the handles of Drew's wheelchair. J.J. held the door open and James pushed Drew out into the hallway.

After arriving at the Raleigh Durham airport, Roy opened the door and helped Drew into the plane. After putting the luggage away and making sure everything was secure, Roy took off on the runway. When they got into the air, they leveled off and headed toward New London, Connecticut.

Drew looked over at James. "Is this your plane?" He asked.

"It's the company's plane, but I use it most of the time." James replied.

Drew had a solemn look on his face as he nodded. James and Drew sat in silence for a few minutes.

"Drew, let me ask you something." James said. Drew looked up. "That day I walked up on your porch. If I had told you and David that I was James Andrew Exum and that I wanted to be your roommate for three months, could you have treated me like a normal person?

"The only reason that I wasn't upfront with you is because I wanted you to treat me like a friend in need. Like somebody you could say 'it's your turn to wash the dishes' and somebody you could teach to dance. I didn't want you to change; I wanted you to change me.

"The only thing I knew about life before I met you, was working 18 hours a day and sleep 6 hours. I'll never forget what you and

David taught me. You two are the only people I can really call my friends, and I hope we can still be friends, Drew. I'm still the same person, just with a title hanging over my head. I hope you can still look at me as a friend and not a title."

Drew looked over at James. "We've been through a lot together. If I think you're an ass, I'm going to tell you that you're an ass."

"That's exactly what I want you to do." James said.

After a couple of hours of flying time, Roy stuck his head in the room. "Okay, fellas', let's buckle up. We'll be on the ground in 10 minutes."

"Are you ready for this?" Drew asked.

"I'm ready to support you, Drew." James said.

"The same goes for you." Drew said as he buckled up.

A few minutes later, Roy had the plane on the ground. When the plane stopped, a limousine pulled up beside it. James looked out of the window. "It looks like our ride is here."

"Man, that thing looks like it belongs in a funeral procession." Drew said.

"J.J. sees to it that only the best is provided, Drew." James replied.

As the door opened, Roy and James helped Drew down the steps of the plane. The driver of the limousine opened the door. James walked over to the other side and got in while the driver was helping Drew get inside. The driver put the luggage in the trunk and handed Drew a package containing David's ashes. It was wrapped in a white silk fabric with an envelope on top.

James watched as the color drained from Drew's face. Drew looked up at James with a face that couldn't be described. James reached over and took the box out of Drew's lap. The driver pulled out of the airport and onto the highway.

James leaned forward. "Are you familiar with the area that we want to go?"

"Yes sir, I think so. It's what they call a viewing area park where you can watch submarines return from being out at sea. There's only one area around here like that and it's small." The driver replied.

James looked over at Drew for confirmation. Drew nodded his head. He didn't say a word during the whole trip. After fifteen minutes passed, the driver pulled off onto the main road lined with trees on each side. When they parked, the driver turned to look at James.

"There is a cobblestone path leading down to the inlet waterway. I'll wait right here until you gentlemen return." The driver said. He then got out to retrieve the wheelchair from the back and helped Drew out of the limousine. James stood beside the wheelchair and waited.

"Are you going to be okay, Drew?" James asked.

Drew looked up at James with tears running down his face. "I don't know, Jim. Give me a minute or two."

"Take all of the time that you need." James said.

When Drew was ready, James started pushing Drew up the cobblestone walk way. As they got towards the end, James stopped pushing just to view the scenery. It was an overcast day. The sky was a light gray and he could smell the sea water. He watched as the cold wind came off of the water, creating small white caps on the waves as they washed against the bank. The grass had turned brown and there was snow covering the trees.

Drew looked up at James. "This is exactly the kind of weather it was when we spread David's mother's ashes. Will you push me over to the three cement benches under the barren trees along the shore?"

"Yes." James replied as he began to walk.

"That's where we sat after we spread his mother's ashes." Drew said.

James pushed Drew near the bench, and helped him out of the wheel chair. "Jim, will you hold his box while I read the letter?" Drew asked. James took the box from Drew and sat down beside him.

Drew opened the envelope, pulled out a one-page letter, and began to read out loud.

"Well, Pal, if you are reading this, that means I have bit the dust before you did. As far as I'm concerned, I'm glad it happened this way. I don't think I could've stood the loss of you before me.

"Before you start getting sentimental while reading this, the whole reason I am writing this letter is just to let you know that being your friend, and you being the brother I never had, has been a pleasure. You've made me laugh; you have shown me life can be fun. You've been a mother and father to me. If you ever feel there is an angel looking over your shoulder, you can bet it's me. Have a good life and one day, I will see you on the other side.

"P.S. Just spread my ashes where we spread moms. Just know that I'm with mom and I'm happy. With love and respect-David."

Drew dropped the letter on the ground and began crying into his hands. James put his arm around Drew's shoulder with tears running down his face. James watched as the letter tumbled into the water and out of sight.

After sitting for about fifteen minutes, watching the white caps of the waves disappear, Drew looked up at James. "It's time to send him to his mom, Jim." He said. Drew took the box out of the fabric case, opened the lid on the box, and stood up. "I want to do this standing up." He placed his arm on James' shoulder. "Let's go slow. I think I can do this without the wheel chair."

James wrapped his arm around Drew's waist and held his hand for support. Slowly, they began walking while Drew shook the ashes out of the box along the edge of the shore.

After spreading David's ashes, Drew threw the box into the water and watched it drift out of sight. "He's with his mother now, Jim. Let's go home, buddy." Drew said. They turned around and headed back to the bench. As Drew sat back down into his wheel chair he reached over and picked up the fabric that held David's ashes. "I think I'm going to hold on to this." He folded it up and put inside of his jacket pocket. "I don't think he'd mind."

"Not at all, Drew." James replied.

After driving back to the airport and getting into the air, Drew looked at James. "For some reason I feel good. I know he's with his mother and that he's fine. There's nothing I can do to bring him back and it would be selfish of me if I could. He's where he wants to be and I'm fine with that, but the Lord knows I will miss him."

When they took off from the New London airport, it was a smooth flight back to Greensboro. When they landed, Linda, J.J., and Brad were waiting for them.

"Hey fella's, what's going on?" James asked after they helped Drew out of the plane.

"Drew and Linda are going to take the limousine and go where ever they want to go." J.J. said. "Brad won't tell me what it is, but he said that it's very important that we go back to the mansion. There's something in mom's will that he needs to discuss with us."

"It won't take long, James. I'll feel better the sooner we get it out of the way." Brad said. "J.J. has called Sandra and she knows you'll be a little late getting home."

James turned to Drew. "I'll be by tomorrow to check on you. This is going to be a new beginning for all of us. Thank you for letting me go with you today, Drew."

"Thank you for being there with me. You can rest assured that if you need my support, I will be there for you. You can count on me." Drew replied.

James turned to Linda. "Take care of him Linda. I'll see you later."

As James, Brad, and J.J. pulled up to the gates of the mansion, Mr. Carter walked out to speak to James. "How are you feeling, James?" He asked.

"I feel fine now, Mr. Carter." James replied.

"It's nice to have you back home, and in good health."

"It's great to be back, Mr. Carter. I'll see you later." James said. J.J. pulled through the gate and around the back of the house. "Do we have time for me to see Grammy's grave?" James asked.

"I don't see why not." Brad said as they got out of the car.

As they walked up the brick path leading to the family cemetery, the sun was beginning to set to the west, throwing shadows on the back side of the headstone. On the right of his father's grave, Elizabeth's head stone read: "There was always a place in my heart for you- James Andrew Exum."

"Your dad wanted that put on her tombstone, James. This is also where he wanted to bury her." Brad said.

"She could not have been buried in a better place." James said. "There was never a question of how much dad cared about Grammy. It was very thoughtful of him to put that on her tombstone."

"Yes it was, James." J.J. said. "I do appreciate it."

"Well let's go inside and take care of business." Brad said.

As J.J. unlocked the door and went inside, James stopped in the middle of the kitchen. He looked around the house and decided that it would never be the same without Grammy.

Brad walked over to the pie safe in the kitchen and opened the envelope he had in his hand. Inside the envelope was a key which he used to open the pie safe door. Inside the drawer was a metal box, which Brad took out. When he unlocked the gray box he smiled. "Yes, it works. Let's go upstairs to the office and get down to business. I think I have everything that I need now."

When they walked into the office, James stopped. "I think I'm going to change this office one day. I think it's time we make a change. We'll get rid of that small desk and make that side room into a play room for kids."

"I think that would be a good move, James." J.J. said. "It will certainly put better memories in your mind."

"Let's step over here to the round table. It will give us more light than sitting around this desk." Brad said.

"That sounds good to me." James said.

Brad reached into his pocket and pulled out an envelope. "I don't know whether you guys knew this or not, but Miss Washington was on your daddy's payroll for about 20 years and she never cashed a check. We kept trying to get her to, but she always refused. The only thing I knew to do was start putting it in stock. I would send her notifications as to what she had monthly. She would just send them back, unopened."

"That sounds exactly like something what she would do." James said.

"You must have invested it well, Brad." J.J. said.

"Thank you. I did the best I could and she did very well with a lot of it." Brad said. "About three months ago she sent me a letter that she requested to be added to her will. I later called her and said that I could do it for her. The letter read:

"'Brad, my two boys have been very successful and I'm sure they are financially secure now. I would like to use the money that you have been putting away for me by giving it all to A&T College where I had some of the best memories of my life. Anything else I may own may be given to the two boys, or given to the Salvation Army. Thank you for your help. Elizabeth Washington.'

"Do you fella's have any questions?" Brad asked.

"It's all fine with me." James said.

"It's the same for me as well." J.J. said.

Brad then pulled out the gray box he had retrieved from the pie safe. He read "'Brad, I would like you to read this to my two boys at the same time.'" Brad pulled out hand written papers with a small sealed envelope.

Brad read. "'Boys, I hope you're comfortable. I'm going to try and answer all of the questions that you may have. I wanted to sit down with you and tell you myself, but a good time never came around.

"'I was born in 1910, just outside of Washington DC. I was told I was born to a white woman that lived on a plantation, and my father was the son of a plantation slave. All I can remember is that I was raised by a black family that lived on the plantation. I can remember a white woman coming down to our cabin and reading to me under candlelight. For years, before she left she would tell me that an education would get me a better life. I worked hard every night after she left, and read until I fell asleep. She would always bring books to the house for me to read and would always be in a hurry and say she could not stay long. Before she left, she would always give Ms. Jenkins some folded money and thank them.

"'One day when I was about 16 years old, Mr. and Mrs. Jenkins were standing at the door. They had a suitcase in the middle of the floor with a brown bag on top. They told me to wash up and get dressed as quickly as you can.

"After I had gotten changed, Ms. Jenkins came in and said, "Child, it's time to go."

They put me into a truck and told me they loved me.

"'We drove for a long time without stopping. Thank God for those biscuits and fatback that Ms. Jenkins had put in the brown paper bag. When I woke up the next morning, the driver was standing outside of the truck talking to a woman. He handed her money and the woman took me out of the truck. I found out later that morning that I was at A&T College in North Carolina.

"'I washed dishes and swept the floor. I did anything I could to pay my way through college. When I graduated as a nurse, I was the happiest person in the world. I found out quickly that there was no room for a black nurse around Greensboro, but to clean bed pans. I did not want to do that because I had a college education.

"'That's when I went to work at Exum Textiles. For two years, I cleaned offices, mopped floors, and cleaned bathrooms. One day a man nearly cut his hand off while he was working on machinery. Because it was early in the morning, no one was at the office but me. He came running down the hallway with blood shooting out of his hand. I stopped him and made him sit down. I took the shoe strings from my shoes and wrapped it around his wrist to stop the bleeding. I stayed with him until someone came to take him to the hospital.

"'The man did not lose his hand, and Mr. Exum was very appreciative that I had the knowledge to know what to do medically to save his hand. After he found out that I had a nursing degree, he gave me the job to be the company nurse. That's how I got to know James.

"'We began to spend time together at the plant, and I guess you could say that that's where I fell in love with him. The problem was at the time, it wasn't right for a colored woman and a white man to be a couple. He didn't care, but I knew it would ruin him and the business.

"'J.J., when you were born, it was such a happy day for James. He wanted to tell the world about you, but I never let him. You boys know the rest of the story. I know your dad always had a place in his heart for me. There was no doubt in my mind, and I think Mrs. Exum knew that too, which is why she wanted me to raise you, James. She knew that I would love you the same way I loved J.J..

"'It was always a pleasure for me to watch you two boys grow to become as you are. Your dad was proud of the both of you, and I love you with all my heart. I hope that I've answered the questions I know you've always wanted to know about your family. I'm sorry there is nothing more that I can tell you. The only blood family that you two have, is each other.

"'I love you both- Mom.'"

After Brad finished the last few lines of the letter, he handed James a piece of paper that was folded up. When James unfolded it, it was the birth certificate of Jonathan Jackson Washington, the son of Elizabeth Washington and James Andrew Exum Jr.

James showed it to J.J., and the two of them stood up grinning at each other. They slid their chairs back with their legs and embraced each other without saying a word.

"I never looked at you as anything other than a brother, J.J.. The only thing that has changed is that we know that the same blood runs through our veins. That makes me so happy." James said.

"To tell you the truth James, I had my suspicions, and they turned out like I had expected. I always felt like you were my little brother, and you will always be even if we didn't have the same blood." J.J. said. "It's nice to know that I can tell people that you are my little brother."

"This is a happy day. Let's have a glass of wine." James said. "We'll make it a toast to brothers."

Chapter 48

Ten months later, in mid-October, a long black limousine crossed over the rail road tracks of Elon College. It was a beautiful day. The sun was shining directly over the college and all the oak trees were beginning to change colors. The streets were lined with Victorian houses with couples sitting in rocking chairs on the front porch. Children played in the yards, passing the football around.

As the limousine drove slowly through town, people stopped and stared. As it continued through town, it pulled into the main entrance leading to the new library. It was a colonial architectural design with a dozen steps leading up to the porch. It was a two story building with six columns.

The car made its way halfway around the circle and stopped. There were folded metal chairs on both sides of the sidewalk that led from the circle drive to the steps of the library. On each side of the sidewalk, nearly 100 metal chairs were arranged in a crescent shape. There was a row of chairs for the distinguished guests from around the state. A microphone stood in the center of the porch with a speaker on each side. People filled the seats as they awaited the ceremonial speech by James Andrew Exum III that was going to be held that afternoon.

The chauffeur got out of the limousine and walked around to the side. When he opened the door, J.J. stepped out dressed in a black suit. He stood at the door while his wife Sally got out holding their baby. J.J. and Sally walked up the brick pathway, passing the monument that was going to be presented by James later in the ceremony.

A few minutes later, a white 1941 Chevrolet coupe with a front license plate that read 'Little Susie' slowed down as it crossed the railroad tracks into Elon College.

James was driving with Sandra by his side holding their newborn baby. As they drove through town, the people outside threw up their hands and waved at the couple. James and Sandra couldn't help but laugh as they drove. James turned into the entry way to the library, and drove around the circle. It was the first time that James had been back since his accident.

"This is beautiful, isn't it?" James said in awe.

"They've done a beautiful job with it, Jim." Sandra said as they pulled up.

Most of the crowd recognized the old Chevrolet and started standing up to clap. When James stepped out, he wore khaki pants, and a black long sleeved shirt. By the time James got out and walked around to open the door for Sandra, they were getting a standing ovation from the crowd.

 As they made their way up the walkway, they shook the hands of the people they knew. James looked up at the top of the stairs and spotted J.J. grinning at him. When he got to the top of the stairs, he kissed Sally on the cheek and shook hands with J.J.. He then gave J.J. a hug and whispered in his ear "You don't have to shake hands with your brother, you hug him."

James made his way down the line and shook hands with the governor and other dignitaries. He turned around and made his way back to the microphone. Sandra smiled and winked at him.

"What a wonderful day it is, to be in a beautiful setting. I would first like to start by introducing my family. Many of you probably recognize this wonderful lady sitting behind me."

James said as he pointed to Sandra. "This is my beautiful wife, Sandra and my new son, James Andrew Exum IV.

"To her right, is my sister-in-law, Sally Washington, and beside her is my brother Jonathan Jackson Washington Exum. I must admit that it is a long name to say." James paused as the crowd chuckled. He then began to introduce the governor and the other distinguished guests.

"I would also like welcome some of my close friends. Let me introduce you to my old roommate, Drew Harris and his wife Linda Harris. They're going to be parents in a couple of months." James looked at Drew. "It's great to see you guys here, and I'm sure I'll see you Monday morning at Exum Textiles in the D & D engineering department.

"I'd also like to introduce to you Kevin Johnson, or Bull as most of you know him. He's one of the best defensive tacklers at Elon, and his fiancée Helen Jones. I'd also like to say welcome to Malia Faulk and her two sisters, Avery and Sydney. David talked about you often, and I know he would appreciate you being here today. Thank you for coming.

"As I stand here today, I would like to give you this small token for what you have done for me. This college has given me a beautiful wife, a son, and true friends." James waved at Drew, Helen, Linda, and Bull. "You have given me a life that I thought I would never have. You showed me that there is more to this world than the world of textiles. A life that I did not know existed until I came to Elon College. I would just like to thank you all from the bottom of my heart." James finished and everyone gave him a standing ovation.

"Now, there is one other thing we need to do. I have asked the president here if I could make a small change in the presentation. Most of you know of the accident that happened at the beginning of the year. I lost of one my best friends, David Keller in that accident. David loved this college and the people here. Drew and I feel very fortunate to have known him. He always gave you that big smile when he met you."

"I stepped up on the porch of 2424 Center Street and David met me at the door with a big smile. In honor of David, I am naming the library The David Keller Library." The crowd stood up and applauded. "I would also like to introduce to you today David Keller's father, who has flown in from Putnam, Connecticut for this ceremony. He is here to honor his son and unveil this statue." James looked at David's father. "Mr. Keller, would you please step forward?"

James moved the microphone out of the way and took a couple of steps backward. When Mr. Keller unveiled the statue, there stood a life-size bronze statue of David with his hair down over his face, with a big smile, and with his hand out as if he was greeting you. Everybody applauded and whistled.

James looked down at Drew. Drew was not standing, but had his face covered with his hands. Linda had her arm around his shoulders, and James ran down the steps. As James placed his arms around Drew's shoulders, Drew stood up and embraced James. They stood there for a moment as the crowd continued to applaud. When Drew let go, James turned around and wiped the tears from his eyes as he walked up the steps.

James walked over to the microphone once more. As he started to speak, the crowd was quiet and sat back down. For a moment, all was quiet until there was a dog barking in the distance. When James looked down towards the sidewalk, Bandit was hopping towards him as fast as he could. Bandit started up the steps, and James met him halfway. James picked Bandit up and Bandit started to lick James all over his face. The crowd laughed and began applauding.

James walked back up the steps and to the microphone while holding Bandit in his left arm. Sandra and Sally walked over to James' right side holding their children. J.J. stood on James' left side. James looked up at the Carolina blue sky and said to himself "Thank you Lord for the great memories of life, family, friends, and of course, a good dog."

Acknowledgements

There are a lot of people I need to thank for the completion of this novel.

First of all, I would like to thank Michelle Morton [Morton's Art Media] after telling her my story of Making Memories; she gave me the encouragement to write this novel, and gave me tips and pointers on how to do it. Thank you so much Michelle.

This novel could not have been possible without the encouragement and the patience of my son-in-law Brad Wilson or Burlington, North Carolina. As a first-time laptop/ computer operator, there were a lot of phone call questions, day and night concerning the computer. How was this done, how can I fix this, how can I change that? Brad was bombarded by all my questions, but he stood fast, kept his patience with me, and kept on encouraging me. He gave me ideas and helped me along the course of this novel. It could not have been done without your help, Brad. Thank you so much.

I also would like to thank my two daughters, Heather and Malia for their continuous encouragement and their assistance in typing and keeping my computer organized. I would like to thank them for having faith and confidence in me. I love you girls.

Also, I would like to give thanks to, Dawn Mitchell for the hard work she did on designing the book cover. You did a great job, and I'm very proud of it. Thank you, Dawn.

Thanks to my two brothers JB Axsom and Roger Axsom for all the research assistance. They gave me the dates, times, and facts that was implemented in this book. Thank you guys so much.

Rudy Barrett, you did a great job on my website, thank you for playing a special part of this and helping me get this book distributed to all the readers.

This book would have been nothing without the great editing job of Adria Smith of Mebane, North Carolina. Adria took this book and made it what it is. Thanks for all your hard work and confidence, Adria.

I'd like to thank Susie Barnes of Greensboro, North Carolina who spent a lot of time reading my book, making suggestions, and corrections. She did a lot of research on the music titles for 1969 that was implemented in this book. Sue, thanks for all of your time and help. I'm looking forward to reading your book someday.